J. S. Strange lives in Wales surrounded by books, and his three cats. With an interest in the occult, the esoteric, and the paranormal, J. S. Strange often finds himself waiting for Halloween, or thinking how he can make his home more supernatural. Author of *The Boyfriend Academy*, J. S. Strange is also working on murder mysteries with gay male leads.

www.jackstrangeauthor.com

- instagram.com/JackStrangeAuthor
- tiktok.com/@JackStrangeAuthor
- x.com/JackStrangeBook
- facebook.com/JackStrangeAuhthor
- jackstrangeauthor.substack.com

Also by J S Strange

Writing as Jack Strange:

Look Up, Handsome

25 Days in Athens

THE BOYFRIEND ACADEMY

J S STRANGE

One More Chapter
a division of HarperCollins*Publishers* Ltd
1 London Bridge Street
London SE1 9GF
www.harpercollins.co.uk
HarperCollins*Publishers*
Macken House, 39/40 Mayor Street Upper,
Dublin 1, D01 C9W8, Ireland

This paperback edition 2026
1
First published in Great Britain in ebook format
by HarperCollins*Publishers* 2026

Copyright © J S Strange 2026
J S Strange asserts the moral right to be identified
as the author of this work

A catalogue record of this book is available from the British Library

ISBN: 978-0-00-871408-6

This novel is entirely a work of fiction. The names, characters and incidents portrayed in it are the work of the author's imagination. Any resemblance to actual persons, living or dead, events or localities is entirely coincidental.

Printed and bound in the UK using 100% Renewable Electricity
by CPI Group (UK) Ltd

All rights reserved. No part of this publication may be reproduced, stored in a retrieval system, or transmitted, in any form or by any means, electronic, mechanical, photocopying, recording or otherwise, without the prior permission of the publishers.

Without limiting the exclusive rights of any author, contributor or the publisher of this publication, any unauthorised use of this publication to train generative artificial intelligence (AI) technologies is expressly prohibited. HarperCollins also exercise their rights under Article 4(3) of the Digital Single Market Directive 2019/790 and expressly reserve this publication from the text and data mining exception.

To those who wish for a better world

This book is entirely written by a human, and a gay one at that.

There are themes in this book that some readers may find triggering. The full list is available on my website.

www.jackstrangeauthor.com

2105

CHAPTER 1

I don't remember the first time I asked myself what it means to be a man, but it is now a question that I think of daily. It's a lifestyle that is expected of me, drilled into me from birth. I may not know the answers yet to what it means to be a man, but I know I'm about to learn it.

Loose stone chippings ping against the paintwork of my father's peach car, and he mutters up front, one hand on the wheel, the other holding my mother's delicate hand. A portrait of the pompous young king swings from the mirror. As we've approached Ganymede's, an elite boarding school for boys, they've both fallen silent, as if out of respect for the fifteenth-century Gothic manor house nestled in the hills of Mid-Wales, with only views of sprawling green and sheep for miles. I press against the window, mouth open, trying to take it all in, but the swaying car makes me queasy.

Underneath a bright blue sky, our peach car glistens, slows as it gets closer to wrought-iron gates and thick stone walls. I think it must be a remnant of a castle wall, the manor built within sometime later, though I'm not entirely sure of the dates.

History is not my strong point, though perhaps that will change here.

Father rolls down his window and the heat rushes in, eliciting a cough from Mother and a prickle of sweat from me. Two twenty-something men in gold chest plates and duck-egg-blue body suits approach. My eyes rove over their sculpted muscles, and I shrink into the shadows of the back seat, glancing in the mirror, hoping Mother isn't watching me. She isn't, thank God. The warmth rising up the back of my neck must be because of the sun. One of the boys, men, peers into the car. He's clean-shaven, a military buzz cut, and his skin is a rich black. His warm brown eyes swoop the interior of the car, but he does not smile. Neither does his companion, a white guy who is circling the car as if he is hungry. The sunlight glitters off his golden chest plate, armour worn as an accessory rather than for its primary function.

'New student,' Father says to the man at the window, as Mother breathes out. 'Dylan Cecil. I am his father, Charlie Cecil, and this is my wife, Mabel Cecil.' He touches her bare knee, and they lock eyes long enough for the man at the window to clear his throat.

I long for the day when I can fondly talk of another like he does my mother. A day that feels ever closer now that we are here. Craning to see up the driveway beyond the gate, I feel a thrill jolt through me, seeing Ganymede's in the distance. Before I can get a proper look, Mother glances back and I take that as a warning that I need to be on my best behaviour.

'Appropriate documents?' the man at the window asks.

Father turns to Mother, who hands him a thick folder; parchment desperate to escape.

'Are the medical records in there?'

'At the back. He passed with flying colours.'

Every student must have a medical exam before entering

Ganymede's. It was rather invasive, but Father assured me it was what everyone went through. We have a regular medical exam every year, with health checks every three months.

Behind me, the familiar crunch of tyres over stone, and I crane my neck to get a better look. A dark-skinned boy my age sits in the passenger seat next to a man dressed in black. I linger upon his features, breaking out of my reverie when the car engine starts and the window rolls up. The chill reaches us again. For now, we are safe from the heat.

Father exhales. Mother pats him on the knee. Neither of them says a word to me as we pass through the gates, under shadows of trees. The wayward grass is alive with buzzing bees, and in the distance, glimpsed through the trees, a green house and raised planter beds. Behind us the car slows, the guards speak, and then within seconds those inside are admitted through. I wonder why no documents changed hands. Do they not trust us?

My mouth drops at my first proper look at Ganymede's. The warm sun beats down upon four rising spiral towers, the slate roof coated in moss. It glistens off the Jacobean windows that line the front of the school, some of them open to let in a breeze, or at least the hopes of one. We get out, and Father claps his hands together in excitement as the bell in the bell tower in the middle of the roof rings out. It rattles my bones, setting my teeth on edge, every joint of my skeleton vibrating. That commanding tone is going to take some getting used to. Father runs his hand over the wisteria that grows over the redbrick facade, saying, 'I can't believe this is still growing,' and shakes his head in awe at the acres of grounds. 'Old keeper Marley still going strong.' Behind the three of us, the gates we came through look miniature.

As I'm staring up at the school, the car that was behind us

has come to a stop, and the driver opens the door for the boy inside. 'Welcome to Ganymede's, Mr Aceman.'

Something itches in my brain as I mull over his name. Aceman meets my eye as he climbs out of the car, which shines brighter than my father's. Father fixes a smile to his face, moving closer to my mother, as Aceman places his hands on his hips and looks up at the school. His clothes fit him well, I think, as I take a moment to watch him, under the guise of curiosity rather than anything else. He's a little taller than me, dressed in a rugby shirt and smart black trousers. His brown hair is feathered in all the right places, thick and healthy like a lion's mane. When he smiles, it's like he embodies the sun.

'I wish Papa was here,' Aceman says, loud enough for me to hear. Meeting my eye, I offer him a small smile, and he takes that as a sign to approach. Holding out a hand, a hand that I still remember touching, he says to me, 'Blake Eric Aceman. And you are?'

Intimidated, I think. Terrified out of my mind. As Father and Mother watch the exchange, I mumble, 'Dylan Cecil.'

'A pleasure to make your acquaintance, Mr Cecil.'

Blake's driver getting his bags out of his car is an opportunity for me to delay entering Ganymede's on my own.

I stand before my parents. Father, with his hair like mine and his kind but solemn eyes. Mother with her proud smile and her wise words.

For the next three years, I plan to come home to them during term breaks as a refined gentleman, kind of like this boy next to me. A man who will learn to support his own family, and the family that has raised him.

'This is where you'll make it, young man,' Father says to me, staring out at the expanse, refusing to meet my eye. 'This is where we all made it.'

He hugs me there on the steps of Ganymede's, for the first and last time.

Mother kisses me. 'Be a good boy. And a better man. We are so proud of you.'

Father pats me on the shoulder, and the silence is returning to them.

'You ready?' Blake asks me, breaking the moment when I wish they would say whatever is on their mind.

But it's gone, burnt to a crisp under the hot sun, and Father and Mother are smiling and getting back in their car. Blake's driver has already left, fading into nothingness as he leaves Blake behind, at least until term break.

A few weeks away, but it may as well be an eternity. I wave at Mother and Father before they drive away, and I want to watch them go, in fact I plan on watching them until they're no longer visible in these Welsh hills, but Blake grips my shoulders and says, 'It's easier if you let them go now.'

His voice wobbles, and his eyes are wet, but he does not let his tears spill. It's our first day, after all, and we don't want to be labelled as the cry-babies, no matter how emotionally intelligent we are meant to be. He pats his chest pocket. 'You smoke?' When I shake my head, he says, 'No, I don't much fancy it, either.'

'You're who I think you are, aren't you?' I ask him.

'Who do you think I am?'

'The billionth child.'

Blake sniffs, his eyes drifting to the cigarette packets in his pocket, but he neither confirms nor denies and I know enough not to push.

∼

A few hours after my parents left, everything changed for me, and by extension, Blake. I sometimes wonder if he might have regretted befriending me on that day. If he hadn't spoken to me, would his life have been different? Would mine?

I was settling into my dorm room, shared with Blake and some other boys, who scared me but I hoped would become friends, when a stressed-looking final year boy came and told me the headmistress wanted to see me.

What followed then, I still cannot fully recall, except for the news that I would never see my mother and father again.

'Headmistress Dwynwen, so very nice to meet you,' she said, *telling me to sit.*

'There's been an accident.'

'I'm afraid it's not good news.'

'We did everything we could.'

All the lessons I'd had in mindfulness came in useful then. Instead of breaking down, I went to my place of safety, breathing through the pain. I meditated that night on the memory of my last interaction with my parents, and whispered my goodbye to the moon.

I didn't tell Blake until the next morning. The first morning at Ganymede's, the day of excitement when our futures were meant to truly begin.

'I've been told my parents have died,' I said to Blake on that bright morning. Watching his reaction. I did not cry. 'They were coming back here, and their car crashed, and they died.'

As Blake hugged me, then fussed over me, all I could think about was how Father would not be around to see me become the man he told me I could become. How cruel life had been to bring me here with such excitement, only to take it away. Perhaps it was a lesson in balance. Perhaps a man must lose to gain.

'You want a smoke?' Blake had asked me.

'No, thank you.'
'No, nasty habit.'

~

Father always said that a boy like me would grow to be a man he would be proud of. He'd delight in telling me that I could be the change I wanted to see, and that to be born a boy was to be born with security.

I'd often scoff at his prophetic musings over our breakfast in the dining room, a newspaper held aloft in his hand, a cigarette burning in an antique ashtray on the table between us. My legs would swing forward and backward as I leant against the breakfast table, eating Welsh cakes, listening to Father remark on the ways of the world. Remarks that meant nothing to a young boy.

'When I was a boy, the world looked different. Look at me now, not like I was. You'll be here to see the world change. You'll be the one changing it.'

Then there would be mornings when he'd say nothing at all. Merely stare out of the window at the green landscape as Mother harvested the vegetable beds. Inside, she'd touch his shoulder, ruffling my dark hair, as unruly then as it is now.

Father's elbow seemed to rest permanently upon the equally perpetual newspaper, and I don't remember the first time I realised that his words, his mood, were always impacted by that morning's headlines.

As I got older, though, and my legs reached the floor, I would grow to enjoy those conversations we had, no matter the mood, playfully rolling my eyes at some of his suggestions of how kind the world would be to males like me. Sometimes I recall that look of pride in his eyes as he watched me reading a book, or climbing a tree in our garden, or even speaking to Mother.

'Not all men are good, Dylan,' he would say to me, usually after supper, when the night was dark and my eyes were heavy. His skin sunkissed from a long day harvesting the land, growing food for the hamlet. 'They're being helped now, but they haven't always been good.'

He'd pat my mother's hand gently at this, and she would look at him wistfully.

Born in a world that was uncertain of itself, rebuilding a society long lost, I was the type of boy that went about his day with questions far from his lips. For my core education I went to an all-boys primary school in a hamlet we'd lived in all my life. The school opposite us was for the girls. Sometimes we would wave from the playground, innocent and free of inhibition.

We did all the usual subjects like English, science, mathematics. I was around eight years old when I realised I had a passion for English and art and that I would gladly see my maths class burn. History wasn't a bad subject, either, but our history lessons were always tinged with sadness. The man who taught us was severe, grey-haired, ancient, even in my father's youth. He oozed a strained energy that I look back on now and put down to the way everything he'd ever known, or thought he would know, had been torn away from him.

On the morning of my fifteenth birthday, the sun unfurled itself like a sleeping cat in my bedroom, rejoicing in its ease of access through the curtain-less windows. With sleepy eyes I took in the cracked ceiling, the bare walls, glancing over at the skirting board and the hole where the mouse lived. Our core education is mandatory until we're sixteen. But every human knew they must strive for perfection, and that education should not stop at the primary level. Not if you wanted the good life.

Everyone who finishes their core education will go to a

finishing school for their formative three years, graduating at eighteen. They are all single sex, something about keeping students focused, and I know that the one all the girls want to go to is Pandora's. There are eleven across the country. All of the schools are run and owned by the Vandervere company, under the instruction and funding of the monarchy. Headmistress Dwynwen is a Vandervere, and Ganymede's and Pandora's are the schools everyone strives to attend, mainly because they carry more prestige.

Father was coiled and jumped at me as I came to the kitchen, hair jutting up, dressed in my flannel pyjamas. Mother had bought a cake, already adorned with burning candles, and together they sang, before Mother embraced me in a hug, kissing me on both of my cheeks, lined with fresh stubble that was only just beginning to grow properly.

'Look at you. Growing so fast,' she had said. 'You'll make a woman proud.'

'That's my boy.' Father clapped me on the back.

I forced a smile and swallowed the bile in my throat. We ate our cake under the portrait of the king.

In the afternoon, Father took me fishing at a lake nearby, muttering over the state of the murky water.

'How do you feel, son?'

'Like any other day.'

Father whistled, before saying, 'There's a letter for you back home. Enrolment papers. There's a spot waiting for you at Ganymede's, should you want it.'

I'd jolted, almost usurping us, plunging us into the polluted water that desperately needed our attention. 'You're joking.'

Father grinned. 'Only the best for my son.'

Ganymede's! A dream I once had, lost as I'd aged. It was *the* top school for boys. Everyone wanted to go to Ganymede's because it was almost guaranteed you'd have a successful life as a man. Your name would be respected, like my father's was, and people would remark on how kind you were, how gentle a man could be. Ganymede's nurtured boys into attuned men. Better men. Perfect men who respected their partners, understood their emotions, bonded with their fellow man. Perhaps more importantly, it was a place where boys *became* men. Found their life partners. Graduated at eighteen with everything waiting for them. A job, a house, provided by the monarchy, in all its splendid glory, and a woman who was your perfect match, as determined by the best technology on earth.

'Are you sure they'd want me?'

He smiled at my innocence. 'They'd be lucky to have you. You will be the perfect student.'

It's nice to reflect on those memories. I often did it, even around Blake. A week into our new friendship, he said to me, 'You can talk about them whenever you want to, you know.' We were standing outside the chapel in the grounds, the doors padlocked shut and the windows boarded up. Some of the boys said it was haunted.

'I know.'

'Do you want to?'

'Not right now.'

'Okay. Nice day. Should we smoke?'

I laughed. 'Not for me.'

'Swim, then.'

We swam in the indoor pool. As the weeks went by, I felt like a bare branch beginning to show its buds. With Blake, I could start to bloom, faster than I would have been able to on my own.

When I did speak about them, he listened.

'I want you to talk to me like you would anyone else,' I said to him midway through our first year. Our relationship was a good one, but I could sense there was something on his mind. Whenever he looked at me, it was like he was observing a wounded bird, one that had fallen from its nest and could not fly. 'None of this treating me differently because my parents are dead.'

'I'm not treating you differently.'

'Maybe not intentionally, but sometimes you do.'

Blake considered this, and then he nodded. Our relationship then changed into humorous banter, full of insults and brotherly love. It was the first time I realised how much Blake listened, and how much he thought about his actions. He made me laugh again, and he didn't judge me for it. He offered me the food off his plate, gave me clothes he no longer wanted, even stayed for the Christmas break because, now that I had no family, I had no one to return home to. It didn't feel like charity. It felt like platonic love.

I probably decided around then that was all it could ever be.

I got to know Blake well over the two years at Ganymede's as we started to change into men.

'I'm telling you, I've got hair growing under my arms.'

'That's new for you?'

'And I've got hair...'

'I don't need to know.'

Blake could be coy, though. 'Mum and Dad are first ministers,' he said to me when I asked him what they did during our second year. I'd realised he'd never spoken about his family life before, and I'd wondered if it was because he thought it might be too delicate a subject for me.

My eyes had widened at that. I'd never met anyone who had first minister parents. 'That must be so cool.'

'Not really.'

'But they make a real difference,' I said.

'I guess they do.'

First ministers are almost as royal as our royal family, and it shows in how much they get paid. It made sense why Blake always struck me as someone with a safety net, though he never held that over me. In fact, he seemed to want to share everything he had. Everything except what his life was like out there. By this point I knew he was who I thought he was, and that being the one billionth child had bought him class nobody else could get. After that talk, I only ever found out he had an older brother, and he very rarely mentioned his family again.

Everything changed in year three, after my lonely summer break at Ganymede's.

'You're back,' I'd said to Blake upon his return.

He said nothing.

'What's going on? Why are you being weird?'

'I've been thinking.' Then he lit a cigarette. The teachers didn't know he smoked, though I'm sure it must have showed up on his medical record.

There was a new teacher, too, who was there to teach us life skills: budgeting, bringing up a family, cooking. We didn't know what to make of that, and Blake hated him. Then, there was a new student. A student who caught my eye and haunted my thoughts like the white lady ghost who walks the second-floor corridor.

All this difference had my body aching. Dread filled me, and one autumnal night, I finally confronted Blake.

'It's nothing to do with you,' he said. 'I don't want to put you in any danger.'

'What exactly do you mean by danger?'

He'd given me a look that I always knew would eventually alight on me. A look that said he knew more, that he was better off without me. That I was just a kid and he was a gentleman. That he'd finally seen me for who I really was.

I'd caught him disappearing out of our room at night, but he never told me where he went. He started acting up in class, making mistakes, causing arguments with the teachers. So unlike Blake, who'd been the aspirational golden child from day one.

One winter night, we were sitting under lamplight in the dark library. We had blankets around us, electric heaters buzzing. The windowpanes frosted, the night carrying a white sheen.

'I know I've left you out in the cold,' Blake whispered, holding a copy of *Nineteen Eighty-Four*. 'It's only because I need to. You'll understand why.'

'Will I?' By this point, I knew I needed to give up. Let him go. He was never supposed to be mine. Just another thing I was destined to lose.

'Dylan,' he said to me, lit by lamplight. 'You'll wait for me, won't you?'

I didn't answer.

I wish I had.

CHAPTER 2

HERE LIES BLAKE ACEMAN, A TRUE MAN LOST TOO SOON.
YMA GORWEDD BLAKE ACEMAN, DYN GO IAWN A GOLLWYD YN RHY GYNNAR.
2088 – 2105

It's written in the Welsh language, beautifully scribed by hand. Instead of sadness wrapping its arm around me like a grief companion, I stand with confusion, staring at those words and the short amount of space between Blake's birth date and his death date. A mere seventeen years, a blip on the world. My hands unfurl to touch the stone, wishing that I'd known not to get too close to Blake Aceman, for he would only go and destroy me.

Blake's grave is unremarkable, surrounded by headstones that date from centuries long before anyone I've ever known was born. This boy changed my life, for better, for worse.

Should I, a young me, be crying now, mourning the loss of Blake and sitting with my feelings? Our school encourages us to feel what is real, to hold on to the tangible, to intuit the imaginable. If I were a true man, like Blake here has been marked as, I would find no shame in crying. Alone in the graveyard, nothing but me and Blake's name, I should have no qualms about tears, but the truth is, I have none to give. I haven't cried since my parents died. I didn't even cry for them.

Birds start to wake, they tweet and they stir, and the tree leaves shake as they wake from slumber. The heat of the morning starts to murmur, and I breathe in the sunlight, praying for thunder. A good storm right now would be just what I need to wash away the chaos of the last few days of April. Though spring, fleeting, burns upon the breeze as the sun threatens to smother us.

Blake always liked the summer. He was one of the few here who did. I still remember the second week of April, early afternoon, when I was told Headmistress Dwynwen had found Blake after two days of missing classes and not coming back to the dorm room. Up until then, I'd began to allow myself to believe he'd gone home, telling myself he had a sickness in the family. Blake would come back healthy, with news that his family were in good spirits. I'd forbidden myself to think the worst, even though such thoughts have grown and prospered in the habitable conditions of my mind.

'Would you like to come with me, Mr Cecil,' Professor Lawrence, our men's studies and mindfulness professor, said as I was walking from English Literature to History. He asked in Welsh.

I've been having private counselling sessions with Professor Lawrence since my second week at Ganymede's Boarding School for Boys, so I recognised the grave tone in his voice and didn't think twice about following him and not attending my next classes. The clouds were a dull grey, and deer crossed the running water that poured through the landscape. Further down was the lake where I always see the same boy swimming in the early hours when he thinks everyone else is asleep.

Professor Lawrence's classroom is in the basement of the school. It's a room adorned with dark blue paint and a gold-painted zodiac stretching across the sloping walls, reminiscent of a buried Roman amphitheatre. He sat at his desk, beneath his large and imposing statue of Saturn, and I tried not to meet Saturn's wild eyes, which seemed to look at you no matter where you sat in the room. The seating behind me, arranged in a semi-circle split into our four school houses, was vacant. I'd listened as Lawrence told me of Blake's fatal fall down a flight of stairs, where he'd hit his head sometime earlier this morning. Dwynwen found him and had the body removed before any student saw him.

A rather unremarkable death for the billionth child.

'But people don't die from hitting their heads.'

'They do when their brain bleeds.'

'Where'd he been?'

'We believe he had been in the school the whole time, evading staff and students.'

And security guards, too, I think.

'Do you want to talk about it now?' Lawrence had asked. 'I have time. If you'd rather we talk about it in our weekly sessions, that is fine, too. Dylan? Dylan. Have you heard me? Do you understand what has happened?'

I agreed we could add this to our regular course of conversation in our next sessions, saying, 'If you'll forgive me, sir, I'd like some time to process this,' and he'd let me go.

A man fit for society would have let his emotions come to the surface, and he would have healthily talked about them and worked through them. A man would talk to his friends without fear. A man wouldn't think twice about being honest about the grief he felt that he'd lost a confidant, a fellow man whom he thought he had more time with. He would remember his friend and carry him through his own life.

But me? There was nothing but vacant emotion.

We get ever closer to our graduation month in June, when we become the men we have been raised and taught to be, and yet I only feel like a boy. A foolish, naive boy.

I stare at Blake's name, and every day I say the same thing, 'I will honour you, my friend, and I will find out the truth.'

Because within two days, Blake's death was a distant memory to everyone else. The boys in school laughed like nothing had changed. Our classes continued the first day without Blake, and by day two our professors didn't entertain any questions about him. By the end of week one, his name had died on their lips. Flowers lay dead upon his grave by the end of week two.

We have no access to news here, but Professor Lawrence gets the papers and occasionally I've had the chance to scan the pages. I've seen no news about the death of Blake at our prestigious school. The grass begins to grow over the earth that has buried Blake forever, and it seems I am the only boy to remember.

A true man would know when to move on and carry on with his life. A boy would only wither here and cling to the past.

There are many reasons why I am not ready to face graduation, and indeed a life promised to the good men of society. Namely because any feeling I have is buried further within me than Blake is in the patch of land I walk away from. With the graveyard behind me, I head to a bridge that crosses the end of the brook, and a few feet away is the lake. Halfway across the bridge, the water of the lake ripples and so do the muscles on the back of the boy that breaks the surface.

I know his name, but I do not think he knows mine.

His red hair is cropped into a buzz cut, and his square face is broken by sharp cheekbones graced with red freckles, a razor jawline and a strong nose. His pale white skin shimmers in the sunlight, already too hot for the time of day. He sees me watching him, turns and treads the water, droplets glimmering upon his symmetrical forehead. His warm brown eyes consider me, his plump lips neither smiling nor scowling. He breathes out before he turns back, away from me, and continues to swim.

I hiss, looking down at the palm of my hand, which has tightened upon the wooden banister. A splinter lodges itself within my skin, but it's my heavy, beating heart that gives me cause for alarm. Having feelings I thought were buried is uncomfortable, but feeling something for the same sex is a danger in itself.

CHAPTER 3

'Yo, Dylan.' My dormmate Johnny Acton joins me in the breakfast hall. 'Caught any worms yet?'

'Ha. Ha. All the good food goes if you get here late.'

Johnny rolls his dark eyes, shaking away a loose strand of black hair. His Bangladeshi grandfather moved to Scotland from the Bhola District with his family due to climate displacement, unable to ever return home. As far as I'm aware, Johnny has never seen his homeland, like many other students here.

Johnny scans the table, crumbs on silver platter, unwanted fruit looking sad, before he settles for orange juice and takes toasted sourdough from the toast rack, lathering his two slices with butter. He rubs his stomach absently with one hand as he loads his plate with remnants of scrambled egg left behind by boys who have already eaten.

'Aye, this is all right,' Johnny says, his Scottish accent seemingly stronger in the mornings. 'Get much sleep last night?'

Thoughts of Blake kept me up all night, and I only got

respite when I sat in my dorm room window watching the red-headed boy swim. 'Same as usual.'

Johnny nods. He learnt pretty quickly in the first year that sleep evades me, and he often wakes and peers at me. It's like me being awake at all hours has become a part of his routine. I asked him once what he thinks when he sees me lying there, but he said he doesn't remember waking. I'm not sure if it's the truth or his way of avoiding talking about his worry for me. Us boys are better at talking about our feelings these days, but we're still struggling teenagers on the cusp of adulthood. We're still human.

He inhales his food, chewing and swallowing faster than I can read a page of a book. He barely pauses to drink, to breathe, to savour the organic tastes of what Ganymede's feeds us.

I wash down my morning vitamin and zinc pills with freshly pressed apple juice, my plate long since empty of breakfast. I reach for a punnet of grapes, taking them off one at a time and popping them in my mouth. Father always loved grapes. Something I've inherited from him, maybe. Even though they died three years ago, I find myself trying to remember my parents, and hating myself for forgetting any detail about them.

'How're you doing?'

This simple question is something we are supposed to ask each other every day, one of our first lessons from mindfulness class. But I know Johnny is asking me not out of duty, but true care.

'I still can't believe he's gone.' Over a month later and I still feel numb.

'I know,' Johnny says, pausing his eating, so it must be serious. 'I looked at his bed this morning and I dunno, it kind of hit me that he isn't coming back.'

His absence is felt by more boys than just me, then? As I sip at my drink, I'm relieved to know he isn't quite as forgotten as I thought he was.

'He would have sailed through these final tests,' Johnny says.

'He'd have been more prepared than the rest of us.'

'Speak for yourself, mate.' Johnny scoffs, grinning. He takes the last bite of his food, barely chewing. I'm surprised he hasn't choked to death yet. He then takes his own vitamins and zinc. We have to take them every day. 'I'm going to ace them. It's going to be a piece of cake. Ooh, cake.'

Johnny rises, walking down the long table in search of cake. That boy is something else.

I rest my chin in my palm as a hum of chatter bounces off the stone walls, and traverses through the vast room big enough to hold seven hundred students.

The Jacobean windows are all closed to combat the heat from the morning sun, manageable now at this hour. The air conditioning that is fitted within the school is only now coming to life, slowly pumping cool, regulated air throughout. It's a lot more environmentally friendly than it once was. The floor is all polished wood and sheepskin rugs. The coat of arms for the school, a beautiful depiction of a curly-haired Ganymede, naked from the torso up, and a separate Welsh red dragon flag, hangs in silk tapestry behind the professor's table. Even at this time in the morning some of the professors sit with their goblets full, dark green bottles of red wine resting beside them.

How relieved must they be feeling that we have moved on from Blake's death so quickly? Do the hamlets even know there has been death at our school?

'We're so lucky to be here,' Blake had said to me on a morning like this one in our first year. 'Ganymede's is the place to be.'

'Yeah, right, mate,' Johnny had said to Blake. 'The professors can't hear you. No need to kiss their arses.'

Blake had laughed at this. 'This school is prestigious. If we graduate, we've made it.'

'You've already made it.' Johnny pointed out.

'Nah, billionth boy don't mean a thing. Doesn't guarantee me a top-level job and all the money and protection a man could need. Not like being a Ganymede's graduate would.'

'Long live the king,' I'd said.

'Long live the king,' the boys had echoed.

'Dad used to say work hard now to have ease later,' I added, seeing their familiar reactions whenever I mentioned my parents.

'Nothing less than perfection,' Blake replied, indicating the school motto underneath Ganymede's iconography.

If you don't make Ganymede's or Pandora's, you have to work a little harder, but you still get the support of the monarchy. We all do these days.

'I thought it would be greater,' Johnny said.

'When you're progressing in careers that are actually useful to society and some poor sod isn't, you'll see otherwise,' Blake said.

'Everyone contributes to society,' I reminded him.

'Not as much as us.'

'Maybe I'll go to the open country,' Johnny had said, popping a grape in his mouth.

Blake and I visibly shivered. Both of us had been driven through the open country to get to Ganymede's, and I didn't see a soul. Mother used to tell me scary stories when I was a child about looters and disruptors who are eternally doomed. Father once likened the open country to being hell on earth. Owned by the monarchy, this land has no use. No farmers use it, no houses are built upon it. Just nature, growing and thriving again like it is supposed to do. But also home to people who want to kill, who disregard rules and order. Who are ungrateful to king and country. Those who never made it.

'You don't mean that,' Blake had said with severity. 'All those wildfires, cold snaps, floods, freezing winters. Johnny, there's nowhere to escape it. Not like there is here.'

'I'd survive. The looters do it.'

'If the stories of looters and disruptors are true, then they have drowned in the floods, their corpses set alight by Mother Nature's touch,' I replied.

When the previous society came to a halt three generations ago, the monarchy saw an opportunity: capitalism no longer serves us. We must be a community once more, where the currency is equality, harmony and care for one and all. We still have a class system, as evidenced by our schools, but at least poverty has been eradicated. Everyone has a home, a partner, food on the table.

But it's not easy to eradicate the world of what was once left over. Our changing climate means the world needs rebalancing, and the effects of the great 2080 plague are still felt in the economy, even twenty-one years later. It's why the monarchy, and all its wealth, has been redistributed to the masses by creating a universal income. Its why people strive for Ganymede's, why they hope to pass, because you'll be better off, and you won't go without.

Nobody wants to be out in the open country.

Graduate from Ganymede's and you need not worry about the open country. Fail, and it's easy to find yourself discarded from society, forgotten and left to the elements. It is certain death, and if not death, it brings shame to your family name.

There are memories of Blake I hold onto, when he was so full of life for this school, when he loved everything about it. But they are fading, tainted with the knowledge that near the end,

Blake was distant from me. That when we did speak, he always left me with questions. During a cold winter night in the library, I'd asked him if he was phasing me out in preparation for his new life in society, to which he'd replied, 'That's a life I no longer want.'

He wouldn't elaborate, and I planned to follow him again, should he sneak out in the night. Blake got lucky, slunk out when sleep got me. I kick myself because of it. How typical it was that that was the moment he chose, because if he hadn't, I might have stopped him, and he might not have disappeared.

All I have is the last conversation I had with him, the evening before he vanished, just he and I in our dorm room. I'd asked him what was going on.

'I keep asking myself why,' Blake said. 'Why are we doing this?'

'Because this is what we have to do,' I replied.

'Do we?' He'd asked me, staring out at the amber sky. 'Humanity has a strange way of trapping itself.'

'Not anymore.'

He'd scoffed and I'd blushed.

'Pay attention,' he'd said. 'Wake up.'

Perhaps I hadn't woken up, because somehow, I find myself here. The end of May. June creeping closer. I've grown to hate June, when the boys return back to their hamlets for the summer break, and Ganymede's is my only familiar companion. I don't dare return home to the family house I inherited. I can't face it. For all I know, it's rotting away, or broken into, or maybe even burnt to the ground. Whatever. It might be mine legally, but the earth can have it.

June's shine brings a silver lining this time around. We've completed our higher level core education exams, and we've done our exams in cookery, carpentry, sports and physical exercises. That last one I'm sure I've failed. But they're nothing compared to the final thirty-day exam period. From the first of June to the thirtieth, us third-years have to pass a series of tasks to graduate. They're the exams that will determine if we're men fit for this world. If we're perfect. If we're not...

'Want a bite?' Johnny asks, shoving some cake on a fork under my nose.

'No, I'm fine.'

'Go on...'

'Get away.' I swipe, knocking the cake onto the table.

'That's the worst thing you've ever done. Almost wasted good cake.'

'I don't know how you can eat. Aren't you nervous?'

Johnny shakes his head. 'Not really, mate. They're just exams, aren't they?'

'Just exams? They determine our future.'

Johnny blows a raspberry. 'Nah. All overhyped.'

This boy never ceases to amaze me.

The bell tolls and my stomach rolls, and the hum reverberates through me. My skin crawls and my teeth chatter, but I convince myself to rise. Johnny makes a dramatic groan, before shoving the rest of the cake all as one into his mouth. I grab my bag, tittering, trying to ignore the fluttering butterflies in my stomach.

It's time.

CHAPTER 4

Morning sunlight pools in the vaulted ceiling of the assembly hall and streams through stained-glass windows, illuminating a naked Apollo, hands outstretched, palms facing outward. Nearby is Pan, sitting upon a tree stump, and Kratos in colours of blue and gold, wrestling an unidentified man. Ten windows, each one telling a different story of the Greek gods. I've always wondered why we don't celebrate the Welsh mythology here.

I take a seat next to Johnny as the lights in the floor lamps flicker. The electricity is weak throughout Ganymede's, especially at this time of year when it is reserved for the air-conditioning units. There are no overhead lights, a remnant from a quirky owner centuries ago, so candles are lit, a faint scent of burnt matches in the air. The hall is split into four sections, each one dedicated to the house we've been put into, chosen for our traits.

There's rule-abiding house Saturn, diligent and hard working. It's the house I'm in, probably because of my rigorous habits.

Across from us is house Mars, assertive, competitive, and the house of boys who need a little more work on their anger.

Directly behind Saturn is house Jupiter, the intellects and the lucky. A lot of Jupiter boys go into work related to foreign relations.

Behind Mars is house Mercury, the communicators, the free thinkers, the boys that need reminding to stay in line.

We are the sons of the gods.

We're all in our uniforms, charcoal blazer and trousers, crisp white shirt and shined black shoes. The only thing that sets us apart is the house crest knitted on the breast pocket of our blazers. Sometimes the boys swap them over, sit in each other's houses, see if they can get away with it. A stupid game, but often they're caught and asked to return to their proper seating.

Not today.

I look around at my other sons of Saturn.

Taylor is leaning at the back row of our house, hands in his pockets, head tilted back to the ceiling. Cameron, his glasses reflecting the glowing candles, leans forward in the front row, staring at the stage where our teachers sit in a row.

Everyone is where they should be. Everyone except Blake.

The chatter in the room subsides, just enough to get my attention. Sauntering down the aisle is the boy I've seen swimming. His uniform strains against broad shoulders, wide chest. He heads straight to Mars, the house of warriors and action-orientated people. He does not smile at those that try to catch his attention, and he does not thank those who move aside to let him pass. He finally reaches his seat, slipping down into his chair. He crosses his arms, leaning back, legs splayed. I bite my lip, eyeing his stance. He holds himself like a man, I think. When he turns to look at me, I snap my attention back to the stage. I've learnt that his name is Roman Edwards, and he's got my heart racing with one look.

My leg jiggles as I chew my bottom lip, trying to erase the image of Roman from my head. He's an enigma, and he is ignorant of me. He's out of my league, surrounded by the type of boys who come from wealth, and the first time I saw him he was the type of person I wanted to look at from afar, as if being too close to him would get me burnt.

There's a rustling from the stage as the professors sit a little taller, and I touch my fiery cheeks and hope they are not too noticeably red. From the shadows at the back of the stage, Headmistress Dwynwen emerges, sleek and soaring, and sweeps to the podium centre stage.

'My sweet, sweet boys.' Dwynwen's hands are held aloft as she surveys us.

Dwynwen's mother, Mother Mai, clears her throat. Dwynwen stands taller. 'Good morning, third-years. I trust you are all well fed.' She's slicked her bright blonde hair away from her pale white skin. Narrow-faced, she peers down at the students, smiling warmly. Her rigid shoulders keep her straight backed, and she clutches each side of the podium, which is carved with wooden flying eagles, with her smooth hands and long fingers. 'You all must be very tired after your last round of exams. They are being graded, but I can say that we are very pleased with what we have seen so far, and we have a good feeling for all of your futures.'

Some of the boys around me start whispering, and it spreads out to all corners of the room. Dwynwen holds up a hand, and the room falls silent.

'But of course, you all know that your exams only make up forty-five per cent of your final result. Knowledge is power, but what matters now is how you pass our series of tasks this coming month, applying what you have learnt. Ask yourself, how have you embodied Ganymede's? Are you as perfect as can be, or do you still need to correct some small errors of your being?' She pauses, allowing us all enough time to think this over. 'Eight tests, to ensure that you are ready to go into this world and do what is most important: repopulate.'

I guess Father wanted me to be old enough before he had *that* conversation with me.

My fists bunch and I cross my arms, tucking my hands away from prying eyes. Cameron nods slowly, hanging on to every word. A boy next to him tuts, but Cameron either doesn't hear or ignores him.

'Ganymede's has been proud to lead you into manhood. But now it is up to you to show us what you have learnt. With our eight tasks, you will all face scenarios that will put to test how you show up in a relationship with your female partners upon graduation. It won't be easy. You will question yourselves, your fellow man, and you will question what is required of you to help society at large.' Dwynwen's eyes brush over me and I try not to give anything away. 'Ganymede's is a wonderful bubble, but it is not forever. As men, you are expected to provide, to nurture, to care and to protect. Ganymede's has done this for you so far, but we will not be your safety net forever. No, you will become the safety net for your families. You've already done so much for the world by getting this far. For that, you should be proud.'

She brings her hands together and leads a round of applause. The professors all join in, and so do I, mouth dry. Mother Mai nods, as if for Dwynwen to continue.

'Eight tasks,' she repeats. 'A task of trust, a task of honesty, a task of survival, a task of mind, a task of strength, a task of teamwork and empathy, a task of intuition and sacrifice, a task that tests it all and confirms you can live independently. I dare say that some of you may want to keep task seven in mind.'

Roman crosses his arms, looking at Dwynwen with a blank expression.

'These boys are now, more than ever, your confidants. Your friendships will be tested. Your personalities stretched. You will question all factors of your being, and you will ponder all that you have known about your fellow student. Ultimately, you must determine when to work together, and when to put yourself first. A balance that humanity once lost, but is now regaining.

'We have a high pass rate for these exams here at Ganymede's. We are the leading school, full stop. What is it?' She puts this question to the professors behind her, but barely looks at them, doesn't wait for a response. 'Ninety-seven per cent of students each year graduate. Graduate, and you will be rewarded with a life waiting for you in the form of a home, a job and, most crucially, a partner. Fail these tasks, or prove that you are not worthy, and...' Dwynwen smiles. Fail, and we lose everything. We're better off dead. 'Well, we won't go there. Because none of you in this room are going to fail, are you?'

'No,' some chant back, half-heartedly.

Dwynwen nods, saying slowly, 'Good, good. Boys.' She pauses, surveys the room. 'Men.' A frisson of excitement ripples through the sitting students. 'Do not be afraid. You are all capable of these tasks. For king and country, you will be better men at the end of June.' She takes a deep breath. 'Some of you may have noticed that there are three empty seats here...' She looks at the back of the room, to her left, and then, to my horror, at the empty seat next to me.

Blake's. An acknowledgement, from her, that he is gone.

'As you know, we are working towards a functioning society. These seats belonged to boys who are unfit for the final exams. Unfortunately, you will not be seeing them again.'

Johnny feigns a dramatic gulp, but I don't smile.

Instead, I stare at the empty spot where Blake once sat, and I wonder, was Blake's death really an accident at all?

Was Blake always going to fail these tasks? Was it coincidence that death came to him first?

'You are dismissed.'

The crowd thins as boys begin to leave, and when there is a direct line to the stage, I rise, walking against the grain of students filing out of the room.

'Headmistress Dwynwen.' I hate that my voice shakes.

She turns, her lips curling into a smile. '*Bore da*, Dylan.'

I nod, a mark of respect for our headmistress. 'I was wondering if what you said was true? About boys who aren't here today being ... gone?'

'I don't lie.'

I glance at the teachers behind Dwynwen, all of them dressed in the same black coats with blood-red inlay, black trousers, black waistcoats. It doesn't matter what gender the teachers are, the uniform is unisex. Professor Lawrence, the only teacher to have dared put white pinstripes through his black fabric, holds my gaze. His lips curve downwards, before he turns back to Professor Omar, our sports teacher and a right thorn in my side.

'I didn't think you were, Headmistress. It's ... has...' I swallow, feeling smaller by the minute. 'Blake.' I choke the word out, cringing at my betraying tone. I may as well have shouted it. I try to ignore the stares of the professors behind Dwynwen, all of them seeming to sense that here stands a boy offering himself to subjection. Dwynwen clasps her hands together in front of her, staring me down.

'What about him, Mr Cecil?'

But I'm a brave boy. I can speak my mind. 'It's just ... why did you mention him not being fit for society when...' My throat bobs. 'When...'

Dwynwen places a hand on my shoulder, leaning forward until she's level. 'Focus on your own tasks, please, Mr Cecil.

It's imperative that you do so. This month will be one of the biggest of your life.'

'But Blake...'

Dwynwen sadly smiles, shaking her head ever so slightly. 'It might hurt you to know the truth—'

'I want the truth,' I interrupt.

She nods, considering my words. 'Very well. Blake was not heading towards graduation, due to some of his previous exams in the spring. However, he was a young man with a lot of potential, and we were hoping he would claw back enough marks within his first two tasks to get him back on the path he was destined for.'

'And we couldn't let the billionth boy fail,' Professor Omar stage-whispers.

Dwynwen titters, taking her hand from off my shoulder. 'Unfortunately, as you are aware, a tragic accident befell Blake before he had the chance to compete.'

I sway where I stand and Professor Lawrence leans forward in his chair, as if he thinks he might catch me should I faint. 'And his partner?'

'What about her?'

'Well, she won't have a husband now.'

Dwynwen's smile is warm as she says, 'I appreciate your concern for others, Mr Cecil, and indeed for a sex that is not your own. Rest assured that our system for pairing partners will always bring up a second and sometimes third choice of compatibility. Blake's partner will have already been reassigned to someone new.'

I scratch my head. Second and third choices? Aren't we supposed to be finding our one true soulmate? 'But what of someone else?'

'Someone else?'

'Won't the second choice have been partnered with a first choice?'

'Not necessarily, Mr Cecil,' Dwynwen says. 'A lot goes into the partnerships and nobody will go without, should they graduate.'

It's only now I realise I have not given much thought to how our partners are chosen. There's no Cupid's bow here or one-on-one matchmaking like the olden days. Technology has been developed to assess humans and their traits, and study them as they mature. These schools observe every personality trait, every little part of us, from our exam results to the foods we like, and they feed it all into a system which regurgitates the perfect partnership. We are moulded to each other from that first year at these schools, and we are raised within the parameters of our chosen perfected future selves. It works, and people are happier for it. The world is happier for it.

'I am, of course, sorry for your loss, Mr Cecil,' Dwynwen says. 'I do trust Professor Lawrence is still offering you guidance?'

He nods, even though Dwynwen can't see him, and I nod in silence.

Dwynwen straightens. 'Good. You are dismissed.'

She turns, her boots thudding across the stage. She exits through an arched doorway, and the professors rise as one, all heading in the same direction.

'If you need to talk…' Professor Lawrence says.

'I know where to find you, sir.'

He nods stiffly, and disappears through the door.

I massage my chest, as if I might slow down my racing heart. The reality of what I'm about to face is sinking in.

I think of the boys I have known to leave this school over the years. Twelve boys in my first year, one day never returning to the classes. We soon learnt it was because Ganymede's expels those who are not fit for this school. We asked where they went, and we were told they were sorted into the lower schools that better match who they are. It very rarely happens the other way around, but it happened with Roman. There are many whispers of where he has come from, but from what I've gathered he was in a school that wasn't quite as prestigious as Ganymede's, destined for a comfortable but less than exemplary way of life. He must have done something extraordinary to be transferred here. Whenever boys go, it's sad but we don't dwell. We accept it. It is, after all, what this is all about. Our futures. Putting us where we're supposed to be. Seven boys faced dismissal in year two, and now, in year three, only three. Two, if you discount Blake. His fall was an accident. He wasn't destined for anything less, even if Dwynwen says he was. He would have come back. I know it.

A shiver passes over me as I think of her who waits for me. Perhaps she has graduated already, making our hamlet home hospitable for my arrival. Or she might be about to graduate, and feels just as full of nerves as I do. She will be from Pandora's, I am sure. There's a part of me that hopes she might fail, so that I can graduate and have an excuse not to marry a woman.

What a disappointing man I will be.

I turn back to the empty assembly hall and my gaze falls on three old portraits of male headmasters of time gone by. Even in paint their eyes are hardened, their jaws rectangular, their dark suits fitting their toned bodies. There's one with thick facial hair, and another with a confident smile, and I wonder if any of them are still alive. Their legacy is felt as much as the sun, which leaves a mark upon my pale skin. They resemble Dwynwen, I think.

I sink, sitting on the edge of the stage, knees to my chest. Good God, why can't I cry? Crying would be such a relief right now. Drawing a rattling breath, I imagine drowning my grief, my anxiety, my worry. Those mindfulness classes with Professor Lawrence are ingrained in me, and I soon feel the circle of calm wash over me. Lifting my head high, I get to my feet and walk out of the assembly hall, not daring to look back, even though I know the stage is empty. That I'm alone.

As I round the corner of a corridor carpeted in deep red, with nineteenth-century gilded mirrors lining the walls, a stinging blow hits my back. Dazed, turning, I'm forced against the brick wall with a thud. A nearby table with brass candelabras rattles. I reach out to steady myself on an old Victorian table.

Taylor Powell smirks, laughing with two of his mates, Lee and Jackson, who flank him on either side. Pale white faces burnt red by the sun. Taylor claps his large hands together, cricking his neck as he faces me.

'Crying to Headmistress Dwynwen, were you?'

'Get fucked, Taylor.'

'Ohhh,' the boys wail, covering their mouths and looking at one another for approval.

Taylor steps closer, closing off my escape route. 'I heard you asking Dwynwen about Blake.' Lee's and Jackson's laughter rips through the corridor as they overreact to Taylor's mimicking tone. 'Do you miss *cwtching* him at night, Dylan?'

Cwtching, the Welsh word for hugging.

My hands shoot out before I can stop them, colliding with Taylor's shoulders. He stumbles, bumps into Lee, who wails when Taylor's foot stomps onto his.

'That all you got?' I shout.

Taylor aims a punch, slow, and I roll under it, punching his gut. Taylor's rigid stomach barely tenses at my touch, but it's enough to shock him. I may not be the strongest lad in this school, but I know how to move fast. Faster than Taylor, anyway.

We shouldn't be fighting. Men should not participate in violence.

'Get here, you little prick.'

'Think you're talking about your own prick,' I say.

My leg gives out from under me as Jackson swipes me with a kick. Fists hit my back as I fall onto the carpet, another fist colliding with my eye, before a hand grips my collar, fingers pinching my neck. Taylor yanks me towards him, my neck snapping back. Spit lands on my face as he hisses, 'You'll be joining him again soon.'

I spit in his face, not my proudest moment. He twists his head away from me, eyes closed. My fist raises, collides with his cheek, his neck, any part I can reach from where he holds me.

'Oi.'

Taylor springs back, letting me go, and I stumble.

'What do you want?' Taylor shouts.

'Get away from him.' Roman storms from the other end of the corridor, his blazer removed, shirt undone at the top. His face flushed red, he raises a hand, pointing to the door at the other end of the corridor. 'Are you thick? Get away from him.'

Out of anyone else's mouth, it might have sounded comical, but Roman's growl, his narrowed eyes, his stature, make Taylor hold up his hands.

And here he is, defending me. *Me!*

'Woah, man, we're just playing.' Taylor taps Lee with the back of his hand. 'Aren't we, boys?'

Lee wraps his arm around me, digging his nails into my shoulder, using his other hand to rub his knuckles over my head. 'Having a laugh.'

'Yeah, lighten up, Roman,' Jackson says. 'All brotherly love.'

'Are you friendly with them?' Roman asks me, crossing his arms.

All coherence exits my brain as I meet his eye. For the first time he's talking to me, and I don't know why. I shake my head, not wanting to speak in front of him, not wanting my voice to betray me and my emotions in any way. What a relief that he cannot hear my thumping heart and the beating of my eardrums.

'Then fuck right off,' Roman orders the three boys.

'*Pfft.*' Taylor waves his hands. 'You got no humour, mate.'

'If this is your humour, it's shit,' I say.

Taylor's look could put me in an early grave. He scowls one last time at Roman before tutting, beckoning for Lee and Jackson to follow him.

Their voices bounce in the stairwell as the door swings shut, and when it closes, all I can hear is Roman's light breathing.

'You all right?' Roman asks.

His sharp features soften as he looks at me.

'Yeah.'

'They shouldn't do that,' Roman says.

'What is man if not domineering over others?'

'Huh?'

'They're just being autocratic.'

Roman tuts. 'They're being fools. That is not how men should behave.'

'Then they won't pass the tests, will they?'

Roman barks a laugh. 'Surprised they're still here, in all honesty.'

I'm not. The three boys don't show that side of them to anyone else. It's an overhang of what men once were, that's what Blake said once when he caught them bullying me. I'd never been able to voice my suspicions about why they targeted me, but it was like their bloodhound noses could sniff the otherness in me.

'I'm surprised they listened to you.'

'Those guys?' Roman scoffs. 'They tried to be my friend when I first got here. I told them where to go.'

'You did?'

'Guys like that won't get far out of these halls,' Roman says. 'You'll do well to remember that. Next time I might not be around.'

'I didn't need your help,' I mutter.

He stares at me. I wish he wouldn't. 'You sure about that?'

The tender, painful throbs on my back tell me otherwise.

Roman holds out a hand, touching beneath my eye. I flinch, wincing.

'Sorry. You're bruised.'

He lightly touches my face, my breath hitching. His fingers grasp my chin, tilting my head towards the sunlight coming through the window at the end of the corridor as he observes me, his plump lips parted ever so slightly. I notice the way they curve slightly upwards, as if he is smiling.

'You want to go to the nurse?' he finally asks, his grip softening until he lets go.

My skin tingles and it's as if the nerves of my body follow his retreating hand, as if crying out for him to touch me again. I rub the spot he'd touched, eyes looking down. 'I'll be all right.'

'At least get some ice on it.'

'I'll be *fine*.'

Roman shrugged. 'Suit yourself.'

Hands in his pockets, he walks towards the door that Taylor escaped through, whistling as he does so. Torn, dazed at his compassion, I say, 'Hey. Roman?'

He barely looks behind him, nodding slightly to show he's listening.

'Thank you.'
His hand waves before he leaves me alone.

CHAPTER 5

Okay, so I have to admit, I was wrong and I should have gone to the nurse straightaway. About an hour after Roman's suggestion of getting ice, my eye is throbbing, and a quick look in the mirror shows a dark purple patch stretching towards my cheek.

But that pain doesn't compare to the panic that pulses through me at the memory of Roman talking to me. Looking at me. Why? Why did he decide to stick up for me? Ever since he got here, he's kept himself to himself. Sure, he's got the people he sits with, the people I've seen him talking to, but seeing him alone in the mornings, glimpsing him walking the halls alone, all of that points to a boy who is lonely. Boys like Roman don't concern themselves with boys like me.

I'm in the library, holding an ice pack to my face that I got when I finally relented in going to the nurse's office, using the shadows as my disguise to get lost in thoughts of Roman. Leaning back into a red leather armchair, I curl my legs underneath me, balancing a Thomas Hardy book on my knee, flipping past the foreword encouraging us to 'think differently'.

The professors allow us to read literature from times gone by, offering an insight into what once was, thoughts that may no longer resonate. Lit by oil lamps and candlelight, the dark library flickers an ember glow as I reach for a mug of tea from the nearby oak side table, breathing in the scent of leatherbound books and ageing pages, all piled high on rigid, dark wood bookcases that line the walls. Floorboards creak above in the oak galleries, as students slink within the shadows.

I sometimes wonder how much studying actually goes on here.

A risky game, if there is something more.

A risk that I've ignored, no matter how many times I've thought about it. Thoughts that Roman has made difficult to discount.

I've tucked myself away in a nook, hoping to attract as little attention as possible. It's not that I mind people here, except for Taylor, he can do one for all I care. Sometimes I need a place to breathe. Being in a school full of boys who mostly feel like family has its downsides, too.

As Thomas Hardy himself once said, *I have no fear of men, as such, nor of their books.*

The library is my safety, the library is my respite.

Everyone will be ready to face the tasks of June, which will put all of our learning to the test. Paper exams are a memory game. Make a note of every possible exam topic, and set time to delve into each one, and if you've done it well you can recall what you've already studied. I do not worry too much about my exams.

But the tests? That's a whole different ball game.

We'll be marked on our three years of study, but we'll also be marked on our personalities. Who we are as young men. Are we ready to step out of this school and start a new life? Are we capable of looking after ourselves, and looking after our girlfriends? Respecting them? Are we right for the life promised us by Ganymede's? These are questions I can't answer, for I feel the version I must sell is a lie.

It all seemed like such a pipedream in that first year of Ganymede's when we were all so excited to become better men, and eventually meet the girl of our dreams. I think we all thought it wouldn't really happen. And yet, here we are.

One month.

Thirty days.

It's all come down to this.

I keep my thumb between the pages of *Tess of the d'Urbervilles*, thinking about all the history we've learnt.

'History can be learnt from, class.' Mother Mai is our history teacher, and from day one of our Ganymede education she let us know we are lucky to even be alive. The history textbooks in front of us have whole chapters dedicated to how touch and go it was that this planet would even survive in its current state. 'If people hadn't ignored history, perhaps we wouldn't have made the same mistakes. Yes, history teaches us all. If only those in the twenty-first century had known that. The beginning of change was coming long before the later stuff, but they continued to ignore it.' She smiled at this, as if the collapse of society itself near the later years of the twenty-first century is now a mere joke. Overconsumption, wars, ultra-processed food, declining fertility rates and climate change have all altered the way of life.

'That's why you are so fortunate to be in a school like ours,' Mother Mai reminded us.

Of course, now we listen to the stories of why Ganymede's, and academies like it, came to be and we yawn, and we doodle and we try to stay awake. 'The effects of a declining population have impacted us, and still do, in the twenty-second century.' She had gestured then to the window, where rain had been constantly falling for three days. The grass, once overgrown and a wild heaven, was sodden; the food growing outside moved inside, though much had been lost. 'Despite this, we're seeing fewer storms.'

The wind howled as if to protest this, but when the winds come, they rage, as if remembering what humanity did. Yes, the weather is still extreme. Still too hot, but it's cooling, apparently. Less consumption, less nastiness going into the air, so better air quality, and healthier diets. It's ingrained in us now.

More importantly, there are healthier men. Educated men. Kinder men. Respectful men. Fixed men.

Families, though? That's a problem. I think back to one of Mother Mai's rants.

'Can you believe that people chose not to procreate? Not to start families?'

All because of the rise of something called a right-wing government, where men demanded control of women's autonomy. Insane, if you ask me.

'If you can believe it, women began to refuse to marry, and even refused to have kids.' Mother Mai shook her head at this, incredulous.

'The entitled lot who refused simply because they didn't want to.' She'd barked a laugh at this. 'This protest, this reclamation, meant that fewer children were being brought into the world. Beyond my own personal feelings, it is worth noting that those that were brought in, by choice or otherwise, were being born into a world of uncertainty. Before collapse, the population rose to over eight billion. Mother Nature herself could no longer hold up under the weight of it all. We're now down to around just over one billion people. Before that, we were dangerously low.'

Blake had revelled in the glory at Mother Mai's words,

always one to remind people that he was the one to bring the population to one billion again.

Mother Mai's stories of men's fertility rates dropping because of air pollution and harmful chemicals are etched on my brain. It's tough to listen to an old professor telling us that our sperm counts need to be higher, and that microplastics were gathering in men's testicles, but at least now that seems to be back on track. Fewer plastics, more fertility.

'But let's not just blame the women, boys. Like I say, learn from history. It wasn't just the women not having children.'

She'd told us of neglected men, ignored men, broken men, angry men. Victims of a patriarchal society, whether they knew it or not. Victims who wouldn't, couldn't help themselves. Ignored, hated. Hostile men, misogynistic men. Violent men, who harmed other men, other women, other people, other minorities.

Not all men, but men.

I remember the first time I heard about the dangers women faced, and how men never took accountability for their actions.

'There was a time when women armed themselves with pepper spray and keys between knuckles and walked in groups for fear of being attacked. Raped. Murdered.' She'd emphasised each word, relishing in the discomfort it caused. 'Political upheaval made women fight for their rights. Men fell into conspiracy and hatred. Men's mental health was ignored, ridiculed, until it was too late and people asked themselves, "Why are men doing this?"

'There were men who sympathised with women, a lot fewer then than there would be now, thank you, Ganymede's. They showed "solidarity"—' she paused here, putting the word in air quotes '—by also refusing to entertain the thought that a family was needed.

'In front of you are case studies on the emasculation of

man,' Mother Mai said. 'Men became lazy. They stopped thinking of themselves as heads of households. It became less important for them to aspire to that. Yes, we can also blame men for not having families. Twenty-first-century men cared more for technology than human connection. Men became weak. They lost their fight. They relinquished control of themselves. That is what we are eradicating from all of you.

'Humans began to realise they couldn't even afford to bring children into the world. By the time they paid their rents and their taxes, or bought highly inflated food, they were broke. Why bring children into it when people could barely look after themselves?'

Yes, climate was a big factor in reproduction, as it was in all walks of life. When families are displaced, they're not going to be thinking about procreation. A struggling economy was another. 'Food couldn't be grown because of extreme climates,' Mother Mai lectured. 'And people had to leave their homes, move away from rising tides. Animals began to decline, and diseases spread.'

We'd learnt how rights were stripped from the disabled, and those who weren't white or who needed help the most, while minorities and those fleeing war-torn countries were painted to be the issue, used as a distraction by corrupt and useless governments and leaders. Factor in lifestyles that were victims of the economy, like people being unable to afford homes at the behest of career politicians who were supposed to be for the people, while the rich hoarded their wealth and got richer as people struggled to get by. It's really no surprise that the world fell apart.

'It simply couldn't go on anymore,' Mother Mai had told us. 'Not the way it was. As people died, others did what they could to survive, but it was clear something needed to change before humanity was wiped out completely.'

The plague came after the collapse, killing off those who were too weak to go on. With humans struggling to make life, humanity was on its knees. Thankfully, our king took swift action. The plague was short-lived, but it did its damage.

Since Ganymede's' conception, and the conception of boarding schools like it, men were kinder. Softer. More empathetic. We were gentle again. Slowly but surely, humanity learnt to be equal. To work together.

Now, we exist to repopulate.

And to save mankind itself.

Which is why someone like me, someone who craves the touch of a man, has to keep that part of himself hidden. A constant battle between what is right and what is right for me. If they ever knew, I'd find myself in the open country. Find myself in jail. Find myself dead. Society, in that sense, has gone way back in time.

And it is why I have to avoid Roman Edwards at all costs, because today he came too close, and he didn't help me. Not really.

I listened with gritted teeth over a few lessons as Mother Mai told us about previous liberating laws regarding sexuality, and their rolling back. 'It all got a bit ridiculous,' she'd said.

Hard to fathom now that the same sex could once marry. Hard to believe that people weren't men or women at all, but something out of the binary, that people were themselves in the face of adversity.

There is no adversity anymore, and so there is no need to fight.

'This world relies on men and women being one in matrimony,' Mother Mai had said only a few weeks ago. 'Flights of fancy should not be entertained like they once were. We crave traditional values.'

It sounded like a religion, though none of us subscribed to one.

People go on marrying because they can't resist natural forces, I'd thought at the time, thinking of *Jude the Obscure*. How I'd wanted to say that to Mother Mai.

But I didn't think she'd be happy with the rest of the sentence.

Many of them may know perfectly well that they are possibly buying a month's pleasure with a life's discomfort.

CHAPTER 6

Professor Lawrence leans over his office desk, his right hand resting on his forehead, fingers combing absently through his hair. Ebbing candlelight casts shadows in the crevices of the walls, and over the whisky glass next to him. His table is in disarray with leatherbound notebooks, old books, parchment and small antique dishes. Some of the boys swear they've seen a small gun on his table, others have said they've seen cigars. The newspaper is out beneath him, and he's absorbed in the words, his eyes trailing through each article, his lips pursed. My fingers pull at my collar as heat greets me, with the scent of earth. He's undone the first three buttons of his shirt, as well as the buttons on his sleeves, so that they flow away from his wrist and reveal the hairs on his arms.

Then he sees me, and he composes himself, quickly closing the paper and folding it up. Blushing at being caught, I approach his table, as he hides the paper away from me.

'Were you there long?' He asks me, voice slightly hoarse, as he reaches for his whisky. There's a half-drunk bottle next to him. But I don't think he is drunk. He watches me steadily, and he seems as composed as ever, despite the look.

'No, sir.' It's the truth. I was there just long enough to watch him, to see how he holds himself when the world isn't watching.

'Take a seat.'

I do, sitting opposite him in the front row of our class. I compose my thoughts as he drinks.

He gestures at my face. 'What's happened here?'

'It's nothing to worry about.'

'Have you been hit?'

'Please, sir. It's nothing.'

It's become a somewhat comfortable thing to come down here and speak with Professor Lawrence, but this is probably one of only a handful of times when I have come here this late.

'Shouldn't you be getting ready?' he asks me.

I breathe out, glad that he seems to be letting the marks on my skin go. 'Figured I've got some time before we're needed in the hall. I've been in the library.'

'Really?' He says with a smile. 'I thought you might want to avoid books now.'

He eyes the one in my hand, and I move it from view, even though I'm doing nothing wrong by reading it. 'I like to read for pleasure, sir.'

'That certainly looks well read.'

'Guess a lot of students have enjoyed it over the years.'

He considers me, the smile never leaving. 'Anything you wish to talk of?'

'Am I disturbing you?'

'Not at all.'

'Anything interesting in the paper?'

He pauses. 'The usual.'

The usual, I think. I wonder what the usual is. But I know

what my typical question is, and so does he, and he's not surprised when I lead with it. 'I can't help thinking about them, and why they were coming back.'

My parents, that is. I've found out small details over the years as I've sought answers for how they could die, as if we aren't all mortals and any day could be our last. But what I knew from that encounter with Dwynwen was that they were on their way back here.

'Any new thoughts this time around?'

I shake my head. 'I have so many. They all blur into one and I no longer recognise what is new or old.' I swallow. 'But there's one that I always ponder on, when I'm not thinking of other things.' Like Blake. Like Roman. Like the life that waits for me. 'Whether or not Father was actually proud of me. Whether he truly wanted me here at all.'

Lawrence sips his drink, the chair he sits upon creaking underneath him as he moves. He does this. Says nothing, only waits for me to spill like the whisky that disappears down his throat.

'They were coming back, Professor,' I say. '*Why* were they coming back?'

'I wish I could know, too. For your sake.'

I nod, biting my lip. 'Were they coming back because I forgot something? Did *they* forget to tell *me* something?' I meet Lawrence's eye. 'Because I don't belong here, Professor. I don't belong to any of this.'

Lawrence lets out a small sigh, and I wince, afraid that he doesn't care for this conversation right here, right now. 'You belong, Mr Cecil. Why do you believe you don't?'

I cannot tell him. I will not tell him. Not the true reasons. 'I should be a confident man, and yet I am afraid.'

'By admitting your faults, you are what a man should be,' Lawrence says. 'For too long men were told they had to be a certain way, and that they should man up and grin and bear it. It is our job to ensure that does not happen again. Ganymede's is always here to help.'

So why do I feel like they can't help me?

'I miss them so much, and yet I can't cry,' I mutter.

Lawrence offers me a sad smile. 'That doesn't mean you're missing them wrong.' We sit in silence for a moment, the only occasional sound is the whisky being refilled and the flicker of flames. Finally, Lawrence says, 'You're in tune with your emotions, Mr Cecil, and for that you should give yourself credit. Almost eighteen, you have suffered more loss and hurt than many before you. What is important now is that you do not let that hurt consume you. Continue to address it, speak through it, feel it, and I will be here to help you when you need me to. I assure you of that.'

His last words seem emphasised, yet final. I give him a nod, before dismissing myself from his room.

'Dylan?'

I turn. 'Yes.'

He's already opening his newspaper, but he keeps the contents hidden from me. 'I'll be keeping an eye on those bruises. If you get anymore...'

'It won't happen again, sir. Boys will be boys.'

'Hmm.'

It's my cue to leave, and within moments he's lost to whatever is before him.

Switching the hand that holds my book, I come out from the basement and Professor Lawrence's office and find myself on the ground floor. There's the aroma in the air of our evening meal, and my stomach rumbles. I'm crossing the hallway, tugging my knitted maroon sleeves closer to my hands to protect against the air conditioning, when the front door opens, Roman steps in, towel wrapped around his shoulders. For one wild moment I think of darting behind one of the plinths and trying to hide myself, and as seconds slip by and he still hasn't seen me it doesn't seem like such a wild idea. But then, halfway to the stairs, he spots me, standing in the hallway like a lost odd sock.

'Hi.' It comes out of me like I'm winded, and rightly so. He's so ... fit. Heat rises to my cheeks, and my body tingles and I seem to lose all memory of where I have been.

Roman adjusts his towel, so that it covers his bare chest. 'Didn't think I'd see anyone.'

With part of his chest concealed I can focus. Kind of. 'No, I suppose I do look a bit odd just ... standing here.'

'Nice jumper,' he appraises.

'It's old.' Why tell him that? He doesn't care.

'What exactly are you doing?'

I cast around, settling on a marble bust of Ganymede himself. 'You know, just paying respects.'

Roman cocks an eyebrow. 'To Ganymede?'

'Uh, sure, yeah. Admiring his ... hair. And, you know, the art. I like art. I've always liked art. Wish we could have studied more of it, really, but I suppose we had to learn all the other stuff, didn't we? And...' *Rambling, Dylan. Stop rambling.*

Roman crosses his arms, his pale red and white striped towel stroking his skin. I try not to look too much, but it's hard not to when he looks as sculpted as the busts of gods that line the halls.

'What art do you like?'

That wasn't what I expected him to ask.

'Oh, um...' Shit. Some of the stuff I don't want to talk to anyone about. Not because they are sordid, but because I don't think people will understand. There's Hippolyte Flandrin's study, young male nude seated beside the sea, but I don't think I should bring that to his attention.

To tell the truth about the art I appreciate would expose me for what I am, and I'm not prepared to do that. Especially not to Roman Edwards. So, I settle on, 'David Ligare comes to mind,' and hope he doesn't ask...

'Why?'

I baulk. 'Well, Greek art is of course wonderful to look at, but...' I swallow, trying to ignore the rising heat to my cheeks. 'But I like that there is work here of someone who was influenced by the classic works of art and could make it current to his time.'

Roman nods, slow, considering. His skin glistens in the candles that burn, and I imagine painting him, how gold and red would cast him so elegantly against the dark browns of the panelled walls. 'How did you find out about him?'

'One of the art history books in the library had him included.'

'Any favourite pieces of his?'

'I liked his *Achilles* and the *Body of Patroclus*.' It's somewhat close to the mark, a painting which depicts athletic, toga-clad men carrying a body. It was painted in a time of AIDs, something I've researched in private along with other health pandemics, and I think that aspect says a lot. I think his other works of the male figure, often nude, depict men at their most human. *Arete*, for example, tells us we can reach our full potential.

Surprisingly, Ganymede's does not shy away from depictions of nudity. When the school is full of Ancient Greek statues, paintings and some of our stained-glass windows, it's not something they can exactly hide. We have a healthy, non-sexual view of nudity, but it's not like we all walk around butt-naked, and no images or paintings in the school depict anyone below the age of twenty-one. It's part of our culture, the belief being that we can have healthy conversations about what is accepted and what is morally right.

'What I like about someone like Ligare's work is his symmetry. This sort of aesthetic look into humankind itself. It's like a reminder that we can be perfect when observed by the right people.'

Roman makes a noise between a laugh and realisation. He sniffs, before saying, 'I like to paint.'

'You do?'

'You seem surprised.'

'I wasn't expecting it, s'all.'

'Oh? And why not?'

'You strike me more as an outdoorsy guy. Good with his hands.'

I look at his sizeable hands and realise what I'm doing, what I've said, and stand back, as if that might separate myself from the past me of a few seconds ago. Good with his hands? Really? I could have said anything else, but now all I'm thinking about is his hands and how they look and how they might feel in mine.

I bet they'd feel good.

Roman holds up his hands, peers at them. 'Huh. These hands? You think they look good?'

'I think you'd be good *with* them.'

Roman looks up at me, smiling. 'I can be good with my hands, yeah.'

Oh, Saturn and gods above.

'What I mean is, you seemed good in the archery and outdoorsy classes we had.'

'You noticed?'

I force a smile. 'Well, I guess I can't deny that I haven't, can I?'

He laughs at this, running a hand over his buzzed hair. 'I guess not.'

'But a lot of people notice the new boy.'

'Ha, that they do.' He sighs, glancing at his hands again.

'Yeah, I don't mind the outdoor stuff. You never know when you're going to need to tie a knot and all that.'

My laugh is dry, but he doesn't seem to mind. We stand in the warmth of candlelight, surrounded by artists of time gone by.

'I've never quite understood Ganymede's,' he says.

'Oh?'

He points at the statue. 'Like, him. Why they've named this place after him.'

I look at Ganymede's face, described as the most handsome of mortals by Homer. 'He was the server to Zeus, but before that he was but a humble shepherd. A boy who crafted the land and became server to king and country as a man. Eternally youthful, immortal, so that we can look to him and embody him at the right time in our lives. Why not Ganymede's, when that is who we aspire to be?'

Roman's eyebrows raise as he smiles slightly. 'That is one way of looking at him, yes.'

'There is no other way.'

'Ah, but there is.' He comes closer, and even though I want to put as much distance between us as possible, I stay rooted to the spot. Every step he takes is in rhythm with my heart, which is going to betray what I feel. Roman lowers his voice. 'Homer writes that Ganymede was noted for his beauty, and gives a rather romanticised telling of how Ganymede was plucked from obscurity to be Zeus's cupbearer, but have you never thought to ask yourself why?'

'Because he was the perfect man.' I blush, feeling like I'm in a class without all the answers.

'Zeus certainly thought so,' Roman says, wiggling his eyebrows. 'You don't get the accolade of being the sign of Aquarius if you're just another cupbearer.'

'Ganymede had distinction, and we are here to be distinct,' I retort.

'But could Ganymede have been something more?'

I am not getting into a debate with Roman about Greek mythology in the middle of the deserted hallway. 'With all due respect, you have only been here a year. I have been here for three, and I have been working towards this life since—'

'Ah, so because I come from a lower school, I don't get to have a say on Ganymede and what he represents?'

'He represents the perfect man.'

'Perhaps he can represent more than that.'

I shake my head, incredulous at his disposition. He might be here because he proved himself elsewhere, but talking like that will not get him to graduation. He pats Ganymede on the head, and even that feels condescending to me. I watch how his body moves as he steps away from the bust, from me.

'My work isn't good, by the way,' he finally says. 'My paintings. They're messy, really. I don't get much time to do them.'

Maybe he's realised the error of his words.

'I've never painted, myself.'

'Oh? And why not?'

'I like to admire rather than partake.'

Roman cocks his head. 'If you ever want to give it a go, we could go to the art studio and see what we come up with.'

My forehead furrows but I nod all the same. 'Yeah, maybe one day.'

It's not like we're going to be hanging out anytime soon. This is the most we've ever said to one another. He steps forward, looks at my face.

'That bruise looks worse.'

'Think of it as a paint smudge,' I say.

His eyes flicker over me, his mouth drawing into a line. 'Hmm, you sure you're all right?'

'I can handle it.'

Roman shrugs, stepping away from me. 'I'd best go and get dressed. Get ready for the evening meal.'

That would be a big help to me, I must admit.

He walks away, and I glimpse his back beneath his shifting towel. He pauses on the stairs. 'You didn't ask me what my favourite artwork is.'

'Oh, right. What's your favourite art work?'

'*The Vitruvian Man.*'

'Why?'

'Nothing less than perfection,' he says, with a nod at Ganymede, and then he's gone, leaving me standing in the hallway rubbing my chest.

I look back to the bust of Ganymede, remembering all I've ever known about him, thinking how that information has never been challenged. I wait a few moments and then head back upstairs myself, a light bounce in my step.

CHAPTER 7

'Good evening,' Dwynwen says. She sits at the top table in the dining hall, in a doomsday throne chair ingrained with the date, 1086. The other professors sit in similar chairs, but without the leather padding and the carvings of crowns and flowers. They all have golden goblets before them, their patterned plates sparkling clean just like ours, only ours are pale, and our goblets are thin glasses. 'I know you are hungry, and my stomach is rumbling just as much as yours, but you are more alert when you haven't eaten.'

My stomach rumbles as if in protest and Johnny nudges me, giggling.

'In front of you are envelopes,' Dwynwen says, looking at our tables where we sit in our houses. 'Inside each envelope is the name of the boy you will be paired with for the next month. Eight tasks, starting tomorrow, the first of June.'

Whispers break out around us.

'Did you know we'd have a partner?' Johnny whispers.

'No.'

'I feel sick,' Cameron moans.

Dwynwen waits for the chatter to subside. 'I know, I know. It's all very exciting, isn't it? Now, before you open that envelope, know this. You are paired to your strengths. Those strengths are the archetypes of the men you are to become. This next month will test you, but it will encourage you to know thyself. Say it with me: "I will know myself."'

'I will know myself,' we chorus.

'Come on, you can summon more energy than that, I'm sure.'

She lifts her hands in a crescendo, and we chant, 'I will know myself.'

'Good, good.' She beams. 'You will know thyself like women know themselves. No longer will you be entitled, or emotionally stunted. These tasks are set to define you. You will know your archetype once you open the envelope.'

'Archetypes?' Johnny whispers to us, keeping his head low. 'What archetypes?'

'They've only done it once before,' Cameron says. 'I remember Mother Mai talking about it.'

'But what's the point?'

'Who we are to become,' Cameron whispers, flapping his hands for Johnny to be quiet.

'You may now open your envelopes. But do not move from where you are sitting. There will be time to meet your partner over dinner.'

Taylor, sitting a few people away from us, rips his envelope open and cheers. 'Lee, boy, looks like we're together.'

Lee grins, turning his paper to show that Taylor is his partner, too.

'Oh, no,' Cameron groans.

'What is it?' I ask, holding my unopened envelope.

Cameron shows me his white parchment paper. Elis Bell's name glistens back at me in gold foil, and underneath the word: sensitive.

'They got your archetype right.' Johnny chuckles.

'I don't want to be with Elis Bell. The guy's a slacker and he quotes Shakespeare too much.'

'Cameron doth protest too much, methinks.'

Cameron glares at Johnny, while I laugh, glancing over to the Mercury house in time to see Elis yawning, his open envelope discarded next to him. He's one of the boys I've seen Roman with. 'Maybe you're meant to bring the best out of him.'

Cameron chokes out a cry, covering his face.

'Ha, nice, I've got Jackson,' Johnny says.

'That's not nice,' I say.

'What's your archetype?' Cameron asks.

'Rebel.' Johnny's eyebrows raise. 'That's ... interesting.'

A stone in my throat makes it hard to swallow as I fumble to open my envelope. Is there still a chance mine might say Blake? What if one of my tasks is to find him? To bring us closer together for whatever reason?

The paper slips out, and a glint of gold makes me pause.

Roman Edwards.

Magician.

I can't be with Roman Edwards, not when this is the month that really requires me to stay on track, stay focused.

'I'm a magician,' I mutter.

Roman's watching me. His arms are crossed, the skin of his biceps rippling. He winks, nodding once, curtly. With a swish of his hand, he brings up his own paper.

Dylan Cecil.

Warrior.

'Mate, you've got Roman?' Johnny gasps. 'You're about to be the most popular bloke in school.'

I force a laugh. Roman is only popular because people love a mystery. Roman grins at me and I hold up my own paper, as if it were an offering of some sort. As if we're close enough to nod at one another.

'Okay, quiet, quiet,' Dwynwen says. 'Good, good. Some of you may be questioning the archetypes presented to you. Your archetypes have been determined by your exams, but also by the way you have conducted yourself over the past three years. Your archetypes are your strengths, your core being. They will play pivotal roles in your tasks. Some of you are the providers, and you will be expected to act as such throughout these tasks. Then there are the warriors, prepared to face any battle.' Roman breathes deeply, and when he looks at me I pretend I was looking elsewhere. A few moments later, though, and my eyes dart to him again, only to see he is still watching me. I clear my throat, reach for my drink, and turn back to Dwynwen, feeling his stare. 'The sensitives...' Some of the boy's chuckle, and Cameron's head bows. 'It is not a bad thing to be sensitive. You should know this by now. Sensitivity is power.' Dwynwen's tone is steely, and Taylor's grin fades. 'Being in touch with the feminine aspects of oneself is a strength. You have to be compassionate to one another. It is its own strength. Some of you are known as rebels.' I smile at Johnny, before glancing towards Roman again. He's watching Dwynwen now. 'The rebels are here to learn when a rule should be broken, and when it should be obeyed. Then there are the magicians. They're the men who can think outside of the box. To have a magician partner is an honour.'

Roman rolls his eyes at me, but the edges of his lips quirk upwards. I flash him a cocky grin.

'Curfew starts this evening. You are not to be out of your dorm rooms after nine p.m., or before eight a.m. Tomorrow morning, you will need to be up bright and early, and we will allow you to be awake and out of your dorm rooms before eight. A professor will be in the assembly hall waiting with instructions.' She surveys the room, smiling warmly. 'Well? What are you waiting for? Get ready for your meals.'

CHAPTER 8

What archetype would Blake have been? A scholarly boy. I would have thought he would be someone high ranking, someone bright. Might he have been a provider?

I guess I'll never know.

Roman sips from his drink, alone in a sea of boys. What the hell am I going to do? Johnny and Cameron talk about the tasks, speculating on what might happen, but I don't say a word. Our food is served to us by male waiters brought in from the nearest hamlet. They're all smiles as they place steaming green goddess soup before us, a scent of chilli in the air. It's full of potatoes, peas, broccoli, green onion and leaks. At the top table, Dwynwen is in conversation with Professor Rory, our newest teacher. Rory's eyes meet mine and he quickly looks away, as if he is afraid of being seen by students.

The chilli burns my tongue, sizzling until I'm numb. The hunger I had before is fed with anxiety of the threat to my security now that I am to be with Roman. For the past three years, I've been able to ignore these feelings that I carry.

Feelings I first noticed when I was younger. Feelings that have made themselves both clear and confusing to me as I have aged. I have tried everything to get rid of them, from the ridiculous to the downright dangerous. Told myself it is a phase that I will grow out of. Drank hot tea as if it might burn it away. Sunk under the bathwater and considered drowning myself. I've even allowed myself to indulge in the feelings, figuring that as men we're supposed to acknowledge what we feel. When I do that, I feel good, and then guilt consumes me and I may as well kiss goodbye to getting sleep even before I rest back on the pillow. I think by doing that, by acknowledging such feelings, I'm correcting myself. Correcting myself enough that eventually I will awake and I will be cured.

That day is yet to come.

As I eat the soup but barely register the taste now that the hot chilli has made my tongue and lips numb, I take some time to watch Roman, trying to work him out. He's everything I'm not. Built bigger, a swagger that I cannot match. His skin is smooth, and puberty seems to have been kind to him with the light dusting of stubble along his jaw. He keeps his arms close to his chest, but all it serves to do is make him look superior, like he could drag me to his chest and squish me with ease.

I try not to think of that.

Slowly, he puts his drink down on the table, his lips drawn into a line. Is he disappointed? Disappointed that he has come here for a better life and he's got to see me during the most important month of his education?

Finishing my soup, Johnny recounts a story about something in his hamlet. I've got this far with no one truly knowing what I am. People might suspect, and that's what I think Taylor's bullying is rooted in, but he can't prove anything. Mostly because I'm careful, and also because I have never been close to someone in that way. I'm sure my relationship with

Blake didn't help the suspicions, but I was always ready to argue that we were as brotherly as any other close friends here. As I look around the hall at all my fellow students, I can't help think that there may be others like me, hiding themselves because they have to.

One of the thoughts that keeps me up at night is the question of what is most important? My answer to that changes all the time, but it always comes to the same conclusion. That I need to graduate and get to a hamlet and live how I am expected to, and any feelings of mine are ignored, dealt with in private. I am not to be selfish. I am to be caring and look after my wife, giving her all that she needs.

I scan the envelop that has magician written on it. A magician knows his tricks, and he is well versed in his illusions. So far, I have been good at smoke screens, at pretending to be something I'm not. What's a few more weeks, or the rest of my life?

I do not need to address what I feel, but Roman makes that difficult. Fear runs its hands across my nerves, playing me like a harpsichord as I think of the wounds he can open. How he can debunk my illusions and threaten my standing.

It's simple, Dylan, I think to myself. *Roman is but a dot on the horizon of your life. All you have to do is keep him at an appropriate distance, work with him when the time calls for it, and keep focused on the bigger picture.*

How hard can that be?

CHAPTER 9

'I've been reading about the archetypes,' Cameron says when the boys are in their beds that evening. His cane is resting against the side of his bed, something he uses to aid with his osteoarthritis in knee and hips.

While the rest of them returned to their common rooms, chatting with one another about the reality of what they're about to face, Cameron retreated to his room. When Johnny and I return to our beds, he has five books sprawled around him, and two clutched in his hands. He turns wild eyes to us, retreating slightly when Taylor comes in.

Taylor yawns. 'Boring.'

'No, it isn't,' Cameron says, keeping his eyes on the pages. 'We need to know why we've been assigned our archetypes. They'll be there for a reason.'

'It's not like this is life or death,' Taylor says.

'Do we know what happens to the boys who get disqualified?' Johnny questions, looking over towards Blake's empty bed.

'Who cares?' Taylor challenges.

'You'll care when you fail.'

'I'll come over there and beat you,' Taylor says, glaring at Johnny.

Johnny pounds his chest. 'Fight me.'

'No one is fighting anyone,' I say, though the bruise on my eyes says enough. 'Cameron is trying to help us and we should listen to him.'

I don't know why I argue with Taylor. Maybe it's because Roman has given me the courage to stand up to him.

'Pity he couldn't help you with that eye. Who did that to you?' Taylor asks me.

'Cameron, what have you found?' I ask.

Cameron nods at me, shifting forward in his bed as if he might get closer to us. 'The world runs on archetypes. I didn't realise the importance of it before, but Ganymede's develops boys into certain roles. Yeah, we knew they did that to some extent, but when they actually assign someone an archetype there's a reason for it. It means there's a lack out there.' He lays down the books he is holding and gestures beyond the boundaries of Ganymede's, boundaries we can't see. 'Turns out the schools choose when and who assigns the archetypes each year. It's why we've all been working on a more general basis the past two years than we are now.'

'But why would we do that?' Johnny asks.

'I guess because it's then easier for them to put us where they think we will do best,' Cameron says. 'You know, like where we'll fit in society. Instead of narrowing their cohort of students from the start.'

'Like this year?'

'Well, yeah, this year, but more importantly, we have the added layer of following our assigned roles.'

'So, I'm going to fuck society up?' says Johnny.

'There's no need for rebellions,' Taylor says.

'A rebel doesn't mean you have to be so literal about it,' Cameron replies, reaching for another book and trailing his finger down a page. 'Think of it all as being something within the boundaries of what already exists. Ah, here we go. It says a rebel's purpose is to challenge the norm, and to challenge his fellow man.'

'Challenge in what way?'

Cameron looks at me. 'Call things out, change some rules – could be anything, really.'

'Aw, but I wanted to fuck shit up,' Johnny moans.

'Well, good luck with that,' I say.

'Do that and you'll probably find yourself expelled.'

'I can handle that.' Johnny leans back with his hands behind his head. 'No biggie.'

'Yes, biggie.' Cameron shakes his head. 'There's no world out there for boys who don't have the support of their institution.'

'Maybe I'm meant to change that.' Johnny grins, making me laugh.

'Don't know what you're smiling about,' Cameron says to me. 'The magician goes hand in hand with the rebel and the warrior.'

'In what regard?' I ask, thinking of Roman. Thinking of his hands.

Cameron peers at the pages, bringing his book closer to his oil lamp. A hardback book falls to the floor with a shuddering thud, but Cameron doesn't bother to retrieve it. 'The magician is intuitive, a thinker, a visionary and a man of knowledge. He thinks before he speaks, observes before he decides.'

'That's 'cause he's got no friends,' Taylor says.

'Mate, you haven't got a friend in this room,' Johnny says.

'Yeah, I have. Dylan's my mate, aren't you?'

'Carry on, Cameron,' I say.

'Those with a magician archetype can lead warriors and rebels into organised change.'

'That's what it says?'

Cameron turns the page. 'Right there.'

'I'm too far away to read that, but I'll take your word for it,' I say.

'You do like to study,' Johnny says.

'And you're always lost in your own head,' Cameron adds.

'Yeah, probably thinking about us naked.'

The lights seem to dim and my blood runs cold. Glad for the darkness, I pretend to plump my pillow, in case anyone sees my red face.

'Dylan's never talked about guys as much as you have, Taylor,' Johnny says.

'Fuck you.'

'He's got a point,' Cameron mutters.

'What did you say?' Taylor rounds on Cameron. 'You fucking weed.'

Cameron feigns pain. 'Whatever will I do with that insult?'

Taylor lobs a pillow at Cameron, who shields it with one of the books. 'What's your archetype, then?'

Taylor waves the question away. 'Doesn't matter.'

'Ohhh, are you bitter?' Johnny asks.

'No.'

'Clearly he is,' I say.

'I'm a provider, all right? A lovely nurturing provider.'

Cameron flips pages as he says, 'A man who is a provider is perhaps the most influential of all.' I grit my teeth. Taylor doesn't need anything else to inflate his ego. 'Every man should provide, but none more so than those assigned the role of provider. Providers have big families, should always have food on the table, and should know when to stop acting the fool. Providers lead, and every archetype falls in line.'

'Surprised there's no fool archetype,' I say.

'There is a whole list of them, but seems we've only been assigned a few this time around.'

'Well, that's a shame,' Johnny says, nodding his head at Taylor. 'He would fly with passing colours if he was assigned the fool.'

'Did you hear what he said?' Taylor asks the room. 'Providers lead and you all have to fall in line with me. I can help you out there, boys.'

Johnny makes a tsk noise.

Why is it that boys like Taylor always find themselves in a role of power? Boys that will become men who expect the world to bow down to them, worship the ground they walk upon. Men who never face consequences.

'I'm thirsty,' Taylor announces. 'Cameron, lad, go get me a drink.'

'Get it yourself.'

'That isn't a way to talk to a provider.'

'Providers should provide us all with water,' Johnny says. 'I don't know about you guys, but I'm parched.'

'Yeah. Me too,' I say.

'Sure, I could use a water,' Cameron says.

We all peer at Taylor.

He laughs, getting to his feet, muttering as he exits the room.

'I'm not drinking anything he gives me, by the way,' I say.

'Nah, it's just fun to make him do something, isn't it?' Johnny asks. 'Listen, Dylan, mate...'

The atmosphere in the room shifts. Even Cameron stops flipping through his pages. My throat bobs. 'Yeah?'

'What he said, about thinking about us—'

'I don't think about any of you naked,' I interrupt. 'I don't think about *anyone* naked.'

I cringe. Wrong answer? *Should* I say I *do* think about people naked? Nudity is in the art I love, after all, so I guess I do think about nudity. Should I pretend to be more interested in girls than I am?

'No, I don't mean...' Johnny sighs. 'Listen, uh...' His eyes slide to Cameron, who is watching me. 'You know we...you know we're okay with it, right?'

I close my eyes, face burning, glad for the shadows. 'Okay with *what*, exactly, Johnny?'

'No, I mean ... it's just, you know you can talk to us, don't you? You know. About *anything*.'

'There's nothing to talk about.'

The door opens, Taylor strolling in. 'Couldn't be arsed to refill the water, so I got one for myself.'

'You really are a dick,' Johnny says.

I'm glad, for once, for Taylor's intrusion. Johnny's words got too close to what I try to conceal. There's no world out there for a gay man, for queer people, if that is indeed what I really am. Right now, I don't need his prying eyes. Instead, I continue to tell myself lies.

CHAPTER 10

'Good morning, Dylan... Sorry, I mean Cecil. Uh, are we expecting Edwards at all?'
Sunlight streams through the windowpanes of the grand entrance. I dab at my sweating forehead. Judging by the thermometer that is at the front door, it's already twenty-seven degrees by midday. I'm dressed in blue shorts and a white T-shirt, with old trainers on. Running a hand through my messy hair, I smell the organic oat shampoo that we are given in our shower rooms.

Professor Rory stands with his hands behind his back, sunlight illuminating his smooth brown skin. When he came here at the beginning of the year, he looked lost. Wide-eyed, wearing a suit that seemed too big for him. He's been a great teacher and has prepared us for our lives outside of these halls. He's not wearing his usual dark suit, but instead wears a white linen shirt and smart heather-grey trousers. He must be feeling somewhat daring to wear a splash of colour.

'I haven't spoken to Roman,' I say. Was I supposed to? Is that part of the task? There are students in the grounds. 'Are we doing the task outdoors? Maybe he's out there.'

'We are, but there is no use trying to see what everyone else is doing,' Rory says to me. 'Each task is different and designed to develop trust between you and your teammate.'

I suppose that makes sense. If I am to spend time working with Roman for the next month, I'm going to have to know that I can trust him not to fuck all this up. Why couldn't I be paired with someone that has been at Ganymede's for the past three years? Someone less likely to make mistakes. Someone who knows the appropriate standards.

I don't laugh aloud, but I laugh internally at that word. Standards. Who am I to preach about standards when most of the time I don't feel as worthy as those around me. You see, Father struck a huge contract with the monarchy and I suspect that is what bought my entry into Ganymede's. Yes, he came here himself, and it's often a given that the children of Ganymede students will normally get a place here, but it is not guaranteed. I know he must have pulled some strings to make sure I got here, and I asked him once why the king favoured our family. 'The king and I understand one another,' Father had said one morning. 'He owes me.' Which is why I don't understand why he was coming back.

I was eleven when I first saw the royal family. They came to visit our hamlet, though not because the hamlet was particularly special. King Carwyn Celyn, the Holly King, and his queen, Sara Celyn, youthful and bright in their beauty, pulled up outside my home and our family farm on a warm October morning. They were fairly new to the throne. My father and mother fretted all week about the big royal visit. I remember being enthralled by the way Carwyn's suit gripped his chiselled body. The diameters of his chest muscles, the real estate of his stomach. I busied myself with potato planting in the field to avoid having to look at the king any longer. My mother and father were now responsible for supplying food to the establishments selected by the crown, which included the schools that created perfect men and women. I remember their joy and the celebrations lasted for weeks, going into Saturnalia. We'd been busy ever since, but I didn't mind. At long last I had something to bring to the family, something I could give back to my devoted parents. I learnt how to farm and I learnt the way of the land and I was always rewarded with beaming smiles from my mother and father.

'I told you Carwyn would look after us,' Father said to us when the contract had been signed, their promotion sealed.

'*King* Carwyn, Charlie,' Mother reprimanded.

I was drenched in sweat and with sunburnt skin when my mother called to me to come to the gates to meet King and Queen Celyn, and their daughter, Princess Cerys.

'Young man, *bore da*,' King Carwyn said to me after I had bowed to each member.

'Hello, your majesty.'

'You do not mean to tell me it is only your son who ploughs these fields?' He asked this of my father, all good humour and jovial. They were familiar with one another, my father and the king.

My father spluttered, insisting it was a family effort.

'I am sure of it. You are doing a good job. Why, he looks just like you.'

His eyes roved over me, and I felt severely underdressed in my hand-me-down vest and the shorts that barely clung to my hips.

'We provide only the best food for the kingdom,' Mother said, when Father said nothing.

'Oh, don't we know it?' Carwyn laughed. 'Students in our schools are reporting they feel less hungry, which is fantastic.

All organically grown, too. We are finding out if nutrition has improved, and I am sure the results will be satisfactory.'

'I can't believe people once ate such rubbish,' Father commented.

'Unfortunately, it was the way things went. But not anymore,' Carwyn said, shaking his finger. 'Our hamlets are thriving and we are recuperating. I know for certain there are fewer microplastics being consumed.'

My eyes never left the king, even though I knew it was rude to stare. Nobody questioned it, if they did notice. I suppose all they saw was a young boy in admiration of a true man, but I had my first moment of questioning what it was that made my stomach feel like it was full of ants.

'It was lovely to meet you, young man,' the king said to me. 'I'm afraid I did not catch your name.'

Father covered his mouth, as if in shock that he'd forgotten something so important. I smiled, and said, 'Dylan, your grace.'

'Dylan,' Carwyn had said, looking at his family. Then his eye met my father's. Something changed in his expression. 'You called him Dylan?'

Mother shifted.

'I did.'

The king held my father's gaze, jaw clenched, before he turned back to me. 'Lovely to meet you, Dylan. Now, Charlie boy, I wonder if we can talk...'

The king began to walk with my father, while Mother went in a different direction with Sara and Cerys, leaving me standing in the field with potatoes waiting to be planted and dirty hands.

There are footsteps on the stairs now, disturbing my memories, and a few moments later Roman comes around the corner, wearing a dark green vest top and loose-fitting jeans. I have to take a moment to take him in, to compose myself. I'm not going to stay focused if I'm looking at Roman's muscles.

'Nice of you to join us, Edwards,' Rory says. He never calls us 'Mr', maybe because he's in his twenties. Maybe he feels closer to us than he should. 'We're running a tad behind, but nothing major. Now that you're both here, I suppose I should say, welcome to task one. Come on.'

He opens the door and heat rushes towards us, joining the warmth that rises on my neck as I feel Roman brush past me. Stepping outside, I'm glad I've lathered my skin with lotion to protect me from the rays. I wish they'd invented something to keep us cool, like outdoor air-conditioning units. Birds tweet overhead, bees buzz as we break away from the school, bound for the edge of the forest. Johnny walks into the maze in the distance, and there are people in the old Victorian greenhouse. I wonder what everyone's doing, how they all might be learning to trust one another, as I side-eye Roman.

I still know little about him, except that he paints and he has controversial views on Ganymede. Mostly, Roman comes here and everyone admires him and he swims at early hours. What is his favourite subject? What was the name of his last school? Where does he live when he isn't here?

Where has he been all my life?

I roll my shoulders and look away from him.

'Bit smoky,' I mutter.

The day is a bright blue, but it's hazy. Breathing in is like inhaling the last remnants of a bonfire. I almost expect to see ash, but there's nothing. Not even black smoke clouds.

'Wildfire in the open country a couple of miles away,' Rory says. 'It's under control but wind has blown some of the smoke in our direction.'

'Not good for air quality,' Roman says, surprising me.

'No, I suppose not.'

We walk a few more feet in silence, me lost in thought about the wildfires. It's another reason why nobody wants to fail and end up in the open countries. I hope nobody who has been subjected to that life has fallen victim to the flames.

'So, uh, yeah, trust,' Rory says, as if he's trying to remember what he's there to do. We're at the edge of the forest, and there's a set of arrows, next to a bow propped against a tree. 'Task one. It's vitally important that...' Rory pauses, looks at us. 'I don't need to do the whole Ganymede spiel to you, do I?'

I blink at this drop of scholarly facade from one of our professors. 'Uh ... no, sir.'

Rory grins, claps his hands. 'What a relief. I hate talking the way they do. It's like we have to be so prim and proper all the time, ain't it?'

Roman barely smiles, and my eyebrows raise. Neither of us say a word. Rory's smile fades ever so slightly, but he clears his throat and holds out both his hands towards the tree. 'Ah, right, so here we go then. This is your task.'

'The tree?' Roman asks.

'Yes. No. Not the tree. Kind of the tree, but no,' Rory says, and takes a moment to breathe. 'Trusting one another is important, but obviously it's even more so when you get out of here. Society doesn't work if we don't trust everyone, from king to neighbour. Your female partners will also be learning about trust, and you will have to trust one another. Trust everything that has brought you to each other. But before all of that, trust starts with you.' Rory peers at us before continuing. 'If there's one bit of advice I can give to you when you do these tasks this month, it's to keep perspective. So, shall we begin?'

I nod, my eyes straying to the bow and arrow. What could we possibly have to do with that?

'Climb that tree for me, Roman,' Rory says, smiling.

'Hmm?'

'Can you climb the tree for me, please?'

Roman meets my eye and I quickly look away, to the tree, focusing on the grooves in its bark that must be centuries old.

'Okay, sure.'

Roman steps forward, placing his hand on the trunk of the tree as he sizes it up. He reaches up and pulls, muscles flexing, lifting both legs from the ground, using his feet to keep himself suspended on the tree. He hovers for a moment, before using his left hand to reach for a higher branch. With ease, he pulls himself up, clambering through the thick branches as leaves rustle after him.

Rory, hands on hips, looks up to the tree. 'That's far enough, mate. Take a seat.'

Roman peers back down, and then straddles a branch. He's already too high for my liking and I sway where I stand, stomach knotting.

'Tell me, Edwards, do you trust me?'

'Trust you?'

'Yes, do you trust me?'

'Uh, I did, but...'

'Now you're not so sure.' Rory grins. 'It's a valid point. I've asked you to climb a tree and you did it without much fuss. Without much questioning. What else would you do without questioning?'

Roman reaches for another branch, as if he's about to climb back down.

'Not yet, Edwards. Stay there, please,' Rory says. 'Have a think about your trust for me, would you? Just a few moments.'

'Um, so...'

'You don't have to voice it,' Rory says. 'Just have a think and let me know when you've thought about it.'

Roman cranes his neck to get a better view of the branches above him. He's shielded by leaves, and I wonder if he's thinking about climbing higher. From the top you'd probably get spectacular views, but I'm not exactly in a rush to find out.

'Okay, I've thought about it.'

'Care to share?'

'Not particularly. Mate.'

He adds this as if it is a barb, but Rory doesn't seem to mind. He strolls to the base of the tree as if he might inspect it. 'What if this tree were loose and I pushed it?'

'It's clearly not loose,' Roman says.

Rory nods. 'What if those branches were loose and you'd got halfway up and you fell?'

'That was my risk to take.'

'What if there is someone in there waiting for you?'

'Do you always live in such paranoia, Professor?'

Rory chuckles. 'Just things to consider.' He steps around the tree and Roman presses his lips together, never taking his eye off Rory. Rory pauses at the bow and arrow, before picking them up.

'What if I shot you, right now?'

CHAPTER 11

Roman swings his legs over the branch and makes to jump. As he's high enough to cause himself damage, I yell, running forward, as Rory yells, 'Halt, Edwards.'
Roman slips, but steadies himself, leaning back so that he doesn't fall. He adjusts where he sits, his hands gripping the bark. Leaves fall, drift with swift ease, as my breathing steadies.

'It is a question, that's all,' Rory says, looking at us both. 'Trust, remember. Perspective. You climbed that tree after I asked you to, Roman. You didn't question it. You are sitting on a branch that I told you to stop on.' The bow whispers as it slides out of the bunch, and as Rory loads the bow, the taut sound makes the hairs on my arms stand on end. Is there anyone to call for help? Rory's gone rogue, I think.

Roman squints around him, weighing up his options, but I know he would never get away in time. Those bows are fast. Hunting bows.

Right now, Roman is prey.

'I could shoot you,' Rory says, as casually as if he were commenting on the weather. 'Maim you. Kill you. The choice is mine. Or...' Rory peers at Roman. 'I could trust that when I loose this arrow, it will hit the bark, and not you.'

Before either Rory or I can say anything, the arrow flies from the bow. A scream rips from me and even though I know it is reckless, I launch at the tree. A sickening thud forces me to close my eyes, and all fight dies from me as I slide down the bark, landing on my hands and knees.

'He all right?'

My head snaps up. Roman peers down at me. Embedded in the bark is the arrow, which Roman flicks.

'He didn't hit me,' he says, though he sounds breathless, and his eyes are wide.

'Trust,' Rory says. 'You are right to trust me, but trust has to be earnt. I won't harm you, and I never will. But you made it easy for me if I wanted to.'

'Weird way to show it,' Roman says.

Rory places the bow back against the tree, and for one wild moment I think about snatching it up and aiming an arrow at him, to see how he likes it.

'Are we done here, then?' Roman asks. 'Can I come down?'

Rory laughs. 'Not quite. You've learnt to trust me, now learn the same thing about each other. Dylan.' He doesn't even bark my name but I flinch. 'Stand beneath the branch, please.'

Considering he's just lectured us about following his orders on blind trust, I hesitate. Rory doesn't push. Just puts his hands behind his back and waits. Roman gives a stiff nod of his head.

'All right.'

I stand beneath the branch, wondering if it's going to snap and land on me. Wondering if Rory's going to produce something from behind his back and pretend to attack me, only to show that he won't because he's a good guy and I should trust him. I trust all the professors, why wouldn't I? Now he's making me wonder if that's wrong to do.

Rory eyes Roman. 'Fall, Edwards.'

'Huh?'

'Fall. Dylan will catch you.'

'I will?'

Roman laughs, and despite it all, it makes me smile. Is Rory for real? He wants me to catch Roman? Roman, with his vast chest and his thick arms and his chiselled face? Okay, so I don't know how the chiselled face adds to the weight, but it's got to contribute to something.

'You will,' Rory says. 'A classic trust exercise, but vital. Will you be there to catch one another should you fall?'

Will I? Will he? I don't know the answer, but I hope he is as focused and dedicated to graduation as I am. If this is what it takes to graduate, some falling task, then I can do it. Surely he can, too.

'Hmm, looks like a pretty bad fall.' Roman peers at the grass. 'I could break my back.'

'Dylan will catch you.'

'Will you, though?' Roman asks me.

'Course.' The courage surprises me, but I hope he doesn't see through it.

His eyebrows raise, and I'm thinking maybe he has, when he takes a big sigh. He looks ahead of him, back to me, and I position myself underneath him, feet spread apart as if in defence. In our strength classes, we've learnt how to brace ourselves, how to carry heavy things. I can carry Roman, at least long enough to break his fall and lay him upon the grass.

'On the count of three, then,' Rory says.

Roman closes his eyes, whispering something. One of his hands splays upon his chest, and I wonder if he might be praying. At Rory's command, Roman tilts backwards, and then he's falling. Falling in a flash of red cropped hair and dark green vest and tumbling foliage.

My arms outstretched, I take a deep breath. I know it must happen at speed but this feels like an eternity, watching Roman cascading towards me like an autumnal leaf. I feel him, all heavy body, and my knees buckle and my breath escapes me. We're toppling, and he's lying upon the grass, and before I know it, I am splayed across him, smelling the scent of him, and earth.

His hand is on my back, and my body is splayed across his chest. I lift my head, realising I am mere inches away from his freckled face of beauty. His eyes flutter as his lips quirk into a smile, and I reel back, scurrying off him and all his rigid charm.

'Are you okay?' I stammer.

'You caught me.' He sits up, his vest riding high enough for me to see the ridges at his hips. I fight the urge to linger. Rory considers us, smiling.

'Good work, Cecil.'

I stand, shaking with adrenaline, wiping my forehead. Roman rises, running a hand over his neck. He's got some grass stains on his vest, and a bit of dirt on his arms, but otherwise he looks mostly unscathed. He peers up at the tree. 'That was kind of thrilling.'

'I would suggest that you do it again, but time is running out,' Rory says. 'Dylan, you're up next.'

I nod, and make my way to the base of the tree.

'Oh, no, you won't be going up there.'

I look back, seeing Roman's confused expression and Rory's smiling one.

'Stand against the tree.' I follow Rory's direction as he comes forward, reaching into his pocket. 'Put this on, please.'

He pulls out a black eye mask, which he hands to me.

I take it, staring at it. 'Why?'

'Good question,' Rory says. 'But can't answer that. You trust me?' He waits for me to answer, and when I nod, he says, 'You trust him?'

Roman stands in the shade with his arms crossed, looking like he'd rather be anywhere else.

'Should I trust you?' I ask him.

He watches me, giving nothing away. 'Up to you.'

Why can't he give me a solid answer? It's either yes and put this mask on, or it's no and fall at the first hurdle. The scent of smoke in the air gives me my answer. I put the mask on, plunging into darkness, and then hear footsteps approaching me.

'Headphones, too, please, Cecil.'

I take the headphones, popping them over my head. They hug my ears and as soon as they're on I hear nothing. Just dead silence and my own breathing.

I feel dead.

CHAPTER 12

How long have I stood here, with darkness as my only friend? My heart rate ascends as a hot breeze plays across my skin, and I think this might never end. This antagonising, drawn-out wait. I wish I could hear what Professor Rory might be saying to Roman. What is he instructing him to do? What if they have both agreed to leave me here under the shadow of this grand oak tree? For all I know, night will fall and I will be here, waiting.

How long do I wait?

The seconds tick into minutes, and before I know it, I've lost all track of time. The headphones begin to make my ears ache as they pinch the sides of my head. I keep my hands behind my back and my fingertips graze the rough bark of the tree for something to keep me grounded and still.

It's odd what happens when you are cut off from your sense of sight and sound. Now, every touch is heightened, every brush of nature upon my skin is louder. Is that a butterfly on my arm? An ant on my ankle? Has a spider begun to weave a web between my ear and my clavicle? I am but one with this shattering, aching, beautiful earth, and I am as delicate and vulnerable as the ground I stand upon. I have to trust that Roman won't hurt me, won't forget me, like we have promised to do for our land, our country, our earth.

I think about asking out loud, but what would the point be? I would not hear a reply. My mouth opens and for all I know, I did ask, though I'm sure I haven't. I can smell the smoke in the air, and I picture the red, angry blaze of fire somewhere I've never been. What if it was in my hamlet? What if my home is nothing more than charred carcass and dead memories? A skeleton that nature can pick upon, until grass grows through the foundations of the floor where I learnt to walk, and birds nest in the rafters of what was once my bedroom.

Has the day always been this hot? Aching from standing too long, I'm not sure. I feel the warmth on my skin. Has the sun moved, and now I am in its rays? Is my skin burning? Should I sink to the earth or take this mask off and give up? Or is this all a play on my mind, and it has always been this warm, and I am only now realising so because I am doing nothing but thinking about it?

'Roman?'

I know I ask it. A deadened sound in my head, as if I am listening from inside my mouth. Of course, no answer. No words. No reassuring touch of his hand to let me know he is here too.

What if he's blindfolded? What if he's next to me? My hand strays out upon the oak, as if I might find his waiting for me. Then what? Would I touch him? Would I explore his hand further?

No, Dylan, no thoughts like that. I shift on my feet, afraid of what I feel, afraid they are watching me and might be able to read what I am thinking. Thoughts of Roman are like wildfire in my head, and the flames are spreading, but so far, I can contain them. They must not get out of control. They must not damage me.

He must not damage me.

Oh, this is ridiculous. Reaching for my blindfold, I let out a yelp as something grazes my knuckles. I feel a rough pull, a sting, and thoughts race through me. Flames? A bee sting? A bite from an ant, AKA, Satan himself?

I don't wait for instruction. I rip off my mask and my headphones, and the world comes rushing back to me. Birds singing, bees humming, and Roman. Roman, running towards me, his eyes wide. He's talking, but nothing is registering, because Rory looks aghast.

I look at my hand. Blood is spreading, but it's just a nick across two of my knuckles. I'm in no pain anywhere else. The bow and arrows are at Rory's feet, and Roman is in front of me, gripping me. 'Are you okay? Did I hurt you?' His intense stare burns me, and his touch is like resting my hand upon an open flame. 'Dylan?'

'Why would you hurt me?'

He swivels me back to the tree, and I gasp.

Inches away from where my head was is an arrow, buried in the bark of the tree.

I erupt into anger like a volcano, turning to Roman. 'You shot me?'

'What? No.' Roman gawps at Rory, whose right hand is massaging the side of his temple.

'You let him shoot me?' I fire at Rory.

He shakes his head. 'No, Dylan. He was never going to shoot at you.' His voice wobbles, he takes a breath. 'I mean, he was, but...'

'You tried to kill me.'

'No,' Roman says, shaking his head. 'Sir? I ... no.'

I point at the arrow, wave my hand, which isn't too bloody

but I kind of wish it was for dramatic emphasis. 'I'm cut, and that is inches away from my head.' I tap my forehead. 'Any lower, and...'

Roman grimaces. 'Oh, God, Dylan, don't. Rory said it would be okay.'

'Now hang on a minute,' Rory says, seemingly coming back to earth. He breathes in and approaches us, standing between us. Two boys, one lit by anger, the other fuelled by fear. 'That isn't what was going on. This is a trust task, and you had to trust Roman. Roman had to trust he wouldn't hit you.'

'You put my life on the line for ... trust?'

Rory nodded. 'Sometimes the limit must be pushed, and—'

'Fuck your limit,' I say.

'Cecil.'

'That could have been so much worse,' I reply.

'I was always here. Roman was always in control,' Rory says, though he looks uncertain. 'Edwards, you were in control, right?'

'O-of course,' Roman says. 'I mean, I meant to shoot it a bit higher than that, but...'

Laughter bubbles upon my lips and I look at the bow with deliriously wide eyes. 'Yeah, well, you kind of fucked that up.'

'Cecil,' Rory repeats, storming towards the tree. 'Come here.'

'No.'

'Come here. Now.'

It's the first time I've seen Rory truly forbidding. He's breathing deeply, eyes narrowed as he watches me. I sigh, trudging over to him.

'Get the arrow.'

I look at him, then Roman. My hand reaches for it, and my head tilts as I feel rubber as I touch it. I pull, feeling it flex more than it should under my grip. 'What the—'

'It wasn't a real arrow.'

Pulling the arrow from the tree, I expect to see the shining blade, but instead it's a dead head, no jagged point. Inspecting the tree bark, there's no sign of there ever being anything deadly. With a bit of effort, the arrow itself bends at my will.

'Are we done here?' I ask, heat rising.

Rory clears his throat. 'We are.'

'Did we pass?' Roman asks.

Rory smiles. 'Yes, you both passed. I hope now you know you can both trust one another to—'

'Not put an arrow through my head? Yeah, really fucking great.'

I stalk off, trying to save face, but really my body is shaking and I'm still thinking about Roman's touch. A few moments later, there's heavy breath, and he appears in my peripheral, jogging to keep up with me.

'Hey. Hey, wait.'

I stop. 'What, Roman?'

He holds out his hands, and for one moment I think he wants me to take them. Just as I'm about to, unsure why, he says, 'I'm good with my hands.'

My own hands drop to my side, and I slip them into my pockets for good measure. If he noticed I was reaching for him, he doesn't show it. 'What are you on about?'

'Good with my hands, remember?' He smiles. 'I was always in control. I was never going to shoot you. You said it yourself, I'm good with a bow, and I'm—'

'Good with your hands,' I mutter, realisation dawning.

We stand there. Me with my shaking hands, Roman with his good ones. Two boys, breathing in the dry, slightly choked air.

'Do you trust me, Dylan?'

Do I? Do I trust the boy with flaming cropped red hair? The boy with eyes that are warm? The boy who appeared in school and has remained cryptic? The boy who makes me afraid to look in the mirror? The boy I've watched swim in the morning, with thoughts of freedom and self-discovery?

'We passed the task, didn't we? This wasn't real. It was never real.'

And with that, I leave him, because I don't trust myself. Not then.

CHAPTER 13

'Can I trust you, Professor Lawrence?'
It's the next day after our first task, and Professor Lawrence is free for our mindful chats. I know he's available for every student during this month of tasks, but I don't know if any of the boys have taken him up on the offer. He's taught us well, made us compassionate and kind men, and as far as I'm aware, most boys are prime examples of his exemplary teaching. I don't ask him about Taylor, don't tell him about the streak I have observed in him. It is not my place to do so.

We are sitting like we usually do. Him at his desk with a newspaper tucked under his arms, away from my view. No whisky for him this time. I suppose that is his evening drink. Though do I imagine it, or do I smell it in the air? He surveys me with those sharp eyes of his, underneath the statue of Saturn, who seems to watch us both.

'You can always trust me, Mr Cecil.'
'I can?'
'Yes, you can.'

Professor Lawrence rarely gives anything away. Perhaps that is why I'm not sure if I can trust him. Up until now, I have. I mean, I do. Don't I? He's always listened to me, always guided me in the right direction. He's made me the man I am today. And yet, I'm not sure if I like who I am to become.

But there's one thing in particular I am now questioning. Yesterday was a task of trust between Roman and me, but that bow was inches from my head and my thoughts keep asking one thing: did Roman know it was fake? A scab is already forming over my wound.

'Rory oversaw yesterday's task, and an arrow scraped my skin,' I say. 'A fake arrow.'

'*Professor* Rory,' Lawrence chides.

'What do you know about *Professor* Rory?'

'What sort of question is that?'

'What's his experience?'

'If you are asking about his work history, Mr Cecil, he has been studying to become a professor since the day he graduated.'

'And where did he graduate?'

'I'm not permitted to share that information.'

'Ganymede's?'

'Mr Cecil.' His tone is final, warning even.

I change tack.

'Who sets the tasks?'

'Headmistress Dwynwen and I work with the board of directors alongside the first ministers of the monarchy,' Lawrence says. 'The king has the final say.'

'The king allows students to be shot at with arrows?'

'No students are shot at with arrows, Mr Cecil.'

'Fake arrows, then. You're shooting fake arrows at all the third-years.'

'Each scenario is different, Mr Cecil.'

'Then who gets to decide who is shot at with arrows?' I ask, my tone rising. Lawrence sits a little taller, his brow furrowing. 'Why was it me?'

'Each task is designed for the particular student's strengths.' Lawrence goes on, but I think of Roman, his skill with a bow, his good hands. He must have known he wouldn't actually harm me. The school must have, too. If they can know who our perfect partners are, it's not much of a stretch for them to have the trust in their students to know what is best for them. 'But of course, it is then up to the student to exhibit those strengths, and how they think and adapt when the task comes to challenge them. Every task you have, Mr Cecil, will be aligned with who you are, and what you can be. Nothing is set to trip you up.'

I nod, unconvinced. What else am I to say?

Lawrence leans forward. 'Why do you ask if you can trust me?'

I glance at him, the newspaper, then back to him. 'Silly thoughts, perhaps, Professor.'

'No thoughts are silly, especially not in my room.'

'It's just ... yesterday I lost trust a little bit in what we are doing,' I say, but I refuse to look at him now, instead focusing on my knees. 'I guess because it scared me. The fact a professor could stand there and let another boy shoot a bow at my head, fake or not.'

'At your head?'

'They said it was never meant to be at my head. Above my head was the target, but...' I hold up my scratched hand, still not looking at him. I hold it there until I'm certain he's seen it, and then say, 'It could have gone so wrong. They could have had a problem on their hands. And I thought, if they're willing to jeopardise that, what else are they willing to do?' I finally look at him, surprised to see that his eyes are wide and his lips frowning. But it's gone so quickly, I think I imagine it. That look of ... pity? 'And then it got me thinking about the boys who didn't make it this far. Boys who were let go before they could graduate. Why, Professor Lawrence? Why are they not allowing boys to graduate?'

Lawrence bites his lip, his fingers absently flicking the edge of the newspaper. 'Some boys aren't equipped for the roles Ganymede's provides.'

'So where do they go? They have given all their time just to fall at the last hurdle?'

'That is the way things go, sometimes, and these are your final tests.'

'So, where do they go?'

'Go, Mr Cecil?'

'They could go back to their hamlets, I suppose.' I try and think about the times I ever saw anyone come back and say they had been let go from their schools. I meet his eye. 'Year one, some boys never showed up to class again. Year two, there was that tragic accident in the lake, quickly swept under the rug. Other boys let go, told they aren't up to scratch. Year three, and Blake ... how quickly he has been left to rot.' My eyes prick, but no water comes, though I wish it would. 'The billionth child, so celebrated, and nobody cares that he's gone? And I think, if Ganymede's lets just anyone in and lets anyone graduate, it would lose its rank, right? But in all the years in my hamlet, I never once saw a boy come back and say he was let go. Never once saw a boy come back and start at a new school. Nothing much changed in that hamlet, except when a family upped and left, or we had a royal visit, or someone changed their job, or new graduates came.'

Lawrence nods slowly, looking to the door, as if he hopes a teacher might come and disturb us. Finally, he says, 'They are, of course, good questions to have. When a boy is deemed not suitable for Ganymede's education, he is assigned elsewhere. Perhaps he goes to a lower school. Perhaps he is put into the workforce where his existing skills are needed. Or, perhaps he is so far gone he is only good for the open country. Ganymede's is prestigious, and only prestigious boys can continue to be here.'

I think of Blake, and the questions he asked. How he started to talk about something... How he seemed uncertain where he was going, and what was expected of him, of us. What if I am now thinking the same? His death, coupled with the arrow Roman shot, has opened my eyes.

'There's one final thing,' I say. 'Everything you have ever told me about my parents, about what you know...' I swallow as my mouth runs dry. 'You promise me, that is all you know?'

Lawrence doesn't falter. 'You can trust me, Mr Cecil. What happened to your parents was tragic. I wish I had more answers for you.'

CHAPTER 14

The days between our tasks are sold to us as days to recoup, to relax, to reflect, to embody free time. It might look different for everyone, but I'm certain they're not supposed to be spent fretting over the meaning of life. I've swum in the indoor pool with Johnny. Gone on a gentle walk with Cameron around the grounds of Ganymede's. Got lost in the pages of art history and literature. Written poetry in my journal. But every time I have a moment where I'm not distracted, I'm reminded of the anxiety that won't let me go.

I sit in the shadow of Ganymede's, lost in the growing grass. A mouse goes scurrying through the growth. Bugs climb the blades. A collared dove coos from the nest it has made in the crevices of the manor house, and a few seconds later another dove responds from the boughs of a branch nearby. Swifts glide past the trees and ignore the grazing deer that conceals itself in the branches' shade. In the distance, black birds blot the blue sky. Shadows move in the greenhouses, perhaps the kitchen staff harvesting our food.

What I feel is normal. Ever since my parents died,

Ganymede's has been my home, and at the end of this month I am to fly the nest and leave it. I should be embracing the change, not dreading it. The boys around me are full of excitement, their laughter bouncing off the halls, their conversations full of whimsical flights of fancy as they discuss their possible jobs, how their archetypes will shape them and, most importantly, the women they are to meet, marry and love. Their next of kin.

When I am asked, I play along. But off comes the mask as soon as they are gone. I look to the tree where I completed the first task, the only memory of the arrow a scar upon the wise old oak, and on my skin.

When people ruined the earth, did they spare a thought for the future generations? Did they know we would be scrambling to get on our feet again? Did they consider the sacrifices we would have to make? Or did they ignore the constant headlines of warning, as they over-consumed and thought of what else they could pollute? Even though it is foolish, I resent those humans of the past, too.

Two black crows come into the shade, landing a few feet away from me. Their strong beaks peck at air, before they inspect the grass. I don't want to see what they come back with, what life they have ended to extend their own. So, I adjust where I sit, planning to lean back and close my eyes and rest in the grass. Roman's voice catches my attention.

He walks with a confident swagger, hands swaying at his sides, and he's deep in conversation with Elis. Why would Roman be talking to Elis? I swear they're complete opposites. Elis, from Mercury, is more likely to be found theorising about subjects and lounging around, while Roman seems more driven. More aligned with what we are taught. Elis is airy, Roman is firmly on the ground. Maybe they complement each other. And why do I care so much?

Why can't I take my eyes off them as they walk away from me, lost in conversation? Elis's hands gesture widely. No doubt he's trying to challenge the way Roman thinks, and, to my surprise, Roman seems to be hanging on to his every word. They walk down a flight of stairs flanked with gargoyles, and neither of them looks around him to see who might be watching. I sink lower where I sit, hoping the blades of rising grass might conceal me somewhat. My movement sends the two crows flying, but they land a few feet away, eyes darting in my direction.

The two boys walk towards the lake and the bridge. Roman is talking now, his hand movements more controlled. Like he's listing something. They cross the bridge and they're heading towards...

The graveyard?

Why are they heading towards the graveyard?

For one wild moment, I think maybe they're going to see Blake. Pay their respects. But Roman wouldn't do that, and Elis wasn't really close to Blake, so I put that thought aside. They reach the gate to the graveyard and Roman opens it, lets Elis walk through, follows and closes it.

He sees me.

I duck.

At least, I think he sees me. I must be nothing but a small blip now, like he is to me, but he hovers. Stares.

Shit, shit, shit.

Nice going, Dyl.

He turns, and I look away, not wanting to look at him again. But I do, but by that point they are both gone.

I consider going there myself. The graveyard is definitely less spooky when the sun is shining. But then, there would be no way I could deny that I was following them. Maybe I could say I finally wanted answers from Roman about that arrow.

I let out a snort of annoyance, get to my feet and trot back into school. I don't want to add another thing to fret about.

Lost in thoughts of Roman, I bypass the main staircase and instead take the spiral stairway. It's only when I'm halfway up that snatched whispers coming from further down the stairs catch my attention.

'I don't know what you expect me to do about it, and I suggest if you have any concerns, you—'

'You're the person I'm meant to go to with concerns, are you not, Headmistress?'

I hover, resting my hand on the cold stone wall. Dwynwen and Rory, I think. The stairwell is lit by lanterns, this being one of the oldest parts of the manor house.

'These are not concerns, these are the disruptive thoughts of a man who must remember his standing.'

She's cutting. If she spoke to me like that, I know I would wither. There's a silence, and I think perhaps Rory has fallen into submission, but then I catch his voice, low, parts of his words lost to the stone.

'You know ... I do that ... boys suffering.'

Suffering? Is he talking about the task? Perhaps he is thinking the same as me, that it was foolish to let another boy shoot a bow at me, no matter how skilled he is with one, and no matter how low the stakes.

'Are we to ... and make the same mistakes?'

I almost hear Dwynwen's sharp intake of breath. 'The only mistake I have made is letting you become a member of this faculty.'

'You don't have to be this way, Headmistress.'

Footsteps, hard and determined, coming closer and closer. I slip away from them, twisting, until I'm out of view. Dwynwen reaches the doorway leading to the ground floor. Her nostrils are flared, her eyes narrowed. She snatches the door, slamming it against stone. Old brick dislodges somewhere nearby. She disappears into the hall, the door banging behind her. I ponder, waiting to see if Rory comes, wondering if I should go down and see if he is still there. 'Fuck,' and another door, somewhere lower, opening and closing, and then the familiar sense of stillness. Loneliness.

I race up the spiral staircase, getting dizzy with each narrow and uneven step I take, until finally I'm on the Saturn floor and tumbling into our mostly deserted circular common room. Breathlessly, I race to my dorm room, taking a few moments to rest upon the closed door and thank Saturn that I am alone.

Incense smoke floats like spectres through the air and I inhale the scent of cedar. I leave the door and I peer out of the window, looking to the graveyard, as if I might see Roman and Elis inside. But from here, it looks deserted, like they were ghosts returning to graves.

What was Rory talking about? Mistakes? Boys suffering?

The door behind me creaks open and I spin. Has Rory followed me? Is he going to tell me to keep my mouth shut?

But it's only Cameron. He walks over to me, frowning. 'You looked worried when you came in,' he says.

'Didn't even see you in there,' I mutter, relaxing.

'Point proven. What's up?'

Should I be truthful or semi-honest? 'What do you know about Roman Edwards?'

Cameron shrugs. 'Seems all right.'

'Just all right?'

'Seems like a bright guy, from what I've gathered in classes. You having doubts about working with him this month?'

'Uh, yeah. Sure. That's exactly it.'

Cameron nods, pushing his glasses up the bridge of his nose. 'He seemed quite intense during your task.'

'What?'

The blue sky reflects in Cameron's spectacles. One of the doves swoops away from its nest. Cameron nods. 'I finished my task and was heading back when I saw you blindfolded by a tree.'

'Not just blindfolded,' I say, pointing at my ears.

'And Roman and Rory were, well, I don't know how to explain it. It looked like Rory was getting scolded.'

'Professor Rory?'

'Know any other Rorys?'

'I mean, Rory was getting scolded? Roman was scolding a professor?'

Cameron holds up his hand. 'That's what it looked like.'

I cross my arms, looking back out over the grounds, like a king surveying his kingdom. Maybe I shouldn't trust Roman after all.

CHAPTER 15

Someone's got hold of me. My bones rattle as I shake back and forth, eyes flickering open, hand raising to shield the light.

'Get up, lazy,' Johnny says, letting me go as soon as he sees me stirring.

He doesn't bother to wait, merely leaves the room. Taylor has already left, and Cameron is slipping his tie through the collar of his uniform shirt.

'Nervous?' he asks me.

'Tired. Is it really time already?'

'Afraid so.'

Another night of near sleeplessness, finally catching some as the sky turned a lighter shade of black. I dreamt of Blake, whispering with Roman and Elis, being discovered by Rory and Dwynwen, and how she told Blake he was no longer useful to Ganymede's, to society. Why wasn't he useful? What was Blake up to before his death?

Dressed, I follow Johnny and Cameron down into the

breakfast hall. But the doors are closed, four professors standing outside.

'Something wrong?' Johnny asks Professor Tania, our swim coach.

'Come with me, please,' she says to Johnny.

'But I'm hungry.'

'No breakfast this morning.'

No breakfast? I gawp at Cameron, seeing him clutch his stomach as if he hasn't had a meal in weeks.

'Mr Cecil.' I turn, seeing Professor Lawrence walking towards me and Professor Abigail eyeing him, probably swooning over him, despite the fact both are already partnered. 'Come with me, please.'

Lawrence walks with a confident swagger, like he knows people are watching him. I can imagine him being a bit of a lad when he was my age. Probably like Roman. I wonder what his life is like away from here with his partner. I wonder what any of their lives are like away from here.

Lawrence opens a door I've never been through, one I always thought led to a classroom, but turns out to lead to a narrow spiral staircase. I draw my sleeves over my hands as a chill bites at my exposed skin. Our footsteps echo on slender stairs as we climb upwards, away from the babble of chatter from the halls.

'Don't tell anyone I showed you this,' Lawrence says, a cheeky grin on his face. 'Old servant corridors. They run throughout the school, strictly for security guards and teachers now, but we're running a little late.'

'I didn't think I was late.'

Lawrence doesn't alleviate my fears. Instead, he slides open another door halfway up the stairs, and we emerge into a crooked corridor on the second floor with painted vines snaking up yellowing wallpaper. The candles are lit in their candelabras, and incense sticks in holders burn along the windowsill; an aroma of fresh nature wafts towards us. The air conditioning chills me, and I notice that the lamps have not been switched on; instead, natural light is allowed in. 'A natural way of life is a good way of life,' I remember hearing the king say in one of his Saturnalia speeches. We've lived by it for as long as I can remember.

Antique tables of dark wood are piled with leatherbound books, and doors to classrooms are open, offering glimpses of dark, eerie interiors.

Sitting on a chaise longue in the hallway is Roman, leaning back like he's soaking up the sun.

'Sit up, Mr Edwards,' Lawrence orders, and Roman does, but slowly, like he's miffed at being disturbed. *What did you and Elis talk about?* I want to ask him. *Why are you friends with him and not me?*

We stand at a chipped black door, with frosted-glass panes either side of it. Lawrence extracts a stopwatch from his inner breast pocket. His shirt is tucked tightly into his trousers. Roman catches me looking, tilting his head. I clear my throat, stepping away from them both, as if I'm already too close.

'Task two,' Lawrence says, his voice carrying through the dim, deserted corridor. 'Honesty.'

'Honesty?'

'Honesty, Mr Cecil.'

'Honesty about what?'

'Honesty towards one another, of course.'

I scratch the back of my neck, heat spreading underneath my clothes. I can't wait to take my blazer off.

'Why is that?'

'You've learnt to trust one another. Honesty complements trust. The aim of this task is to learn to be honest with one another, to communicate openly and to be vulnerable. Men must be intimate with one another. We're looking for *emotional* intimacy here, Mr Edwards, so you can wipe that smirk from your face.'

He says this with a small smile, and Roman laughs. 'I don't know what you mean, Professor.'

Glad to see that Roman is finding all this funny. Oh, sure, I'm almost certain he no longer cares about the fact he could have killed me with his bow. Anyway, I'm moving past that after what Cameron said. I waited for so long, long enough to reach for my mask and attempt to take it off. All that time Roman was arguing with Rory? About what, exactly?

Lawrence reads me. 'Sound okay?'

I nod.

'You will be placed in this room here,' Lawrence says, tapping the black door. 'You won't be allowed out until I am satisfied that the objective has been met.'

'We could be in there forever,' Roman says, half-joking.

'Hopefully not,' Lawrence says, all dry humour.

Roman looks at me as if to say, 'You hearing this?' I shrug.

'But why does that intimacy matter?' I ask.

'By being emotionally raw, you are creating a stronger bond. A bond that is vital to your relationship with your partner in the outside world,' Lawrence continues. 'But with tasks ahead of you, together, you need to know when the other is being honest.'

'Question. How do you know we are lying?' I ask, trying to keep my tone cocky and casual. Roman grins, so it must work.

'You'll see once you get inside,' Lawrence says.

The smile drops from my face, all feigned confidence gone. My palms sweat and I rub them together, feeling an icy chill descend upon me. Now I feel like I'm not wearing enough layers.

'Be as honest and real as you can be with one another, please,' Lawrence says. 'It will only benefit you in the long run.'

Roman stands, cricking his neck. 'Shall we get this over with, then?'

Now? Already? And why does he act like he can't wait to be shot of me? He's already halfway to the door, and all I want to do is run in the other direction.

Instead, I grin, clap my hands together and say, 'Piece of cake.'

CHAPTER 16

Inside the room, the dark blue ceiling brushes the top of my head, and Roman crouches to avoid hitting his. The only light comes from a library lamp, which sits upon the wooden table in the middle of the room. No windows offer a welcome glimpse of the outside world, only four dark walls. Roman heads across the rough floor to the further side of the desk and takes a seat on a wooden stool, angling his long limbs underneath the desk. The door groans behind us as it drags shut, and the locks churn, sliding into place. Harsh metal on metal, vibrating through the room.

Only one door.

Just a dusty, cracked mirror behind Roman in the wall.

No escape.

'Do you know what this is?' Roman asks me, his voice quiet, as if he's afraid to break the silence between us.

The table is empty except for what looks like a vice to hold something in place. Two wires trail across the floor, disappearing into the wall underneath the mirror. I linger, looking not at my distorted reflection but instead at the glass.

'There's instructions,' Roman says, looking at me. 'On the table. It says we need to put our arms in here and put this thing on our finger.'

He holds up a grey finger-shaped clip, and I swallow.

'Do you think Lawrence is watching us?' I whisper, nodding towards the mirror.

Roman turns, looking at the glass. 'No.'

'Hmm,' I say, taking my seat. 'So, I guess this is what he means by being able to tell if we're lying or not.'

Roman grins. 'I don't know. Shall we try it out?'

Roman puts his thick arm in the vice, using a lever to tighten it. He tries to move, but his arm is wedged, and he stretches out his fingers, as if to get feeling back into them. With his other hand, he hooks the clip onto his finger, nodding at me to do the same. I can't help feeling like he's willingly led himself into a trap.

'Does it hurt?' I ask.

'No, not at all.'

I gulp, glad that he doesn't seem to mind that I asked if I need to fear any pain. My leg dances under the table as I put my left arm into my own vice, and tighten it in with my right hand. I lift the clip, cold to the touch, and see an indentation inside where my finger is supposed to go. Roman's right, the clip doesn't hurt; there's only pressure as it weighs upon my finger.

There's a sound of whirring, like something powering up. A moment of sizzling air makes my hair stand on end.

Roman nods slowly. His eyes dart around me, as if he's reading my aura or something. Is that something he can do? Read auras? I remember Mother telling me once about those who travel between hamlets, offering esoteric services. We even had classes in our first year about divination practices – you could choose whether to go on taking them in year two and three. I did a divination class until year three. Did Roman? Did he like it? All these things I don't know about him, I think. He's not too far away from me on the other side of the table, and with this room seemingly closing in on us, it feels strangely intimate.

I guess that's all part of the test. My chance to get to know him.

'So, uh, how do we start?' Roman asks.

'No instructions on the paper?'

'Nothing.'

No clock, either, counting us down. 'A bit anti-climactic, really, isn't it?'

'I guess so.'

Lawrence said we had to be honest. Honest about what? Roman is leaning on the table like he's bored, and all I can think about is whether I'm going to have to out myself in front of this boy whom I'm relying on for my graduation.

I don't know what Roman's going to ask, and I can't lie.

I could guide the questions, take control of the situation. The magician thinks outside the box, right? As long as we stay on a level footing, we can get through this and pass this task. Maybe we don't have to know each other deeply, just know each other enough?

Roman looks at me. 'You okay?'

'Yeah, sure. Piece of cake, remember?'

I yelp as my body jolts at what feel like tiny needles ripping into my fingertip. I try to pull back, but my arm keeps me rooted as a sensation of burning fire seems to claw its way right to my marrow. But after a few seconds, everything stills, though my finger stings. Roman's shocked expression at the other end of the table is almost comical.

'What the hell was that?'

'I ... don't know.'

Was that meant to happen? Is my clip faulty? I try to spot a break in the wires, something that might offer a glimpse of the problem.

Roman frowns, already moving on. 'Uh...Where shall we begin?'

I eye the clasp on my finger. 'Well, how deep do you want to go?'

Roman thinks for a moment, that thoughtful expression back on his face. 'Do you like school?'

I laugh in relief, catching my reflection in the mirror. 'I mean, I like it some days and other days, not so much. What about you?'

'Adore it. My favourite place on earth—'

He breaks off, eyes widening as he reaches for his hand. His body judders forward, and he whacks his knee under the table. And then there's silence, and he wobbles where he sits.

'Bloody hell, what the hell was that?' he gasps.

'The needle feeling?'

'Needles? That was a bloody electric shock.'

My stomach drops and I grip the leg of the table. 'What?'

'I swear,' he says. 'That felt like an electric shock.'

'You've been shocked before?'

'Course I have, I'm a boy.'

I stutter a laugh, unsure of what being a boy has to do with any of that, but I accept it nonetheless. 'Say it again.'

'Say what?'

'What you just said. Do you enjoy school?'

Roman blinks at me. 'Adore it. Best place on—'

He lurches forward, mouth stretching into a pained cry, but no sound comes out.

'Stop doing that,' he yells to no one, when he's no longer juddering. 'What the fuck?'

I close my eyes, shaking my head in wonder. There's no way this can really be happening.

'Dylan, talk to me.'

'Don't you see? We're being shocked when we lie.'

CHAPTER 17

'Fuck that.' Roman reaches for the wires, anger blazing in his eyes.

'Don't.' He pauses at my shout. 'I mean, I don't think that's a good idea.'

'I'm not getting fucking electrocuted, Dylan.'

'Will you bloody calm down?' He stares at me like I've grown another head. 'I don't want to be shocked, either, but it's clearly not enough voltage to kill us.'

'But I was only joking about school.' He sounds young when he says this, and for the first time I see something other than the swagger he projects to the world. Perhaps this is his true self.

'Roman. Please.'

I think of the situation we're in. The vice we can take off ourselves, the clip we can remove. Hell, I'm sure we could stand up right now and leave if we wanted to. 'This is part of the test. If you want to get up and go, be my guest. I don't think Lawrence will stop you.' I glare at the mirror for good measure. 'But if you walk away from that...' I bite my tongue.

'What?'

'You walk away from us.'

Roman's angry expression slackens, and with his free hand he touches his chest.

'What's the use in lying when we could just be honest with one another instead?'

Roman rolls his tongue over his teeth before speaking. 'But what is there to be honest about?'

Plenty I could be honest about with you, I think. *Like how the freckles on your cheeks make me feel funny. Like how I want to run my finger over your jawline. Like how you make me think about things I'd rather not think about.*

'Lawrence said we have to be emotionally raw,' I say, hoping that the machine can't read my thoughts. 'Be honest with one another. I don't think whether we like school is going to cut it.'

'But what else is there to talk about?' Roman asks me. 'I'm not being funny, but what have we got to be emotionally raw about?'

I nod, following his logic. He doesn't know me. This is the most we've ever spoken, the longest we've been together. I know he likes art, and that he knows how to avoid killing a boy, but that's about it.

But there's plenty I could be emotionally raw about, and after seeing his mask slip ever so slightly, I'm sure there's something else to him, too. I want to know who Roman Edwards really is.

'I suppose we should talk about who we are,' I say. 'At least, who we think we are.'

Roman looks at his hand with the clip attached to his finger. He sighs, his shoulders heaving. 'Well, I'm not who people think I am.'

He doesn't judder. No yowling pain.

'In what way?'

'Well, let's look at it this way,' Roman says, his shoulders slumping as he looks at his hand. 'What do you see when you look at me?'

So much for guiding the conversation how I want it to go. What the hell am I supposed to say to that?

'You know, like, a cool guy.'

'Cool? Is that all?'

'Uh, yeah, and, you know … you're popular and I see someone who I could be friends with.'

The burning pain rips through my body again and I curl my body, hoping it will subside.

'You all right?'

I want to say yes, to fake bravado in front of Roman, but instead I simply shake my head – no.

'It's tough, isn't it?'

'Yeah.'

'So, you *don't* want to be friends with me?' He's smiling, jovial almost.

Of course I want to be friends with him. I don't know why the machine thought that was a lie. I peer at it, thinking it's faulty. Thinking maybe it sends out random shocks for the sake of it.

I try a different tack.

'You scare me.'

'Huh.' Roman's smile fades into wounded animal.

'I mean that positively.'

'Doesn't sound positive.'

No, I suppose not. 'But it's because I envy you.'

He looks at me, cocking his head. The light from the lamp sets his sharp jaw on edge. I know I'm losing him. *Stop beating around the bush, Dylan, and tell him what you're thinking. At least some of what you're thinking, anyway.*

'I mean, look at you,' I say, using my free hand to gesture

towards him. 'You're handsome, you're fit and strong. But ... you have this cocky arrogance to you that I hate...'

'Hate? Wow.'

'We're meant to be honest,' I say with a shrug. 'Sometimes that means hearing things we don't like.'

'Hating me because you envy me sounds like a you problem. Any other reason why you hate me?'

'Not really.'

Pain, searing hot, blinding pain. I lurch forward until I'm pressed on the table.

'Hey. Hey, enough. *Enough.*' Roman's shout comes in and out, and the white subsides from my vision as I feel the cold roughness of the table. My head is spinning, light dimming. Why are they doing this to us? Why is the place I call home feeling inhospitable? Roman's hand is on my head, stroking my black hair as he leans across the table, his arm stuck in the vice twisted awkwardly beneath him. His fingers lace through my strands, a delicate touch from someone so strong. Too intimate. 'Dylan, you all right?'

Bile stings my throat. I'm sure I'm close to fainting. 'That was a hard one.'

'Maybe they're upping the voltage.'

'Are they going to kill us or something?' I mean it as a joke, but my laugh is weak.

A horrible silence spreads between us, before Roman says, 'I don't know.'

Something in his tone makes my breath halt. His eyes are dark, his mouth stretched down.

Leaning up, Roman lets his hand stray towards me. 'We can get through this,' he says. 'Together.'

Together. Huh, I suppose we are together, whether I like it or not.

I want to be courageous like him. I want to have the feeling that everything is going to work out fine. So I say, 'Tell me a truth, then.'

CHAPTER 18

I've gone too far. He's looking over my shoulder at the blank wall and he's not said a word for, oh, I don't know, too fucking long. Maybe he'll tell me what he was doing with Elis. Maybe he'll explain why he was seen arguing with Rory while I stood and waited like a fruit nobody wanted to pick. I wait him out, at least that's what I tell myself I'm doing, and it has nothing to do with the fact that I'm too scared to say anything else. He makes a sound, something like a groan and a sigh, and finally looks at me.

'My father raised me to be a man's man,' Roman says. 'I'm the only boy, youngest to two sisters, and so he saw me as the man that would carry on his line. He's very proud of the Edwards family tree. From since I can remember he would always be telling me how to stand up for myself, how to fight. He'd tell me that I should be glad to be born a boy.'

When Roman says nothing, I say, 'I suppose my dad meant the same thing.'

It's a realisation that's only coming to me now. Father always talked of how happy he was to have a boy, how lucky I was to be born a boy. How he fought for me to get here. How he had some relationship with the king that I can only begin to fathom. A relationship that is only now dawning on me as being unusual.

I think of my father's desire for me to come here. To Ganymede's and its insistence on creating better men.

'But I never felt like I should be proud,' Roman says. 'I felt like a weak man overcompensating to fit in. Dad caught me playing with my sister's dolls once.' He chuckles, but it's cold, and his face looks dark. 'I honestly think I can still feel the sting from his belt.'

I wince. 'Roman—'

'Honesty, remember?'

It's true. I wanted to get to know Roman, but I'm not prepared for sharing our life stories. Our trauma.

'It's hard, isn't it, when you realise you're a disappointment to your family?' Roman goes on, though I'm sure he doesn't want me to answer. His eyes are unfocused, lost to a memory I may never be privy to. 'Dad would never say it, but I think he worried that he only had girls. Not that he thought there was anything wrong with girls, of course not. He's a good man, I promise you. It's just ... well, I think he wanted a son. A project.'

A project. Was I a project for my father? The only child, the one to represent the Cecil name. The boy who would become a man my father could be proud of. I bet he had thoughts of growing old and seeing me mature, leaving when the time was right. Are you happy with me now, Father?

'You sound like you resent that,' I say.

Roman shakes his head. 'I don't resent anything. My parents raised us well and we had comfortable lives. Ordered lives.' He pauses, and I say nothing. 'But when I didn't get into Ganymede's, well...' Roman chuckles. 'I think that was the final nail in the coffin. They tried to put brave faces on it, but I knew they were thinking, "what went wrong with me?"' He holds up his free hand, stopping me from saying anything. 'Please, I don't want your pity. It was yet another long line of disappointments. One school below Ganymede's wasn't good enough. Not when Dad had come here, and Mum and my sisters went to Pandora's. I couldn't be the only Edwards not to go to Ganymede's. So, Dad came to me once. Sat me down. Man to man, you know.' He smiles, but it's a wry smile, rather than fond. 'He said I need to really excel in my schooling. There's still a chance I could transfer. Well, year one, no transfer. End of year two, I've done enough. It was the first time I truly saw happiness on my dad's face.

'I always thought my parents were happy, you see,' Roman says. 'But that moment made me realise I'd never seen true happiness in him. Dad told me many times that he graduated here, met Mum, fell in love the first time he saw her. That this was something I should aspire to, even when he thought I'd never walk through the front door and get educated here. Both of them are historians, so they like to tell me about the past, about the meaning of things. The meaning of this place. But Mum ... she didn't love him. Not straightaway, anyway. At least, I don't think she did. But over time she did love him, or she at least learnt to.' His eyes meet mine. 'Or she was very good at convincing us kids that she was in love.' He bites the edge of his lip, a quirk that immediately makes me want to scream at him to stop, because the way my stomach somersaults is enough to make me want to never look at him again. He stops, as if he knows what he's done to me. 'It's hard to believe in society when you see the flaws of it.'

My heart rate is fast, and I adjust my aching arm in the vice. 'Roman...'

'Dad took everything away from Mum when she had children. She stayed home to raise us, even though society encourages everyone to make their own choices. She could still do a bit of her work, but Mum liked to get out there, network, and she lost all of that. Consigned to reading the old books in our library, while Dad contributed to discoveries and whatever else he liked to do. Then I saw the same thing that happened to Mum happen to my sisters. They had all these hopes and dreams. Then they went to school and met their partners and they ... lost something. Sure, each one of them did what they are meant to do, and I include my father in this. They strengthened the population by having us, worked in respectable careers, boosted the workforce. They repopulated our hamlet, made the biggest contribution they could make. We might have wanted a bit more, but we certainly had enough. We're told we're living in a free world, that Ganymede's is raising us to be men sensitive of our girlfriends' feelings. I believed it, Dylan, until I realised that it was not like that in my family. Dad wasn't sensitive to how my mother felt. And once you notice that contradiction, you notice it everywhere.'

I want to tell him to stop talking. If Lawrence is listening, surely this will get Roman into trouble. But there's also a part of me that wants him to carry on, to tell me everything, because for the past year I have wanted to know him better. And now I know what he has been carrying.

Roman shakes his head, shoulders hunched, back turned to the mirror. 'You asked me how I feel about Ganymede's? I hate it.' No jolt comes, and his thumb rubs mine. His touch sending its own shockwaves through me, but calming at the same time, like a restful ocean. 'I hate everything we're going towards, everything we're supposed to be. Am I a warrior or a brute? Are you a magician or a con?'

'Shit, Roman.'

He flinches, offering me a sad smile.

'I don't think we should talk about this,' I whisper, rubbing my hand on my trousers. Not because I don't want to. But here, some things are better left unsaid.

'Fine. Tell me about you.'

I'm scared of the question. 'There's nothing you need to know.'

The jolt runs through me and I grit my teeth, trying to breathe through it. When it subsides, I shake my head. 'Fuck's sake.'

Roman smiles. 'Come on, Dylan. You can tell me anything.'

Anything. I am a magician, not a con.

'I haven't been happy since my parents died,' I blurt out, already wishing I didn't.

Now Roman stares at me in the way everyone does when I mention my parents. Sad, with wide eyes. Like I'm vulnerable. The way Blake did, until I told him not to.

'They dropped me off here on my first day, so full of hope for me, and then they died. The same day. A car crash. I learnt later their car was travelling back here when it happened, back to Ganymede's. Like I'd left something behind they needed to give me, or they wanted to remind me of something.' I stare at the wall, shaking my head. 'That haunts me, you know? Wondering why they were coming back here. I've asked Lawrence, Dwynwen, but nobody has ever told me why. If they hadn't turned around and come back, they wouldn't have crashed, and I would be happier and I wouldn't be so fucking confused about everything.'

'Confused about what?'

I can't lie. But I can twist the truth. 'Becoming a man.' I hesitate, awaiting a shock, but nothing comes. 'Stepping into what is expected of me.' I flex my fingers. 'It's scary, isn't it? We have to be these stoic, empathetic, resourceful men. We're encouraged to trust our feelings. To speak about them. But if we mention what frightens us ... if we truly talk about our fears, like we are now, we're told to just get over it.'

'Why fear what is perfect?' Roman asks me.

I shake my head. 'I don't know.'

'I wasn't asking,' Roman says. 'Ganymede's is creating the *perfect* life for us, right? For all of us. Our partners will be safe with us, we will be safe with them. We'll live perfect lives with perfect wives, and we'll be honoured and happy.'

'Exactly.'

'Perfection scares me,' he says.

He holds my gaze, and I nod slowly. 'Me too.'

'Why?'

'I think because ... because I'm not perfect.'

'No, neither am I.'

'So why do you fear perfection?' I ask him.

Roman thinks, then says, 'Because someone else's perfect isn't my perfect.'

We fall silent, Roman watching me. I didn't expect to talk to him like this so openly. To talk of my parents, for him to nod, listening to me. Sure, he can't go anywhere, but I'm so used to people not wanting to talk about it that it touches me that he's done so. I haven't been this open, this honest, since Blake. And even then, Blake never got all of me.

'I wish I was normal,' I finally say. 'I wish I could step into the role expected of me and make my father proud.'

'You can. You are.'

I shake my head. 'I don't think I can.'

Right now, it doesn't matter if Lawrence is on the other end of that mirror. It doesn't matter if he's listening. All that matters is passing this task, being honest with Roman, and him being honest with me. Maybe we could have done that in a different way. But emotional men are necessary to the fabric of our being.

'Did you know?'

'Know what?' he asks.

'Did you know the arrow was fake?'

Roman lifts his strapped hand, licking his lips before answering. 'Yes, I knew it was fake.'

Holding my breath, time seems to stand still as I wait for a jolt to come, but Roman nods slowly as the moment stretches between us, and I know he's told me the truth. My shoulders relax as I exhale.

Right now, we are at each other's mercy. I bravely ask, 'Will you tell anyone? About what I've said? About how I feel?'

Roman shakes his head. 'I won't tell a soul.'

No jolt.

'And you won't tell anyone about how I feel?'

'About Ganymede's.'

He spreads his hands. 'About Ganymede's. Society. This.'

I hesitate, before nodding. 'I won't.'

Roman waits. Perhaps I'm lying. But I'm not. He raps his knuckles against the wood. 'Can I ask you ... what do you want from Ganymede's?'

I swallow. 'I want to graduate.'

'And meet your partner?'

'And meet my partner.'

His tongue roves over his teeth, his free arm resting on the table.

'Your *female* partner?'

Heat prickles my skin. What is he doing? Why is he asking me this? I think of my embarrassment at Taylor's words, at the way Johnny tried to coax out of me something I can't think about.

We're supposed to trust each other, and he's assured me he won't tell a soul what I've confided in him so far. But in the grand scheme of things, all I have shared with him is fears. Truth about my fears. Not what I want. Not the truth about who I am. Not something illegal that could get me in trouble.

Society is built for heteronormativity. It's not built for my truth.

I pause, because I can never take this back if I tell the truth. 'Yes.'

My whole body rocks and I want to rip the thing off my finger. It takes everything I've got not to visibly react, but tears still sting my eyes, and I quickly wipe them away before Roman can see them.

'Are you sure about that?'

Eyes tightly shut, I nod. The magician must think outside of the box. He must weave his words carefully to cast the perfect spell. Finally, I mutter, 'I want to honour my partner and make sure she has the best life she can have with me. As much as I can give her.'

No jolt comes, but it doesn't give me the courage to meet his eye, to see what he thinks of me now. I have not told him what I am. I have given him enough.

'What about you?'

He gazes at me, his expression is hard to read.

'What about me?' he says.

'You want to meet a female partner, too?'

He hesitates and my whole body tenses.

'I ... want to find my perfect,' he says.

My muscles unclench. A perfect answer. And I have no idea what it means. Does it involve a woman, or—

'Whatever that is,' he adds.

He must have his own reasons, his own idea of what he wants life to be. A solitary man like him might struggle to live with someone he doesn't know. Perhaps he's protecting himself by hoping to be without another, for fear he might end up like his father.

'You want security? Stability?' I ask.

'I don't want Ganymede's help.'

I pray for a jolt, anything that tells me he's toying with me. When none comes, I shift, my hands clenching into fists.

'But you have to.'

'Do I?' he asks, cocking an eyebrow. 'Do *we*?'

'Roman,' I whisper. 'Stop this. You could be costing us the task already.'

Roman heaves a deep sigh. 'I'm sorry. I don't want to ruin this for you.'

To my relief, he isn't shocked. In that moment, I know he's on my side.

CHAPTER 19

The lock clicks, and the door handle rattles, and Roman gives me a wink as I'm breathing a sigh of relief before the door opens. Lawrence stands in the doorway, looking in at us. I shield my eyes from the light pouring in, realising just how dark it is in here. Lawrence's expression is blank. Has he heard us? Does he think differently of us?

'Good work, boys,' he says.

We unclip and take our arms out of the vice, massaging our wrists. Roman comes bounding towards me, and for one horrible moment I wonder if he's going to do a Taylor. But instead, he throws his arm around my shoulders, bringing me tighter to him.

To Lawrence, it must look like a brotherly bond. Perhaps that's what it is, now. Roman has told me he hates this place, and I have to pretend to be okay with that.

'Yes. I think we know each other better now, don't you?' Roman looks at me, smiling.

It's true, but I want to say that it's not enough. I want to know more. He's always so resolute. Stoic. I've glimpsed the fire growing underneath him. How does he cope with feeling he's been a disappointment his whole life?

But Lawrence is watching us, and I fake agreement. 'Yeah, absolutely. You're as much of a dick as I thought you were.'

'Language, Mr Cecil,' Lawrence scolds, as Roman laughs, patting me on the back.

'Sorry, sir. Is "sod" better?'

Lawrence cocks an eyebrow. 'Join me outside, please.'

In the hallway, Roman wipes the corners of his eyes, blinking in the light. My stomach flutters watching him, and I cross my arms, trying to keep myself standing tall and confident in the effortless way that he does.

'You were in there just over an hour,' Lawrence says. 'I'm hoping you both were open and honest with one another?'

'Ah, quite,' Roman says, adopting a posh accent.

'Why did you shock us?' I ask.

Lawrence turns to me slowly. '*I* didn't shock you.'

'Well, someone did.'

Lawrence holds out his hands, as if to say, 'Eh, what of it?'

'It hurt,' Roman adds, peering at his hands. 'Surprised it hasn't left a mark.'

'Yeah. Perhaps we need to see a nurse,' I say.

'Maybe a night in the hospital wing,' Roman suggests.

Oh, God. A night in a hospital wing with Roman? I definitely wouldn't be able to sleep having him so close.

'A little shock never hurt anybody,' Lawrence says. 'You had to be honest with one another. If you weren't, the test picked up on it. Every time you were shocked, you were being deceptive. Hopefully you didn't lie too much.'

I smile swiftly. 'Not too much, sir.'

'Do we get marked down if we did lie?' Roman asks.

'I can't share those details, Mr Edwards. Besides, the

technology behind that test is almost foolproof. Unless you are an exceptional liar, it would have detected you.'

'Hmm, are we done here, then?' Roman asks, hands in his pocket. Back to his nonchalant self, it seems.

'Just one more thing,' Lawrence says. 'Your words have been recorded, and may be used for future tasks.'

My eyes bulge, turning to look at Roman. He nods slightly, as if he's shaking something away. The spark of cheeky bravado fades from his warm eyes. Eyes he keeps fixed on Lawrence, hanging on to his every word, words which sound like a blur of nothingness to me.

Lawrence turns his attention to me and I try and zone in on what he's saying '...in three days' time, task three will begin, but for now, please head to my classroom and fill out the papers waiting for you.'

Roman goes, and I follow, away from the room of truth, away from Lawrence, who goes back through the secret corridor, no doubt to snare another boy in a task that could risk his whole existence. We stay quiet, walking side by side down the main staircase and to another set of stairs leading into the depths of the school. I shiver as we take the darker stairs, the walls no longer mahogany-panelled but redbrick, as if whoever built this place didn't bother with the finer details underground. We emerge into a corridor lit by lanterns on antique tables.

'It's always like we're not supposed to be here,' I whisper.

There is no artwork here, no warmth, only a wall of mirrors that distort our features, making us seem taller and then shorter than we are. Despite coming here to speak with Lawrence, it never feels welcoming. At the end of the hall is a door, leading to Lawrence's classroom.

In the front row of amphitheatre seating, parchment paper sits on the old-fashioned bark, polished into small desks, just big enough to hold our books and our arms and our papers.

Judging by the fact that only two desks have paper, Roman and I take our seats side by side.

Neither of us reads the ten questions waiting for us. Instead, Roman whispers, 'How're you feeling?'

'Like your days are numbered.'

'Yeah, maybe.'

'You don't care?'

'If they are, they are,' Roman says. 'These tasks exist for a reason.'

'Yeah, but come on, Roman, you don't want the life of nothingness.'

Roman laughs at this, warmly, and it echoes through this cold chamber of a room.

But I glower. 'It's not funny.'

Roman sighs. 'No, it's not. None of this is.'

I turn my attention to the questions, scribbling down answers on the paper:

Do you feel like you know your partner better?
What surprised you most about your partner?
Was your partner open and honest?
Could you tell your partner anything?
Do you feel emotionally connected to your partner?
Would you trust your partner to keep a secret?
Do you feel safe with your partner?
Would you trust your partner with your life?

That one is a strange question, I think.

'You think we've passed?' I say.

'Aced it.' Roman finally looks at me, smiling. 'Come on, we can't dwell. We've done nothing wrong.'

'It doesn't feel like that.'

'If the task is to be truthful, then truthful I was,' Roman

says. 'If they even try and expel me for that, I will argue my case.'

'How very sanguine of you,' I mutter.

Roman nudges me, making me look at him. 'Are you nervous around me?'

'Excuse me?'

'It's like you think I'm in the wrong.'

'I'm just worried about you, that's all.'

Roman leans back, his hands falling to his lap. His paper is half complete, and I almost want to tap the next question – *What surprised you most about your partner?* I want to know what his answer may be.

'Don't worry about me, Dylan. I can handle myself.'

Roman takes a breath, and I do the same, recalling our lessons in mindfulness.

He moves the paper closer to him, reading the questions.

'*Do you feel emotionally connected to your partner?*' Roman asks, his voice carrying in the dark room. 'Yes, I do feel emotionally connected to my partner, thanks for asking.'

How can he be so calm?

His pen scratches the paper.

'These are weird questions,' he says, brow furrowed. 'Like this one. *Do you feel safe with your partner?*'

'I just said yes to all of them.'

'Very expansive.'

'I'm not writing more than I need to,' I mutter.

Roman shrugs, before writing down the answer 'yes' to the final question.

Papers finished, we lean back in our benches. Without the rest of the boys here, the classroom feels imposing. Our voices echo, and I worry that maybe someone is in the hallway, listening to our every word.

'What surprised you about me?' I ask.

Roman leans forward, looking at his paper. 'That we seem to have more in common than I first thought.'

'We do?'

'I think so,' Roman says, then shrugs. 'Maybe. To be honest, I wrote something that might act as though I've seen another side to you.'

I bite my lip, looking at Lawrence's room, at his table, absent of any newspapers.

'I'm nervous about this. All of this.'

Roman angles himself so his knee touches mine. I let my hand rest on the bench, hidden between us.

'You should be,' he mutters. 'We all should be.'

CHAPTER 20

I don't know how long we've been here, but footsteps approaching the room make us break apart. We hadn't moved from where we'd cosied on the bench, as cosy as it can be when you're on stone seating, but lounging there was the first time I've felt truly relaxed.

Roman leans back over his paper, pretends to be finishing his answers, and I rest my face against my fist, dragging my lip up for good measure.

The door opens. It's Taylor and Lee.

'Aye, here he is, look,' Taylor says, slapping Lee on his chest. 'Oh.' Taylor pauses, puffing up his chest. 'And the other. Numbskull and blue balls.'

'Which one's which?' Roman asks.

'I'll let you figure that one out,' Taylor says.

'Why? Too much of a strenuous task for you?'

Taylor ignores him. 'Did you create a stronger bond? Are you *emotionally raw*?'

'Probably more emotionally attuned than you two,' Roman replies.

Lee shakes his head. 'We already know each other.'

'Do you, though? Do you really?'

Taylor and Lee stare at each other, momentarily confused, but Taylor's confidence restores first.

'Get up, then. We need to do our papers.'

Roman crosses his arms, leans back, legs spread. A stance of defiance, I think. 'You hear something?' he asks me.

I shake my head. Taylor's eyes narrow as he considers Roman. I wonder what he's thinking, what he makes of him. I doubt anyone has spoken to Taylor in this way before.

'What you going to write? Today I learnt the word empathy?' I ask.

'Want another bruise, Cecil?'

'Yeah, I need to accessorise.'

Roman laughs, loudly. It's probably his way of trying to show me he's on my side, but I wish he wouldn't.

Taylor and Lee approach, and I stand, Roman following me a moment later. If they want to intimidate us, I'll stand up to it. But neither boy makes to attack. Instead, Taylor considers us both. *Stand down*, I think. We take our papers, leaving behind others that Lee hands out to Taylor and himself.

'Those shocks hurt, didn't they?' Lee asks our retreating backs. We turn.

Lee grimaces. Taylor, leaning against the bench with his arms outstretched, gives Lee a confused look.

'Shocks?' Roman says. 'We weren't shocked.'

'We have no reason to not be honest with one another,' I say.

I turn back before I can see what Taylor or Lee have to say, but a scrunched-up piece of paper hits me on the head, and laughter rings in my ears all the way down the corridor. It's such a childish move, but that is Taylor. In front of Roman, though, it feels like public humiliation.

'I know we're not supposed to, but I would gladly smash their faces in for you,' Roman says. 'If you want me to.'

'As much as I'd like to see that, I don't need you to fight for me. You've already done enough.'

'Suit yourself.'

We're halfway up the uneven, dank stairs when Roman blocks the doorway leading to the main foyer of the school.

'What are you doing?'

'I wanted to say something before we ... go back out there,' he says.

'Okay?'

'I wanted to say thank you for telling me about your parents.' His face is cast in shadow, so I can't see his expression.

I sigh, sitting down on the step. Roman checks over his shoulder again before he joins me. The only light comes from the crack beneath the door.

'Can I also tell you about Blake?'

Roman watches me carefully, finally nodding.

'He was my best friend.' I swallow, already feeling the sting of tears. 'I could tell him anything. Beyond Blake, you're the only one I've been able to talk to about them.'

Roman smiles, touching my shoulder. His grip is tight but it knocks me off course, head reeling. 'Thank you.'

'Don't flatter yourself,' I say with a laugh.

'I'm going to.' Roman grins.

He lets me go, and I feel him shift closer to me. 'I think a lot about them. I think a lot about Blake. Your mind goes all sorts of places when you can't sleep. I've thought of all possibilities. But there's one thing I keep coming back to.'

Roman's breathing steadies and he turns to me. 'Which is?'

I grit my teeth, wondering if I should speak of what Blake confided in me before he disappeared. 'The lead-up to Blake's disappearance. He was acting odd. He started talking about students that dropped out. Said he wanted to find out where they went. Wouldn't listen to me when I told him it was just boys not being cut out for Ganymede's. They're probably just transferred to other schools and...'

'No.'

I stop. 'No?'

'No Ganymede boy was ever transferred into my school, before I came here. Boys can only go up.'

My body vibrates with worry, and I don't say anything for a moment, replaying my last few weeks with Blake, and the way his paranoia seemed to consume him.

'Sorry, I interrupted,' Roman finally says. 'Tell me more about Blake.'

'Right, Blake.' I nod, but now I'm unsure. 'When he didn't come back, I thought anything was possible, that there was an explanation for where he was. But then of course he was found dead. It all felt so ... neat. Where had he been? Why did he appear at the bottom of the stairs? Where could he have been hiding, with no one accounting for him? Surely he would have been seen?'

Roman nods, crossing his arms over his knees.

'And then you start to question that. You question why his death has been so glossed over. They folded his death neatly in a box and threw away the key. And then you think, if they could do that with Blake, what of the other boys that have been leaving the school over the years? How can they be the top school if boys aren't completing their full education?'

'I see.'

Trust. I have to trust him. I can trust him with this.

'There was a boy who went missing in the lake,' I say. 'First sign of summer he goes swimming and he never comes back. No body found. Nothing. Some of the boys said he couldn't handle the school, but I remember him struggling with his lessons, asking too many questions. Questions the professors didn't seem to like.'

'Like what?'

'Like, challenging some of the history. Some of the methods.' I shrug. 'Then there was the boy who failed our mock exams in year two. Never really bothered with him and I have to admit it took me a while to realise he'd actually gone, but, yeah. He stopped showing up to lessons one failed mock and that was that.'

'Expelled?'

'But why expel someone over a failed test result? Why waste talent like that?'

Roman nods slowly. 'Back in my school in my second year I was friends with a guy called Peter. I remember him having a few health issues and stuff. Nothing major, he just always seemed to be down with something. Like a low immune system, I guess,' Roman says. 'Anyway, one day he said he was worried about something he'd found, um...' Roman gestures below his waist. 'Went to the nurse for a check-up and came back looking very pale. He wouldn't talk to any of us. That night he was called to our headmaster's office and...'

'He never came back,' we say together.

'So, it's not just Ganymede's, then,' Roman says, more to himself than anything. 'But I'd be lying if I said I hadn't noticed these things, too. Both of my sisters casually mentioned their friends leaving out of the blue. We never see them or hear from them again. It's like they vanish into thin air.'

He holds his hand out, as if it is smoke lost to the breeze.

'I didn't pay much attention to these vanishers, because I think we've been led to believe that it's innocent. Accidents.' I turn to face Roman, imploring him to understand my next words. 'But Blake started to question some of the things going on here. He felt as though the boys were being taught the wrong sort of emotional intelligence, that they were picking up bad habits in their attitudes. In Lawrence's class he started asking all these questions about what happens if boys don't conform, don't fit in to the way of life expected of us. Lawrence answered all of them but I could see him getting angry. And then Blake started answering questions wrong, and in one of our exams he refused to answer questions on history.' Roman looks away from me. 'I saw him writing something else, some long spiel, but he never told me what it was. After that...' *Poof*, I say with my hands. 'They celebrated him so much when he was born. Celebrated him when he came here. You'd think he'd get some state funeral, being the billionth child, but nothing. It's like he was nothing.'

Roman crosses his arms, staring into the darkness. 'Can I ask you something?'

'Yes, of course.'

Roman inhales, cast in the shadows. 'Do you think Blake's death was an accident?'

Of course I had wondered about that in the nights after Blake's death. It's why I go to his grave, as if he might rise from the dead and tell me exactly what happened. 'I have no evidence,' I say, carefully. 'But they seemed to cover up his death way too quickly. Moved on from it too fast.'

'Well,' Roman says, taking a breath. 'We're smart men. We get answers. Knowledge is power, Dylan. Let's find out what really happened to Blake.'

'How? We can't—'

'We can,' Roman says, getting to his feet. 'If we've been taught anything, it's that our intuition should be listened to. You're telling me you think something doesn't feel right with Blake's death...'

'Yeah, but—'

'No buts,' Roman says. 'Your best friend died.' I wince and

Roman puts his hand on my shoulders. 'Sorry, a bit blunt of me, maybe. It might still be an accident, but you said it yourself, it felt neat. To show up dead here means he was still in the school, and yet no one saw him. Don't you want answers?'

'Yeah, but I don't know where to start.'

'You're a magician, Dylan. You can make anything happen.'

I bite my lip, lost for words. This changing landscape is littered with landmines; one wrong step will lead to destruction. But with a warrior by my side, together we can navigate it like explorers, documenting truth.

'Then let's do it,' I whisper. 'Let's find out the truth.'

CHAPTER 21

My mouth waters as I walk into dinner that evening. Running a hand over my adequately empty stomach, I barely register Johnny and Cameron sitting at the other end of the room, opposite one another.

'How do you think you did?' Johnny asks as I sit.

Since telling Roman what I felt, what I thought, I'd started to convince myself I was wrong to have done so. What if Roman was telling his friends about me right now?

Fingers click and I turn to see Johnny's hand raised. 'Earth to Dyl.'

'Sorry. Uh, yeah, I think it went all right.'

'You do?' Cameron asks, his voice laced with worry.

'You don't?'

Cameron bites his lip. 'I ... well, I was as honest as I could be until—'

'The shocks,' Johnny and I say together.

Cameron gives a sad nod. 'I didn't think they would do something like that.'

'It didn't hurt that much,' Johnny says, though he doesn't sound convincing.

'What did you tell him?' I ask.

Cameron's answer falls flat as waiters come to the table, carrying fresh soup, this time tomato. Standing either end of the professors table are two security guards, still in their familiar blue armour that glints in the light.

'Elis said he likes to keep secrets,' Cameron says, keeping his voice low. I keep my expression neutral, but inside I want to prod for more information. Elis is keeping secrets? I knew something was odd about the way he talked to Roman. Theirs did not look like a natural friendship. 'I tried to ask him what they were, but he said he wouldn't tell me. Not yet, anyway. Said that he only needed to be honest. You know what he's like. Thinks he's some philosopher, started saying all this stuff that sounded like he'd learnt a bunch of words but didn't know how to use them yet. Made a Shakespeare reference that's gone in one ear and out the other, too.'

Cameron rolls his eyes and Johnny laughs.

'And then he asked me how I'm feeling,' Cameron said. 'I told him I feel fine and then...' Cameron held up his hand, shaking it. 'I told him some things I'm not proud of and now apparently it was all recorded?'

What could Cameron possibly have to say that he wasn't proud of? He comes from humble roots, a charitable family that give back to their hamlets. The boy is the kindest, sweetest boy here. I often look to him to see how I should be feeling. Some equilibrium.

So the idea that he might have said something he thinks was too raw and vulnerable has me questioning everything I've said to Roman.

'This was all about trust,' I say, trying to keep my voice

devoid of any emotion. 'If Elis goes and spills to other boys, then he's not graduating, is he?'

'Do you really think that?'

'I do. A partnership is all about knowing the parts of ourselves we want to keep hidden from the rest of the world.' I don't meet their eyes as I say this. 'If Elis is a good man, he will respect what you've said and accept you for who you are.'

Cameron takes a delicate taste of his soup, nodding slowly. 'I hope you're right.'

'And what did you get from Jackson?' I ask Johnny.

'The boy's a laugh when he's not trying to dick-measure with Taylor.'

'Well, that's all that matters, then, I guess,' I say.

'Yeah, sounds like you really got the emotional scope of him,' Cameron says, smiling.

'We passed, so I'd say so.'

I peer at Johnny. 'How do you know you passed?'

Johnny lowers his spoon, soup spilling over the edge. 'You haven't heard?'

I shake my head, and Cameron looks away.

'Two of the boys from Mars failed. They've packed their bags and left.'

At the Mars table Roman ignores his food, staring at the flames of the candles that line the table. His hands are clasped, his jaw set. The boys next to him sombrely eat their soup, shoulders drooping. Dwynwen watches them from the top table, a goblet raised to her lips. Her eyes glint.

This suddenly got real.

'How did they fail?'

'Didn't tell each other anything, I guess,' Johnny says with a shrug. 'Or maybe they refused to be honest. Either way, they've been expelled.'

Expelled.

I bite my tongue, trying to remain level headed. More boys expelled. More boys left behind, discarded, told they're not fit for Ganymede's. Am I reading too much into it? Am I thinking about things too deeply? I wonder if Roman's thinking about what I said to him in the stairwell. I want to ask him, but I know it would draw attention. I don't know the rules on speaking with your partners between the tasks. I'm sure it would be allowed, but why risk it when I already feel like I risked too much talking to Roman about how I feel?

Dwynwen wipes her eye, as if trying to hide tears. When she looks at me, my heart drops, and I refuse to look at her again.

When we've finished dinner and our desserts have been wolfed down, we're dismissed by Dwynwen twenty minutes before our curfews begin.

'You go on up,' I say to the boys. 'I'll see you later.'

'Where are you going?' Cameron presses. 'You'll get in trouble.'

'Don't worry about me.' I pat Cameron on the back and make a beeline through the crowd as they file out of the hall, firmly set on my target. Halfway up the stairs, I tap Roman on the shoulder. 'Can we talk?'

CHAPTER 22

'We've got to get back.'

'It will be quick,' I say. 'I promise.' When he says nothing, just hovers in the thinning crowd, I insist. 'Please.'

Roman groans. I'd not put him down as a rule follower.

'Where's your Mars spirit?'

What's really the big deal in breaking this brand-new curfew?

'Fine, but not here,' he says, looking to the food hall, where Professor Omar is leaning against the door, arms crossed, stifling a yawn. Two security guards patrol the end of the corridor.

He beckons for me to follow him up the stairs, and I'm glad that Omar isn't watching because if he was paying attention, he'd know Roman is going the wrong way. On the next floor, he drags me away from the stairs that would lead to my dorm room, and down the corridor, straggling behind some of the Jupiter boys. I wonder if we're going into one of the classrooms, maybe some of the lounges. To my surprise, he stops at a grand six-foot gold-gilded painting of the zodiac constellations.

He looks around him, hands in his pockets, before crouching down and slipping his fingers underneath the frame.

'What are you doing?' I hiss. That painting is centuries old.

He waves me away, returning to the painting, and a few seconds later there's a click. The painting swings towards us, and I cover my mouth, expecting to be crushed by frame and paint and canvas.

But instead, it's hinged, and behind it is a long corridor, lit with dim strip lighting.

'Old servants' corridor,' he says. 'Come on.'

'But we're not—'

He takes my hand and drags me into the corridor, pulling the painting, the door, closed behind him.

It's darker now, quieter, the dim lights barely cutting through the gloom. Outside, the boys' voices have faded into nothingness. There's a density to the air we breathe, and as his shoulders brush mine, he takes a few steps further into the corridor, where it widens ever so slightly as the walls curve. It's here we stop, in this small nook between one corridor meeting another. I can smell something earthy here, mixed with burning, like incense and lamplight have been transported through it only a few moments ago.

'How do you know about this place?' I say.

'Saw one of the security guards use it once and thought it would be good to explore it myself,' Roman says, looking slightly proud of himself. 'It cuts right through the school and takes you to the other side.'

'Have you ever been caught in here?'

Roman shakes his head.

'Are you okay?' I ask him.

'Why wouldn't I be?'

I swallow. 'You looked sad earlier.'

'You watching me?'

My cheeks heat, but I power through. 'I heard about two of the Mars boys being expelled. Did you know them?'

'Course I knew them,' he says, his clothes rustling as he slips his hands in his pockets. 'Doberman shared a room with me.'

'Uh, Doberman?'

Roman chuckles, low, and I feel my lips tug into a smile. 'His father rescues dogs, his mother provides Dobermans to people who want them. He was the first of his family to come here. Just a stupid name we came up with.'

'What's his real name?'

'Does that matter?'

I shrug. Changing tack, I ask, 'Were you close?'

'Ah, I liked him. Cool dude. Smart. Switched on.'

But not close. Not friendly.

There's silence as we fall into thought. Maybe Doberman and the guy I don't know simply weren't good enough. They lied, or weren't honest enough, or didn't click together, and their team work wasn't good enough to take them further. This month was always going to be the make-or-break month. We knew it from day one.

But why are seemingly bright, young, perfect men being expelled?

'What's his family life like?' I ask. 'And the other guy's?'

'They seemed happy. Same as you or I. Parents who have come through Ganymede's. Looked after, supported. Kids with potential.' Roman clears his throat. 'James was the other guy. Kept himself to himself, mainly. Everyone thought he might go into some security role.'

'Why?'

'Family in security,' Roman says. 'Usually the way.'

'Roman,' I ask. 'What's it like out there?'

Roman cocks his head. 'Out where?'

'In the hamlets.'

'Don't you remember?'

'I remember my home, how it seemed to be falling apart though Mother and Father wouldn't admit it. I remember sleek cars and everything we could ever need within a fifteen-minute walk. I remember that it was like a circle of Victorian homes, with trees in the middle. I remember wishing we were closer to the sea, but I could smell it on the air sometimes.'

'I'm close to the sea,' Roman says. 'Tenby. Well, what used to be Tenby, anyway.'

'Do you like it?'

'My hamlet is the same as yours, I guess. Everything you need close by. Clothes, food, shops. All there. Everyone works from their homes, and if they don't work from home they work in the town, where there are buildings where people hot-desk. Big fishing industry, now that the sea is starting to thrive again. But mostly people just exist. They live. Because they know they will always be supported. Always be looked after. Everyone gets along and everyone has what they need and everyone is healthy and happy. It's ... perfect.'

'And you like it?'

'It's where I'm going to end up, isn't it?'

'Won't you go somewhere else?'

'Most people stay within their communities all their lives,' Roman says.

I think of my hamlet, my home that has sat empty. Will I return? Move in to the home that was full of family memorabilia with a young woman I don't know?

'I heard my parents talking one night, arguing over drinks,' Roman says. 'The summer before I came here. I hadn't been feeling well and I came down to try and see if we had any medicine. I heard them saying that Ganymede's were streamlining boys. Becoming more selective. Before they could say any more, I bloody made a noise on the step I was sitting on and they stopped talking. But that was enough for me, Dylan. That discussion. They sounded ... worried. I asked my mum about it a few days later. She said I was hearing things. Blamed it on my illness, said I had a temperature, hallucinating.'

'But you weren't.'

'Nah, course I wasn't,' Roman says. 'Now that I'm here, I keep thinking about that word. Selective.'

Roman joins me on my side of the wall. His shoulders brush mine, and we stare at the blank wall in front of us.

'They've just been expelled, right?' he whispers.

'Like the boys from before. Do you ever think of just getting expelled?' I ask. 'Just getting expelled and living away from all of this?'

Roman turns to me, and I realise just how close he is. I think of stepping back, putting some distance between us, but I wonder if it might be odd.

'Then I'd lose everything,' he says.

'Don't you want to lose everything?'

He shakes his head. 'Perfection is power.'

CHAPTER 23

'What time is it?'

Roman shrugs. 'Who cares?'

'I care.'

'Why?'

'I don't want to face the wrath of Dwynwen.'

We've been standing in this corridor, mostly in silence, for the past ten minutes. We're cutting it fine. Now that I've adjusted to the dark, I can make out that the walls are brick, with carvings from long ago. There's a film of dust coating the surface, like the security guards merely pass through and no one looks after the maintenance of the corridors, or their secrets.

'What do you think our parents thought about students leaving?' Roman asks me.

'I've wondered.' I notice how he speaks about his parents in the past tense, as though for my benefit. I think of correcting him, but I leave it.

'I have, too.'

'Have you asked?'

'I've mentioned the boys being expelled,' Roman replies.

'And what have they said?'

Roman shifts, leaning on his shoulder so that he faces me. I turn my own body so that I mirror his, both of us inches apart, reading each other's expressions.

'That they've moved on to where they need to be,' Roman says. 'Like, different lives.'

I nod, then stop. 'Then why have we never encountered them again?'

Roman smiles at me, eyes widening. 'Exactly what I've wondered.'

'Why has no one questioned any of this?'

'I think there are a few reasons,' Roman says. 'One of them being that before, it may have been once in a blue moon that a student didn't graduate and their families have moved on. But more recently, the number seems to be getting higher. Across all the schools, too, not just here, but all under the eye of Vandervere. And even then, why question it? Why pay it any mind? What does it matter if one or two boys lose everything, when the majority of us have it all? Poor souls, but at least it's not me. Mum tells me to keep my head in the sand. To graduate. Because that's what I need to do. And I will graduate, of course I will. It's just...' Roman looks down at his feet. 'Look, these boys ... what do they all have in common? They all started asking questions. They got cocky. They stopped caring. They tripped up somewhere along the line. The reason people aren't speaking up is because they don't want to let their families down, let society down, or lose what is promised to them from the day they were born. But those who do—'

There's a creak at the other end of the corridor, and our heads whip round. Roman stands taller, and I brush up against him, dwarfed by his stature.

'I don't think you understand. Nobody is looking our way,' a voice whispers.

'I still don't like it,' another voice says.

Other students, I think, sneaking away for quiet moments. I wonder what they might think when they see Roman and me hidden here too.

'We did the right thing. He got out of hand,' the first voice says, gruff and low.

'That was your fault.'

The footsteps are closer now, and Roman grips me as I sink back into him, as if he might hide me.

Two boys emerge before us. One is tall, as if he's been stretched, all bone and sinew and spots across his white face. I put him at around twenty-five. The second boy is shorter, a little rounder in the middle, around the same age, I'd wager. His white skin is blotched with red. They both wear the familiar armour of security, their hair cropped short. They squint as they stare at us, lifting their lamps closer to us to see us better. The daggers at their waist glint.

'You're not security,' the taller boy says in his gruff voice.

'Good spotting, Ieuan,' the shorter one mutters.

Ieuan nudges his friend. He looks at us. 'Last warning, boys. Curfew is almost up.'

Roman remains silent and I follow his lead.

'We'll be on our way,' Ieuan says, eyeing us up and down. They brush past us, the shorter one sniffing the air as if he is smelling us. It's oddly terrifying. Their backs retreat into the darkness, their bodies illuminated as they open the door and disappear in the corridor.

Roman exhales. 'Maybe we should get a move on.'

But before we can, footsteps hurry towards us, a light bobbing. Roman takes a breath, shakes his head. He nudges me into the wall and he slips to the side, away from me, as another face looms out of the darkness.

Blinking at us like he's seeing humans for the first time, Rory opens and closes his mouth. Finally, he says, 'You're not supposed to be in here. This is a violation.'

'We got lost,' Roman says. 'Forgive us.'

Rory looks at us, Roman leaning against the wall, me with my arms crossed around my stomach trying to shrink into the dark shadows. Maybe this is the time to ask what the two security guards were arguing about. But I can't ask my professor that. Even if right now he looks like he's doing something he shouldn't be doing.

The lantern swings in Rory's dark hand. The warm glow of the candle illuminates Roman's self-assurance, his casually calm face. Rory looks him over, before turning to me. 'Please. I must ask you to leave.'

'We're going that way,' Roman says, nodding behind Rory. Where's his respect for him? 'You're heading the other way. Go. Don't let us stop you.'

'Did you see two security guards?' he asks.

'We did,' I say.

'And they went that way?' Rory points behind us.

'They did.'

'Fine job they're doing, then.'

Rory moves on, eyes firmly set on the back of the painting that we walked through.

'You didn't see us, are we clear?' Roman asks, and I stare at him and then at Rory.

Rory halts, observes us over his shoulder. 'It's none of my business what you are doing here.'

'And it is none of ours what you are up to,' Roman says.

Rory looks like he wants to say something, but seems to think better of it. Shaking his head, he walks away. Light cuts through the dark as he steps out into the corridor of the school. When it closes with a thud, Roman exhales.

'What the hell was that about?' I snap.

'What?'

'You talking to him like that. He's our professor, Roman.'

'I did it for us,' Roman bites, pointing to the painting. 'They aren't on our side, Dylan. He saw us here and he would have told on us and then what?'

'We would have lied. We would have—'

'We're two boys hidden in a corridor after curfew. People are going to talk.'

'What do you mean?'

'Didn't you catch the way those security guards looked at us? Even Rory seemed to consider us as something ... other.'

With shaking words, I say, 'And why would that have mattered?'

Roman blinks, brow furrowed. 'Huh?'

Shit. There's no point pushing it, even if I want to.

'Nothing. It doesn't matter.'

'You think I'm worried about ... about that?'

The words hang between us, until finally I say, 'It's illegal. It's damaging, if someone were to start a rumour like that.'

'Yes, it is, and that's why I wanted to make sure he wasn't going to tell anyone,' Roman says. 'A rumour like that would get us expelled, Dylan. Neither of us wants that, do we?'

I step away from the wall, heading to the painting. I don't know what's going on. Back turned, I hardly hear Roman following me.

'Dylan?'

'What?'

It comes out harsher than I intended, but I don't care. I don't want to walk this shaky ground with him.

'Actually, I really don't care, you know,' he says. 'I mean, if someone started a rumour like that. About me. Us. I'd stand by it.'

My grip tightens on the wooden beam, and my mouth runs dry.

As blood rushes to my face, pounds in my ears, I say, 'Goodnight, Roman.'

I hope I don't see a soul from here to my dorm room.

CHAPTER 24

On the next bright summer morning, Professor Lawrence leads a check-in class, an opportunity for boys to talk openly about their experiences with the tasks so far. When I enter the room behind Johnny, Taylor and Cameron, most of the seats are already taken, despite the class being optional. The room is big enough to hold all of the third-year boys, and split into four sections according to our houses. I shiver at the two empty seats in the Mars cohort, Roman sitting on the end of the row, leaning forward, chin resting on his fists.

There's a Saturn seat empty across from him, which I take as I offer him a curt nod. He does not return it.

My brow creases, but I look away, as if that moment hasn't happened between us.

Last night, another restless night, I thought about Father. He wanted the world for me, and I'm doing everything for him. It's like all this time I've been going through the motions, living in a bubble, because it hasn't been for me and it hasn't been for my wants. It's been for Father. Now Roman is the jagged edge that could burst the bubble I've made home.

Home.

Ganymede's is home.

And now here I am. From boy to man. And my thoughts are leading me down dark paths with wild theories, and Roman is telling me everything is perfect, but he's unhappy, and I'm starting to think differently. Starting to wonder about the what-ifs.

Starting to question things.

Questioning is dangerous.

Don't ask questions, unless it's to learn more. No questions must be asked unless they are about widening the mind, parching the thirst for knowledge. I've learnt so much in all my seventeen years. About wars started by men, who took over countries. Male leaders, dictators, who cared only for profit, and not for the environment. About how countries led by women were few and far between but had better performing economies. I've learnt to embody empathy and love and compassion. I've learnt what's right and wrong. But now I'm learning that *I* am wrong. That I truly don't fit in, that I don't belong. Because, tossing and turning in my bed, my thoughts always went back to Roman, and the quiver of excitement I felt at being in a dark, secluded corridor with him, where nothing else existed but us. Where I could have done anything. I don't know if he feels the same, in fact I am certain he doesn't, but that hasn't stopped the wild thoughts of possibilities that have grown like buttercups in the grounds. But the fantasies die when I think of Professor Rory. Roman and I have learnt to trust one another, but should we have also learnt to trust Rory? I think of Taylor, and how he seems to have sniffed out that part of me I've tried to hide for so long. The part I didn't even know existed until recently. I've never told a soul about my same-sex attraction, and yet there seem to be boys who just know.

Does Roman know?

Why did he want me to know that he wouldn't mind? Was he letting me know I was safe with him? Was he trying to coax it out of me, to trap me? I dare not look at him, for fear of my thoughts racing again.

Then there are the security men, Ieuan and the shorter one. What were they whispering about? They sounded harried, the shorter one sounding troubled.

Operating on two hours' sleep, I know I need to battle to stay awake during Lawrence's talk. He stands behind his mahogany desk, heaped high with notebooks and leatherbound books and loose papers with sketching on them. I think I can see a bunch of newspapers stacked at his feet, and wonder how old they might be. It's almost like looking at stolen contraband.

'So, how are you all feeling?' Lawrence asks. The room is still, silent, and I peer around at the heads of my classmates, wondering if anyone will break it. 'Come on. These classes are for us to talk... So tell me.'

He stands so refined before us, not a hair out of place. There's almost something ethereal about him, and indeed all of our professors.

But still, no one talks. No one even moves. I wonder if they're all in on some prank and any moment now they might burst into laughter.

'Why were we shocked?' Elis's voice is loud in the quiet room.

Lawrence smiles at him. 'Thank you, Mr Bell, for your question. Did you not wish to be shocked?'

'Why would anyone want to be shocked?'

'I can assure you, it was perfectly safe. No lasting damage.'

'Then why shock us?' Elis presses.

'These tasks exist to push you to your limits,' Lawrence says.

'Are they going to get worse?' a boy at the back of the room asks.

Lawrence's smile doesn't falter. 'One boy's worst is another's best. You are all perfectly capable of passing these tests. Your education has led you to this moment.'

'If you want to know how we're feeling, read our expressions, Professor Lawrence,' Elis says. 'I can only speak for myself, some of my dorm mates, too, but none of us were expecting shocks. That surprised us.'

'You might even say shocked us,' Johnny calls out, and the room laughs lightly.

Lawrence nods, walking around the table. His black coat ruffles behind him, the red lining catching the burning light. He leans against the front of the desk, hands either side of him resting on it. 'I understand that it must have been surprising to you, and I do wish I could have told you myself so that you were better prepared. However, as your professor, I cannot interfere in your outcomes, because it is your future on the line.' He peers around the room, his smile fading so that his expression becomes serious. He's not our friend, I have to think. Not our older brother. He's our *professor*. 'Do you want to be serious for a moment?'

Some of the boys nod.

'To be the men society needs, you have to go through the lows to get to the highs,' he says. 'When I was your age, I went through all of these tasks myself. One particular task sticks with me, and I'm not going to bore you with the details. But it made me question who, what, I was doing this for.'

I bite my lip. I feel Roman's stare. He won't get any indication from me that I'm thinking along the same lines as him. I wait for Lawrence to continue.

'I imagine, right now, that some of you are feeling hurt? Confused? Maybe even betrayed?' He observes the room. 'Come on, boys, we've talked about harder stuff than this. You can tell me. Do you feel any of those things?'

There are mutterings of agreement, before Elis says, 'I'm angry.'

'All right, sure,' Lawrence says with gusto, smiling. 'Be angry. Be confused. Hate me. Hate us. Hate yourselves. Hate the school and the world. I'd be worried if none of you were feeling that.' He strolls across the platform his desk sits upon, hands behind his back, walking the width of the room. 'The tasks are designed to bring up all the dark matter you've been dealing with. They're designed to make you think differently and engage parts of yourselves you didn't know you had. The reason for that is we want to ensure you are prepared for the world out there.'

'But why shock us?' Elis asks. 'We'll have it all out there, so why make us feel like this when we're expecting greatness when we graduate?'

'A good question,' Lawrence replies, but his smile at Elis is tight, not quite reaching his eyes. Alarm bells ring in my mind. This is what he was like with Blake. 'We have to be sure this is really what you want.'

'It's better than the alternative,' Elis mutters to his friend, but his voice carries.

'Yes, Mr Bell, it is.' Lawrence stares at us all with severity. 'The world isn't against you, boys. Neither is Ganymede's. To think such means you are in a dangerous mindset.'

'Can we expect to be shocked further down the line?' Elis asks, his sleeves rolled up, bare arm resting against his table. 'Maybe burnt alive by fire, or fed to sharks?'

'Please, Mr Bell, we are landlocked, there are no sharks here,' Lawrence says, and one or two of the pupils laugh. 'You can expect these tasks to shape you further into healthy, refined men.'

Elis tuts.

Lawrence steps down off the platform until he's level with

Elis's row. He looks over at him. 'Do you require an apology, Mr Bell?'

'Sorry, sir?'

His friends laugh. Roman grimaces.

'Do you want me to apologise to you on behalf of Ganymede's?' Lawrence asks, voice clear. 'I'm serious. I'd like an answer.'

Elis swallows, running a hand over his crooked tie. 'No, sir, I don't require an apology.'

Lawrence considers him, before stepping backwards, turning and heading back to his desk. He switches on his desk lamp, and he takes a seat in his leather chair. 'Here at Ganymede's, we know these tasks can be strenuous, both mentally and physically. Which is why these check-ins exist.' He nods at Elis. 'Please, all of you, don't feel as though you can't speak your minds here. You are free to say whatever you want and it will not leave this room. You have all, after all, been through your tasks of trust and honesty, and you have passed this component...' He's interrupted by elated cheers, boys clapping one another on the back, thudding the tables in joy. Johnny hugs me, and I laugh with him. Lawrence holds a hand out, calming the noise. 'But you all have to learn to trust *each other*, too. No judgement. We are here to listen and learn and look out for one another. Am I making myself clear?'

'Yes, sir,' we chorus.

Lawrence smiles. 'I am, of course, available anytime you want to talk privately. My mindful classes may well be over, but I am still your mindful teacher. Now, rest up, boys. Task three is a good one.'

CHAPTER 25

On the morning of task three, I awake feeling surprisingly relaxed. Exhausted with running thoughts, I'd drifted off to sleep at an earlier hour, when the night was the blackest black, and the stars were winking at me as if to reassure me it was okay to let go. Not even Taylor's snoring had kept me awake.

I'm sure I'm the first to wake and the sun has barely risen in the sky. A strange tinge holds both dawn and night suspended in a stalemate. Not quite dark enough to conceal secrets, not bright enough to bring them to light. With a yawn and a stretch, I lower my feet to the floor, staring out of the window at the lake.

The surface of the lake ripples, and Roman is a dot upon the landscape, navigating the breadth of the water. His disregard of the curfew is inspiring, though curious. We haven't actually spoken since that night in the corridor. The night we talked about Blake. I'd been so fired up about finding out what happened, but there's been no time, no opportunity. It felt like something shifted between us in that corridor, and I've been too afraid to look at it.

Johnny sleeps on his side, breathing softly. Taylor's arms are spread either side of him, his mouth open. Probably drooling, but I don't dwell. Cameron has fallen asleep with two books either side of his lithe frame. One is on the folklore of Wales. Cameron has always believed in the paranormal, in something other. He once tried to tell me that he thinks vampires are real and live amongst us. When I asked him for evidence, he told me to simply open my mind.

I dress in wide black trousers, black loafers, a crisp, off-white short-sleeved shirt. Heading to breakfast, I tread slow, soft, over the rich carpets, taking in the paintings on the walls. The hallways are lit with electric lamps, but the lights flicker and dim, as if one of Cameron's supernatural beings follows me, taking the energy source as their own. Beyond the Jacobean windows, a tinge of orange spreads across the canvas-white sky like blood running through arteries. There's a scent in the air of recently burning fires, of incense being relit, of matches being struck.

With a twisting stomach, I descend the stairs, barely registering the old Baroque artwork depicting Venus and her chariot pulled by swans. When I first saw this artwork, a replica of Lanscroon, I'd allowed myself to sit on a step and take it all in. The dark colours seemed to swirl, like a current dragging me closer and closer. The brazen nudity of Venus that stirred no desire within me, only appreciation for detail. The hallway is interspersed with the same style of artwork, of muscled men with fear and anguish and desire etched on their faces. I've looked at it so many times, eyes always drawn to the torso of a faceless man. Look too long and people might start to notice. Privately, I can dwell on the brush strokes, appreciate the story and what it stirs within me. Art is my escape, and I'm lucky to be surrounded by it in these hallowed halls. I tear my eyes away from the painted humans, wishing I could stay for longer.

Arriving in the breakfast hall, I'm not surprised to see it's just me and another boy from Mercury, who is slumped over the table asleep. I smile, wondering if he'd tried to get up early for whatever reason, only for sleep to finally catch up to him. The professors' table is deserted, just their wine bottles and their goblets and their empty plates. I think of going up there, sitting in one of their chairs, eating my meal and surveying the room. What would happen if I did? Such rules I have never thought of, now swimming to the surface of my mind.

Settling for my usual seat on the Saturn table, I go through the motions of my breakfast routine. There's comfort in familiarity. Security, even. The food is as good as ever. My eyes glaze over as I stare at nothing, unfocused, relaxed.

The sleeping boy hasn't moved the whole time. Poor guy. Must be exhausted.

There's a rustle somewhere out in the hall. Roman. His towel is wrapped around him, and he's wearing a damp T-shirt. He does not look into the breakfast hall, but the glimpse of him has me smiling. It's just enough for me. I'm able to briefly forget what transpired between us. As he disappears, I long to run after him. But my legs do not move, merely ache.

The goblet of half-drunk apple juice slips from my heavy hand, and my eyes flutter open and closed, lids feeling like weights. I grip the table, thinking it's moving beneath me, like I've been on a ship and the land is swaying. But my thoughts are slow, all feelings registering as if rising through cement. I look up at the moving room, asking for help, but is my mouth opening? Am I forming the words I think I am? Is help coming?

I only just remember the cold touch of the table as I slump forward, before darkness engulfs me.

CHAPTER 26

Birdsong, sweet and lyrical, reminding me of home, of summer days working the farm. Warmth on my skin like I'm blanketed in front of a fire. The bare skin of my arms, my hands, is dusted with tree leaves and pine needles and dropped seeds and gritted earth. Eyes flickering open, twisted branches come into my view. Bright blue sky glimmers through. I inhale the scent of earth, hot days and sizzling sun. Sweat prickles across my forehead, and I look at my body, half shaded, half exposed.

I jolt up. Roman turns to me, leaning against the trunk of an oak tree.

'Morning, sleepyhead.'

'Morning?' My tongue is heavy, my eyes still blinking away sleep. I let my hands sink to the dirty earth, taking small breaths, allowing my swimming head to settle into calm waters. 'What... Where are we?'

'In the middle of the fucking forest in fuck arse of nowhere,' Roman says, throwing a twig away from him and reaching for another, starting to pull off the dead bark. 'Welcome to task three.'

The forest floor is nothing but roots, a bed of pine needles and pinecones, and the occasional chopped down, burnt tree. I sniff the history of flame upon the air. This must be replanted forest.

'You were just coming back from swimming.'

'Think that was a few hours ago now,' Roman says.

'Why are we in the woods?'

'Hm, I don't know, maybe for a laugh,' Roman says. 'Maybe it's so we can come up with the answer to if a tree falls, does it make a sound? Maybe it's...'

'Your sarcasm grates on me.'

'Look around us, Dylan,' Roman argues, hands splaying out. 'Nothing but trees. No water, no food. Just this.'

He reaches behind him and raises a small black satchel. I shuffle over to him, looking at the bag in his hands. It glimmers in the sunlight, free from any marks or signs of wear. He unclasps the flap and pulls it back. Inside, there's nothing but a wad of paper and two small steel bottles.

'"Boys. Welcome to task three",' Roman reads. '"You find yourselves in the woods. There are only three rules: Survive. Provide. Protect. You will be here for three days, until the day of the next task. A professor will collect you when your task is over. With kind regards, Headmistress Dwynwen."'

'Well, how lovely of Dwynwen to write us a letter.'

'Now whose sarcasm is grating?'

Roman scrunches the paper in his fist and I gawp at him. They're really going to leave us out here to survive? To live in the elements? In this heat? It's not even the middle of the day yet. It is soon going to become unbearable. But we're shaded, and we're safe, and that's all that matters.

'Thank God I ate breakfast,' I say aloud.

'Hope that tides you over for the next three days,' Roman comments.

I gasp. 'What about washing, and...?'

Roman cocks an eyebrow. 'Don't think there's an en suite out here.'

I fall back onto my hands, sitting on the earth. Our ancestors long ago would have lived like this, I think. Our king has spoken about the country needing to go back to basics, to community living. But even when we live communally, we have our home comforts. Perhaps that is what this task is serving to us. Preparing us for what could happen. Every day, they monitor our impact on this land. If we're still doing damage we have to resort to extremes.

Roman gets to his feet.

'Where are you going?'

'We can't stay here all day and night, can we?' he asks me, rolling his eyes. 'We need shelter and we need food.'

'Of course we can stay here.' I jump to my feet, trailing after him. 'We're covered by trees and it's warm, and we're in the shade here.'

'The three rules, Dylan. Survive. Provide. Protect. That last one doesn't sound jolly to me.'

'Neither does the first,' I mutter.

I bite my lip. Ganymede's isn't going to put us in any danger, are they? Professor Dalia, our survivalist teacher, knows we're here. And the rest of the boys must be here somewhere, too. They're going to come back for us and check on us. They're just pretending that they aren't, so that we can emulate being alone in the wilderness, emulate a real-life scenario.

That's what I have to tell myself because the other option scares me too much.

'All right, fine. Let's find somewhere to sleep,' I say. 'We can find food along the way or ... I don't know, later.'

'Got any ideas?' Roman asks. I get up too and we start to walk aimlessly.

I do have some ideas, actually, but I'm not going to talk him through the process. He grabs a stick and starts trailing it through the earth, occasionally whacking it into shrubs, but I break off and go deeper into the forest, where all sound is deadened by the trees I peer at, childishly wishing I was small enough to live inside the trunk itself, thinking that I wished Cameron's notions that faeries exist were real, because I could use a miracle right now.

'Roman, over here,' I call.

He heads my way, peering at me.

'What?'

I point at the hole in the base of a hollow tree. At the circle of earth underneath it, sinking into the ground. 'We sleep in here.'

'In a tree?'

'Got any other suggestions?'

'I don't know, maybe they've left a tent for us or something.'

'If you find one, good luck to you, but I think this is going to be it,' I say. 'Look'—I start to crawl in—'it's quite roomy when you get inside.' My voice echoes as I angle my body around so that I rest my back against the inside of the tree. The earth here is moist, and I try not to think of the critters around us as I disturb something and bits of bark flake over my head, lodging in my hair. Roman sighs, climbing in, too. His knees bump against mine and his weight shifts, and I try and adjust where I'm sat, slipping my feet under his legs. We look at one another, sunlight creeping through the holes in the bark, washing us in a warm glow.

'It's certainly cooler in here,' he says, his voice hollow-sounding.

'It's cosy,' I say, and immediately wish I hadn't.

His look at me is fleeting, before he watches the woods. 'But it's open. We're sitting ducks in here.'

'You speak like we're going to be attacked.'

His knuckles rest against my thigh where he's crossed his arms over his stomach. He stretches out a leg, and the cuff of his trousers rolls up at the ankle, revealing hairs on his skin. I try not to stare, try not to think how the sun highlights his copper strands.

'I think we should make fake shrubbery,' Roman says. 'Attempt to conceal the entrance.'

'Wouldn't that draw attention to us?'

'It might, but...'

'Shh.' My hands find his mouth, palm covering the softness of his lips. His warm breath caresses my skin, and our eyes meet. His arms uncross, and he places a hand on my knee, a frisson of shock coursing through me.

Outside, footsteps crunch over the ground, and we hear voices.

'We ransack their supplies and we make sure we keep a hold of them.' Taylor. His voice is animated, excited, even. 'Why work hard when we could think smarter?'

'You're a genius, Tay,' Lee's voice carries to us. I hold my breath, thinking they must be a few feet away. 'I wouldn't have thought of that.'

'I'm a provider, remember? Why does it matter where I got it from, as long as I get it?'

'So, where do we start?'

'Keep an eye out. They'll be around here, somewhere.'

CHAPTER 27

I murmur to Roman, 'What do we do?'
He moves closer to me, so that my hands slip away from his mouth, fingers trailing softly over his T-shirt, which is already stained with dirt. His breath catches my ear, the hairs on the back of my neck rising. 'They don't know we're here,' he whispers to me. I can see the way his jaw angles as he tilts his head. See the way his teeth align, and I smell soap on his skin. 'They're plotting against us all. It isn't personal.'

A whack of sound makes me jump, but it's Roman's turn to cover my mouth. I push back against the bark as if I might become one with the tree.

'Boys?' Taylor's voice rings around us. 'Where are you? Come on, let's work together.'

Another whack, something ricocheting. Taylor and Lee step into view, their backs turned to the tree. They're at least fifteen feet away, but I feel like they're angled in too good a position. If they turn, if their eyes scan the forest, they're going to spot us.

'Roman,' I whisper. We have to conceal ourselves better than this.

'Don't move,' Roman says. 'Not yet.'

Not yet? What does he mean, not yet? It's like the boy has smelt blood and wants more of it. Is this really what he's doing already? No attempt to survive on his own? Just pilfer from his own classmates? So much for empathy. So much for compassion.

'We might have to fight them if they don't hand food over,' Taylor says to Lee.

I look at Roman, who whispers, 'Good luck with that, Taylor. We haven't got any.'

'Does it have to come to that?' says Lee.

'Yeah, boyo, it does,' Taylor hisses.

'We should help each other, if we can,' Lee says. 'No, hear me out. What if we all join together and … and form an alliance with someone?'

Taylor tuts. 'No. We're not doing that. This is survival of the fittest.' He flexes his arm, showing off his bicep. 'And I'm pretty fit.'

Lee laughs, punching Taylor's arm. 'Yeah, bro. You wish.'

Roman snorts, and I look at him.

'He's such a…'

But his words falter, and a look of horror crosses his face. I peer out into the wilderness and my mouth drops. Cameron and Elis are walking behind the boys, lost in conversation. Only snatches of their whispered conversation reach us. They must be strategising, thinking how they can survive three days.

'Oi,' Taylor yells, and I jump.

Cameron steps behind Elis as they take in Taylor and Lee. Elis lifts a hand, shielding his face from the sun. He drops it when he sees who has called them, turns away from them, puts a friendly hand on Cameron's shoulder.

'Don't ignore us,' Taylor says, beaming. 'How're you boys doing?'

'Crazy stuff, right?' Lee adds, following Taylor as they approach Cameron and Elis.

Don't stop. Keep moving, I urge the boys.

'You got any food?' Lee asks, circling the boys, who have come to a stop. Roman nudges me, feeling around the floor, never taking his eyes off the four boys in front of us. 'Any water?'

'Not yet,' Elis says.

'That's a shame,' Taylor says with a sigh. 'We're hoping to find some.'

'Looks like you got a plan, though,' Lee says. 'Got any shelter?'

'We're going to gather some sticks and make a small tepee.'

Taylor smiles. 'Not a bad idea, boys. Good luck with it, yeah?'

He's so effortless with his fake charm, with the smile that disarms you. Both Elis and Cameron nod and continue on their way, but as soon as their back turns Taylor's smile drops.

'Let's follow them,' Taylor says. 'Stay hidden.'

I want to stop them, want to distract them, but Roman shakes his head. A few moments later, the woods are clear.

'Come on,' he says. 'We need food and we need water.'

'Before we do that, I think we should talk.'

Roman looks torn between wanting to get out in the wilderness and waiting to hear me out. Finally, he says, 'Talk about what?'

'You've been distant with me since...'

'Have not.'

'The fact you defended it so quickly says you have.'

Roman shakes his head, poised to leave our tree. 'This isn't the time. We need to get ourselves some supplies, Dyl.'

But I grip his shoulder, stopping him. 'You ignored my smile in Lawrence's class. You haven't spoken to me since that evening in the corridor. I think you've been avoiding me.'

'Avoiding you? No. I've just been ... busy.'

'Busy with what?'

'You know.'

'No, I don't know.' I'm being ridiculous, I'm sure, but when my future lies on the line, I can't let him jeopardise it. 'Listen, what you said to me in the corridor...'

'Forget I said anything,' Roman says. 'I don't want to talk about it. I don't want to talk about any of it. None of it matters right now.'

'It always matters.'

Blake matters. Mattered.

'What matters is trying to survive,' Roman says.

He crawls out and I have no choice but to follow him. There are no voices on the air, no sign of Taylor waiting to ambush. It's the familiar feeling of loneliness hidden in the shrubbery. 'I need you to work with me, Roman. I need you to want to get the best for us both. Not avoid me.'

Roman rolls his eyes. 'I want the same for us, too. Believe me on that. Was our trust task for nothing? Our honesty?'

'No, not for nothing, but...'

'But nothing. You're acting like you don't trust me and you're acting like I'm not being honest when I say to you I am not avoiding you. I don't regret what I said in that corridor, but I worry I overstepped the mark, and yeah, maybe I thought the best thing to do was to give you more space. But I have not been avoiding you. Sometimes I need my own space, too.'

I soften, seeing his shadowed expression. He's looking around him, but like he doesn't really see what surrounds us.

'You need a lot of space?' I ask him.

'What do you mean?'

'Well...' I think of what to say, how to phrase it. 'I've not seen you be friends with many people, and I wondered why that was.'

Roman looks at me now, sighing. 'It's hard to be the new kid.'

'Right. But you seem to spend a lot of time by yourself.'

'I have friends.'

'I know.'

'Just not close friends.' He says this with a shrug. I think of how hard these years would have been if I hadn't had first Blake, then Johnny, and Cameron. 'I don't need close friends.'

'You don't?'

He shakes his head, brushes a thumb over the edge of his nose, then swipes his hands through the air, as if swatting away a fly. 'Friendship has never really been my priority.'

There's a moment of silence before I ask, 'Why not?'

'I guess it comes down to the fact that most people don't think like I do,' he says, then gives me a smile. 'I don't mean that in a pretentious way. Sometimes I think I'm the wrong one for thinking the way I do.'

'How do you think differently?'

Flapping wings and rustling leaves make us flinch, until we realise there is no threat. 'It doesn't matter,' Roman says. 'Some thoughts and opinions should stay as that.'

I change tack. 'But what about your friends back in your hamlet?'

He grins. 'No friends, Dylan.'

'None whatsoever.'

'Nope.'

'Not even neighbours.'

'No,' he says with exasperated laughter. 'No friends other than my sisters and my parents. I've lived a solitary family life, and I'm happy with that.'

'Not even friends from your last school?'

Roman places a soft hand on my shoulder. 'Are you worried about me?'

'What? No. I'm just ... trying to understand.'

Roman cocks an eyebrow, a small grin spreading. 'This isn't a get-to-know-and-understand-me task. But if it were, I'd tell you this. I like to live my life by my own rules and by my own thoughts. I don't like to share those with others, or let others dictate how I should react. You might see it as loneliness, but I have not felt lonely. Not really. I've felt free. Now, if you want to stay in that tree, we should maybe make it more hospitable. Then we should forage for food.'

We take tentative steps away from the tree, and I think how all his friendships must have been fake. How other people have tried to get close to him, only to feel his distance. I have felt that. His withdrawing after he seems to bring you close, his way of letting you think you know him and then changing. Maybe he likes being a mystery, but I want to know the other side of him. Because I've seen it. Those small looks of his, and the way he seems to internalise what goes on around him. Maybe he doesn't know how to share it yet, but maybe that's what I can do for him this month.

I know he's not completely lonely here, though. Not really. As he points out nettles and talks about harvesting some to see if we can make nettle soup, I say, 'But you seem close to Elis.'

He freezes, halfway between me and the nettles. 'Huh?'

'I saw you and Elis walking together. To the graveyard. I didn't realise you were friends with him.'

Roman clears his throat, approaches the nettles, seems to survey them. I think he's not going to say anything, and then he says, 'Elis is a good guy. He thinks like I do.'

He says nothing more, a sting stronger than the nettles we wrestle out of the ground.

'Is that all you're going to say?'

'There's nothing else to say.'

'Are you angry?'
'Oh, very. But not at you. Never at you.'

CHAPTER 28

My hands and arm itch. We've got nettles, and now I'm scrambling to assemble a makeshift fire. I've found rocks and placed them in a circle, putting dry logs and sticks together, avoiding those that are wet or with moss on them. The less smoke the better, I think. I don't know what the need is to protect, but I don't want to find out if I can help it. I'm trying to get a spark going, taking my mind off where Roman could be. He said he was going to find water, but for all we know there could be none. I haven't heard any water running. The thought of going without water makes me panic. My mouth is dry, my throat catching every time I swallow. My stomach is starting to rumble now, breakfast clearly wearing off. I've shed my shirt and I am hiding in the shade so my back and torso don't get burnt.

There's crashing from behind me and I leap up, stone and bark in hand, when Roman appears. He's smiling, topless, sweat dripping down his face and his neck and his body. His skin looks like it has caught the sun, flushed with red, and I wonder if it hurts him. There's a part of me that thinks of abandoning the fire and going to find some plants that I can use to make a serum. There must be some aloe growing around here.

'I found water,' he says, slightly breathlessly. He holds up the steel bottles, stepping closer to hand one to me. 'It won't be the best water, but it's something.'

'Where did you get it from?'

'There was a small pond. I think maybe in the winter water runs through this forest, but it has dried up. I followed damp moss until I came across it,' Roman says.

'We better boil it, then,' I say. 'Get rid of any contamination.'

'If you can't get the fire going, we'll have to run it through our clothes.'

'Last resort. I'm working on it,' I mutter. 'It's hard to get it to catch.'

'Want me to have a go?'

'You can try.'

Our nettles are gathered nearby, and the hope is we can get nettle soup going. It won't be the best meal ever, and I'm sure we'll still be hungry, but it's something.

Roman crouches, and starts trying to get sparks flying. The pieces of wood scrape against one another, and I take a moment to rest my aching and energy-depleted body. Roman's taut stomach flexes with his breathing. His biceps bulge with each thrust of his hands, and his tongue sticks out at the corner of his mouth as he focuses on getting the fire lit. I can't stop looking at the curvature of his arm, or the way his light red hair looks almost golden when the sun that creeps through the trees catches him. The brown freckles across his chest disappearing into the crevices of his sternum. He adjusts where he kneels, angling his back towards me, and I have to stop myself from watching the ripple of his back muscles.

'Yes, yes, yes!' he shouts, frantically scraping the wood together. There's the gentle sound of crackling. Kindling catching alight. When he stands back, the flames are small but spreading. I rush forward, bringing dry leaves and sticks, helping the flames spread. With relief, they lick upon the thicker branches, growing brighter and taller with every second.

'Who do you think discovered fire?' I ask him, when the flames are healthy and we begin to assemble something to heat the water.

'Hm, a woman, probably,' Roman says.

We heat our steel water bottles over the flame for two minutes, then put them aside to cool down.

'All right, so far, so good,' I say. 'But we need something to make the soup in.'

Roman places his hands on his hips, lunging forward as he stretches. I try to distract myself, but any thought of trying to find an adequate vessel is gone. Does he have to do those exercises now? Does he have to do them topless? Every move he makes looks as fluid as water, and I need to drink.

'Bamboo,' he says, during one particularly strenuous-looking stretch.

'Right, bamboo,' I say. Where can I get bamboo? Am I going to have to search for miles? I have no idea what time it is, but the sky is still blue, so I estimate it must be late afternoon. I could get back before it's dark, couldn't I?

'We can turn it into a base and then put the water in there and soak the nettles,' Roman says, right arm over his head as he angles his body to the side.

'Do you have to do yoga now?'

'You should always keep your body in good condition.'

'Yeah, but now?'

'Why not now?'

I sigh, turning away from him. I'm halfway towards the thickest of trees when Roman calls, 'Where are you going?'

'To get bamboo.'

'See if you can get a bit extra, so we can make a door for the tree.'

I nod, taking in the opening in the tree where we're meant to sleep tonight. Going further into the woods, my mind eases somewhat. Without Roman's topless, stretching body, I can focus. Our survival classes regularly touched upon the wilderness, and I think there must be enough here to survive on, otherwise Ganymede's wouldn't have sent us here. I have no idea where we are, but it must be somewhere in the open country. The nightmare stories Mum used to tell me come rushing back to me. Thieves and traps and skeletons left behind. So far, none of that, but I still don't like being here.

I harvest some blackberries, using my shirt as a makeshift bag. I keep an eye out for water, though I can't see or hear any. We have been taught how to hunt animals, but I'd rather leave that as a last resort. Hopefully we can find food that won't result in me having to take a life.

I breathe a sigh of relief at the sight of thick, healthy bamboo. Some stragglers, too. I take the stragglers, thinking we can find some use for them, and then repeatedly kick at another trunk until it breaks. Breathless, leg aching, I do the same with another, until I have all that I can carry. I think it's just about enough for fashioning a door and cooking with.

I'm about to turn back when something snaps. The hairs on the back of my neck stand on edge, and I freeze, looking over my shoulder. No sound, no movement, except for leaves. Yet I know someone is there, out of view, watching me. It's unmistakable. My heart thuds and despite the heat I feel a chill creep over me. I consider asking out loud, to let them know that I'm aware of them, but I decide against it. Whoever it is, they have the power here. I almost expect something to be in the branches above me, but there's nothing. Only glimpses of the blue sky.

CHAPTER 29

Crashing through the trees, I stumble out into our humble clearing, where the fire still burns and Roman is sitting on a fallen tree trunk, away from the flames. His bottle is at his lips and he rises when he sees me. 'Everything okay?'

'There are people in those trees,' I say.

'Yeah, other students.'

'No, not students. It didn't feel like students. I felt like I was being watched.'

He faces me, nothing but his solid chest, freckled, and his smooth stomach; his body athletic. And in that moment, my teeth sink into my tongue, a taste of iron in my mouth. *Look away, Dylan. Look away.*

'Yeah, by students,' he repeats. 'I felt the same.'

Exasperated, I throw down the bamboo and slump down on the tree trunk too. It feels good to sit down, but I keep looking towards the trees, expecting to see people come after us, but there's nothing, and the feeling of being watched has gone.

'All right, take a breather,' Roman says to me. 'You're on edge.'

'Of course, I'm on edge. How can you not be?'

'There's no point, we have to do what we have to do,' he says. 'Let me deal with this bamboo, and then we can make our door.'

'I'm exhausted, Roman.'

'Me too, but it has to be done.'

He's a whiz, I'll give him that. He puts his left foot on the bamboo and hacks away with his other foot, until he's made enough of a hole in one side. He switches over, doing the same to the next. All the while he huffs and he groans and oh, my God, he's doing so much to me without even trying to. How my stomach tightens and my eyes follow him like they're on strings tied to his fingers. He lets out slow, deep breaths. I drag my eyes from him, trying to occupy my mind with something else. It feels wrong to stare at him, yet I can't help but admire the warrior skills that ooze out of him like sap from a tree. Professor Dalia would be proud, I think.

He hooks his fingers into the split bamboo and pulls, slowly breaking it open. Finally, a slab comes loose, revealing a hollow base. He takes a deep breath, before grinning at me, holding it up for me to see. 'We can put some water in here, heat it up, get the soup going.'

'I got us some berries, too.'

'Snacks,' Roman says. 'Not for the soup.'

'Obviously.'

We have one full bottle of water left and pour it into the bamboo; it's shallow, but enough. Then we add the nettles, wincing each time our skin stings. While I've been gone, Roman has fashioned a spit out of branches, and we place the bamboo across the flames. The water begins to boil. My shoulders relax as I know I'll have something to eat at last. I spread out my shirt, and Roman comes to sit next to me as we pick away at what I found, washed down with water from his bottle.

'I'll refill the water tomorrow morning,' he says.

I nod. 'I saw some mushrooms when I was looking, but I didn't pick them up.'

'Why not?'

'I wasn't entirely sure what was what.'

'We'll have another look tomorrow.'

I nod, tilting my head to the sky as it becomes a dusty red, the sun setting. I feel like it's been the longest day on earth.

Roman fashions two smaller bowls out of the discarded bamboo and pours thin soup into them. I feel the heat and raise my bowl to my lips, taking tentative sips.

'Better than nothing,' Roman says when we are done.

We sit together, across from the flames, as the sky turns from red to indigo to black. The flames crackle and pop as Roman stokes them, glowing in the embers that fizzle in the air. Ash drifts, smoke rises, and despite everything a sense of calm washes over me.

'Do you want to keep watch tonight?' I ask him, after a lapse in silence.

'I don't think it will be necessary,' Roman says, pulling on his T-shirt. I'd already put mine on when I went to a pee behind a tree. Leaving the flames made me realise how cool it is when the sun is down. 'We'll need all the rest we can get. Besides, we'll have our door and we'll be fairly safe.'

'You really did pay attention in survival classes, didn't you?'

Roman considers this. 'I like the outdoors.'

'I got a stomach ache once when I ate a conker and I kind of gave up on it all,' I admit. 'Spent enough time outdoors growing up, so I guess I got lax when it came to our classes.'

'I suppose you never thought you would be in a situation like this.'

'No, I guess not. I'd rather not be like this any time soon.'

Roman nods. 'What is it you want, Dylan?'

It's a loaded question, though I wonder if it's meant to be. He has his hands behind his head, and the fabric of his T-shirt hugs his bulging arms.

'To survive.'

Roman turns to me, smiling. 'And after that?'

'Happiness,' I say.

Roman nods. 'Yes, I suppose I do, too.'

'What does happiness look like to you?'

Roman sighs, dropping his hands and crossing his arms across his stomach. 'Well, happiness to me is a home where I have a little garden. I'm not green-thumbed like you are, but I'd like to be.'

'Could have fooled me,' I say, nodding at what's set up around us.

'Right, but this is survival. I can't grow plants and tend them for shit,' Roman says. 'Believe me, I've tried. I killed a cactus once.'

'Goodness.'

Roman nods. 'I'd like to have a little patch I can tend. Maybe a pond. I'd like ducks and chickens, and I want some cats.'

'Oh, I'd love cats, too.'

'Yeah. Cats would be cool,' Roman says, not quite meeting my eye. 'I'd like to walk to the bottom of my garden where I have a little shed, and in that shed, there are paintings. My paintings. I want the wood to be flecked with paint drops and I want my canvases to be against the wall, and then I want to sell them and provide art to those in the hamlets. So I know I will never go without, and I know every day will be happy.'

'Sounds achievable.'

'Does it?' Roman says.

'Sounds like it to me. It sounds like a dream.'

Roman nods. 'Exactly that. Because in that happy life of mine, I don't have what Ganymede's is promising me. I don't have a wife, or children. I live alone, and I'm unbothered by my neighbours, and if I want someone to join me, then I have the choice of letting someone join me.'

'So, what are you saying?' I ask. 'You don't want a family of your own?'

'Not really,' Roman says. 'At least not the way I'm expected to, anyway.'

'I don't quite follow.'

Roman gives me a sad smile. 'No, I suppose you wouldn't. I guess what I'm saying is this. Happiness, to me, is my choice. My choice to live how I want to live. Alone. No wife. No children. A choice to wake up and paint and sell my art. A choice to change my career if I want to. A choice to move away and do whatever I want to do.'

'But you can do that.'

Roman shakes his head. 'If I get my way, yes, I will do that.'

I swallow and reach for what's left of the water in his steel bottle, which we have begun to share without mentioning it. I watch the flames, wondering why he would tell me this.

'"The power of finding beauty in the humblest things makes home happy and life lovely,"' Roman says to me. 'Louisa May Alcott. Did you know she was a big fighter for women's rights? She wrote in an essay that women did not need to marry. I wonder what she would think about this now.'

'About what?'

'Our free and equal society, of course,' Roman says, sarcastically. 'Who knew that what she said back then would still be as relevant today? And it goes further, these days. What if we had the choice to say no to marriage? What if we said we wanted to live differently? What if Jo got Louisa's intended ending?'

I shake my head. 'This is more than just marriage, Roman. It's saving society.'

'Does saving society make you happy?'

I pause, finally saying, 'It is our duty.'

'I see.'

'You don't agree?'

Roman shrugs. 'I have many thoughts, but now is not the time for such debates.' He yawns, stifling it with his hand. 'I think we should hunker down for the night.'

Though I want him to continue, want him to speak further about what he means, I'm distracted. A night with Roman in that tree stump sounds like heaven on earth.

CHAPTER 30

In the dead of night, I focus on my breathing in the hollow base of this tree. The earth sinks in, slopes at the side, and what seemed like a good spot now seems like a bad idea. Roman and I sat side by side at first, but quickly realised that it wasn't practical. When my feet and legs started buzzing with pins and needles, we shifted to sit opposite one another.

'I still think you should let us stretch our legs,' Roman says. We're mostly in darkness, but moonlight finds her way in, illuminating half of his features.

Our knees are bumped up against each another, my hands in my lap. Rolling my neck does nothing to alleviate my aching back, which has some knobbly bit of tree digging into it. My bum has gone numb, and I need to move, but stretching out over Roman is the only option, one I'm reluctant to take.

Loose vines and pine branches that have fallen to the forest floor cover parts of us. Roman's idea of a bedspread. There's a definite chill, but the warmth from the day has captured itself within here, and our body heat seems to be rising.

When I've waited long enough, I sigh. 'Fine. Let's stretch our legs.'

He chuckles, and I feel the warmth of his breath, my body buzzing with something else. Heat rises, pinching my cheeks, and I'm glad of the darkness. Roman shifts where he sits, and within seconds, both legs come to rest either side of mine. He lets out a sigh of relief, and all I can think about is how his calf muscles bulge against his trousers, and how the warmth from his legs warms my thighs, my hips.

'Well? What are you waiting for?'

'Oh, right.'

I stretch out my legs, and I've got to admit it really is worth it. My thighs sing and my calf muscles stretch, and I roll my feet to feel something. It's still somewhat cramped, but this feels better. He rests his hands on his stomach, above the little blanket he's made for us, and I feel his fingers brush my knee.

'Sorry,' he whispers.

'No, it's fine.'

He doesn't remove his hand, and I breathe through his touch, as my body sizzles. Just one little touch like that and he's sent me reeling. I stretch out my arms, feigning a yawn, and let my own hands fall at my side. My knuckles touch what must be the side of his thigh, just enough to seem almost accidental. He smiles, but says nothing.

'What time do you think it is?' he asks me in a whisper.

I shrug, before realising he probably can't see it. 'I've no idea. Must be close to midnight.'

'You tired?'

I'm anything but, with the warmth of his body touching mine... 'A little, yes.'

'Let me know if you want me to shut up while you get some sleep.' Outside, a branch snaps somewhere in the distance, and I let out a shaking breath. His hand reaches for me in the dark, clumsily finds my hand, and then slips his fingers in my palm.

'It's okay.'

He goes to pull his hand away, but I let my fingers lock around his hand, and he nods.

'I've thought about getting weapons,' Roman says, breaking the tension. 'Maybe we should find something tomorrow.'

'You think we'll need some?' I ask him.

'It's always good to be armed.'

'I don't think Ganymede's would put us in any scenario where we actually need to arm ourselves.'

A stillness falls over us, matching the serenity that hugs the tree. Roman breaks it by clearing his throat, enough to get me riled.

'You don't agree?'

'I think it's worth thinking about,' he says, ever the diplomat.

'In what way?'

'Ah, I don't know. Shooting arrows at your head.'

'Wasn't a real arrow.'

'Ah, all right then, what about electric shocks? Now this. Putting us in open country where anyone could be roaming.'

I focus on the palm of his hand, the warmth that spreads in mine.

'If you trust Ganymede's, I'm glad you do,' Roman says to me, his voice soft. 'I would, too, if they'd looked after me.'

'What's that supposed to mean?'

'How many other boys get to live their lives here all through the year?'

'I don't know. I don't think many people were only children who lost their parents.'

'I'm sorry.'

'No apology needed, it's the truth.'

Roman nods, his thumb brushing the back of my hand. I flinch, and his grip slackens, but he doesn't let me go.

'Have you never wondered why you were the one that has been looked after? Did you never wonder why they never forced you to go back to your home?'

'Because I was a kid?'

'Sure, I guess,' Roman says. 'But maybe it's more than that.'

'How could it be?'

'I guess when you're an outsider all your life, you pick up on things. I'm quite observant,' Roman says. 'And I've noticed you, Dylan. I've noticed things about you.'

I swallow, before biting my lip. Do I tell him I've noticed him, too? His aloofness, his swagger, his difference?

When I don't say anything, Roman says, 'The teachers treat you differently, I feel. They encourage you to talk in class, and when you don't seem to understand something, they help you grasp it more than they would another student.'

'That isn't true.'

'Isn't it?'

Is it? I think of my archery classes, where my aim had never been too good, and how I had time given to me to improve it. How foraging wasn't my strong point, but Professor Dalia always had patience for me and recommended extra reading materials. I think of Professor Lawrence, and his guidance over the years. How Headmistress Dwynwen always says hello to me in the corridor, and asks me how I am. How Mother Mai always smiles, always catches my eye when she talks history. But isn't that what the professors are supposed to do? Help us?

'It's like you're being watched. Like they are guiding you. For a while I thought maybe you were the golden boy or something. Thought you were the smartest, brightest, best boy to walk through the halls.'

'You don't think I am?' It's meant to come out as arrogant, but I laugh halfway through and Roman cracks a smile.

'Hey, you don't always have to be the brightest.'

'I know.'

'You shine bright enough as you are.'

He holds my gaze, long enough for me to flush with warmth. Every nerve in my body seems to crackle with excitement, and I think about my next moves. His brown eyes hypnotise me, his eyelashes fluttering with every blink. He rests his head against the bark, surveying me, smiling ever so slightly. He doesn't look away, and I can't pull away. Drawn to him and his magnetic look, his touch. I've never felt this before. This mouth-watering ache, this pang of hunger, a need to taste something new. Roman is a delicacy unexplored. One bite and I know I wouldn't stop. Couldn't stop.

His look, his touch, his body heat. Even his voice, the lilt of his sweet accent. He's flavours I can't quite place. Flavours that make me see the world differently. I cannot return to the monotonous, when his sweetness is all I crave.

And I shouldn't crave him in this way.

And I shouldn't want to know if he craves me.

Hidden in this tree, we could indulge. Nobody need ever know.

But I would know. I would live with it. I don't think I could.

I sag a little. Say nothing.

Roman leans forward, misunderstanding my silence. 'Look. All I wanted to make you think about was why Ganymede's has shown a loyalty to you.'

'But what are you implying?'

'I'm not implying anything.' He smiles, but when I glare at him, he stops. 'Honest. I just think ... well, without family, you're easy to discard, aren't you?'

'Discard? No one is getting discarded.'

'Aren't they?'

His imploring eyes search mine, and now is not the time to get lost in them. What he stirs within me is confusing enough.

We lapse into silence, hearing the whisper of wind, before Roman adds, 'Dylan?'

'Yeah?'

'I'm sorry.'

I peer at him. 'For what?'

'For making you doubt things,' Roman says.

'It's okay.'

'You sure?'

I pat him on the leg. 'I'm sure.'

Roman looks at my hand, watches it withdraw. He smiles, then closes his eyes.

I lie across from him, so close I can feel his breath. I sync my own with his, like he's a meditation, an antidote to my racing thoughts. At some point, the temperature drops. I try and nestle further into the earth, strain and pull the stupid leaf blanket closer to me, but it only brings brief respite before the cold seeps in again.

'You're cold,' Roman says at some point, when I've heard more twigs cracking in the distance and the hoot of owls in the dark woods. He shifts. 'We could share body heat?'

My eyes fling open and I look at him, expecting to see his jovial, joking smile. But there's only a calm, controlled look on his chiselled features.

'What?'

'Survival, remember?' He asks me. 'Turn over, I'll hug you.'

'Roman, I...'

'What you worried about?' he asks, then considers me. Softly, he whispers, as if he has read my thoughts, 'Nobody needs to know.'

I want to tell him why I can't do it. Why the thought of him hugging me frightens me to death. But the chill is settling into my bones, and he's so close, and he's so warm, and...

'Okay, fine,' I say, turning around. He shifts closer to me, heat pressing into my back, and his hand lightly touches my hip, before moving up my stomach. I shiver, hoping he doesn't read into it, hoping he thinks it is just because I'm cold and nothing more. His body against mine, pressing into me, is divine. My eyes flutter, and I sink into his embrace, losing myself to his scent. 'If you tell anyone about this, you're dead.'

'Our little secret,' he whispers into my ear as he puts his arm over my chest, and slides his other hand under my neck. A frisson makes me tremble, my head tilting to his ever so slightly. I let my hand find his and listen to his steady slumbering breath.

That night, I sleep better than I ever have before.

CHAPTER 31

'What was that?'
Roman lets out a groan.
I whack him with my fist, right in his burly chest.
'Hey,' Roman groans.
'Shh.' My fingers press against his soft lips, and my breath catches. 'There's something out there.'
'Maybe it's a bear.'
'No time for jokes,' I hiss. 'There's—'
Roman bolts upright at the sound of something dragging across earth, forest peace disturbed, finally taking me seriously. His arm links around mine, and I think about how mere moments ago we were lying against one another, entwined in warmth.

Debris shudders and lands in our hair, on our upturned faces as the bark is pelted with something solid, over and over again. Roman is on his knees now, approaching the shrubbery he and I assembled to conceal the entrance. I picture hailstones hammering against the bounty of the open country. We sometimes get wild weather in the height of summer, in polar opposite to the heat, but this, whatever it is, seems different.

Roman yelps as an arrow lodges itself in the base of the tree, and I grip his shoulder and pull him back to me.

'Okay, that one was definitely real,' I say.

'Out,' yells a voice from outside.

Roman shakes his head. I hold my breath, letting it out with another exclamation of fear when another arrow hits the tree, the sound of it wobbling as it sets.

'Out, now.'

A man's voice, deep and foreboding. Roman bites his lip, eyes wide with fear. 'What do we do?'

I stare at nothing, eyes losing focus, trying to summon calm. Hard to do when my mind is flooded with fear, and when I still remember Roman's touch. The footsteps seem to approach us, but at least the hail of arrows has stopped. But what if they have bows raised, ready to shoot us as we climb out of here? There's no escape other than where we came in. We have to face the music, otherwise I think whoever is out there is going to get us out by any means possible.

Students? It can't be. The voice seemed older, and unless all the students have banded together to shoot at us, I can't see it being them. Which means what?

The stories of the open-country people are true.

'Follow me,' I whisper.

'You crazy?'

'We have to. Come on.'

I'm a magician, Roman a warrior. We have to play up to our strengths. I tentatively crawl out into the open. Birdsong rushes to me, and I feel a warmth different to Roman's. I blink up at the blue sky, thinking it must be dawn.

Standing a few feet away, in a semi-circle that faces the trees, are a row of people. Various ages, I think. Men who are just a few months older than us, and men who look like they have seen better days. Women, again in various stages of age, watching us with bows and arrows poised. They all have on the same attire. Hand-me-down patchwork and frayed clothing.

'At ease,' I say, as if I'm some commander. 'Lower your weapons. Please.'

I'm surprised at my own courage, at my tone. But to be a magician means having the ability to direct this situation how I need it to go. The people look at one another, before a woman at the front nods. The weapons go down. Roman stands a little taller besides me.

'Can I help you?' I ask.

'Return what you have stolen,' the white woman at the front says.

'All of it,' a tanned man next to her says, the booming voice we heard earlier.

'Stolen? We haven't stolen anything.'

Some of the people whisper, as if annoyed by my words, but the woman quietens them with her hand. 'We saw you.' She's staring at me. 'You took from us.'

'I didn't take anything,' I say, annoyance lashing at me, but I try not to show it.

'Why are you here?' the man asks.

'We're students,' I say. 'From Ganymede's...'

The bows raise again, and this time Roman steps in front of me. 'What the hell do you think you're doing?'

'Return what you have stolen and leave,' the woman orders.

Their accents are Welsh, from what I can gather. Perhaps some whispers from the others could be traced back to some of the bordering English hamlets. I wonder if I vaguely recognise one of the boys across from us, barely in his manhood.

'Tell us what we have stolen,' Roman says. 'Then maybe we can help you.'

'You can't help us,' the man says.

'Why not?'

'We don't want your help,' the man-boy I think I recognise says. My eyes widen. He's one of the boys who disappeared in year two.

'You...' I begin.

'What did we steal?' Roman asks again, clearly not seeing what I have seen.

I try to listen, but I keep eyeing the boy, who seems to be staunchly evading my eyes. I think he was in house Mercury, a friend of Elis's.

'Bamboo?' Roman's voice breaks my concentration, and I turn back to the man and woman.

'The bamboo was wild.'

'You came to our patch of the woods and you took it,' the man says.

'Forgive me, but I thought this was wild land.'

There are tuts and mutters, and the woman lets out a laugh.

'Ganymede boys think they are entitled to our things,' someone mutters. The boy isn't smiling.

'Izaaz?' I say, uncertain. The boy looks at me. 'It is you, isn't it?'

They all turn to him as he chews the inside of his cheek, narrowing his eyes.

'How does he know you?' the man at the front asks him.

'Ganymede's,' says Izaaz.

'You're from Ganymede's?' Roman asks.

'Was. Obviously not anymore,' he says.

'We've been placed here on a task,' I say to him, hoping he will understand. 'I think they drugged us.'

The realisation comes as a shock. But I think of breakfast, and how after a few bites and a drink I fell asleep. The boy who was asleep in the refectory when I came in. Out of it. It wasn't normal sleep. It was not because I woke up early.

They drugged us to move us here.

How could they do that to us? Are these tasks really meant to toy with death? Are we supposed to accept that? Be grateful that we survived?

'We've been put here as part of our task to ... graduate,' I say, wishing I'd chosen another word when Izaaz winces. 'And we have to survive. We've been given nothing but bottles to get water. We needed food. We needed something—'

'Enough,' the man says. He walks away from his group, towards the fire, circles it and then walks towards us. 'If you want to survive, you do not make yourself so easily discoverable. Here, look. Footsteps from the fire, straight to your tree. But those shrubs. They don't grow there. They look out of place. You want to survive? You listen to the land, not adapt it. You respect the earth you walk upon.'

'Yeah, we're respecting—' Roman begins.

'You make a good fire,' the man says, as if Roman hasn't spoken. 'But last night we saw smoke rising. You,' he says, pointing at me. 'We followed you when you took our bounty. You want to survive, but you have given yourself away in such easy ways?'

I nod, even though his words make me bristle.

'We're doing our best,' I say. 'Just trying to survive until we can go back.'

'Ah, yes, go back,' the woman says, grim-faced. 'It's easy to have fun out here when you know you are able to go back.'

'Don't be bitter, Bonnie,' the man says. 'You should pity them, instead.'

These people. How dare they?

I don't like the way some of them are inspecting their bows. I don't like the way Bonnie watches us. I don't like the way this man speaks of us, like we are a disease that plagues the trees.

'Take it back, then,' I say.

'Dylan,' Roman snaps.

'No, if they want to take what they think we stole, then they can take it.'

'What are we going to do?' He looks at me.

'I don't know. Starve. Find something else to cook with. We don't need their supplies.'

'We've got another night here. We can't just let them take what we've got.'

'You heard them,' I say to Roman. 'I stole it, and so I must give it back.'

Roman looks like he wants to fight, and honestly, can I blame him? I'm sure he could wrestle the weapons from some of them, but he'd only be delaying the inevitable arrows through our bodies. We started with nothing, we can continue with nothing, until we find something else.

Bonnie nods, and the group take the leftover bamboo and kick at our fire until it collapses. One girl even knocks over Roman's spit, but doesn't take it. A particularly cruel move, I think.

The man is about to take our makeshift bamboo cooking bowl, when Bonnie says, 'No. Leave it.'

Uncertain, the man asks, 'Are you sure?'

Bonnie looks at us. 'Yes, I'm sure. Leave it. They're going to need it.'

The group head back towards the woods, in the direction I came from yesterday. I don't feel reassured that I wasn't out of my mind for thinking I was being watched.

'Are you going to leave us alone, now?' Roman asks Bonnie.

I hold my breath.

'Just don't steal from us again,' she answers.

Izaaz stops at the edge of the clearing. He nods for the others to go on. Stepping towards us, he says, 'They won't protect you, you know.'

'What?' Roman asks.

Izaaz holds his hands out, gesturing to the expanse of trees. 'There's a life out here. Run while you can. Don't go back.'

He turns, darting into the trees, ignoring our shouts for him to come back.

CHAPTER 32

'There.'

Growing in circles are mushrooms. Blooming, tall, white mushrooms.

My pointing hand makes Roman smile. 'Don't get too excited.'

'Do you always have to be so pessimistic?'

He ignores me, crouching down. His shoulders flex as he touches the mushrooms and peers at them closer.

He looks around him, before shaking his head.

'I don't trust them.'

'What? Why? We have mushrooms all the time,' I say.

'Not these ones. Look, they've got red on the cap, some on the stems,' Roman says. 'And these ... well, they look okay, might be an agaric, but they're too close to these ones here, and the trees, look at the trees, Dylan.'

'What about them?'

'They're yew trees.'

I peer at the gnarled trunks, the twisting branches, so thick and rough. 'So?'

'You ever paid attention in any of our foraging classes?'

I titter at this, running a hand through my floppy hair.

'Professor Dalia always says to pay attention to the surroundings, not just the subject,' Roman says. 'Nature always has a way of talking to you, and the yew trees are a message.' He stands, running a hand across his stomach absentmindedly. He's shed his T-shirt and I have to stop myself from counting his abs. All six of them. 'Let's skip the mushrooms, keep walking. There's got to be berries around here or something.'

I linger longingly on the mushrooms, but Roman's adamant, I heard it in his tone, read it in his expression.

'You know, I wouldn't be surprised if this place is full of poisonous stuff,' I say, trudging after him.

'I've thought the same thing. Already seen some belladonna,' Roman says.

I pick some berries, adding them to the bag we've fashioned out of his shirt, which feels so soft in my fingertips. We've gone in the opposite direction, away from the bamboo and the people from the open country.

We're distracting ourselves with foraging, but Roman flinches at the sound of something moving beyond our vision. He looks over his shoulder, back into the shadows. My stomach is in knots and my heart feels like it is feathering as it beats, as the anticipation of attack courses through my blood.

'What do you think Izaaz meant?' I ask Roman, as he's looking through shrubbery to see if there's anything worth harvesting.

'What do *you* think he meant?'

'Don't throw it back on me.'

'You said he was a student at Ganymede's? Sounds like he had reasons for not wanting to come back.'

'What, you think he voluntarily put himself out here?'

Roman shrugs, abandoning what he was looking for. 'Something like that, yeah.'

'But he can't really believe we'd be safer out here than in society.'

'Why not?'

'Don't know if you saw them, Roman, but they had nothing. If they're fighting over bamboo then they can't have much, can they?'

'Maybe we're being given too much,' Roman suggests. 'Maybe the monarchy promises us too much.'

'Roman.' I act as if the king himself might charge out at us and demand Roman to take back what he said.

'Hey, look at this,' Roman says, pointing to a tree across from us.

My mouth drops when I realise what it is. 'Apples.'

'Here, take some and let's get them back to base.'

'You want to go back there? It's not safe, Roman.'

Roman shrugs. 'They can't intimidate us out of the woods when we've been placed here for a task.'

We gather the apples and an hour later we're back at our camp. I almost expect to see it trashed, but to my surprise our fire has been reassembled, and the stake that Roman set in the ground has been fixed back into position. But it's different now. Leaning against a tree, I feel as though it is tainted.

'What the—' Roman starts, moving forward.

I look around, trying to see any sign that we are being watched, but as far as I can tell there is no one nearby. No boys lurk in our makeshift bed. No one hides behind trees or in branches. It's just Roman and I in the woods, alone. But then I notice bare footprints, sunk into the earth and disappearing into the overgrowth. I shiver.

'Do you think it was them?' I ask Roman, walking towards him as he looks at the fire.

'I don't know.' He lays down our harvest from the day. Some mushrooms he found that he says are edible, half a dozen apples, berries and some wild garlic. He's also refilled our water bottles. 'You light the fire. Get us a soup on. Garlic and apple soup ... not sure what it will taste like but it's better than nothing. We can save some apples for us to eat as well. I'm going to go and see if there's anything else I can find.'

'You're leaving me here?' I ask, glancing at the arrows that still stick out from the tree.

'You'll be fine. I promise.'

He steps to me, places his hands on my shoulders. We watch one another, before he lets go and then heads into the trees. I bite my lip, wishing I could call him back, while also wrestling with the idea that I should be brave. I can handle this.

I do the usual. Lighting the fire, setting up our bamboo pot, boiling the water. My hands tremble, and hot water splashes and scalds my knuckles and I swear. The apple scent rises and my mouth waters, stomach rumbling. Every other second, I check that no one is running towards me. We've used so much energy today scouting around for something, anything, that we can eat to keep us going. If the tasks get worse after this, I don't know if I'll make it. The daylight begins to ebb, lost to the wildness of the trees, and I think of how I haven't seen another student since Taylor and Lee passed through. I wonder if Cameron is okay. I wonder what Elis might be telling him.

Darkness is coming, and I wonder if I am about to succumb to the open-country people.

The soup is boiling, bubbling away, and I don't know how much longer I should leave it to cook, when footsteps approach. I pick up one of the open-country people's discarded arrows. It's sharp, and I think it is sensible to be armed. Not that I could actually attack someone with it. It might even get me arrested.

To my relief, Roman appears, now with his T-shirt on.

A slight shame, but at least he's here. He nods at me, but doesn't smile.

'What's wrong?'

'Hmm? Oh, nothing.' He waves a hand. 'Couldn't find any food. How's the soup?'

His hands fidget. He doesn't sit, but paces around the fire.

'It's done.'

'Great. Let's eat. I'm starving.'

Later that night, back in the tree, Roman munches on an apple saved, and a core from an apple already devoured sits at my side. 'You look like something is up,' I say to him. 'Anything you want to tell me?'

'Nothing, no,' Roman says. Quick. Too quick. 'It's all fine. It's been a long day, that's all.'

It sure has, I think. And now, to add to my woes, I think Roman is hiding something from me.

CHAPTER 33

'Morning.'

Roman's deep voice rumbles through me, his whisper brushing over my ear. I tilt my head, my chest heavy with his draping arm, and I smile at him. 'Good morning.'

Sunlight filters through, the outside world trying to claw us out, back into a place where I have to hide this part of myself. The part where I enjoy lying with him, having his arm over me.

'Sleep well?' He leans up, resting on his arm, peering down at me.

'I was warm,' I say. Because telling him that I adored sleeping next to him would probably be a step too far. 'But I kept thinking...'

'Me too.'

He grins, and I feel a wrench when he leaves my side, crawling out into the world.

I exhale, trying to compose myself under the pretence of slowly waking up. Waking up to his voice, to his warmth this morning, felt intimate. Here in the tree, it's almost like we are in a fairytale. A world where two boys like us can do that. Is that what Izaaz was telling us? That out here we can be free?

For a moment, I imagine that life. Roman and I, here in the woods, sleeping underneath the trees. Over time we would make it homely. We might build something semi-permanent, and fashion a bed out of fallen timber. One big enough for us both to stretch out in. We could live off the land and we could make each other hot drinks, and we could spend a lifetime together ageing with the oak trees.

Does he want that?

I have no idea.

But the way he held me, like he didn't want to let me go, like I was an indulgence, has lit a fire of hope within me.

But just like when I think about it too much, and when I consider the art I like, and when I catch myself daydreaming about a life with another man, the guilt comes rushing. The rot from my core spreads out like wild mint, taking over, destroying every part of my ecosystem that could bloom into something beautiful. Guilt threatens my very existence.

'You coming out?'

Ha. As if.

I don't want to face the world.

When I do, he's made us breakfast in the form of stewed apples. I take it, listening to him talking about going back to Ganymede's. 'Someone will eventually find us,' he says. 'Take us back.'

After a while, he says, 'What's wrong?'

'Hmm? Oh, nothing.'

'You've barely eaten, and I don't think you've heard a word I said.' He watches me with some concern, and I wish he wouldn't. I wish he would turn away. It's a danger to be under his scrutiny. 'What's concerning you?'

'Can I ask you something?'

'Of course.'

I take a bite of apple, playing for time. My heartbeat is getting faster, palms beginning to sweat.

'I just...' I bite my lip. 'You were hugging me; we were so close.'

'Okay?'

I brave looking at him, and to my surprise, he's smiling. Does he find this amusing? 'And that, just now. What was that?'

'What was what?'

'That good morning. Asking me how I slept.'

'Exactly what it was,' Roman says, smile fading ever so slightly. 'Why?'

Why, indeed. I can't tell him why. I don't know what he will think. To me, every boy here has been brought up in a society where they are told men like me are wrong. That people like me no longer exist, not when we are here to repopulate. I try to think of anyone I've ever met, and how nobody has ever given me a sign that they feel the way I do.

Until Roman.

The touch of his hand. His kindness. The way he holds me. I can't be reading the signs wrong, can I?

'Should I not have hugged you?' Roman's voice makes me look away. 'Did I do something wrong?'

I turn to look at him. 'You didn't do anything wrong.' I close my eyes. 'You asked me what is concerning me. Roman, so much is concerning me.'

'Tell me.'

'I can't.'

Roman shifts towards me, so that he's opposite me now. 'You can tell me anything, Dylan. Me and you against the world, all right?'

My dying fantasy of us in these woods together revives, burns brighter, though it's fleeting.

Trembling, I swallow the fear that rises in my throat. But we have to trust each other, and we have to survive together, and I have to tell someone. 'Roman.' My throat bobs, mouth running dry, as the words rise like bile. 'I'm gay.'

Trees stay standing. The earth doesn't split. Sweltering heat presses in on me, and I imagine it rising, engulfing me in fire, damning me to the once believed-in hell. During it all, my eyes remain clamped firmly shut as the thud of my heart makes my ribcage vibrate.

'You are?'

He's still there, looking at me with an expression I can't read. I nod, hesitant. 'I shouldn't have let you hug me. Not when ... not when I liked it. If anything, I've done something wrong. *I'm* wrong.'

'Don't you dare say that,' Roman says, voice stern. 'Don't you ever think that.'

'But—'

'No buts. The world is wrong, not us.'

I almost believe him.

I look away, crossing my arms. 'That's why I'm scared. I know that when we hugged, you did it to keep us warm. I know that we have to survive. But how wrong am I for wishing you'd hold me, wanting you to hold me, being happy that you held me the way you did because I liked it? Because I liked your touch, and your warmth, and I liked that for once I could let myself be held by another man. I'm disgusting.'

Hands touch my shoulders, making me jump. Roman's grip softens, and he slowly spins me around. 'Look at me,' he whispers.

I do, with sad, hopeless eyes.

'You are not disgusting,' Roman says, anger tinging his tone. He cups my face, slowly shaking his head. 'There is nothing wrong with you, Dylan. And we did nothing wrong.'

'But would you have hugged me if you'd known what I am?'

'Who you are,' Roman says. 'Not what you are.'

'Is there a difference?'

'I think so.' Roman smiles. 'And to answer your question, no, I wouldn't have done anything different.' He removes his hands from my face, resting them on my shoulders. 'In fact, if we had another night here, I would do it all over again, and this time I'd hold you tighter.'

I don't need flint to start the fire, because it rages wild, taking out everything in its path. I can barely focus on him after hearing those words, and I hate the hope that rises in me fresh from the ashes. I can't think straight, and all I can focus on is how he's still here, and he's watching me, and all I want to do is reach out to him and hug him.

I've told this man I'm gay, and he's still here.

'Do I not disgust you?' My voice cracks and I hate myself for it.

Roman lets me go, and for one horrible moment I think I do. He lets out a groan. 'This is why I hate what this world has become. This is why I hate what we are taught. I'm angry and I'm furious that it can make you feel that way about yourself.'

'It's illegal. It's wrong.'

'It's natural,' Roman says. 'Tell me this. Will you be truly happy, allowing yourself to be paired with a stranger and live a life with her, when you can't love her?'

'Roman.' I cover my blushing cheeks.

'I'm not arguing with you, I'm asking you,' Roman says, softening his voice. 'I'm trying to make you think again. What do you expect to happen when you leave this place?'

Words evade me, but Roman doesn't say anything. 'I guess I thought nobody need ever know. That I can hide myself, forever.'

Roman shakes his head, looking away from me. His eyes are

closed, his jaw tense. He takes a breath, finally looking at me, softening his sharp features. 'Don't ever feel like you have to hide yourself from me, Dylan. Okay?'

'Even though—'

'Ever,' Roman stresses. 'We're more alike than you might think.'

'What...?'

'Come here. Give me a hug.'

He pulls me to him, so that I can feel his strength wrap around me, and any question I have about what he means dies upon my lips. With shaking hands, I touch him, and he pulls me closer, hugs me tighter, and his hand brushes the back of my neck, making me shiver. My eyes flutter closed as I rest my head against his neck, and this is what I want. What I need. He is the ultimate hunger, and yet loving him would destroy my chances at survival.

'Well, isn't this lovely?'

He doesn't move to let me go, but I push away from him, looking with horror at Professor Lawrence.

CHAPTER 34

'Congratulations, boys, you have passed.'
I start, looking at the warm and inviting Ganymede's that basks in the sunlight. 'How did we get here?'

'You fell asleep,' Lawrence says.

We are sitting in the back of a car, Lawrence in the passenger seat, a security guard driving us. When Lawrence came upon us, breaking us apart, he didn't flinch. He smiled, asked us how our nights were, listened to Roman recount some tales of foraging, and then gave us both fresh, chilled water. A few sips later and I don't remember a thing.

The bottles lie between Roman and me. Roman considers me, nods at the bottle and then looks back at me.

Lawrence opens his door, then opens Roman's. The security guard opens mine. I step out on Ganymede's soil, breathing in the air, feeling somewhat relieved to be back in a place with hot water, a comfortable bed and food.

I force a smile.

'I hope you're ready for task four,' Lawrence says. 'There's no time to get changed, though I'm sure you're all aching to do so.'

'My whole body is aching,' Roman says. 'Sleeping underneath a tree has made my body go to shit.'

'Language,' Lawrence says.

'Sorry, sir.'

'Can we at least get some food?' I ask. 'There wasn't much of it.'

'There were plenty of options in the forest,' Lawrence says.

'I didn't trust a lot of what was on offer,' Roman replies.

'Probably wise, Mr Edwards. We almost had one fatality.'

My head snaps up. 'Who, sir?'

'Milo Spires,' Lawrence says, and I hate myself for breathing a sigh of relief. At least it wasn't Cameron or Johnny. 'He ate poisonous berries. Spent the night in the hospital wing.'

'Why are there even poisonous berries available to us, sir?' Roman asks.

It's asked casually, almost curiously, but I sense something underneath it. Like he's questioning their motives.

'Because nature is neither friend nor foe to us,' Lawrence says. 'But we must respect it and live with it. This was a survival task, after all. And Professor Dalia taught you how to spot poisonous things.'

Milo may not have learnt to read the land the way Roman has, but that doesn't mean he deserved to suffer the consequences.

'Can we visit him?'

'Oh, Milo has gone home now,' Lawrence says, his voice low. 'He won't be coming back.'

I exchange a quick look with Roman before asking, 'Why not, sir?'

'He failed.' His tone is final.

'What is required of us for today's task, sir?' Roman asks after a beat.

'Debate, my boy,' Lawrence says, with a peppy flick of his finger. His smile is wide. 'A test of your intellect, your values and your morals.'

'Sounds easy,' Roman comments.

'I detect sarcasm, Mr Edwards, but yes, actually it is the easiest task you will do. There are no wrong answers on this task. No right answers, either.'

'What will we be debating?'

'You will all be given a subject when it is your turn,' Lawrence says.

'We can't even prepare an argument?' I ask.

'If you've been paying attention, you will know what to say.'

I look up at Ganymede's, in awe of its architectural beauty. Birds flit around it, diving into the growing shrubbery.

'You two looked as though you were bonding, out there,' Lawrence says with care.

I don't dare look at him, heart in mouth.

'We learnt a lot about one another,' Roman says. My furious stare seems to roll off him. 'And Dylan told me something that I was very glad he told me, and I wanted him to know I was here for him.'

Lawrence observes me. 'Is that right, Mr Cecil?'

'It might have been a task of survival, but I also felt as though I got to know Roman better,' I say.

'You feel as though these tasks are beneficial for you?' Lawrence asks of us.

Roman shrugs. 'I'm certainly enjoying them more with Dylan as my partner.'

He smiles at me, and despite everything I grin back.

Lawrence's coat flutters behind him, the crimson flashing against the green grass that strokes his black boots. He looks between us, before saying, 'Come, boys. You do not want to be late for task four.'

CHAPTER 35

We gather in Lawrence's classroom and sit in our houses. There are no more empty seats than the last time, though I suppose there must now be one fewer. Cameron smiles at me from two rows down, and I wave, glad to see him here, glad to know he survived.

We all survived. To see us all here reinforces that Ganymede's was never going to allow us to die. They were never going to forget about us. We were always under their watchful gaze.

Professor Lawrence stands at his desk, one hand propping himself up, another hand on his cocked hip. 'Congratulations, everyone. You have passed task three. But don't get too excited, because it's straight into task four. When I call your name, you will come up here and you will debate a topic. These topics have been chosen specifically for you. Don't fret. Don't overthink. Say what comes to mind. Say a lot or say little. What matters is that you say anything at all.'

Murmurs go around the room, and Cameron sits a little taller, rising to the challenge. This task has Blake written all over it. Articulate, thoughtful, he would have been able to discuss any topic at all. Another reason why I hate how it ended for him, and how nobody seems to care.

'Roman Edwards,' Lawrence calls. 'Your topic is the monarchy.'

All eyes turn to Roman. He rises slowly. He rolls his shoulders as he takes the stairs, standing at the podium, facing us all. His eyes meet mine, as if he's been searching for me, and I give him a reassuring nod.

'The monarchy,' Roman says, somewhat uncertainly. 'What exactly do you want me to say about it?'

Lawrence shrugs. 'Whatever you wish to say.'

Roman swallows, turns back to the room. It's like we're being baited. 'Before I tell you of the king, I need to give you context on the hamlet I'm from. Would that be okay, sir?'

'Of course.'

'So, yeah, hamlets. What I like about my hamlet is that we have a lot of community there. People who look out for one another. There's the man who tends to the boats. The sailor who teaches people how to sail the boats that have been tended to. The sailor's wife who studies marine biology. The houses and the shop fronts, full of freshly baked bread, locally grown food. Nobody goes hungry. Nobody goes without.'

'God save the king,' Lawrence interjects. A few of the students murmur the same.

'Ha, right. I promise I was getting to him, sir. The king,' Roman says. 'He came to our hamlet once, with Princess Cerys. Well, the lads fawned over her, and the dads pretended not to, and the wives pledged their sons as suitors, and the king laughed it off and looked like he'd never struggled a day in his life. When I look around the hamlets, do you know what I see? I see people who are living under the rulership of a man who couldn't care less about them.'

There's a gasp from the room. Lawrence is smiling.

'And what makes you think that, Mr Edwards?'

Stop talking, I want to tell Roman. This is definitely, most certainly, a trap.

'Ah, don't get me wrong, it's perfect,' Roman says, his tone light and jovial. He's even smiling back at Lawrence. 'All you could ever want. Enough food, enough money. We drive electric cars and they arrive in gold horse-drawn carriages. They shake our hands, which are free of jewellery, while they wear diamonds thieved from other countries. We have just enough, so that we don't ask for more. We're honoured and privileged and given equality, but when I look at my hamlet, I see only existence, and not fulfilment.'

'I asked you to discuss the monarchy, Mr Edwards, not your hamlet.'

'Hmm, but that's my point, isn't it?' Roman asks. 'Because we only have hamlets because of the monarchy. We only have our lives because of the monarchy. God save the king, indeed, because without them, what would we have? Freedom of choice? A say in our futures? A brain?'

The room goes silent. I grip the edge of the table, almost anticipating that Roman will be expelled right there and then.

'The monarchy loves our hamlets because the monarchy will always know where we are, what we're doing and who we're doing it with.' Roman looks in my direction, before looking back at Lawrence.

If this were a game of chess, Roman might have pulled a checkmate.

'Oh, but don't get me wrong,' he continues. 'I don't believe it's a bad thing that he doesn't care for us. How could he, when we are strangers to him? He's got enough on his plate, hasn't he, what with saving society and all that? No, I don't expect him to care for us like we are his own flesh and blood. I am pleased we have a monarchy, and not a government, because the responsibility to choose and vote for an ethical government is much too large an undertaking. Much too divisive. With the monarchy taking over for the greater good, we are able to relax, aren't we? We don't have to think about it. They take the pressure off us and allow us to live together, work together, so that we can do something beneficial while they make the relevant and much needed changes for us. The ideas he had for education like ours have been expertly executed. Everything we learn here goes beyond enriching our minds. I'm so grateful to live in a country where the monarch has such a pivotal role in repopulating the earth, getting our country back on its feet, bringing back law and order and correcting what their ancestors watched happen.'

'Is that so?'

'Oh, yeah, course. Started with King William, didn't it? I appreciate that they know what it is that we want, what's best for us. The monarchy has helped humanity realise that nothing is worth doing if it is not beneficial to society.' Roman beams, and I feel as though it lights my soul on fire. 'I feel comfort in knowing that if the world were to start crumbling again, King Carwyn could make decisions in his palace to ensure it does not happen. I am firmly on the side of the monarchy and its overriding rule of democracy, because I don't think democracy ever existed. The king doesn't have to care for us, because he cares for the earth.'

Lawrence's expression is hard to read, his smile not quite as bright as it usually is. His brow furrowed, he nods slowly. 'You certainly make an interesting point.'

'I love what the monarchy affords us,' Roman says. 'I'm glad you find what I say to be interesting, sir. If the king were to walk in now, I would bow at his feet as a loyal subject in his kingdom.'

Roman sounds sincere, but there's a harder glint in his eyes. I fix a smile to my face, trying to read my classmates' thoughts.

'I am grateful for my existence. I'm grateful that we are all here together. God save the king, for he grants us this life.'

Lawrence tilts his head. 'Is that all, Mr Edwards?'

'That's all,' Roman replies.

'Please return to your seat.' He watches Roman go in silence. 'Next, Cameron. Your subject is water.'

Cameron stumbles through his talk on why water is important, followed by a boy who talks about education, opening with 'thank you, Ganymede's', using Roman's words on the monarch's role in education as something to elaborate on. Johnny is asked to discuss sleep.

'Without sleep, life wouldn't be worth living,' Johnny muses, adopting a profound expression that leaves us all grinning. 'It is my favourite moment of the day.'

'Elis Bell. Secrets.'

Elis rises, takes to the podium. 'I cannot discuss secrets with you, for if I did, they would no longer be secret.'

He bows, and Lawrence claps.

Taylor talks for almost half an hour about tennis, and Lee is asked to discuss death, where he shares a story about finding a dead bird, which has me covering my ears by the end of it. Jackson talks about politics, while another boy follows it up with a heavy debate on the separation within our schooling system. 'Where does that leave those who are neither male nor female? Where do they fit in this binary society?'

Professor Lawrence nods slowly at this.

There's only a handful of boys left to speak, and I've been sitting here trying to listen, trying to steady my nerves, when Professor Lawrence says, 'Mr Cecil. You will be discussing same-sex attraction.'

CHAPTER 36

My footsteps echo in the deathly quiet room as I step up to the podium, and white static fills my head. My stomach aches with hunger, and my head still feels fuzzy from whatever was in that water Lawrence gave us, and here I am, expected to be sharp, expected to discuss something so hugely controversial in front of a room of boys with their own thoughts and opinions on such a topic.

Standing in front of them, the boys at the back look barely recognisable, all staring at me, waiting to see what I have to say. What do I say? Do I say what they want to hear? What they expect me to say? Or is this a test of my will, my own beliefs? Is Lawrence expecting me to go against the grain? Does he *want* me to go against the grain?

Roman's expression is blank, but an eyebrow raises and his lip quirks into a flash of an encouraging smile. I take a shaking, deep breath.

'Uh ... same-sex attraction is a ... big topic, isn't it?' My voice trembles. I can feel Lawrence's eyes burning into me, but I dare not look at him. The man has betrayed me. 'Well, as we all know it is illegal, and, uh...'

'Why do you think it is illegal?' Professor Lawrence's voice makes me flinch.

'I don't know, uh...'

'Have you ever wondered?'

Why is he prompting me? Am I not supposed to talk about this topic of my own accord? Is his interference enough to get me expelled?

I don't see anger or distaste from Lawrence. Only curiosity, even a hint of kindness. Between his look and Roman's encouraging one, I relax my shoulders and feel my shaking knee relax slightly.

'I'll be honest and say I have not given much thought to sexuality,' I say, voice a little stronger now. This is true only in that I haven't thought much about why same-sex attraction isn't legal. Of course I've thought about my own lack of interest in girls, and how that might look upon graduation. I've questioned myself, hated myself even, thought about it enough to establish that I am gay, but nobody needs to know that.

'I've heard Mother Mai talk about it in history classes. I've skipped ahead to some chapters and read all about sexuality and gender, even though we weren't going to be tested upon it. But still, it's learning, isn't it? Knowledge.' I say this directly to Lawrence, hoping it might score me some points, if that is even what he is doing. 'My understanding is that same-sex attraction is no longer permitted because the world needs more people. Society cannot have threats.'

'Do you see same-sex attraction as a threat, Mr Cecil?'

I swallow, look out into the room. Jackson smirks at me.

'A threat, sir?'

'A threat to society.'

I consider this, making a show of it by tapping my chin, fluffing my hair. 'It depends, sir.'

There's a small intake of breath in the room and I almost lose my cool. I can't see who did it. I hope it wasn't Johnny, or Cameron. I hope it wasn't Roman. Lawrence doesn't react. A small smile creeps onto his scholarly features. 'Elaborate.'

I nod. 'To me, sir, my understanding, at least ... is that sexuality, gender ... it was all liberated. But that was outlawed with the last government and has since been kept as a method for boosting our population. Am I correct, sir?'

Lawrence nods.

I smile. 'Fairly recent, then. A few generations. Society might treat it like it no longer exists, and they might believe they have stamped it out, but is it not natural within society?' I look to the room, as if addressing them. 'It is only *this* society that believes it is no longer around. What of those who are still alive who went from liberation to seclusion? Statistically, a number of us in this school will have same-sex attraction.'

'You're one of them,' Taylor shouts.

I flush, my cheeks sting, the smile fades. Not one person has laughed along with him, so that his laugh echoes and dies in the room. Lawrence's narrow eyes glare at Taylor, hold him in place, before he looks at me again. 'Continue, Mr Cecil.'

'I am not saying I am gay,' I tell the room, hoping they believe me. 'A mature man can discuss topics that do not affect him.' At this, Lawrence nods. 'Is this not the point of the task, to prove we can debate such topics, and discuss them at a healthy level, and not,' I look at Taylor, 'by shouting out childish words hoping for a cheap laugh?'

Roman claps, and a few others follow suit. It's Taylor's turn to flush red, and he shakes off Jackson's whisper, glaring at me with a look that could kill.

'To me, society is simply not allowing same-sex *relationships* because of their desire to save themselves. They are confusing it with same-sex desire,' I say. 'But what is the difference if a man or woman were to partner up as they are supposed to? And they provide families like they're supposed to? And they do what society wants them to do? Then why does it matter if that person is attracted to someone of their own kind? Why does it matter if they love another? Because you might think we are going out into society with love in our hearts, and you might believe you will love your partner, but what if you don't? Consider, for a moment, that people, same-sex attracted or not, are living with partners and not truly in love, but doing it out of necessity. Historically, marriage was always a way to survive. This is just another example of it.'

Lawrence clears his throat. 'You stray into the dynamics of relationships and marriage, Mr Cecil, but I understand your logic.'

'Sorry, sir. It is all intertwined.'

'Perhaps,' he says. 'Would you allow same-sex attraction, Mr Cecil, if you were influential enough to do so?'

A room of boys, all waiting for my answer. An answer that will surely upset a few. But what if there are some in the room waiting, hoping, for someone to speak for them? Someone to give them courage? What if I could help be the change society needs to see, at least a little bit?

'Yes, sir. Yes, I would.'

Lawrence's eyebrows rise, and a few people mutter and whisper to another. Johnny grins at me, and Cameron claps his hands together, caught between mild surprise and what I think is admiration. But it's Roman who makes me feel like I've done the right thing, despite the risk. His arms are crossed, his legs splayed, and he's beaming at me. When he sees me looking, he nods.

'Thank you, Mr Cecil.'

CHAPTER 37

I leave Lawrence's classroom in a daze, trying not to look at the boys who quickly move out of my way, or the whispers that plague me as I go by. As we emerge from the darkness of the basement, back to ground level, light pouring over us, Elis comes hurrying over. He's been waiting against the wall, watching the door from the basement. He's followed by Cameron, and both of them are bright-eyed and smiling.

'What a topic,' Elis says, as he approaches. He puts his arm around my shoulder, pulling me closer. 'And you handled it so well.'

'I can't believe how ... how ... daring you were,' Cameron says, nodding enthusiastically. 'Can you believe how bold he was?'

'I wasn't bold...' I protest.

'Dylan, bloody hell.' I turn to see Roman throw his arms open. Elis breaks away as Roman engulfs me in a hug. It's strong, and I'm pinned to his chest. Warmth hits me, and I sigh into him. I dare not link my own arms around him, because it wouldn't look like a brotherhood hug. It would look like something else. 'You did fantastic.'

'Didn't he just?' Elis says, voice loud, drawing the attention of boys around us. God, I wish he had a bit more tact. I try not to look at those who are watching us as they pass.

Elis Bell has never been a friend of mine, and that isn't because of any bad blood. It's merely because the Mercury boys tend to be the boys whom nobody can contain. Elis stands with his hair stuck at odd angles and his sleeves rolled up and his shirt creased. You might be able to excuse it as clothes wrecked from the survival outside, but Elis and indeed all the Mercury boys are always like this to some extent. They crunch up paper and throw it in class. They yawn and are the first to look bored. But, equally, they're the first boys to ask questions, some wilder than others. We've been conditioned to ignore the Mercury boys for their eccentricities.

'I think he tried to trip you up,' Elis whispers, putting his hand on my shoulders and guiding me away from the centre of the hall, towards one of the back walls, where there is a bench we can sit upon. 'It's a weird topic to give to someone.'

'Is it?'

'It is,' Cameron whispers. 'Why would a professor want to encourage us to debate same-sex attraction? He must have known you could have said something that wouldn't have gone in your favour.'

I groan. 'Oh, God, did I?'

'Yes, you did,' Elis says. 'Oh, don't look so anguished, Dylan, bro. You spoke your mind and I think Lawrence respected you for it.'

'Spoken like a true magician,' Roman says with a grin.

On the bench, Cameron stands, while I'm sandwiched between Roman and Elis. It's like they're consoling a patient in the hospital wing. I stare at the flagstone floor, boys' voices drifting away from us as they filter out.

'Do you want a seat, Cameron?'

He shakes his head. 'No, I'm good.'

'Where's Johnny?' My stomach clenches, worried that he's avoiding me as he hears the boys whisper.

'I don't know,' Cameron replies.

'Do you think I'm going to be expelled?'

'Expelled? Why would you be expelled?' Elis searches my expression.

I can't voice my fear that I sealed my own fate by saying I'm essentially in favour of legalising same-sex attraction. What if Professor Lawrence is relaying that right now to the other professors?

'I think you know why he gave you that topic,' Roman says.

I look at him, biting my lip. Not now. Not in front of Elis.

'Really?' Elis has tasted blood, and he's sniffing it out.

'When Lawrence came to find us at the survival task, Dylan and I were hugging.'

'How interesting,' Elis remarks.

'I think, if it was on purpose, it's not because of that.'

'Then what would it be?' Elis asks.

I swallow. 'You must have heard what Taylor says about me?'

Elis shakes his head. 'What does he say about you?'

I don't look at any of them when I say, 'He thinks I'm gay.'

I say it so quietly that when nobody speaks, I think they must not have heard me. But eventually, Elis asks, 'Is it true?'

'Elis,' Cameron admonishes.

'Sorry.'

'No, it's not true,' I say through gritted teeth.

Elis considers me a moment. 'Frankly, I don't care. I think I underestimated you, Dylan. You surprised me with your tenacity in that room.'

I perk up, despite the compliment coming from the lips of Elis, who isn't exactly the best person to want to please. The truth is, I'm proud of myself for what I said. For standing up there in a room full of people who have been told same-sex attraction is wrong, and actually speaking up on the topic. For consolidating my thoughts, thoughts I wasn't wholly aware that I had. Thoughts that now won't stop spiralling in my mind.

'Should we ask him?' Elis says to Cameron and Roman.

'I think we should,' Cameron says with a nod.

'Really?' Roman asks. 'I've been saying this since the start.'

'Now is not the time,' Elis argues.

'But—'

'Listen,' Elis cuts Roman off, leaning towards me. Roman joins, so close I can see his eyelashes flickering. 'Let's hang out.' He smiles. 'Tonight, nine fifteen p.m. I'll be in the graveyard. Look for Death.'

I gawp. 'The *graveyard*?' I look at Roman. 'Past *curfew*? Death?'

'I'll take them there,' Cameron says.

Elis leans back, rising to his feet. 'You're in good hands with Cameron.'

'But Elis...' I begin. What does he mean, meet in the graveyard?

Elis waves. 'See ya.'

We watch him go, Cameron grinning. 'You going to tell me what that was all about?' I ask.

Cameron taps the side of his nose. 'All in good time, my friend.'

'Roman?'

'Trust me, Dylan,' he says.

CHAPTER 38

Something's shifted among my peers. All day, shifty looks, whispers behind hands, wide berths. For the last three years, I've only ever had problems with Taylor and his two mates, and mostly flown under the radar. Performed well enough in classes to get by. Spoken to people politely, as expected. Now, I enter rooms and people leave. There are those who are brazenly against me, whispering, 'He said he would legalise same-sex attraction.'

At supper, the professors all sit as usual at their tables, with their goblets and their half-drunk green bottles of red wine. They watch me. Dwynwen, mainly. She sits with Mother Mai, and they talk, and yes, they could talk about anything, but their gazes always alight on me. I wonder if this is what the boys who asked too many questions felt like. I wonder if I'm to be told I've been expelled.

'But what did he mean, look for Death?' I whisper to Cameron.

'This supper is delicious, isn't it?' he says, smiling.

'You been replaced with a robot or something?'

He ignores me, and doesn't even say goodbye when he finishes his food and exits the room.

I'm about to leave for my room, a full hour before curfew, fretting over this idea that we are going to sneak to the graveyard of all places past the imposed times, when Dwynwen's voice echoes through the food hall. 'Mr Cecil. Would you be so kind as to accompany me to my room?'

The room has thinned, but those that remain fall silent, watching, waiting for my reaction.

I nod, and Dwynwen rises, saying her goodbyes to the professors, who raise their goblets, before sipping their red wine.

I walk with Dwynwen in silence. Nothing but the rustle of her dark clothes that cling to her tall, slim frame. We see no one on the way. Just long corridors of antique furniture and burning candles and the occasional lamp lit by electricity. We enter her office on the top floor of the school, close to the Mars corridor. I wonder if she chose it on purpose so that she is always nearby to curb the boisterous energy of the Mars boys. The room we walk into is her office: a walnut table with a lamp, candles and notebooks, surrounded by three walls of bookshelves, stocked high with leatherbound books that look like they should belong to the library. I suppose when you're the headmistress you're not fined for taking the books out too long. Judging by the light layering of dust, these books have been here for a while. She has three windows, arched, and they look out over the lake, towards the graveyard, and I shiver, fearing crossing the expanse of open land later tonight. If I live to see tonight, that is. There's another door, frosted glass, dark oak. It's open a crack, revealing carpeted corridor, more books, this time stacked on the floor, and in the distance a room with a sofa. She sees me looking, and shuts the door with a light snap. 'My apartment,' she says. 'Please, take a seat.'

Opposite her table are two armchairs, next to a small table made out of a tree trunk, and I take no seat in particular, sinking into the dark green plush cushion.

'Am I being expelled?' I blurt.

Dwynwen pauses in her seat, peering at me. 'Why would you think you are being expelled, Mr Cecil?'

I pause. Best to say nothing at all.

Dwynwen sits tall, her arms resting on either side of her chair, her hands gripping its arms. 'I had a conversation with Professor Lawrence today.'

I close my eyes. This is it. I've failed. All of this has been for nothing.

'You chose to tread on uncertain ground,' she continues. 'I find it interesting that you did so.'

'I'm sorry, Headmistress, but please, get it over and done with.'

Dwynwen cocks an eyebrow and regret plagues me. 'Excuse me, Mr Cecil?'

'Sorry, Headmistress.'

'I should think so,' Dwynwen says. 'You are not being expelled, Mr Cecil.'

My head snaps up. 'I'm ... not?'

Dwynwen shakes her head, but does not smile. 'Professor Lawrence gave you a topic and you debated it as you were instructed, and we would be remiss to ignore that.'

'Did he tell you what I said?'

'Yes, Mr Cecil, he did.' She watches me carefully. 'Tell me, what are you hoping for when you graduate?'

'*If* I graduate, Headmistress.'

She bows her head. 'If you graduate.'

I think about it. There's definitely no way I'm going to tell the truth to Dwynwen. I've already risked enough talking to a classroom full of my year, and letting Professor Lawrence witness it. 'I'd like to be a journalist, Headmistress.'

Her eyes widen. 'Oh?'

'Yes. I always found our English lessons fascinating, and I particularly liked the module we did on media studies in year two,' I say. 'And Mother Mai's history of the news was one of my highlights.'

'It's a pleasure to hear that, as most boys do not compliment my mother.'

I smile, uncertain. 'It is history, after all.'

Dwynwen nods, stiffly. 'You're correct. A journalist. How interesting. And what else?'

'Well, of course, to graduate and live and provide for king and country, Headmistress,' I say. 'A home where I can live out my days with my partner.'

Dwynwen nods, before rising to her feet. 'I would have thought you would have liked to continue your parents' legacy.'

I look away from her, lip quivering. When I summon enough courage to speak, I say, 'I'm not sure that's my role, Headmistress.'

She turns her back on me, and I exhale, trying to steady my nerves. She uses a long-boned finger to trace over the books, before pausing at one and taking it out. 'And why not?'

I settle on shrugging, hoping she doesn't ask any more. The truth is I can't face it. Can't face going back to a home that was shared with my parents, and finding it empty, devoid of love and life. I can't run their business on my own, and why would I when the food has continued to arrive at Ganymede's? Clearly someone else took over, so why would they need me to take over when they have done okay without it?

'I never quite understood my father's relationship with the king,' I say, when Dwynwen stands with the book in her hand and says nothing. 'He did everything for him. Every decision was made with him in mind. There were photos of him in our house. I would see the king's portrait every morning.'

'A lot of people live with the monarch's portrait in their home,' Dwynwen says. 'I have one in my apartment.'

'I know. It's just, well, Father treated it like it was a shrine.'

Dwynwen nods, as if she understands, as if maybe she does the same thing, too. 'Your father had a wonderful relationship with the king and benefited from it greatly. Your families have been intertwined for years, Mr Cecil.'

'Not anymore. That relationship died with my parents.'

Dwynwen brings the hefty book to her chest, before dropping it on the table with a thud. A scent of dust and old pages wafts to me, and I peer at the blank black leather, thinking how curious it looks. She lifts the cover, and there's a sticky sound as she leafs through the pages, full of written notes, typed notes, all crammed into the tome. She pauses a quarter of the way through and looks at me.

'Do you know what this is?'

I shake my head.

Dwynwen sits, keeping her hand on the book so that she doesn't lose her page. 'This is your file, Mr Cecil. All of these books contain a file and a record of every boy that has ever walked through these doors. In it, we document the observations we have made, your grades, any conversations we have had.' She looks at me here. 'Our personal conversations have been few and far between, I can see.'

'That's right.'

Dwynwen peers at me. 'This is what helps inform us of your perfect partner. Tell me, Mr Cecil, would you like to know who your perfect match is?'

I sink back into my chair. Have I misheard her? Nobody knows their matches until the day of graduation, when they are taken to their hamlets and shown their homes and their partner awaits them. So much trust goes into the whole process that it has become normal, a simple moment of definition in a young man's life.

'Is that allowed, Headmistress?'

'I am offering it, and that is all that matters, though I ask that you do not tell your fellow students,' she says. 'They will all be lining outside my door begging to be told their own partners. No, it is best that students do not know who their partners are, for men have gone insane trying to change their fates.'

'Then why tell me, Headmistress?' I ask, keeping my tone polite. 'I don't want to know, if I'm going to start doing things differently. Isn't it better if I carry on oblivious?'

Dwynwen considers this. 'Do you not trust having the knowledge?'

I shake my head. 'No, Headmistress, I don't.'

'Intriguing. I thought as a journalist you would always want to know the truth.'

'I do, Headmistress, but not my own.'

She closes the book with a gentle touch, sliding it aside. 'You fascinate me, Mr Cecil. You always have.'

I don't think swearing in surprise would get me on Dwynwen's good side, so instead I breathe out, unsure of what else to say. Me? Fascinate her?

'Most boys would jump at the chance of having a leg up on the rest of their students. Knowing your partner may come at a cost, but it also has an advantage.' She stands, lifting the book. 'But it is no matter. You have made your choice.'

I almost worry that this is some secret task, that me saying no has cemented my fate. But as Dwynwen turns, another idea occurs to me. She walks to the left corner of the room, putting the book back where she found it. I eye it, seeing the candlelight flicker over it.

Inside these books, information is stored on every boy that has walked through this school.

Inside these books, somewhere, is the truth behind Blake's death.

'It's a hard role, to be your headmistress.' She looks out of the window, at the still night. 'There are times when I wish to get more involved in your education, but I must remember my place.' She exhales, offering me a small smile. 'I'm sorry to talk so openly to you, but I rarely get the chance to wear my heart on my sleeve in front of the students.'

'That must be difficult, Headmistress.'

She looks back at the night, her face reflected in the glass. 'Thank you for meeting with me, Mr Cecil. You are dismissed.'

'Thank you, Headmistress.'

I rise, heading to the door, but as I'm about to open it the door swings and Lawrence stands in the frame.

'Professor Lawrence,' I say, somewhat surprised.

He nods his head.

'Run along now, Mr Cecil.'

Lawrence's usually composed face looks strained, and Dwynwen's expression is fixed. I hover, before nodding and stepping out into the hallway. The door shuts with a snap, and I make to move, but then I stop.

'The sickness is getting worse,' Lawrence's voice says.

'Will you be quiet?' Dwynwen replies.

I lean against the wall, holding my breath, as if they might hear me.

'Hamlets are reporting that people are going down with it. They're bedbound and deteriorating.'

'Has the death rate increased?'

'Not yet, but—'

'Then do not panic.'

'And what about—'

'All under control.'

'Headmistress, with all due respect—'

'You underestimate me, Lawrence,' Dwynwen says, her voice stern. 'Aid is on the way.'

The room falls silent, and I wonder if they know I'm here.

'At what cost?' Lawrence finally asks.

The door handle rattles, and I bolt, trying to run lightly, trying to stay calm. I only stop at the end of the hallway, breathing out when I confirm that Dwynwen's door is still closed.

CHAPTER 39

'Ready?' Cameron whispers in the communal bathroom adjacent to our dormitories. He is leaning against the sink, dressed in a blue jumper that's too big for him, and brown trousers that seem to drown him.

'Are you serious?' I frown. I have no idea why he got me to meet him in here.

'Deadly serious,' he says. 'Trust me, Dylan. But we haven't got much time.'

He turns away from the door that leads out into the corridor, and instead goes towards a broom cupboard.

'Where are you going?'

'You'll see. Now hurry.'

He opens the broom cupboard door, pushing aside cleaning paraphernalia. He catches a broom from falling, and moves aside a steel bucket, getting into the closet and crouching down.

I shake my head but I follow him in, my curiosity getting the better of my confusion. Of course, I've never been in here. Why would I when it's just some cleaning supplies cupboard? To my surprise, there's another door right at the back.

Cameron twists the handle and steps through. I follow, finding myself in a stairwell, dark. I shiver, crossing my arms, and Cameron, holding a lantern, shuts the door behind us.

There's a stillness in this damp dankness.

'Old, servants' access,' Cameron says. 'Don't ask me why they wanted a secret entrance into the boys' lavs.'

He descends the stairs, me behind him, both of us light on our feet. I mimic him and fall into a rhythm. There are old cigarette butts littering the stairs, and even old pages from a long-lost textbook. When we're at the bottom of the steps the cold chill seeps into me.

Cameron crosses a small expanse of stone and pushes at a door I hadn't seen, painted black. It creaks open, and red and gold light drifts in as one of the hallways of Ganymede's reveals itself to us. To my surprise, Roman stands before us, dressed in a thick knitted jumper. But he's not alone. Framed by a painted pastoral landscape, holding a pillar candle, is someone with a familiar face.

'You,' I say.

Professor Rory nods. 'Quiet, please.'

Cameron gives Rory a smile and a wave, and then I eye Roman with a questioning gaze, but he ignores my pleading stare. What the hell is going on? All of us fall into step, and I realise we're at the back of the school, in a corridor that leads out onto the grounds.

'Candles out,' Rory orders.

Cameron does as he's told, keeping the lantern close to him. Rory blows out his own candle, where wax has trailed and hardened down the side into a sharp pattern. He pushes open the door, and we step out into the warm night air. It shouldn't be this warm in the evening, I think, as Rory and Cameron turn to face Roman and me.

'Keep your heads forward and follow me. Do not look back. Stick to the shadows.'

Rory leads us around the school, not bothering to tread lightly over the asphalt and loose stone chippings. We descend the steps that drop onto the field, and I know the front of the school is behind us, life inside it, boys kept in solitude. The lake comes into view as it glistens in the half moonlight, the sky spotless except for glittering stars. We take the bridge, single file, and I want to ask why we're walking so steadily, and not rushing to get out of view of whoever might be looking out of the manor right now. The graveyard is upon us, all black iron gates and weather-beaten gravestones. There's the odd statue of a rising angel and mourning, cloaked figures, monuments and relics of people long gone.

'Aren't you worried about that?' I whisper, pointing to the old gatehouse in the distance. Light flickers, a shadow inside.

'They won't see us,' Cameron says. 'They can't see us in the dark.'

We stick to the path and cross through the iron gate, which groans on its hinges. Cameron brings up the back, making sure the gate is closed and locked. I feel a pang in my chest as we pass Blake's grave. The grass whispers around us, and the trees sway. I hadn't realised it was so vast and went back so far. The further in we go, the quieter it seems to get, as if out of respect for its inhabitants.

'What the—?'

We emerge onto a medium-sized, circular patch of land, where five Gothic mausoleum crypts all face a patch of grass, where flowers bloom. I gawp at the stone crypts, each one big enough to be an adequate dwelling for a small family. Why, they may even be the same size as my house back in my hamlet. Moss grows upon the walls and on the arched rooftops, and medieval spires twist to the sky. Each one is decorated with flying cherubs and atop each is an animal. A crow mid-flight, large and mighty. An owl on the second, stone eyes staring at us. Snakes on the third wrap themselves around the supporting stone pillars, before accumulating in one big snake upon the globe. There's another with a sleek cat, paw raised as if in curiosity, and finally, there's a dog.

It's this dog that makes me stare in awe, neck craned to take it all in. It has three heads, and it accompanies a dark-robed man, staring forebodingly at those who dare to approach the entrance to the crypt he sits upon. He holds a sceptre in one hand, with two prongs, his other hand patting the back of the dog.

'Look for Death,' Roman whispers.

'Welcome, boys, to the House of Pluto.'

CHAPTER 40

The stone floor is littered with brown curling leaves, and things that crunch under my feet. With the sight of burial tombs, I can't help but imagine stepping on the bones of dead people. There's a scent in this room that I wasn't expecting: lavender and cedar. Five-foot wrought-iron candelabras stand in each corner of the room, each with four candles burning brightly upon them, casting light around the crypt. It's like an open-plan living space, if you wanted to live in a morbid shrine to death. The big tomb in the middle, about four feet tall, is surrounded by cloaked figures. There are more tombs built into the walls, fashioned with lying bodies looking restful and regal, hands clasped over their hearts.

'This is so goth,' I mutter.

Rory leads us forward, and I move closer to Roman, wishing to take his hand, even though he knows more than I do and hasn't told me a thing. He holds my gaze, a smile spreading across his handsome face, and my breath quickens, pulse races.

There are eleven cloaked figures, heads bowed, hoods drawn to obscure their identities. Rory has put on his own robe, but he doesn't lift the hood. Instead, he considers Roman and me. Cameron has already joined the boys. He's rolling on a cloak.

Rory beckons for us to come to the tomb. Behind him is an altar, lined with candles burning in various states of decline. There's a large gold-dusted mirror, and there are crystals that glitter in the light. There's imagery of Pluto, including a particularly forbidding statue of him that seems to glare at me as if I'm daring to intrude.

'Lower your hoods,' Rory instructs, once Roman and I are shoulder to shoulder with the cloaked boys, who do as he says.

Cameron is next to us, grinning. The two boys beside him I recognise as friends of Elis's from Mercury, and indeed Elis is with them, standing beside Rory, who is flanked on his other side by two boys who I think are from Jupiter. I peer at the boy next to me and it's my turn to gasp.

'Surprise, mate.' Johnny grins at me, face bright in the candlelight. He gathers me into a hug.

'What the hell is going on?' I ask. Him, the room. Anyone who is willing to answer me.

The boys are all staring, and I can't read their faces, except for one of the Jupiter boys, who is shaking his head slowly.

'Sorry I couldn't tell you sooner,' Johnny says. 'I wanted to, honestly. But Rory wouldn't let me. Elis said he'd invited a new person but I had no idea it would be you.'

'I still think there are too many of us,' one of the Jupiter boys says, whose accent sounds Ukrainian. 'How do we know we can trust them?'

'We need as many people as we can get,' a dark-skinned Mars boy says.

'That's Ben,' Roman says to me.

'You've changed your tune,' the person next to him says.

'Grady,' Roman says.

'Nice to meet you,' Ben says, and Grady nods.

'You sure we need him?' The Ukrainian Jupiter boy asks.

'Enough, Petro,' his companion says. 'I'm sure there's a good reason Elis invited Dylan.'

'Is there?' Petro asks. 'I'm not sure about that.'

'You don't have to be sure,' Elis replies. 'Just trust me.' He turns to me. 'Petro and Kim here are second-year Jupiter boys, so they didn't see your performance in the last task.'

'We're still on site for extra-curricular activities,' Grady says, using fingers to air quote. 'Felt like a good way to still be involved without going home.'

'Heard it was a good one,' Rory says. 'It definitely panicked some of the professors.' He laughs at this, much to my surprise.

'Look, I don't know what I've walked into here. I know nothing,' I say. 'If you don't want me here, I can turn and walk out of the door and leave this place and pretend I never saw anything.' At this, Petro looks at Rory. 'I mean it.' I'm pouncing on their uncertainty, because all of the candles and death and Pluto shit has the hairs on my neck standing up. 'I'm trustworthy, I can assure you of that, and I can keep secrets. You boys have your own ... club going on, and that's...'

The boys are laughing at my word choice, and I falter, words dying upon my lips.

'Dylan is right,' Roman says. 'If you want us to leave, we'll leave.'

'Us?' Elis asks.

'I go with him.'

I turn to Roman. 'You don't have to.'

'But I will,' Roman says.

'You have the choice to join us or leave us,' Rory says. 'But let us tell you first what we are and then you can make your decision. Either way, we will require your trust.' He looks at Elis, then at the Jupiter boys. 'He's in too deep here. He's seen enough already.'

Petro gives an exasperated sigh, almost theatrical.

'Elis, make your case.'

Elis grins. 'This is Dylan Cecil. Saturn. Some of you were there when Dylan gave his speech on same-sex attraction.' The Mercury boys and the Mars boys nod, along with Cameron and Johnny. Petro looks surprised. 'You'll know how brave he was to do that. But it caught my attention. That, and Roman's talk on the monarchy. Our great and loyal king.'

The boys scoff, Rory pretending to be sick. My eyes widen at the blatant disrespect to the royal family, who give us everything.

'Sometimes, boys – sorry, Grady, I mean Plutonians – you have to listen and read between the lines,' Elis says, in typical Mercury fashion. 'And that is what I did when I listened to Dylan talk. His was by far the most fascinating, but he offered a glimpse into a different way of thinking, an undercurrent of something other, and isn't that what we are all about?'

The Mercury boys nod enthusiastically, proudly, almost.

'What is it, exactly, that they said?' one – his name is Kim, I think – asks.

Elis recounts my debate, me interjecting to correct him once or twice, but mostly he's accurate. Rory's eyebrows rise, his features softening into something that resembles friendliness.

'Fascinating,' Rory says.

'I'm sorry,' I say, politely. 'But I don't understand why what I said has anything to do with whatever gothic fantasy you're living here.' Some of the boys laugh, and I say, 'No, I'm serious. It's like I've stepped into the mind of Bram Stoker.'

'We prefer Oscar Wilde, here,' Elis says, 'and Shakespeare, but don't you see? Him talking of Bram alone should be enough.'

Rory nods. 'I can see it. If what you said is true, and people here agree, then I can see why Elis stepped out of line and recruited Dylan without telling any of us.'

Recruited? I don't like the sound of that.

'I was there,' Cameron says.

'Elis has always been a bad influence on you.'

I didn't even know they were close. It must be the partnership. Maybe Elis called Cameron into whatever this is when they were paired up to compete in the tasks.

Oh, God, the tasks. This is going to jeopardise all of it. I don't know what's going on, but it doesn't take a genius to work out that whatever these boys and Rory are doing, it goes against all of Ganymede's rules. Why else would they be meeting in a crypt, wearing robes, and have a whole shrine dedicated to Pluto?

'Can someone please tell me what's really going on?' I ask.

'We're disrupting society,' Rory says. 'Starting with destroying Ganymede's, from the inside.'

CHAPTER 41

'Sorry, what?'

It's all I can ask after too long a silence. I stare dumbfounded at Roman, because out of them all, he is the biggest betrayal. Is he going to laugh, to tell me this is one big joke? Is anyone going to break this confusion?

I've trusted a boy who has double-bluffed me from the off.

'We've got to start from the inside, but essentially we see ourselves changing society,' Rory says.

'Oh, very easily done,' I snap.

'Nothing worth doing is easy,' Rory replies curtly. 'We've been careful about whom we let into the fold, because we need to make sure we play it right. But our plan is to disrupt Ganymede's.'

'And how do you plan to do that?'

'We want them to know that we are waking up,' Elis says.

'Waking up? What do you mean?' I ask.

Elis leans against the counter and rests his chin in the palm of his hands, tapping the side of his face with his fingertips. 'Everyone in this room doesn't belong, in some way, to the society we're being told we have to join. We're putting ourselves through all of this, just to graduate and join a society which at the first sniff of otherness will want us destroyed.'

I scoff. 'Destroyed sounds serious.'

'It *is* serious,' Rory says. 'Take me for example. I was once a student of Ganymede's, eager to get out in society and meet my partner. Graduation was the best day of my life, or at least I thought it was. But I arrived at my home and it became clear that my partner despised me. I took the life from her, she said, and daily she would remind me that I was not her choice. I was to become a teacher, and that is what I did, while she refused to comply with what we were supposed to do. She would sleep in a separate room, and at first, I felt lost. I would not do anything she was not comfortable with, but I also felt as though we were breaking some sort of law by not...' He gestures, but doesn't elaborate. 'Then I respected her, because who was I to think I had some sort of right over her? That's when I started realising that everything we've been taught here is self-serving. I wasn't prepared for a woman who didn't, couldn't love me. I was led to believe that both of us would be happy together, and we weren't. Every day I went out to work as a teacher, telling the world I was happy, pretending everything was fine. I might have had my home and money and everything I could need, but my mental health completely fell apart. Ganymede's raised me, they made me who I was supposed to be. I thought everything was supposed to be grand. I couldn't live with myself that I was upsetting my wife. Then there was my brother. The brightest boy I ever knew. The world at his feet.' Tears glisten as they roll down Rory's face, and we all stand sombrely shoulder to shoulder. 'Ganymede's failed me but they betrayed my brother. I know for a fact that they took him because he knew too much. He knew something. He was going to tell the world the truth, and they killed him.

It's why I'm here. For the truth. To expose them. To bring them down.'

He pauses, then his gaze settles on me.

'My brother was Blake.'

My mouth drops, and my world breaks. I don't recall sinking to my knees, but the next thing I know, Rory is helping me up, nodding. 'I'm sorry, Dylan. I know how much you treasured him. And I know you want to know what happened, too. Don't you?'

Words evade me, my mind lost to the truth. This man before me, only a few years older than I am, who has been teaching us about life skills, preparing us for graduation, is Blake's brother? How haven't I seen it before? The same shade of hair. The similar eyes. Even some of Rory's vocal inflections – they are reminiscent of Blake's.

I want to scream. Want to punch at their chests and knock over every candelabra and set fire to this whole place. Maybe then I can feel at ease.

'My mum isn't Blake's mum. I'm his half-brother, the result of an affair our father had. Infidelity is hugely prohibited out there, though it is known of. But to admit they know about it is to admit that their system does not work.' Rory looks at each of us before continuing. 'My father and Blake's mother and my birth mother all agreed to keep it quiet. If our hamlet were to find out that I wasn't the son of Father's assigned partner, our family would be ruined. I probably first learnt the truth when I was eleven. It became even more important to keep it a secret when Blake came along. I mean, having the billionth child be your brother? What a way to make me feel inferior. But with Blake came our family's realisation that we had power. We had to keep it secret, because we were influential. We had to keep them on side. There were ten years between Blake and me. I told him when he was old enough to comprehend his situation, our family tensions. He hated me. He refused to play along. Became the rebel of the family, behind closed doors.'

I remember Blake refusing to elaborate on his family, the brief mention of his brother.

'I taught at Roman's old school, when I was ready,' Rory continues. 'I discovered students going missing. It prompted me to look at the other schools, to analyse the data. In each school I saw the same thing, and came to the same conclusion. Vandervere are discarding students in all of their schools all over the country.'

I shake my head.

'I mean, when you discover that, what do you do?' Rory asks. 'It's my first job, and I'm presented with all this evidence. Do I go straight to the headmaster at my school? Do I go to Dwynwen? Bloody hell, do I go to Carwyn? I told Father, and Father told me to act like nothing had changed. After much debate, that's exactly what I did. It was my job to play along, and make note every time a boy disappeared from the school. In the meantime, I also kept abreast of any other disappearances. For a while, there wasn't much. But I started noticing a pattern.

'I believe the crux of it is coming from this school,' Rory says. 'But I needed someone on the inside. Naturally, I asked Blake. I told him everything. I knew I shouldn't, not when he was entering his third year, but I couldn't let him go back knowing what I knew. He was my brother. With the evidence in front of him, he saw it. Saw the truth. I saw everything change for him in that moment. But Blake was unpredictable, and I hate to say it, but I didn't trust him wholly, and neither did Father. Father said, to be safe, that I should get transferred to Ganymede's as a teacher.

'I got the transfer approved. Blake hated that I was coming here to teach. I think I ruined his plans. When Blake disappeared, I felt responsible.' His voice shakes. 'I knew he'd been acting strangely, doing things without telling me. My fears of him going rogue came true. When, after he disappeared, nobody would tell me anything, I was driven insane with worry, and yet I knew the outcome because I'd seen it all before, and then Dwynwen finds him dead, and I can't show how I really feel. I don't even get to see him to say a proper goodbye. Can't let this anger erupt or burn this school to the ground, even though it's what I want to do. Dwynwen offered me all sorts of support, but all I want to do is tell her that I know, somehow, that she's responsible. That this school is responsible for what happened. Father has made me furious because he still plays along like this was all accidental. It's been hard, Dylan, to see you upset and alone, knowing I've wanted to tell you from the start. It's been gutting to see him forgotten.'

'I haven't forgotten him,' I whisper.

'No, and neither have we,' Elis says.

Rory nods, closing his eyes, wiping his cheeks. 'It's Father that wanted to keep Blake's death out of the headlines. The monarch was more than willing to oblige. Father doesn't want Blake's death to be seen as something tragic. He says it would be an insult to his memory.'

'Not talking about him is an insult to his memory,' I say.

Rory nods. 'The truth will prevail. I'm adamant about it. But first, we need solid evidence, and someone to trust us. I need to know the why behind the disappearances. The House of Pluto is bigger than this crypt. Throughout the school system, students meet and report back on what they've discovered. I'm in close contact with people outside education, too, building up a group that can eventually come together and destroy this school and every school Vandervere owns. We are here to break the system to fix the system.'

'Pluto is the god of transformation, and the underworld itself. We are the death of perfection,' Elis says, grinning.

I look at Johnny, always happy-go-lucky, no complaints. Cameron, who has so much going for him. How can they both be here, risking everything?

'You think Blake was murdered?'

'I know he was, because I think he found out the truth,' Rory says. 'He told me he needed to speak with me urgently. I think they knew he was on to them, and I think they needed him gone before he could tell anyone. And I know for certain that they are paranoid that Blake told someone else. I know he didn't. He wouldn't have told anyone without telling me first. But I'm letting them live in that paranoia, hoping it drives them to make mistakes.'

I lean against the tomb before us. Rory peers at me with worry, but I can't think of him right now.

'But why are the rest of you here?' I finally ask the cloaked boys and Elis.

'Well, I'm Mercurial,' Elis says. 'They're the house they're most scared of. From day one here I asked why we were being partnered up, why we had no say in it. From there it sort of spiralled, and I started getting my hands on books they'd banned, and then, at the beginning of the third year, Rory caught me trying to read a book on liberation in the twenty-first century, and he started to ask me questions, and I asked him and he recruited me.'

'He's underselling himself,' Rory says. 'Elis is my right-hand guy. I should have known, though, that having a Mercury partner would create some volatile situations.' He looks at me.

Elis says, 'I have been known to bring people in without asking Rory first. Cameron was one of them.'

Cameron looks at me. 'My story is similar to Elis's, although – and he won't mind me saying this – whereas Elis tends to dive into things on instinct, I needed time. I've listened to every lesson, and I've studied every topic, and I've believed every word they've said – right up until this summer.' Cameron smiles at Elis. 'There have been little seeds of doubt as I've gone on, but I've always explained it away. That we're the generation that has to sacrifice some things for the greater good.'

'We've all thought it at one point or another,' Elis chips in. 'Conform or die.'

'But then straight after task two, Elis tells me his truth, and for some reason I decide to tell him mine,' Cameron continues. 'I'm probably one of the only people here who would genuinely be happy with what I think I'm supposed to do. Graduate, cultivate the land, live with my partner in some homestead somewhere and never have to think of any other person's plight or struggles. But what a privileged position that would be, where I don't have to worry about someone else's wellbeing because mine isn't compromised. When Elis told me about this place, well ... it was an eye-opener.'

'What about you, Johnny?' I ask.

'I'm here by accident.'

'What?'

'I overheard Cameron talking to Elis once and then I saw Cameron sneaking out one evening, and I followed him and they had no choice but to bring me in.'

'Actually,' Rory says. 'This is the only place we do have a choice.'

'That's exactly what swayed me,' Johnny says. 'I realised that all of this has always been leading to a defined path, one set out for us by people whom we trust, people who know best. Then I started thinking, where's our autonomy? Why can't we have a say? Why do we have to be yes-men?'

'The girls feel the same,' Rory says. 'We're taught that the girls we'll meet want this. That they want to raise families with us and be happy in marriage and be happy with the jobs assigned to them. We've been taught to respect women, and then we are confused when they don't want what they're told they're supposed to want. They have lost as much choice as we have. There is no freedom, not really. We're all under his command.'

Roman puts a hand on my back, rubbing me slowly.

'We're here because we trust Elis,' one of the Mercury boys say.

'Owen and Stan are smart guys,' Elis tells me. 'Free thinkers. Did you know Stan's father was once a liberal prime minister? Liberalism runs in his veins.'

Stan blushes at this, but he nods sheepishly.

'For me, I'm here because how am I supposed to be the perfect man when I am not one?' Grady says. 'I've felt uncomfortable within myself all my life, and society has told me that someone like me doesn't belong unless I conform. And I'm sick of it. I proudly say that I am not a man, and I am not a woman. Ganymede's has always filled me with dread, as has this society, and it's all coming to a head now. I want to get away from it all.'

'But we also want to survive,' Petro says. 'We don't want to lose everything just because we dare to fight for what is right.'

'That's why we're playing it carefully,' Rory says. 'Causing enough chaos to begin with until you all graduate and start changing things from the outside, too. My plan is to keep recruiting while you go and create a system outside that we can all join. Our own society, if you will, until it's so big they can't ignore us. We have to do it strategically and slowly.'

'It sounds like you're talking of uprisings,' I say, paling. 'Of civil unrest.'

'So be it,' Rory says.

'This school isn't creating emotionally intelligent men,' Elis says. 'It's participating in emotional manipulation. Yes, it's great that we have gentlemen these days, and even better that men's emotions are being addressed. But at what cost? The cost of compromising who we are? The cost of losing individuality and our truth? The cost of stamping out true rights for women?'

'It's almost Victorian how the women are expected to be the ones who stay at home and carry our children and smile and be thankful that they're doing so,' Rory says. 'I'm also very conscious there are no women in this room right now. We are kept separate from them for too long, and then never truly understand them.'

'We're told society is equal, but how can it be equal if we are not deemed to be perfect by their standards?' Elis asks.

'And then there's the ones who get expelled,' Ben says. 'My brother, for example.'

'The ones who aren't fit for society?'

'All are fit for society, it's just people in power who deem some aren't. Split, divide, conquer,' Rory says.

I bite my lip, feeling as though I have a grenade in my hand and my finger on the pin. Looking at Roman, I say, 'And what about you?'

CHAPTER 42

'I didn't tell you the full truth about my parents,' Roman says, watching me with intent. 'Not all of the truth, anyway. They're historians, but they haven't been happy for a few years now. What I told you about that conversation I heard from them one night, that is true, but I also know that they have been censored on what they can document.

'My parents pride themselves on their attention to detail, and they started to notice that some of the records when the monarchy took power looked tampered with,' Roman says, now addressing the rest of the group. My palms sweat and I have to stop myself from interrupting. 'There were more questions than answers, especially around some of the families who banded together right at the start of all of this to rebuild society. Names that simply faded away, families who disappeared without a trace. No record of them whatsoever. History tells us it was simply Dwynwen's Vandervere family that changed the course of history, alongside the monarchy. Mum and Dad didn't believe this to be true. But then they started to realise that old history books were being destroyed, banned. They knew for certain that Dwynwen's ancestors burnt history books. Mum and Dad were employed to write history, and at first they thought they were, until they were asked to make changes, and then told that they had to omit some true accounts of lived experiences to better fit the narrative.'

'So, what are you saying?' I ask. 'That the climate isn't a mess? That the population didn't decline? That we've been sold a lie?'

Roman shakes his head, brow furrowed. 'The change of the climate is a very real issue, and people have died because of it, and they still are. What you've been told about a decline of population, about the health of those that lived before us, that is all true. What we aren't being told, though, is how people ended up in the open country. We aren't allowed to talk about them. We have no record of the families who came together to try and establish some form of efficient leadership when society crumbled. We're told the last prime minister simply conceded and the monarchy took over, but Mum says there was a lot of aggravation around that, and that it was taken by force. That there are people out there who didn't want the monarchy to take over. We've been told it was all fine, that the monarch was our saviour. What if they weren't?'

I think of Roman's talk about the monarchy a few days ago, which takes on a whole new meaning now.

Cameron nods. 'Our history books are biased.'

'And my parents have contributed to that,' Roman says, 'and they don't want to. They want to establish the truth. So, I told them I could help them. I told them I will do what I can.' Roman looks at me before adding, 'My parents are part of the House of Pluto, as are my sisters. They are observing the outside world and trying to assemble those in the hamlets who might want to join us, but like Rory says, they have to be careful and not draw attention to themselves. Ultimately, they are trying to document the truth.'

'Dwynwen also comes from a long line of historians,' Rory says. 'There are portraits, too, of her family. Little plaques about who they were. They've been responsible for collectively assembling our history.'

It's not surprising, I suppose, considering Mother Mai is still going strong and letting us know what once happened. Dwynwen's collection of books is record-keeping, essentially.

'Without her family we'd know nothing,' Rory concludes.

'A bit of a stretch,' Johnny says.

'But Roman's parents...' I begin.

Rory shakes his head. 'You ever looked at your history books?'

'No.'

Cameron rolls his eyes with a groan.

'Ever looked at who publishes them, and your study material?'

Johnny blinks. 'Again, no.'

Some of the group laugh, including me.

'The publishing company is Vandervere,' Cameron says. 'Dwynwen Vandervere.'

'It's run by Mother Mai's husband and their sons. Dwynwen probably thought of going into it, but they're quite a traditional-values family, from what I gather,' Rory says. 'The men run the business; the women go into teaching. That sort of thing.'

I turn to Roman. 'Your mum and dad?'

'Employed by the Vandervere company.'

My stomach twists and my head pounds. Roman has always been hard to fathom, and now I know why. He's been keeping a secret. No wonder nobody has been able to get close to him. No wonder I haven't been able to work him out.

'Blake.' I say his name in a whisper. 'Did you know him?'

Roman shakes his head. 'I didn't. We never spoke.'

'I wanted to protect him,' Rory adds.

I suppose it is some solace that Roman hasn't had a secret friendship with my best friend and kept it from me. Though it still hurts, because the three of us could have been in this together.

'Roman and I became allies back in our previous school,' Rory says. 'So, when I transferred, I wanted to bring Roman with me.'

'It wasn't because you worked hard?' I ask him.

Roman sighs, shakes his head. 'I worked hard, but only to get here to continue to help Rory.'

'But you said your dad wanted you to transfer. That he wasn't happy unless you were a Ganymede's student.'

'I know. Please, know that I told you what I could. A half-truth. I wanted to tell you more.'

All the new emotions threaten to overwhelm me, and I close my eyes, wishing to blot out all that is before me.

'What worries me,' says Elis, and I'm thankful for his interruption, 'is that if one family controls all our history books, and publishes all of our study materials, does that not mean they can print whatever the hell they want and none of it gets fact-checked?'

Maybe Dwynwen isn't to be trusted, after all. But how can we be certain? It's not like we can go and corroborate history with those from the past. The climate has changed. Our lifestyle has changed because it has to. It's lived experience, not lies.

But, I think, what if Vandervere *are* obscuring the truth, as Elis suggests? What if they feed us what we need to know, and leave the bigger picture out of it? What if the bias of the press, the rise of misinformation from unregulated media organisations, has spilt over into our history, our education? How do we distinguish fact from fiction?

What is the truth?

My vision clouds as I think of the lessons with Mother Mai, and our textbooks full of history. History I've never questioned, merely accepted.

'But why come here and risk *your* future, Roman?' I ask him. 'If your parents are trusted by Dwynwen?'

'I wanted the truth, and I found people here who wanted the same,' he says. 'We all have our different reasons for pursuing it...' Like Rory, I think. 'And we all have our different ways. But ultimately we have to put a stop to whatever it is Vandervere, Ganymede's and perhaps the king are doing.

'Take the tasks, for example. Rory and I were arguing over task one,' Roman says. 'I wanted to recruit you, then and there, but Rory said we had to be careful. Then, during the survival task, we saw Izaaz. When I wandered off, I went to look for him, and I found him. He wouldn't speak, but he showed me a scar, right above his kidney. He said he would not join us, too afraid to come anywhere near Ganymede's again. He wouldn't say why. We're going to try and recruit those in the open country. I believe you can help us, Dylan.'

'But how...? I don't know anything.'

'You might not think you do, but your father seemed to have a connection with the king, and I want to know why that is,' Rory says. 'Like, have you ever wondered why your seemingly average family were given the contract to supply food to all of the schools? You don't question why you have been housed at Ganymede's with nobody forcing you to return to your hamlet? You don't think it odd that you have asked bold questions, made mistakes that the other boys who disappeared have made, and yet you are still here, thriving?'

I think of Roman's conversation with me on our survival task. 'You were trying to tell me about this all along.'

Roman gives a sheepish shrug. 'Rory wouldn't let me tell you, so I wanted to guide you towards us in some way. But when Elis decided you were worthy of bringing in, I let it happen. You're here now, as you should be.'

'And you want me to take action? To do something?' I ask. 'But what?'

'We're piecing that together,' Rory says.

'But even if we ... I don't know ... protest or something, we'd be arrested. It's illegal.'

A recent memory comes into my mind.

'There is something,' I say. 'After my same-sex talk, Dwynwen took me to her office. I thought I was getting expelled. But she showed me a book...'

'We know about the book,' Rory says.

'You do? Okay. When I was leaving, Lawrence was there, and they closed the door on me. I was going to leave, honestly, but then I heard them talk about the sickness.'

Rory nods. 'There are lots of whispers right now about the sickness. I'm sure it must be connected.'

'What is the sickness?'

'It's a virus, somewhat similar to one that came many years before and took people out,' Rory says. 'People are coming over sick and weak and some aren't surviving. Healthy people, like us.'

'Should we be worried?' I ask. 'Is there anything we can do?'

'About the sickness? Not really,' Elis says. 'Nobody comes in or out except at term breaks, so the chances of the sickness reaching us here are slim. But as for everything else, yes, there are things you can do. Right now, Dylan, you have influence. Your words resonate with people, whether they want to admit it or not. You're a strength to us, Dylan, and we need to start getting the school to be aware. If we all woke up, we could win, but the likelihood of that happening is slim. Instead, we have people distributing what we learn. Anonymously, if need be, or, in your case, you continue to voice your thoughts. For some reason you're allowed to. People like a leader, and you, Dylan, have the potential to be a leader.'

'I don't know why you think that.'

'Really? You never looked at yourself in the mirror? Checked how you carry yourself?'

'Can't say I have.'

'Totally normal thing to do,' Johnny says, flexing his arms.

Elis smiles. 'It is, actually. You speak diplomatically, and your confidence has grown, even if you don't realise it, and it isn't too jarring. You carry people with you, your words and your steadiness and your courage.' He pauses. 'What we are attempting has its dangers, but you won't be alone. We'll support you and protect you and keep you safe.

'It all comes down to this,' he says. 'Are you happy to leave here tonight knowing what you know, and continue walking blindly into society hoping that you'll be happy, that it will be how you expect it to be? I'd have thought you would want a society where you are free to be who you are.'

I shake, my head dropping, afraid of meeting anyone's eye.

'Do not be afraid,' Grady puts in. 'We're working for a society where everyone belongs, because we are already here, and we always have been.'

'You're safe here,' Elis says.

I look up at them all in their robes, glowing red and amber with the candlelight. Am I really that transparent? I think of Cameron and Johnny, who have asked me, who have been friends with me, who have surely suspected something at some point. How Taylor is like a shark to my bleeding wounds.

Perhaps I'm not as subtle as I thought. Perhaps everything I've tried to conceal is my strength and power.

I don't want to dwell on it. I want to change this subject to something safer.

'Professor Lawrence has newspapers. Rory, what's in the news?'

'Our news is just as biased as our history books,' Rory says. 'But Professor Lawrence seems to be getting newspapers that he doesn't want anyone to know about, including the professors. I suspect he has print media that is forbidden.'

'Then we must see what is inside it.'

Rory nods. 'I've been trying, but Lawrence trusts nobody.'

'He seems to trust Dwynwen.'

Rory thinks about this. 'Only so much, I would say.'

'Do you think he is loyal to Ganymede's?'

'I don't know where Professor Lawrence's loyalties lie,' Rory says. 'But I know he has been looking after you, Dylan, and I suggest you keep him close, but do not tell him of us.'

I swallow, thinking things through. If Lawrence has been protecting me, why? If boys are being expelled, if families are disappearing without a trace, why am I still here? Is everyone in this room preoccupied with conspiracy theories they have conducted in their heads, or is there something to each theory? The sickness, Blake's death, missing people. Somewhere amongst it all is the truth, buried under lies and manipulated stories.

'Together, we can make a change,' Rory says to everyone. 'We can grant freedom, truly make people happy in their new lives. We need equality, not class schooling systems which result in a class of living. We're at the cusp of something here, and we need to look out for one another and band together. The truth will prevail.'

Roman looks at me, offering me a small smile. 'So, are you in?'

Influence is suddenly mine, and yet, do I want it? What influence can I truly have? Men with influence come with a streak of danger.

Influence is dangerous in this society.

'I'm in,' I say.

CHAPTER 43

'A task of strength.' Omar's voice echoes even outdoors. 'You can outsmart your opponent, or even knock him down, but beware of doing so, for you might not like what comes of it.'

There are cast iron pots before us, medium-sized, old as time itself. They remind me of ancient woodlands and witchcraft. Positioned in the grass, they look rather tame for what Omar is saying to us gathered third-years. Every shuffle or huff of breath is magnified as we stand in shorts and vests, gym gear provided to us in colours of black and silver, and my knees knock against each other as I survey the crowd, seeing muscled boys, hoping I get someone more aligned to my own body strength and type.

'You have debated and fought for your right to speak,' Omar says. 'Ganymede's does not condone violence, and indeed, society does not encourage it. A man should diplomatically alleviate grievances, rather than use his fists. So, your physical strength will be tested in another way.'

He looks at us all, and I cross my arms.

'Dylan, you're first,' Omar says. 'Step up to a cauldron,' he orders. 'And ... ah, Taylor. You will be Dylan's opponent.'

Taylor turns to me, a wide smirk, eyes alighting on his next victim. I try not to look like I've been cornered. Instead, I accept, walking to the furthest cauldron, in the hope that maybe fewer people will see my defeat. Omar orders more pairs of boys to more cauldrons, and then he crosses the grass and takes a whistle out of his pocket. and stands by a large bell. 'You must lift a cauldron above your head, and you must stand with it above your head until your partner gives up, or until time is called.'

Is that it? I eye the cauldron, lid atop it. How hard can this be? Taylor shrugs his shoulders, jogs on the spot, ready to go.

'I'm intrigued by the outcomes,' Omar says, smiling. 'On the count of three, then. One ... two ... three...'

The whistle blows, and a Mars boy lets out an almighty roar, lifting his cauldron like it's a kettlebell. His opponent, a Jupiter lad, is hit with it, falling to the floor. Omar calls time, and the Jupiter boy limps back into the castle, the Mars boy grinning. What a dirty tactic, I think, and yet Omar is nodding and making a note in a journal. I hope Taylor doesn't get any funny ideas, and I think that once I lift my cauldron I'm going to get as far away from him as possible. Thankfully, everyone else seems to be following the main idea: holding their cauldrons above their heads, with looks of pained concentration.

Taylor cricks his neck. 'You ready?'

Strength, strength.

I can do this. I crouch, putting my hands either side of the cauldron, feeling the rough chill. Taylor heaves his with a huff, holds it to his chest, crouched low. Then, with one fluid push, he stands tall, cauldron above his head. For one horrible moment, he sways, as his lips press together and his eyes squeeze shut, but then he seems to root himself to the earth and the cauldron glistens in the sun, and there he stands, like a statue carrying the world.

Heat on my skin, I whisper a silent prayer to Saturn, and I put all my effort into lifting the cauldron. Something slides inside it, towards me then away, hitting the sides of the cauldron with a dull thud. I try not to think much of it, somehow lifting it above my head. My arms tremble and I lock my elbows into place, stumbling ever so slightly. Omar watches me, almost waiting for me to fall. Taylor, now fully in control, grins wickedly at me.

Strength, Dylan. Summon your strength.

I ground myself, using techniques from Lawrence's class, and I think of all the time I spent in our strength classes with Omar, using the weights. I've lifted heavier. Granted, I've not had to hold it above my head, or think about how painful it would be to drop cast iron upon my skull, but there we are.

Something moves again in my cauldron as sweat drips down my forehead. It feels almost like liquid. Liquid carrying something solid, I think.

'Two minutes gone,' Omar says.

'Do you hear something?' Taylor asks.

I try and ignore him, thinking this is his way of distracting me. If there's one thing I'm certain I can't trust, it's posh toff Taylor.

Hisssssssssss.

My eyes fly open, peering at the bottom of my heavy, shifting cauldron.

'You do, don't you?' Taylor asks me. 'You hear it too?'

'Something the problem?' Omar asks us, as he strolls on by.

'I can hear hissing,' Taylor says.

'Oh, yes, that will be the snakes.' Omar walks on, ignoring the shouts of protests from us and those nearby.

Flared fearful eyes look around the group and peer at the

cauldrons above our heads. Snakes. That's what is inside these cauldrons. No wonder they're so heavy, and no wonder something seems to be moving. I'm holding snakes above my head.

'Are they poisonous?' Cameron whimpers.

'Hopefully you won't have to find out,' Omar says.

Someone yelps, and I turn in horror to see a boy falling, cauldron crashing to the ground. The lid pops off, and those nearest run, yelling, as two thick brown snakes uncoil onto the earth. The boy on the ground scurries back as one of the snakes begins to wrap itself around his leg. He breaks free and runs to safety, standing at the entrance to the school, waiting for Omar to say he can go.

The snakes slither through the grass, flicking their tongues at ankles and the jumping feet that are trying to avoid getting anywhere near what must be boa constrictors.

'Don't worry about them,' Omar says. 'Security will find them later.'

Holding my cauldron, I move as far away as I can without looking like I'm trying to avoid the snakes, but all the while I think about them above my head, waiting for me to fail. What if they wrap themselves around me? What if I were to die under Omar's gaze? My skin protests at the burning on my neck and my exposed skin. My shoulders scream in agony as the muscles feel like they're being ripped, shred by shred. Taylor follows me, grinning.

'Just drop it, Dylan,' he says. 'You're weak. Boys like you can never be strong.'

Boys like me? I know exactly what he means, and he doesn't mind who hears it. I peer over his shoulder, seeing Lee struggling with his own cauldron, and Jackson standing stock still as if in meditation. What do they see in him?

As something moves within my cauldron, something shifts

within me. Taylor stands before me, a boy who thrives upon the misery and fear of others. I think of the Pluto group, what they expect of me. And suddenly, Taylor seems like a mere blade of grass, easily stamped beneath my feet.

Because, as he follows me, straining with his own cauldron, I see him for what he is. A broken, fearful boy. A boy who will gladly stay within a society built for his kind. All of this is for boys like Taylor, I think.

No more.

If I'm to make a change, it must start with how I see others. And what power I let them have over me.

'You, Taylor, are a bully,' I say, voice loud enough to attract those who are watching, including Roman, whose muscles strain, even though he holds his cauldron with confidence. 'You have always been a bully.'

Taylor guffaws, but it's weak. Shallow. Pathetic.

'Only you could be educated in emotional intelligence, and still be unable to control your emotions,' I say, and Omar is coming closer now, listening. Elis grins, and for a second, I despise Pluto. I have a stage of my own, another platform, another way to talk, to be heard. 'Boys like you don't belong in society.'

It's like I've slapped him. Taylor's mouth drops as he looks at me, whispering, 'What did you say?'

'There is no room in society for boys like you.' I turn to the crowd. 'Everyone, listen up.' My voice echoes, and for once I'm glad. 'Taylor is a bully. He gets his kicks from stamping upon those he deems weaker than him. Men like Taylor are the old men,' I say. 'The men who had to assert their dominance by intimidation and scare tactics. Machismo. But what Taylor has failed to grasp is that in the long run, it won't help him survive.'

Omar tilts his head. I can't tell what he might be thinking.

Strength, Dylan, I think. 'Strength, to me is mental

resilience. It's being able to stand up for what you believe in. It's being able to wipe the smirk from your opponent's face without lifting a finger, keeping your honour and dignity intact.

'I do not want to be part of a society that has men like Taylor in it.' I raise my voice so that it reaches those in the back. 'Because, to me, that will be a signifier that society has failed. I address this to you, Professor Omar.' Everyone turns to our teacher, and Omar stands tall. 'You are witnessing my strength right now. I do not fight. I will not fight. It is beneath me. Instead, I tell you this. Taylor does not belong in society. You, Ganymede's, have the power to make sure he doesn't join us.' I pause, seeing some boys peer at me with abject fear. Elis's throat bobs. Taylor doesn't move, even though I'm sure he wants to knock my head clean off my shoulders. If he wasn't holding constricting snakes above me, I'm sure he would be wrapping his hands around my neck. 'Unless, of course, he changes his ways.'

I hold my breath.

'Taylor?' Omar asks.

I finally look at him. The boy who has made my three years hell here. The boy who has targeted me in private, when nobody else is watching. Exposed, on display, raw.

Taylor grips the cauldron as if it is the only thing keeping him standing upright, his eyes glistening with tears.

'Taylor. Do you agree?' Omar presses.

Taylor, realising that all eyes are on him, clamps his mouth shut and with an upward thrust throws the cauldron as far as he can, darting with speed from underneath it. The lid bursts open, and two more snakes tumble out, twisting to orientate themselves. Then Taylor wipes at his tears before considering me. He steps closer, and despite every nerve in my body telling me to bolt, I stand still, as mightily proud as I can. My cauldron wobbles, but I keep firm. He spits, right in my face. Hot, wet, sliding from my nose. I flinch, but I don't move, not even when some of the boys make sounds of shock. Taylor narrows his eyes, and says, 'If you've fucked this for me, you're dead.'

He turns, pushes through the crowd and slams through the entrance doors, which slam just as hard behind his retreating figure.

Left standing with snakes at my feet and cauldron above my head, I see Elis nodding, Johnny's amused expression, Cameron's look of wonder. But it's Roman who makes me smile. He's laughing, silently, attracting the looks of those nearby.

'If you don't mind, Professor Omar, I believe I am done here.'

'Quite,' Omar says, and watches me set down my intact cauldron, hop neatly over the two constrictors and leave the boys standing displaying their strength, while I am in awe of my own courage.

CHAPTER 44

'That was incredible.' Roman shields his eyes from the sun, which is a relief because he doesn't see my face turn to thunder.

Since the House of Pluto meeting, I've avoided him. The heat of the sun presses upon my neck, and I stomp away, hoping Roman doesn't follow, knowing, though, that he will.

'Honestly, Dylan, everyone was talking about it.'

'I thought of one of our first divination lessons,' I say, petulantly. 'I remember going through the meaning of each card. Strength always stuck with me.'

'Internal strength.' Roman nods. 'Taming a situation. Strength comes in many ways, and it isn't just physical.'

We round the school and find a small Italian-style courtyard shrouded in shade. There's a water fountain here, a rugged statue of Neptune rising from the ocean, horses with their mouths open around him. His trident spouts water from its three points, landing in a white and blue tiled basin. Roman looks at me and my chest heaves. Is that admiration I see? 'You showed guts. Did you see Taylor's face?'

'I think he wants to kill me after that.'

'He'll have to go through me first.'

We look at one another, perched upon the basin, a few feet apart.

'Were you ever going to tell me?'

'I knew you were being weird with me,' Roman says.

'Uh, yeah. You take me to a crypt and suddenly you're this whole other person.'

'I'm not a whole other person, Dyl. I've been honest with you. As honest as I can be.'

'How do I know I can trust you? How do I know who the real you is?'

Roman chuckles at this, but it quickly fades when he sees I'm not smiling. 'Go on, then.'

'What do you mean?'

'Ask me anything. I don't know what else I can do to make you trust me, Dylan, so ask me anything.'

'There's plenty I could ask you, but what I keep thinking about is who you were before Ganymede's. You're ... dangerous. A rebel.'

Roman smiles at this, as if I've complimented him. 'I like the sound of that.'

'Be serious.'

Roman puts his hands either side of him, leaning back as if he might tip into the basin. 'I have been a lonely boy, Dylan, and I will be an even lonelier man. That thought doesn't frighten me. It never has. To be alone is nourishing to the soul. To be alone is a power in itself.'

'It's dangerous, Roman.'

'What's dangerous is being moulded into what someone else deems to be perfect,' Roman says. 'The fact they're trying to stamp out people like us because they think it's for some greater good. I'm sick of it, Dylan. Sick of all of this.'

'Keep your voice down, will you?' But my ears are pricked at his words. 'People like us?'

Roman looks at me. 'If you're not ready to talk about what you said in those woods...'

'No, it's not that. *Us?*'

Roman swallows, looking afraid. I shift closer, imploring him to speak, knowing I shouldn't probe, and yet I have to know.

'I've never fitted into this world, Dylan. It's like I've been awake in a world of sleepwalkers all my life. People parroting the same thing, the same dedications to the king, the same gratitude for a life they think they've chosen but that has really been chosen for them. How can I be happy in a society that has always made it clear that I should not belong? That I am some anomaly? Society would have me think that we no longer exist. That they have rid us of our desires...'

What are your desires, Roman? I think.

'We have to be the change we want to see,' he continues. 'We have to speak up when things are wrong. We belong, Dylan. You and me.'

He stops and looks at me, and my heart threatens to burst out of me.

'I'm gay, too, Dyl,' he says. 'I've known it since I was fifteen. And you know how I felt when I realised it to be true? I didn't feel afraid. I didn't even feel ashamed, which society wants us to think. I felt free. Happy. Like I had all the answers. And I was angry. Angry at the world, not at me. Angry because to them I wasn't right, but to me I am perfect already. And it's that anger that fuels me to make this change. Because I have nothing to lose. If nothing changes, then I walk out of here come graduation and I refuse to repopulate and I make some poor woman miserable, and I'm done for anyway.'

I feel a burst of happiness but try not to show it in my

expression. I envy him his courage. How I wish I could be as brave as him, as open as him, as accepting of myself as he is.

Call it riding an emboldened wave, but I close the gap between us, my hand slipping behind him. He looks at me, uncertain, and it makes me reconsider everything. But then his hand comes behind me, rests upon my waist, and he pulls me ever so closer.

'I'm really proud of you,' Roman whispers, eyelashes fluttering as he observes me.

'Are you?'

'Oh, yeah,' Roman croons. 'When Omar put you together with Taylor, my heart dropped.'

'Hey, I held my own.'

'You did.' I catch Roman's gaze drop to my lips, back to me again, and any reservations I had after our Pluto meeting melt. 'You're going to destroy me, Dylan.'

'Not if you destroy me first.'

My head tilts, and Roman's does too. He leans in, and I stay where I am, allowing him to touch his lips upon my own. It's a light touch, uncertain, and I nod, whisper 'Yes', but he pauses.

'I can't,' he says, pulling away from me.

'Roman...'

'We can't. This isn't...'

'If you don't want to, I won't make you,' I say.

'No, I know.'

'But I have to ask ... where do I stand with you?'

Roman shakes his head, angling his body away from mine. 'I wasn't afraid until I met you, Dylan.'

I laugh, thinking back to our first task. 'It's you that's supposed to scare me.'

Roman considers me. I'm dying under his stare, wishing he would do something. 'I don't think so. Not anymore.'

His right hand comes up and massages his chest, an

unthinking move on his part, I guess, but I imagine he is touching his heart.

'I've never felt this way before,' he says. 'I've never been more certain of who I am than I am right now looking into your eyes. For the first time, my true self scares me. What I am prepared to do scares me. It's like everything has been waiting dormant inside me, and you're the catalyst. I thought I was driven to make change before, but now I'm in full flight. If change gives us a chance to be together, I'm prepared to risk it all. Let the world burn, if only to allow us to rise from the ashes as glorious phoenixes.'

His warm eyes are alight with desire, his words scorching my soul. I touch his hand, linking my fingers through his, and I lift it to my lips, kissing his knuckles. He watches me, shivers at the brush of my lips. He bites his own and I want him to bite mine, want to feel him take over every rational part of my survivalist brain.

'Charlotte Bronte once wrote, "Prejudices, it is well known, are most difficult to eradicate from the heart whose soil has never been loosened or fertilised by education: they grow there, firm as weeds among stones." That has always stuck with me,' I say, voice cracking. 'I discovered it once in a library, lost in the hedgerows of old books. I remember that quote rooting itself within me, because I thought we have been educated to be prejudiced, whether we know it or not.'

'A prejudice is taught; it is not innate.'

I nod, letting my hand slip from his, because if I go as far as I want to go, we will never come back from it. 'Thank you for telling me who you are.'

'Thank you for listening.'

I can almost reach out and touch the shift that has transpired between us. He kept a secret from me, but his secret went deeper than I could have thought. I don't know what is right, but I know I cannot leave Roman. He is my life source, my driving power.

'We should probably go back,' Roman whispers, his hand finding mine, linking with it, and we rest them upon the wall between us.

'I don't want to,' I whisper. 'Not yet.'

Because I know I would be leaving this open, vulnerable side of him. As soon as we are back out there, he will be that masked, ambivalent mystery again. We spend time merely sitting comfortably together, occasionally holding hands, other times listening to the pollinating bees, the flying birds, the hypnotising water. We enjoy the benefits of the warmth without the searing sun. But as time goes on, the shadows creep closer and closer, and we know our sanctuary cannot remain so for much longer. I can't help glancing at him, wanting to tell him that all I want to do is taste him.

We head back to school, climb the steps and walk into the grand entrance. Our walk is slow, as if we are reluctant to leave the courtyard behind.

Halfway up the stairs, Dwynwen's voice rings behind us.

'Mr Cecil. A word, if you don't mind.'

CHAPTER 45

This time I'm done for. Sitting in the same chair across from Dwynwen again, who's observing me like I'm putting on a show for her, when all I'm doing is waiting for the inevitable.

'Professor Omar told me about your performance in today's task.'

Huh. This wasn't what I was expecting. My close call with Roman has my mind elsewhere, and that adrenaline I felt from standing up to Taylor, and even tentatively stepping into the role Elis has suggested to me, has now become a distant memory.

'He has?'

'He thought your interpretation of strength was interesting,' Dwynwen says, but she isn't smiling. 'But you humiliated Taylor in front of his classmates. No man should humiliate another.'

'Yes, Headmistress,' I murmur.

Dwynwen sighs. 'You've been an A grade student up until this point, Mr Cecil, so tell me what happened?'

'What happened, Headmistress?'

'Why did you speak to Taylor in that way?' Dwynwen considers me carefully. 'It seems out of character for you.'

I ponder this. Maybe it is. Or maybe Dwynwen doesn't know me, or even the students, as well as she thinks she does. I can't tell her about the House of Pluto, and I can't tell her that all of the thoughts I've had about my parents' death, around the tasks, around some of our education, are now coming together to form a bigger picture. I can't tell her that I'm thinking differently than I ever have. So, instead, I say, 'I wanted to show that there is such a thing as emotional strength, and that standing up to your fellow man does not always have to be physical. Instead, I showed diplomacy and maturity, and I think that should be noted.'

'And you don't think we have noted that?'

'Forgive me, Headmistress, but it seems as though I have done something wrong.'

Dwynwen sighs, clasping her hands together. 'Not entirely, Mr Cecil. Though I would like to know the bigger picture.'

I look around me, at the shelves of books, pretending like I'm taking it all in when really I'm waiting to naturally come across the book with my name in it. All of my details, my history. My partner. And every other student, too. Blake, Roman. I think I see it on the shelf, where Dwynwen put it back before. I try not to look too long, aware that Dwynwen is waiting for me to speak.

'For three years I have been bullied by Taylor,' I say, meeting her eye. 'You might not be aware, Headmistress, but there are bullies in this school, despite all our education.'

Dwynwen takes a deep breath, sitting a little taller. 'Have you told anyone of this?'

'I didn't see the point,' I say.

'And why is that?'

'Taylor, and his friends ... they're clever. It's like to everyone else they can do no wrong, and I've seen the way he switches. He puts on the good boy, the emotionally intelligent boy, the boy he's supposed to be. But then when he gets me alone...'

'Why is he bullying you?'

My hands start to ball into fists, but I unfurl my fingers, sliding them underneath my legs. 'I don't really know.'

Dwynwen's lips purse. 'There must be a reason.'

'You'd have to ask him.' *Please don't ask him.*

'If I were to call Taylor into my room, he would tell me that he is a bully?'

I laugh, knowing I shouldn't, my head dropping in defeat. 'I don't think so, Headmistress.'

'Then how do I know who is telling the truth?'

I snap up. 'There's a witness, Headmistress.'

'Oh?'

'Roman Edwards.'

Is that discomfort on Dwynwen's face? Or am I reading into it with my guilty conscience?

'What did he see, exactly?'

'Taylor being a bully.' Roman won't say that I was fighting back. He needn't say he offered to help. Unless he wanted to. What's important is he can back up the story. 'And Johnny and Cameron share a room with us. He's made some comments there, too, if that helps.'

Dwynwen leans forward on an elbow, her fingers and thumb rubbing together. 'Thank you for telling me this, Mr Cecil.'

'Of course, Headmistress.'

My palms sweat and my foot won't stay still. She's watching me but the silence kills me.

'You're a good pupil, I want you to know that. Society will be lucky to have you. However—' Dwynwen pauses here and I wish she wouldn't. I almost beg, almost try and tell her to leave it on the positive, but there's no time. 'I'm going to have to give you a warning. You must abide by the tasks as they are set out. You trod a thin line between your version of strength and what was actually required. You scrape by with a pass.'

I wait to see if she's going to say any more, as anger begins to simmer within me.

'Thank you, Headmistress. I ... appreciate it.' I put on a fake-grateful smile.

'You may leave,' she says, and smiles.

My eyes flick to the book, back to her, and I nod and rise, leaving before she can change her mind or ask me anything else.

CHAPTER 46

'A warning? Really?'

We stand, all of us in robes, in the House of Pluto crypt.

Elis paces, shaking his head. 'Why would she just give you a warning? If anyone else had done something like you did, they would be expelled, I'm certain of it.'

'Not necessarily,' Rory says.

'Oh, don't play the devil's advocate with me,' Elis says, finger wagging in Rory's direction. 'Why is Dylan getting special treatment?'

I blush, despite it all. 'I don't think it's special treatment, as such—'

'I think it is,' Ben says, and I think of his brother.

'You shouldn't have passed the task. End of,' Elis says, swiping his hands in a cross.

'She told me I was a good student,' I say. 'Maybe that's why she's giving me another chance.'

'Bullshit,' Elis mutters.

'Hey, I am a good student.'

'Oh, not that,' Elis snaps. 'No, there's something else going on.'

'Maybe let it lie, Elis,' Johnny says. 'Just be thankful we still have Dylan with us and that he hasn't let on about what's going on here.'

I'd told them about how Dwynwen had asked why I'd seemingly changed, why I was standing up to people like Taylor. I'd even told Roman that his name had come up in conversation as a witness to what Taylor is really like.

'If she believed it,' Elis says.

'Why wouldn't she believe it? It's true,' I say. 'Taylor is a bully and it's about time he was called out on it.'

'Dylan's here, he's safe, and so are we,' Johnny says to the group. 'Elis, chill out.'

'Yes, Elis,' Rory says emphatically. 'Please.'

Elis takes a breath, then shakes his head and stops pacing. 'Fine. Whatever. Not my problem.'

'There's something else,' I say. 'I think there's a way I can get information for you.'

'There is?'

'Have you ever been in Dwynwen's office?' I ask Rory.

'No, she doesn't seem to let anyone in.'

'Even though you're a professor?'

'Seems Lawrence is the only one she trusts.'

I sigh. 'I can get the book tonight,' I say. 'And I'll find the papers.'

'No, Dylan,' Roman says. 'That's ridiculous.'

'I have to,' I say. 'I need to know.'

There's an itch crawling over my skin, a weight in my chest, twisting coils in my stomach. Safety doesn't feel obtainable anymore. I need the truth on whether or not I belong. I need to know why I am being looked after. I need to know if there's information on my parents. And I need to discover what really resulted in Blake's death.

It's all in that book.

All in the school.

It's been there all along.

'I think he should go,' Petro says. 'A perfect opportunity to prove himself.'

'Or, to put it in a politer way, I think we need solid evidence,' Ben says. 'If Dylan is happy to get it for us, then why shouldn't we let him?'

'Because...' Roman says. 'Because he will get caught.'

Roman told me that change is worth the risk, worth the danger. Maybe he feels differently when it comes to me, my safety? I hide a smile and turn back to the others.

'I won't get caught,' I tell them, hoping someone agrees with me. 'Look, you all seem to think that I have a shield around me, and maybe I do to some extent, but I don't think I will be protected if I am caught. And I am willing to risk finding out. Because after all, I have come to realise that I have nothing. Nothing to lose. No one to disappoint. I have been living for a dead man, and now I am living for me. I can be careful. I can be as elusive as my magician archetype suggests I am. You've said it yourself, the newspapers carry true information, and something tells me those books in Dwynwen's office haven't been censored yet. I think she documents true history, and it all comes from her collection.'

Roman nods, though he still seems hesitant.

'Let me do this. I promise it will be worth it.'

There's silence, like death itself has entered the room.

'Then let's all do this,' Rory says. 'Plutonians, it's time for action.'

CHAPTER 47

'Dylan.' Roman grips me, spins me around. 'Dylan, you're not thinking straight.'

I shrug his grip from my shoulders. 'I'll be careful, I promise.'

'You're acting the fool.'

'All those who were considered fools were so until they were proven right.'

'What are you going to do? Just go in there and break into Dwynwen's office?'

'Uh, that's exactly what I'm going to do, yes.'

'Dylan.'

Our group left two at a time, so as not to draw attention to ourselves. We agreed that I would get the book, and the others would focus on distracting Professor Lawrence if needs be, keeping an eye out for other rule-bending students, professors or security guards, and getting their hands on newspapers. Roman was not supposed to come with me, because I need to focus, and I can't focus after our afternoon in that courtyard.

'Dylan.' Roman's voice is insistent and I turn around.

'Are you coming or not?' I turn back and start heading to the creaking gate, Ganymede's silhouetted by the moonlight and clouds that drift across the dark sky. It's not that late, not even midnight, and yet it feels later. Windows aglow with candlelight. Dwynwen's office is pitch-black. She could be there, right now, I think, watching us.

Behind me, Roman says, 'If we get in trouble...'

'There's no "we".'

'I'm coming with you, you fool.'

'Okay, but stay quiet.'

I've got to keep focused. There's a confidence within me, telling myself I can get a hold of this book and bring it back to the crypt, so that we can explore the contents and find answers.

There's freedom in the realisation that I can only live for me. Only answer to me. It's this or nothing.

My heart thuds as we cross the expanse of grounds, past sparkling lake and over uneven terrain. We take the servants' door back into the castle, not wanting to walk into the main foyer when we're past curfew.

'What's the plan, then?' Roman asks me, racing behind me as I take the servants' stairs two at a time.

'You're really going to do this?'

'I'll do anything for you,' Roman replies. It halts me. 'I mean it. What are we going to do?'

I fight back tears, composing myself with a deep breath.

'Get the book, get out.'

Roman nods. 'I'll keep watch.'

'Do whatever you think is best.'

Roman's hand reaches mine and grabs it. He strengthens his grip and I pause, the door leading to the floor I need only a few feet away.

'Dylan,' he breathes. 'I'm on your side. You know that, right?'

I soften, nodding my head. 'I know that.'

He steps closer, taking my other hand in his, and we look at one another through the dim darkness.

I soften, and whisper, 'I'm sorry. I'm just...'

'Take a few seconds, take a breath. Slow down. Charging in there is going to do more damage than it's worth. You can't just run in. What if she's in there, sat at her desk?'

'I...' I wince. Because I hadn't thought of that, which is reckless.

Roman smiles. 'And what if there are professors or students hanging around in the corridor?'

'Good point.'

Roman chuckles. 'So, let's do this properly. Come on.'

He lets go of my hands and slips ahead of me. He tries the door first, opening it so that a sliver of candlelight penetrates the dark stairwell. Tentatively, Roman steps forward, holding the door open for me to follow. We walk the corridor, take one flight of the main stairs and emerge on the floor of Dwynwen's office. The brown doors are closed.

I almost expect to see someone, anyone, who might stop us. We approach Dwynwen's door.

'I'll do it,' I say. 'Keep watch for me.'

Roman's eyes flicker between me and the door. Finally, he nods.

I place my hand on the door, allowing myself a brief moment to collect my thoughts. An excuse ready on my lips, I twist the doorknob, wincing as the metal makes a clicking noise. I hold my breath, tense, and open the door, feeling it lighten in my grip. I push it away from me, inch by inch, almost expecting it to groan beneath my fingertips. If Dwynwen's in there, she's going to know I'm up to something by how long it's taken me to open this office door. I poke my head through when it's open wide enough. Darkness rushes at me, my eyes struggling to adjust. There's no movement, no response. Just one solitary light glowing behind the frosted glass that leads to Dwynwen's apartment.

The moonlight glimmers through the windowpanes, illuminating her desk, where an empty goblet sits next to a half-drunk bottle of red wine. These professors are so brazen with their drinks – I wonder if any of the students have secretly swiped some alcohol for themselves over the years. You can make better men, but you're still going to have mischief.

I don't dare look back at Roman, in case I lose precious time. I dip into Dwynwen's office, the door slips from my grasp, and I quickly stop it from thudding shut with my knee and foot. The wood hits me hard, and I bite through the pain, steadying the door so that it hovers open enough for me to get out. Embers glow in the fireplace, a scent of extinguished smoke in the air. The spectre of the graveyard on the green landscape is beyond, blighting the greenery like a disease.

Get the book, get out.

I cross the threshold of the room, leaving behind the safety of the corridor and Roman, and the innocence that comes with it. I scan the shelves, heading to the corner where the book with all my information is contained. The truth about Blake. The rest of the boys.

I stop dead.

There's a gap in the shelves where the book should be. I crouch, peering at the lower shelves, before standing on tiptoe and looking above. They all look the same, these books full of history, but I specifically remember that this was the shelf she put it on. So, where the hell is it?

At random, I pick up the nearest one, feeling the weight almost topple me. I rest it on her table, careful not to disturb anything, peering in at the pages that rustle too loudly for my liking. Names I'm not familiar with, boys from five years ago.

Nothing out of the ordinary, from what I can tell. I pick three more books. The names blur into one, though I occasionally pause to study the pages stamped with 'expelled' but with no more information than that. By the fourth book, I let the pages flutter between my fingers, knowing almost immediately this isn't what I'm looking for. There's a musty smell, and the pages crack with dust, which puffs into the air. I lean back, covering my mouth, almost sneezing and giving the game away, my hand resting between the pages. Then a name catches my eye. My hand stops the page from disappearing forever, disbelief rooting me in place.

Charlie Cecil.

I look down at the page, all caution dispelled by a gust of desire to read about my father. It's the closest I've been to him in three years. The year he enrolled, a whole paragraph on his strengths in his previous studies as he's matured. There's a profile of who he should be, and, indeed, what he became. Farmer, archetypal provider, partner to Mabel. My mother. I blink away tears, thinking that even from his first day at Ganymede's, he'd had his life planned out for him. There are notes scribbled in ink that talk about his years at Ganymede's. He liked history, he 'developed emotional maturity', and he didn't like carrots. I almost laugh at this. I run my finger over the page, as if I might touch him again, feel him close. At the bottom, a hastily scribbled note:

Death upon return to Ganymede's. Belief he was coming back to take back his boy.

My knees give way and I find myself collapsing into Dwynwen's chair, staring at the handwriting, the words blurring and dancing around, and I can't make sense of anything. I knew he was coming back, but here is proof he *was* coming back, for *me*. Why?

I lean forward, aggressively wiping the tears from my eyes,

when there's a click. The dark room gets darker and my head shoots up. Before I can register what's happened, shuffling at the door of Dwynwen's apartment sends my stomach plummeting to the ground. Without thinking, I rip my father's page from the book, grasp the book and now the loose page to my chest, and duck underneath Dwynwen's table.

Just as the door to her apartment opens.

CHAPTER 48

Shit. Shit. Shit.

Movement in the room makes me press as far under the table as I can. My only exit is where I ducked in. Logic tells me I should have hidden to the side, rather than under. Footsteps trail around the table, slow, purposeful, as if the person on the other side senses a disturbance in the equilibrium of the room. To my horror, the door to the corridor is tightly shut, a key in the lock.

I press my face into the book to stifle my breathing. Cramped underneath the table, I pray that the person – Dwynwen? – is locking up for the night and will leave and then I can think properly and find a way out of here.

Footsteps approach the table and there's a clink above me and I jump. A bottle cap twists, and there is the movement of liquid pouring into a goblet. The person on the other side of the table breathes lightly, before sighing. The person sips, breath getting deeper, slower, mindful, even. Please, Saturn, get me out of here alive.

The footsteps start to come around the table, and I glimpse

movement in the darkness as the person in flowing black trousers approaches the window. It's definitely Dwynwen, with her silver hair glinting in the moonlight, and if she comes any closer, if she turns, I'm dead.

She's shaking her head, sniffing. Crying?

Knock, knock, knock.

The rap on the door makes me flinch, and Dwynwen's shoulders bunch up. She quickly wipes her face.

She turns, thankfully, in the other direction, heaving a sigh. She has the goblet to her lips and hesitates before walking out of view.

I take a slow breath, as quietly as possible. The door is unlocked and I feel the draught as it is pulled open.

'Mr Edwards? You do realise it is past your curfew?'

'I know, Headmistress, I'm very sorry.'

Roman? Oh, Saturn, I hope he's shed his Pluto robes at least. I bite my lip, not daring to move.

'It couldn't wait until morning,' Roman says. 'I've been meaning to tell you this for some time now, but I've been chickening out.'

'Is that so?'

'It's about Taylor. Would you have a moment?'

Dwynwen sighs. 'I'm about to settle down for the evening, Mr Edwards.'

'It won't take long, I promise.'

There's an excruciating silence, before she finally says, 'Okay, come in. Make it quick.'

There's noise as Dwynwen walks back to the desk, and I scuttle back as she sits on the chair, legs inches away from me. I pray she doesn't put her feet further under. 'What is it you want to say, Mr Edwards?'

'I ... I am ... nervous about telling you, but I think you should know.'

'I'm listening.'

'I caught Taylor bullying another student.'

'Dylan Cecil.'

'That's right, Headmistress, Dylan Cecil. He's a good kid. I like working with him on these tasks. He brings out the best in me and...'

'Mr Edwards?'

'Sorry, Headmistress.'

I stifle a laugh.

'While I'm glad to hear it, I would like to know what you have seen.'

'Of course. Taylor, Jackson and Lee, his friends, they've been targeting Dylan. Pushing him, hitting him, even. I caught them doing it recently. I asked Dylan why they were doing that to him, and he said they've done it since he started here. They get him alone, wind him up.'

'And how did Dylan seem to fare in this circumstance?'

'Meaning, Headmistress?'

I want to tell him to lie, but I'm too concerned that Dwynwen is so close I swear I can make out the pattern on the trousers that I thought were black only.

'Was he fighting back?'

'Dylan stood his ground, but he did not get violent,' Roman says.

'Good, good.'

I wait, holding my breath, afraid that something will give me away. Finally, Dwynwen says, 'Is there anything else, Mr Edwards?'

'No, Headmistress. That is all. I just thought you should know.'

'Okay.' Dwynwen doesn't say anything else. There's no movement. Until she says, in a light voice, 'Are you enjoying your time at Ganymede's, Mr Edwards?'

My heart turns to ice.

'Y-yes.'

'It is unusual for a boy to come to Ganymede's from another school.'

'I know, Headmistress.'

'Are you well? Are you happy?'

I wish I could see Roman's expression.

'I am, Headmistress. I'm eternally grateful to Ganymede's.'

She inhales. 'Eternally, is that so?'

Dwynwen stands, and I rest my head against the table as she walks round it. I don't dare believe it when she disappears from view.

'Thank you for telling me, Mr Edwards. All of it. Thank you.'

'Sorry to disturb your night, Headmistress.'

'It's fine. Please, do see yourself out.'

'Uh ... yes, Headmistress.'

Footsteps, one in the direction of the office door, the other to the apartment. One door clicks shut, then the other. Then...

'Come out. Now.'

CHAPTER 49

A trick. She's found me out. I'm done for. My heart thudding, I scurry out from under the table, foot colliding with one of the legs, and I curse under my breath. Dwynwen is going to kill me.

But it's not Dwynwen.

Roman beckons hurriedly to me, holding the office door open, looking anxiously at Dwynwen's apartment door. He clocks the book and loose page in my hand, and I shake my head, knowing there's no time. He follows me out, closing the door behind him, not bothering to stay quiet, and together we pelt down the hall, feet pounding the carpet, skidding to a halt and crashing through the servants' quarter doors.

Breathless, we hurry down the stairs, two, three at a time, me pushing ahead.

'Where are we going?' he asks, catching my shoulder before I can run out into the night.

'Back to the crypt,' I say.

'No, not yet,' Roman says.

'Then where do you suggest?'

Roman pauses, looking at the door that will take us outside. 'Come with me.'

He takes my hand, and pulls me up the stairs. I follow him, to the first floor, where we step out into the hall. He crosses it, pushing open a door I've never paid much attention to: bland and chipped with paint. Inside is a bathroom, and we pass the cubicles, heading straight to the communal showers.

'Uh ... I may have been sweating through my fear but I don't think a shower right now is good for me.'

'The plumbing doesn't work in here, hasn't for years,' he says, and I look properly around.

The tiles at the back of the showers are covered in sketches, drawings. People have scribbled their names or harmless jokes about one another. Some tiles are missing, broken on the floor, and rails have been taken off the wall, leaving the shower taps hanging, broken.

'Why have they let it get like this?' I ask.

'Beats me,' Roman says.

It's surprising to see something like this in Ganymede's, which is usually so refined and clean. It's like underneath the facade of what they project here is chaos and disrepair.

I turn to Roman. 'You told them about Taylor.'

Roman crosses his arms, cocks an eyebrow. 'I was trying to save your arse.'

'I mean, thanks, but bloody hell, that was close.'

'Bloody hell is right,' Roman says. 'I saw the door close and it locked and I thought the worst, so I crouched to listen. I knew you hadn't been caught, because there was silence, so I thought, fuck it, and I knocked. I had no idea where you'd bloody gone. I can't believe you hid under her desk.'

'It's not exactly like I could style it out by sitting behind it, could I? But underneath it, I caught a glimpse of Dwynwen crying.'

'Crying?'

'Yeah. It's not the first time I've seen her look sad.'

'Interesting.' Roman runs a hand over his head. 'I thought it was interesting that she asked me about my time here.'

'Me too.'

We stand together in silence, until I say, 'Also, I think these professors have a drinking problem.'

'You think?' He smiles wryly and looks at the book still in my hands. 'You got it then.'

I shake my head. 'This isn't what we were looking for.'

'What?' Roman gasps. 'You stole another book? Where's the right one?'

I shrug, sliding down to sit on the floor. 'It wasn't there. At least not in the place I saw it earlier.'

'She moved it?'

'Looks like it. I picked up as many books as I could, went through them to make sure, and then...' I put the book in my hands down on the tiled floor, staring at it like it's said something offensive. 'I saw my dad's name is in there.'

Roman crouches down by the book.

I hold the paper up. '*Was* in there, I should say.'

'You ripped it out?'

'I panicked,' I protest. 'The light went out and then she was coming to the door and I thought of running with this page, but I knew there was no time, so I grabbed the book afterwards. Couldn't leave it on her desk.'

Roman pinches the bridge of his nose, taking a moment to think. 'So, what does it say?'

I look over at him, sudden tears stinging my eyes. 'My ... mind didn't process it when I read it, but I saw the sentence, "Death upon return to Ganymede's. Belief he was coming back to take back his boy."'

Now, years of holding everything in, of dry eyes, begin to

ripple into emotion I can't control. My shoulders shake, and my face contorts into an ugly red flush. Roman leans across and hugs me to him, my tears dampening the clothes on his chest. He's ditched the Pluto robes, and this T-shirt of his feels so inherently him. He strokes my back and doesn't say a word as I sob.

'Let it out,' he whispers, breath catching my hair. 'Let it all out.'

I do. And it's glorious. When the tears finally dry and my aching face relaxes, I allow him to let me go, and when he does, I scuttle to the back wall and sit down, knees to my chest, clutching the loose page. 'They were coming back for me, Roman. Why do you think they were coming back for me?'

'I don't know. Does it say?'

I heave a shuddering breath, smoothing out the paper before me. There's the sentence I read, the one that has set me off course. But above that, there's more. The context leading up to it. A full documentation of the most important highlights of my father's life.

The first: *Charlie alerts Ganymede's of his son's birth.*

The second: *Charlie and Mabel awarded contract to provide food to Ganymede's, complementing suppliers from other hamlets.*

The third: *Cecil food farm visited by royal family.*

It continues like this, notes of how my parents functioned in society. To my surprise, at one point Dwynwen has made a note that Charlie asked if they could bring another child into the world. There's no answer from Dwynwen, but another note remarks that the couple *decide to remain with one child.*

Then, there's another note, handwriting less refined. *Keep an eye on the Cecils.*

'Weird,' Roman remarks when I relay all this to him.

Cecils' standards slipping, reads another entry, and then, *Cecil farm pulls out of contract, refusing to work.*

I stare at nothing as I think of this, never once realising that my parents had refused to work. They always seemed so happy.

Dylan admitted to Ganymede's. Charlie pressing us on his partner. Answer not given.

I scan the next entry, unable to devour it quick enough, *Cecils' correspondence ignored. Days away from son starting.*

And then the next. *Charlie meets Dwynwen. Partnership confirmed by both parties. Charlie and the king's relationship remains a mystery. Charlie insists a bond exists between him and the monarch.* I touch this part, as if it might tell me more.

Then the other. *Dylan starts Ganymede's.*

The next entry is the one I've already read, about their death. When I turn over, half the page is scrawled with notes. They read, *Parents' bodies disposed of. Money is absorbed into the crown. Estate remains in the possession of next of kin. To be discussed upon graduation.*

I truly have nothing. No inheritance, other than the home. Why has the crown absorbed all my parents earnt?

'What are you thinking?' Roman asks, when he's read the page.

'We really need to find the book that we're in,' I say.

'Then we have to go back.'

I blink. 'Really?'

Roman nods. 'Why not? We're already here, aren't we? Come on. Let's see if we can find it. I'll help you this time, too, and we can...'

He's already halfway to the door, voice drifting away from me. 'Roman, wait.'

'Yeah?'

'I'm scared.'

He crosses the room, helping me to my feet. 'I'm scared, too.'

'It's too much. All of this. All at once. My father was hiding something, something he wouldn't even tell Dwynwen. What if she's keeping me here because she thinks I know what that is? What is she going to do when she finds out I don't know anything about him? Because I don't think I ever knew my father. I've been living my life for a man who might as well be a stranger.'

Roman shakes his head and engulfs me in another one of his sturdy hugs. I sink into him, inhaling his sweet scent, relishing the way my body seems to fit every crevice of his.

'Come on,' he says. 'Let's hope they've got the newspapers.'

He's at the door, stepping out into the dimly lit hallway. I hurry after him and he takes my hand, linking his fingers in mine. The buzz of his touch sends shivers down my spine, and despite everything my lips quirk into a smile. My thumb brushes his, daring yet confident, and he looks back, winks, and I could melt right then and there. We're in the stairwell, when voices drift from below.

'The parents are getting louder. They're not letting this go.'

'And you're worried because?' It's Professor Lawrence's voice, calm and measured.

'Too much attention is being drawn to him.' Ieuan, the security guard. 'Gareth agrees with me.'

'Yeah, I do. And if there's attention drawn to him, there's attention drawn to this school, and what—' Gareth is cut off by Lawrence's voice.

'All right, I can see this is concerning you, but I promise you there is nothing to be worried about.'

'No, we have it under control.'

Roman swivels to me, looking shocked. My mouth has dropped, and I cover it with my free hand, my other hand tightening in Roman's.

'The media are not sniffing around the story. Trust me, I would know if they were,' Mother Mai says. Her voice is low, so I step onto a lower step to hear her better. I crane my neck, but

Roman holds me back from going any further. 'Since his death, there has been very little media attention.'

His death? 'Blake's?' I whisper to Roman.

He nods slowly, but looks unsure.

'But that isn't good enough,' Ieuan says. 'It's only a matter of time before—'

'We have good relations with the media,' Mother Mai insists. 'You needn't worry.'

'But we *are* worried,' Gareth says. 'What if they send someone here? Some investigator or something?'

'The king would not allow it,' Mother Mai answers.

My legs wobble, and I step closer to Roman, as if he might steady me. His face is thunder as he glowers down the stairs, towards the sound of the voices.

'Are we protected?' Ieuan asks.

'Do you really have to ask?' Mother Mai questions.

There's a still silence, the only sounds Roman's soft breathing and my beating heart.

Finally, Professor Lawrence says, 'What happened to Blake was a tragedy, but nobody will know the truth.'

CHAPTER 50

Nobody will know the truth.
What happened to Blake was a tragedy.
These thoughts echo in my head all night as if they're shouted from the top table in the breakfast hall. The sharp words crack and snap as the fission of thoughts sends shockwaves to my brain. Now I know, for certain, that Blake's death is a cover-up. It has to be. And if it is a cover-up, does that mean my parents' deaths are, too?

When dawn breaks, I look out to the lake in time to see Roman shedding his top and submerging himself in the water. He disappears under the surface, and I hold my breath as if I'm the one losing oxygen. When I don't think I can hold it any longer he disturbs the stillness of the lake and begins his swim.

It's the morning of our next task, and I wonder how he might be feeling. I consider waking Johnny and Cameron, to tell them what I've discovered, but that runs the risk of Taylor hearing us and getting involved. So I change into my own swim clothes, grab a towel and a bag, and a few moments later I find myself at the lake.

The air is warm, and it's almost as if I can hear the sizzle of the sun. Looking at Roman's rippling back sends heat through my body. He turns, a quick flash of surprise, and then he grins, giving me tingles of excitement, which steady my mind.

I breathe in as he approaches.

'Ah, you broke curfew.'

'I'm risking it all.'

He laughs at this, eyeing my swim shorts. 'You joining me?'

'Can I?'

It's a stupid question. He doesn't own the lake. I can do what I want. But this feels like his private ritual that I'm disturbing.

'I'd welcome it.'

I shed my loafer shoes and my socks, touching my T-shirt instinctively. But then I look at Roman, and I think of how his body is built differently to mine. Stronger, broader. I let go of the fabric between my fingers and step into the water.

'You're going to get your T-shirt wet.'

'I don't mind,' I say.

He considers me, but says nothing more about it. The water makes me gasp, and my teeth chatter as I get lower and lower. The water splashes against my waist and I consider running back out, feet numbing, the tingle of excitement I felt when seeing Roman no longer registering in my brain now that it is kicking into survival mode. Roman chuckles, watching me, and my T-shirt gets wetter and wetter, the fabric waterlogged. Finally, when my shoulders are under, I let out a shaking breath, moving further into the water.

'You do this every morning. Are you mad?'

'It clears my mind. You get used to the chill.' Roman nods towards the sky. 'Especially this time of year.'

He moves off and I follow him, because if I stay still, I will become ice. With more movement I feel the resistance of my body flow into acceptance, and the morning sleepiness change into something akin to invigoration.

'I want to show you something,' he whispers. 'I want to show you what you mean to me.'

Together we climb out of the lake, dry off. Roman leads me inside, back to the abandoned showers.

'Here,' he says, and beckons me inside a cubicle, which is dark and painted with indistinguishable shapes. He crouches, sliding a tile. He beckons me over, and I see the foundations of the school beneath the tile.

'Wow,' I say. Leaning up against the wall are some small canvas prints and parchment paper. Ones he can easily hide. Roman bends and starts riffling through them.

He takes out a framed A4 canvas.

'What is it?' I ask him.

'I know it's strange, but remember we spoke about art?' Roman says, holding the canvas away from me. 'It inspired me. You inspired me. I couldn't get you off my mind, and so I came down and I ... well.'

He hands me the canvas, and I take it with shaking hands. There's a faceless boy with wild black hair, dressed in a knitted maroon jumper. A jumper I recognise. A jumper I wore when he spoke to me at the statue of Ganymede.

'This is me.'

My painted, faceless features hold a single daffodil, glowing bright yellow. Judging by some of the sketching that hasn't been painted over yet, I think he might once have planned to paint me in a field of daffodils.

I loosen the grip I have on the canvas, not wanting to damage something so special. 'Why daffodils?'

'When I saw you that evening you filled me with joy,' he says, voice wobbling ever so slightly. 'Everything about you. It was like seeing you properly for the first time. Up until that point I'd been able to keep you at a distance, put any stirring thoughts aside. But that was when I knew, Dylan, that you had me. You are sun-soaked days after dark winters. You are blue skies instead of grey. When I saw you, I knew I wanted you, no, needed you, and I knew that you were my hope for a better future. You, to me, are my daffodil. My symbol of hope and rebirth. You are a beautiful youth and it is a wonder you do not fall in love with yourself when you see yourself in the mirror. If I looked like you, I would. You are Dylan, a Welsh man, and I am a reader of Dylan Thomas. I felt as though no flower has ever represented you better than a daffodil. You are my daffodil, Dylan.'

With a delicate move, I step to the shower and place the painting back where he found it. When I turn, Roman looks hurt, trying to recover. 'You are a beautiful man, Roman Edwards.'

'I probably shouldn't have painted it, but...'

'I want to live in a world where I can put that on my wall and not have to lie about the meaning behind it,' I say. 'You must keep it safe. Do not let it get into the wrong hands.'

He steps towards me hesitantly and I reach for him, placing my hands on his forearms, sliding them to cup his biceps. His eyes rove over me as if in exploration, and I stand before him and let him inspect every inch of me. He pulls me closer.

'Can I kiss you?' he whispers.

I look up at him, rising to meet his lips.

My eyes roll back before closing and as his lips part I grip him tighter, tilting my head, relishing his soft lips under my own. A lick of his tongue brushes mine, and he lets out a small groan. He pauses, and we break apart, peering at one another, his deep-set brown eyes twinkling as the water runs around us.

'That was...'

'Kiss me again,' I whisper, practically begging. 'Please.'

He does, his hand snaking from my waist, up my spine, sending shivers down it, before he cups my head, fingers splaying through my hair. We kiss once, twice, moving our heads, meeting each other at new, exciting angles. His tongue brushes my lips, and mine his, and he gives me another before his kiss breaks into a smile, and mine a laugh.

It's reckless, daring, but here in the decaying shower room, it feels safe. Right now, I don't think about the professors, the students, what it might mean if they see us kissing, see something forbidden and deemed wrong. Because every touch of his lips feels right. My heart rate has steadied from the initial rush, and my body is warm and buzzing with desire.

I just kissed Roman Edwards and it was fucking incredible.

Roman sighs, resting his forehead against mine. 'Dylan…'

'You're everything I hoped for,' I whisper.

'We can do it again, if you like,' Roman breathes.

I lean in this time, using my hand to bring Roman to me, clutching at his collar, pulling him my way. He sinks into my kiss as my want for him pours from me, as we swim in one another's desire.

'Incredible,' Roman breathes, when our breath has escaped from us and our kisses fade. 'Why didn't we do this before?'

'If I had known…'

'I know,' he says. 'But we're here now.'

'Let's go back to the lake,' I say. 'Before everyone wakes up. I want to feel like it's just me and you on this earth.'

We slip back outside and into the lake, floating, touching hands underwater, for a while, until we see the lights coming on inside.

'People are waking,' Roman says. 'Sometimes I think of these lights like stars. The people inside orbiting like planets, pulled to something or other.'

'You should paint this.'

'Yeah?' Roman asks.

'Yeah.'

'Maybe I already have.' He grins.

'I could kiss you again right now.'

'In the light of Ganymede's,' he says.

We're close, his fingers brushing against my T-shirt. 'But I best not.'

'No,' he says, though I can tell he doesn't mean it.

CHAPTER 51

'This is all about teamwork,' Professor Tania tells us, the morning of the next task. She addresses us in the assembly hall, and we all sit within our houses, bored expressions on our faces. I wonder if half of the boys are waiting for these tasks to end, wishing they could graduate and be done with it.

It all seems so mundane, now, to sit here and act like I haven't changed. That I haven't kissed Roman. Every time I'm brave enough to look at him across the room his mouth quirks into a little smile, the corner of his eyes watching me.

'In this task, you will be required to work with a partner,' Tania continues. 'You will be put into a house environment, and you will be observed. Tasks will take place in the outhouses, so come to me in the entrance hall and get your time slot.'

One by one, we head to Tania. Johnny is called first, and it's a tedious wait as each boy is called to be given their instructions for the task. Inside, my heart is thudding as I wait, realising how many students there are here. I'm frightened, but determined to be strong, to confront whatever's coming. I think of Roman, of what we've shared, and a brief feeling of invincibility comes over me.

Cameron nudges me an hour or so in to our wait, after Taylor has left. 'Feeling okay?' he asks, his body language telling me that he's genuinely unbothered.

'Sure,' I say, calmly, though I want to push him away from me, because now I feel like he's being too placid. After my near escape last night, it feels as though there are more eyes on me than ever.

Cameron is called, and ten minutes later, I am called. Roman flashes me a thumbs-up as I leave.

'Ah, Mr Cecil,' Tania says to me. 'Please do head to the outbuildings. Your task will begin shortly.'

I nod, and do as she says. I've been in that room near on two hours now and my body is stiff. I briefly consider waiting for Roman, but I can't. I have to keep a clear head and work on a fake scenario, and carry on acting like I'm the old Dylan. The morning sun prickles my skin as I step outside. The outbuildings are near the far end of the lake, close to the school boundaries. They date back to the days when Ganymede's was an aristocratic manor house, and were used as guest houses for those who would come to visit the old lord and lady of the manor. Now they stand furnished but mostly empty, occasionally hosting important visitors to the school. In the summer, I sometimes see unfamiliar faces come to stay for a week or two. I've never spoken to them, however.

There are four buildings, all joined, with crumbling beige stonework. The roofs curl in on themselves as if in pain, and the windows look as if a child has drawn them without a ruler. Bees buzz through the lavender that lines the garden and the path that weaves its way to the front doors, which are all closed. Professor Lawrence waves me over to him at the furthest end, and as I walk, I allow myself to enjoy the sound of the waterfall in the distance, and the swallows that swoop overhead and fly to nests built within the crevices of the rooftops.

'There's a task currently going on with some other students. Once they've finished, there will be a change-over, and then you can step inside,' Lawrence says to me, the sunlight illuminating his features. 'How are you feeling?'

I stare at him, thinking of his nightly whispers, knowing I can no longer trust him at all. 'Why do you ask?'

Nice way to play it cool, Dylan. Totally not suspicious of you, at all.

'You're not afraid?'

I shake my head and lie. 'Not really.'

Lawrence watches me, hands in his pockets. 'Are the tasks taking a toll on you?'

I don't dare look at him. He's trying to freak me out. 'No, sir.'

'Are you sure?'

'Yes, sir.'

'Hmm.' He scratches his chin. 'You haven't been to talk with me in a while.'

'No, sir.'

'Why not?'

I gesture vaguely towards the school. 'Lots going on.'

My gaze remains fixed upon the door of the house, as if willing it open. My teeth grit together, and I resist the urge to ask Lawrence to look away. It's hard hiding my fear from the mindful teacher, but I tell myself we're not in one of his classes right now.

'You can tell me anything, Mr Cecil.'

'Thanks, good to know.'

There's a small intake of breath. 'It is completely confidential. You can trust me.'

I almost let out a choked laugh. Yeah, right. As if I'm going to confide in him again. I cross my arms, feeling the intense burn of Lawrence's stare.

Finally, the door opens and out walks a breathless-looking Taylor. He stops halfway up the path when he sees me, but Lawrence calls for him to hurry up. Already the boys waiting in line at the other houses are walking in.

'Dylan,' Taylor says to me, curt and polite like he always is when there's a professor around.

'Taylor.'

'How did that go?' Lawrence asks Taylor.

'I guess I'll see.'

Lawrence nods, signalling for Taylor to leave. He treads slowly over the grassy terrain.

We wait another ten minutes, and I ignore Lawrence's attempts to make conversation. What's taking so long?

Lawrence checks his wristwatch. 'Whenever you're ready, Mr Cecil.'

With a nod, I cross the garden path and step into the home.

The door closes behind me, and I don't know if it's my imagination but it sounds like the locks are motorised. For good measure I test the door, finding it locked into place. I'm standing in a narrow hallway, and the house is silent. I've never been in here before, but curiosity gets the better of me, and I walk slowly through the hall, not bothering to remove my shoes. Part of me thinks maybe I should. Maybe someone is watching me and marking me on how I make myself at home, but I'll take the risk. There are no photo frames here, no coats on the rack. Just a chill and a whisper of a happiness long gone. I can either walk through an archway further into the house, or take a door to my right. I try the door and it opens into a dark study, the curtains drawn over a view of the lavender garden and, indeed, Professor Lawrence. There are shadows of animal heads on the wall, but I don't dwell on them, preferring not to surround myself with barbaric death. I head to the window, treading over carpeted floor, and peer outside. To my surprise, Roman is locked in conversation with Lawrence. I step back from the window, afraid that they might see me. The room reveals no secrets, so I leave it and head further into the house.

That's when someone screams from upstairs.

CHAPTER 52

My feet bound up the stairs, which slope and groan underneath my weight. The hallway is densely packed with jagged brick walls and three doors that I'd need to crouch to walk under. From directly ahead, the person screams again.

I push open the door, stepping down into a decent-sized bedroom. The window is open just a crack, a pathetic breeze coming through, and the sunlight brightens brown painted walls. Antique furniture is spotlessly decorated, there's a single bed in one corner with its sheets pinned tightly underneath the mattress, and an old wardrobe that looks like it hasn't been touched since the last lord died.

Something pushes me from behind, gripping my shoulders and pinching my skin. I yelp, trying to shrug off whoever is behind me as panic floods my nervous system, alerting me to an attack.

The grip slackens and I duck from under it, stumbling back until I crash against the bed and fall onto the mattress. 'Johnny?'

Johnny stands before me, holding his hands out in front of him, squinting. 'Dylan, mate? Is that you?'

I lean forward. 'It's me.'

He falls to his knees, hands grasping the rug beneath him. 'My vision is fucking blurry. My head is pounding. I don't know how long I've been here. I've tried getting out but the windows don't open fully and the doors are locked.'

'I know, I know,' I say, trying to override my fast heart rate. Is something going to happen to me, too? 'What's going on?'

He clutches at his hair, his mouth twisted into fear, letting out a groan. He begins to rock, back and forth, and I hurry to him, reaching out to console him. He flinches at my touch, and I manage to avoid his fist. Adopting a stern voice, I say, 'Johnny, control yourself.'

'Do they know, do they know, do they know...'

I cover his mouth, glancing around, remembering that they're watching us. 'Quiet. You're not of sound mind.'

They've drugged him, I think, like they did us for the survival task. But why? An unsettling dread creeps through me at the thought that this is a different test disguised as harmless observation. And so soon after the close escape with Dwynwen.

His whimpers slow before subsiding, and I think of what they might be hiding. We cannot speak openly, trapped in this building, but Johnny needs some water.

I get to my feet, thinking I'll get him a glass, but the sound of ticking makes me stop.

Soft, rhythmic ticking. Johnny's not wearing a watch. I pat at his chest, as if he might have a pocket watch, but there's nothing. The table is devoid of a clock, the walls, too. I inspect the room, quickly but as thoroughly as I can, trying to spot anything that might tell me what is really going on here.

A floorboard creaks by the wardrobe and I note the ticking seems louder. I test the doors, which rattle but do not open.

There's a keyhole, but no key. 'Fuck's sake.' Determined, I begin to root through the desk drawers, open books and shake them, move the rug around Johnny in the hopes of finding a key. I peer under the wardrobe, use the chair from the desk to look on top of the wardrobe, and I even shove my hand out of the window, fingers splaying on the windowsill, trying to reach the edge. My hand gets stuck and I have to breathe through the panic as I wriggle it free from the sliver of opening.

Johnny is whispering, but I can't make out what he's saying. I hope he knows, even in his state, not to give us away. What if they know what we're doing? What if they suspect it? I won't walk into that trap, should it exist.

The one place I haven't checked is the bed. I shake the pillow, take off the cover, do the same to the bed spread. I pull back the mattress cover, see bare mattress underneath. I flop onto it with a sigh and hear a metallic scratch.

Getting to my knees, I lift the mattress with all the strength I can muster. 'Yes,' I shout, reaching one hand under and propping the heavy mattress up with my shoulder. My fingers grasp the cold metal key and I run to the wardrobe, relief escaping me in a shaking breath when I open it.

The ticking intensifies as I breathe in dust and musky clothes. The fashion is certainly old, and must definitely belong to the dearly departed. I feel around, hitting dead air, until right at the back my knuckles touch wood. I pull out a shining walnut box with a touch screen on top, fashioned with the emblem of Ganymede's. This is new, clearly, and the ticking comes from inside.

Grazing the touch pad, I shake, and a note flutters from underneath. I set the box aside and reach for the note.

Beauty is in my colours,
It's something we all share.

You wear me every season,
Some say that I am fair.
I'm with you when you waken,
Though you leave me everywhere.
I'm fragile yet I'm stronger,
Adorned but often bare.

As I reread the note, my brow furrows. There's another handwritten note underneath.

Time is ticking. Solve the riddle to open the box, and get out before what's inside explodes.

I throw the box from me, seeing it land upon the rug. Johnny shakes his head sadly. 'What is it?'

'A bomb,' I gasp. 'They're trying to blow us up.'

CHAPTER 53

'Here, read this,' I say, shoving the note at Johnny.

He reels back, brow creasing in frustration. 'I can't make any of it out.'

I want to scream. 'Nothing at all?'

'Just colour and blur. It's like my eyes are full of tears.'

'Your pupils must be dilated,' I say. 'What do you remember?'

'They called me to my task, and I was buzzing that I was first. I went to a room and there was a hissing noise and then it all went dark. Then when I wake up, I'm being bundled into this house by a security guard.'

'Terrifying. Did you see Taylor?'

'No, thank God. It's a bit much for the sake of graduation, ain't it?'

Yes, it is, I think. Furiously, I reread the riddle.

'You still there?' he asks.

'Yes, reading the riddle.'

'Not worked it out yet?'

'No.'

'Time's ticking, mate,' Johnny says with a panicked grin.

'Well, let me read it to you, then, and you can solve it.'

'Mate, I've never been good at riddles,' he says, massaging the side of his head.

I read the riddle to him anyway, hope draining from me with every sentence.

'I'm sorry,' Johnny groans. 'I've forgotten what you said at the start.'

'Okay, let's start again,' I say, turning back to the box. My mouth drops. On the screen, a timer has begun. Fifty-five minutes. 'Shit. Fifty-five minutes until what?'

Johnny peers at me, as if trying to make me out.

'It's just a task,' I say.

'Yeah.'

But what if it's not? I know Johnny can't see me, but I'm trying to convey what I'm thinking to him without saying a word. What if they know we are rebels, and they are eliminating us under the guise of a task gone wrong? What if Roman is in the same situation? Elis and Cameron, too? We will merely be boys who failed, when really, we have been killed. Killed like Blake. Killed like Ben's brother. Eliminate us now before we become the true threat.

No, they cannot. Will not.

'We have to think,' I say. 'Focus.'

'Not my strong point.'

If it wouldn't waste valuable time, I'd shove him.

'*Beauty is in my colours, it's something we all share,*' I mutter. '*You wear me every season, some say that I am fair.* Well, that must be clothes. Do you think it's clothes?'

'I'm sorry, Dylan,' Johnny mutters. 'Maybe it is.'

'*I'm with you when you waken, though you leave me everywhere.* Yes, it's got to be clothes, hasn't it? I mean, unless you sleep naked, but no, maybe that's too literal. Because when you waken, you're still surrounded by clothes. And maybe you do leave your clothes everywhere. Yes, I think it's clothes.'

I reach for the box, peering at it. 'Clothes,' I say. 'It's clothes.'

The box doesn't do anything, so I touch the screen, and the numbers are replaced with a digital keyboard. I type in clothes, and there's an agonising wait, before the screen flashes red.

'Fuck.'

'What?' Johnny asks.

'They've taken ten minutes off for getting it wrong.'

'Bastards.'

I look at the window, thinking I could smash it, break through and escape that way. It would surely forfeit the task, but better that than being blown to smithereens.

But then I think of the fight for freedom, the fight for truth. The belief that we can change things. I have to play their game to play my own.

'What else could it be?' I ask. 'Think, Johnny. Please.'

'If you wear something every season, and you leave it everywhere, could it maybe be perfume?' Johnny asks.

'Perfume. Sure, why not?' My breath stills as I type it in, waiting for the screen to say this is all over. But then it flashes red, and another ten minutes disappear, and I drop the box, finally screaming.

'Calm, Dylan.'

'Don't tell me to calm down.'

'We have to stay calm.'

'You haven't been calm this whole time.'

'I'm scared, all right?' he says. 'I can't see anything. I didn't think they were going to make me lose my sight. It'd better be bloody temporary. My eyes are too gorgeous to be diluted permanently.'

I look at him.

Then I look back at the timer and my leg begins to jiggle.

My hand tries to steady it but the movement only gets worse. I rethink the riddle, coming to answers like underwear, dismissing them almost instantly. 'What is fragile but stronger? It must be a material.'

'Could be fibres,' Johnny suggests.

When the screen flashes red again and I lose another ten minutes, I know I can't keep guessing aimlessly. *Think, Dylan, think*.

I leave Johnny in the bedroom and go and fetch him a glass of water before heading back out of the room. Walking through the house brings back memories of my own. The hallway is similar, and the outlay of the downstairs is almost identical. The decor makes me think the lord and lady left and will return. A museum to their memory and a shrine to their lives. I stand at the kitchen sink, staring out at the back garden, where flora grow and bask in the sun. How beautifully coloured the plants are, each one a different shade of green and yellow, purple and red. An idea forms. The strength it takes to grow and bloom, to stand tall, to survive the struggling climate. Yet if I were to go outside and snap the stem, I could do so.

Yes, I think, letting my gaze soften as the plants bob in a breeze I long to feel. I rush upstairs, find the box, certain that I have solved it. 'Plants,' I type.

The screen flashes red, and ten minutes remain.

'We're doomed.' I shake my head. 'We have to break out of here.'

'No, Dylan, that's foolish.'

'We're going to die if we don't,' I say.

'Maybe that's for the best.'

'Are you serious?'

'Are we not dead men anyway?'

'No, I don't believe we are.'

Johnny puts his head in his hands, and I think that if he had a clearer head, he would be more use, but he can't see through his own panic.

It must be staring me right in the face, I think, as I sit across from an old mirror fashioned into the wardrobe. The time slips by, to the single digits. Is this how I am to go? Willingly?

'Nothing's going to happen,' Johnny whispers. 'It can't happen.'

Do I trust Ganymede's enough to believe him?

I've wasted time focusing on the clock, on that incessant ticking that has fallen into rhythm with the bouncing of my knee. I should be decoding the riddle.

Beauty is in my colours, it's something we all share. You wear me every season, some say that I am fair. It's not clothes. Not perfume. Not underwear. What do we wear every season? *I'm with you when you waken, though you leave me everywhere.* I eye the box. *I'm fragile yet I'm stronger. Adorned but often bare.*

Suddenly, it clicks in my brain. Of course. It's obvious.

'I've got it, Johnny,' I say. 'I've got it!'

'Cool,' he says, lazily.

My hand grips the box. I type the words in, holding my breath.

'What is it?' Johnny asks, as the seconds get closer to zero.

They pause at one minute.

The screen goes green.

The lock pops.

Inside is a small ticking clock, no wires, no sign of a true bomb.

Deliriously, I laugh, shaking my head.

'It was skin,' I say. 'Skin.'

CHAPTER 54

I come out of the house, and Roman spots us, grinning, but falters when he sees my expression. I'm clutching Johnny, refusing to leave him behind.

'How did that go?' Lawrence asks.

'Who did that to him?'

'Excuse me?'

'Johnny. Who put him through that?'

Lawrence cocks his head, taking a moment. 'He agreed to the task, whatever the outcome. It was as much his task as it was yours.'

'You did something to his vision,' I say, aware that I'm shouting, aware that others are looking at me. 'I think he was in pain, too. Nobody should be in pain for this ... this game.'

'On the contrary, Mr Cecil, you are tasked with adapting to a scenario given to you, and'—Lawrence raises his voice, overpowering my protests—'and you worked to save your fellow man. Johnny worked with you, even when in turmoil.'

'Will I see again?' Johnny groans.

'Yes, Mr Acton, you will see again,' Lawrence says.

Roman places a hand on my shoulder, trying to get in front of me. He's saying something, but blood rushes to my ears, and the serene bees and the birds and the water aren't registering with me anymore.

'You frightened us. Did you see what I had to do?'

'I am not the one observing,' Lawrence replies, calm.

'Did you know?'

'I am not the task master.'

I shake, annoyed at his demeanour, wondering how he can be so collected about all of this.

'Who is?'

'It is devised with the board, and so...'

'Who came up with that task, and who came up with that scenario?'

'Lower your tone when you speak to me, Mr Cecil.'

I step back from him, and a jolt of fear takes a hold of me. *Be careful, Dylan*, I think. *Do not get so far into this that you do something you regret.*

'Dylan,' Roman begins.

'No, Roman. They made us believe a bomb was going to go off.' As I say it, it sounds foolish, especially when some of the other boys snicker. I blush red as a rational, logical brain takes over. We were always free to leave if we'd smashed the windows. We were never going to fall victim to a detonated bomb. Yet it felt so real. Death felt so close. Closer than it has so far. Are all these tasks sadistically meant to bring us close to death? How does that make us better men?

'There was a riddle, and a ticking time bomb, and Johnny was distraught. All for us to graduate? Come on, it is not worth it. The hurt, the pain and turmoil you're putting people through.' Lawrence's lips turn into a smile, and my mouth drops. 'How can you smile, Professor?'

'I am passing you both on the spot.'

'What?'

'I can see how much this affected you, and I can see how much you care for people. You are a selfless man, Dylan, and we need more of those.'

'Professor Lawrence—'

'Mr Cecil, do you want me to revoke what I have just said?'

Lawrence and I stare at one another, student and master, and I hope I convey everything I can't say to him. That I'm on to the school, that I know something is being hidden, that I will discover what it is.

Finally, Lawrence turns to Roman, 'Your task is ready, Mr Edwards.'

Roman turns to me, fear in his eyes and I want to take his hand in mine and tell him not to do it, but he quickly recovers. He steps to me and pats me once on the back, and then turns away from us both, disappearing into the house.

'You must be careful, Mr Cecil,' Lawrence says, his tone threatening.

'Whatever. Goodbye,' I snap.

'I mean it,' Lawrence says, grabbing my elbow. I gasp at his touch, at the blatant disregard for rules and our standing. His eyes scan the field, the houses. The crowd has dispersed, heading into their rooms, and the three remaining professors aren't watching us. 'Protection will only get you so far.'

'I don't know what you're talking about.'

'Think about it.' He stares at me, then lets me go.

CHAPTER 55

Since the near miss in Dwynwen's office, I haven't had time to speak with any of the House of Pluto members. Only Roman knows of the record I found of my father, of his potential history with the king. Now, under the crescent moon, we all gather in our crypt, the Jupiter students looking too relaxed for my liking, lounging under candlelight, reading books banned by the school.

'How're you doing, mate?' Johnny asks me, wincing, though focused on me. He holds a copy of *The Tenant of Wildfell Hall*, finger on the page to hold his spot.

'How am I doing? More like how are you doing?'

Johnny waves his hands, fluttering his eyelashes. 'I'll be back to breaking hearts in no time.'

'We've got lots to talk about tonight,' Rory says, the last to arrive. 'I got here as soon as I could.'

'Did you get the papers?' Elis asks him.

'I got the papers and they're eye-opening.' Rory pulls a wad of folded newspapers from his inside jacket pocket and starts to lay them out upon the tomb we gather around. 'Most of these papers are the ones owned and operated by the monarchy. You can imagine the content inside. But there's another paper, which seems to be issued four times a year, that Lawrence has been reading, called the *Jolly Jester*. Look at the logo.'

He unfurls a well-read newspaper, where a crudely drawn image of King Carwyn's head is flanked by the words 'Jolly Jester'. Some of the group gasp at the image. A huge photo of hamlet homes graces the front page, with the bold headline **'GROAN SWEET GROAN'**.

The newspaper is thin in my hands, the text slanting ever so slightly to the left, as if printed on a wonky printer. There are five pages inside, but it's the double page spread in the middle I stop at.

HOW THE KING IS MONITORING YOUR HOME
Written by the Jolly Jester

Did you thank your Oak King portrait this morning, my friends? This Jolly Jester stuck their middle finger right up to him when they awoke, and they took jolly joy in breaking every rule they are supposed to follow from the moment their eyes opened from a nightmare-ridden slumber.

It's how I start every morning in the house graciously afforded to me by my great saviour, King Carwyn. How grateful I am to not be able to choose how comfortable my mattress is. That every morning I wake lying on pillows provided by the monarchy, branded with the name of the business of their mates. I open my front door and see my breakfast parcel waiting for me in a measly basket, because the local bakery has closed after a family simply disappeared one day.

Hacking coughs make me cover my mouth as I see the rain clouds coming in. Or is that yet another wild fire? Another day indoors, I think. I close the door on the world of perfection, and look adoringly at my perfect home, and at the second portrait of the king above my mantlepiece that I must not move, must not touch. My furniture is antique, because we can't have anything new. Reuse and recycle what already exists. I cannot paint them in a solid colour scheme. I cannot make the chequered cloth that covers my kitchen table complement the colour of my fridge or the material of my work surfaces. I wish to repaint this whole house in bright colours of red and purple and pink. I want garish and I want brash and I want people to come in to my home and wrinkle their noses and gossip to their friends later about how horrible my design choices are. I want to sleep in silk, not hemp. I want my curtains to be cotton, not linen. I want to be able to distinguish my house from every other house in this hamlet.

I kiss my wife good morning. We are still sleeping in separate rooms. But she is my rock and I am her joy. The king watches us breakfast in silence from his perch above my kitchen window.

We go to work. My wife to hers, where I am sure she is having an affair. I cannot blame her. I encourage her. I am a disappointment to her. I finish my job, rush to assemble this paper. My wife does not know where I go, and I am sure she thinks that I too am having an affair. This Jolly Jester only has love for a free world. A world where we are not constrained. Where we have individuality and spark and hope and colour again.

This Jolly Jester needs you to take pride in yourself.

We are almost ready for print. I come home with my face covered in the darkness of night. How I long to ring my bells and play pranks on my neighbours. To hear true laughter again. Under the shadow of the statue of the king, I skip around his plinth imagining that I am tying a rope around his neck, and I mime pulling, and pretend to cheer as he comes crashing to the ground. My great and mighty king, *Carwyn ap Mawr Celyn*, I wish to spit upon your handsome face. I wish to expose your corruption. Signed dearly, your lovely servant.

My wife is home. She obediently greets me. I help her cook in silence. I cannot bear to listen to the radio. Not anymore. We eat and she goes to bed, and I listen as people saunter by coughing, pretending they are well.

In bed, I stare at the king as he waits for me to drift to sleep. My king, a grisly fate you shall meet.

'What are we looking at?' Roman flips through another paper; more of the same. All articles written by the Jolly Jester, and each one as sarcastic and scathing as the last.

'Someone getting illegal material into the hands of professors, clearly,' I answer.

'Do we know who this Jester is?' Ben asks.

'No idea.'

'Wonder what the sickness is doing to people.'

'Sounds like a flu thing,' Rory says. 'It is killing people.'

'Not good for population.' Elis is flicking through a media outlet that I recognise. A paper full of positivity for the king's new world. 'There's some horrible stuff in the so-called trusted newspapers. You seen this?'

He spins the paper around so we can all see it.

KING'S LATEST SPEECH PROVES PERFECTION IS WITHIN REACH
Written by Maxwell Abse

'Imagine a world where humans aren't sick. Where empathy is in your DNA. Where bright thinkers are not a rarity. That, to me, is a truly perfect society.' Those were the words of the king this week in his latest address to his country, and yet another reminder of his strive towards perfection. Of course, it comes when worry abounds at the sickness that is spreading through homes like the eradicated wildfires of the past. It also comes after recent concerns that people are starting to stray into old ways. RE: see my previous article on two men spotted kissing in a hamlet. Speaking in the shadow of illness, the king assures us once more that we don't need to worry much longer.

The king has not been shy in sharing his desire for a society that is cherry-picked with perfect qualities, across all the sexes. Since taking to the throne, the once shy prince has flourished into a beautiful flower, taking up the space he so deserves to occupy. His father, and indeed the father before him, were the seed bearers of the new golden age we are finding ourselves in. A world that I will be proud to live in.

King Carwyn has not been coaxed into his true vision for his country. Indeed, when he has been asked about what he wants to see in the hamlets, he rather coyly talks of the positive roots his family achieved before him. Though I suspect that King Carwyn is in favour of what a lot of us are: genetic modification to achieve a perfect population.

Ask your neighbours their thoughts on their lives, and you will get the same answers. They feel safe. They have wonderful children. They are fulfilled knowing they are perfecting and correcting the earth. We all know none of this would have been possible if the monarchy hadn't stepped back in, and the king's family hadn't firmly put their vision into plans.

The king sat upon his throne this week and told us that our population continues to thrive. All of whom are working, all of whom are repopulating. We have order back in a world that descended into chaos. I, for one, know that perfection is already within reach. I would not be surprised if King Carwyn already has a firm grip upon perfection, and is waiting for the right time to infuse it into our thriving hamlets.

For me, here is what perfection is. A happy home, where children grow into smart thinkers, with IQs to rival those of the greatest men. A husband and wife in love. Where everybody is a leader. Where those fulfil their roles, contributing to society. Taking less and giving more. A world with no sickness. A world where perfection is in our DNA. Who wouldn't want that?

My stomach churns reading the opinion piece, and my mouth drops as I flick through the pages seeing articles celebrating new hamlet creations, and eradication of people in the open country. I try to remember the newspapers Father read, wondering if he ever read anything like this before. They'd never interested me; I never picked them up. Now I wish I had.

'They're eradicating people they don't deem perfect,' Elis says.

'I'm not sure,' Ben begins.

'Not sure? How can you be not sure?' Grady asks. 'It's there, plain as day.'

'It's an opinion piece,' Ben argues.

'Based on a speech by Carwyn. He's read between the lines. Obviously there have been talks or speculation before for this Maxwell dude to come out with that.' Johnny shakes his head, looking sick. 'That is horrible.'

'It's really dangerous rhetoric,' Elis says. 'It opens the doors to all sorts of ethical questions.'

'There's lots like it,' Rory says. 'Lots of propaganda about boosting the workforce and being able to choose how a society will function. It's all fashioned to be a good thing. Another step forward for society.'

'But where does that leave us?' I ask the room.

'I've said it before, and I'll say it now,' Roman says. 'What they deem to be perfect probably isn't what the rest of us deem perfect. What's scary is they're in a position to enact the changes they want to see. At what cost?'

The silence stretches between us as we all digest what we have discovered. I think of all the students in the school, unaware of what these words really mean. I imagine them stumbling as if sleepwalking, unable to hear us as we scream and make a racket and plead for them to wake up.

'We need to find the person behind the Jolly Jester.' I finally say. 'We don't know where this paper goes, but I'm betting it's getting into the hands of people who aren't happy. If we can get to the person behind the Jolly Jester, we can get the truth out. About Blake. About missing students. All of it. Find the Jolly Jester. Get the truth out.'

CHAPTER 56

I haven't been able to focus all day, to the extent where too much pointless interaction is getting to me. In the corridors, in the hall, at breakfast and lunch, it's like I'm wearing a mask and pretending to be something I'm not. Outside, I have to act as though all is well. So I've escaped to my room, where I look out over the grounds, watching students below mill about, aimlessly wiling away their hours before the next task tomorrow.

Behind me, the door opens, and I resent having my quiet time disturbed in this way. I turn, expecting to see Johnny or Cameron, but my stomach drops when I spot Taylor.

He closes the door behind him, leans against it, blocking my exit. 'Can we talk?'

'About what?' I turn away from the window, crossing my arms, feeling like I'm vulnerable to whatever he intends to do.

'I've been thinking about what you did to me in that task,' he says, tone light. 'It wasn't nice. Not nice at all.'

I shrug. 'I know.'

'And you don't care?'

'What makes you say that?'

'Where's your empathy? Your concern for my welfare? It's not very mindful of you, is it?'

'It wasn't a wellness task.'

'Dwynwen spoke to me,' Taylor says. 'She gave me a stern telling off.'

'Oh?'

I look away, knowing what's happened, who is responsible.

'She said evidence had come to light that I have been bullying you.'

'That's interesting.'

Taylor charges across the room, so quick I don't even have time to react. He pushes me against the wall, gripping me, fingers pinching my skin. I yell out, try to escape him, but he only grips me tighter. Face in my face, his spit lands on me as he says, 'You went and fucking told on me, Dylan? Are you stupid?'

'I didn't say a word.'

He pushes me again, my head hitting the wall. A pain rushes in and my head swims, and for one horrible moment I think he's going to keep beating me against it until I lose consciousness, until I die.

'You could have jeopardised everything for me. Do you know that? Answer me.'

'I didn't say a word.'

He hits me then, fist to my chin. I bite my tongue, tasting blood, and something overwhelms me. A primal need to fight back. I kick him and he yelps, stumbling back. Getting to my feet, shorter than him, I tap my chest. 'Come on. If you want to hurt me, do it. Give them more evidence of who you really are.'

'Who I really am?' he screams.

'A bully. A brute.'

He tackles me, my body going over his shoulders, and we land on the floor in a thud. The wind escapes me and I try to turn over, but he's upon me, pounding his fists into my skin. I try to call out for help, try to tell him to stop, because he won't let up. He keeps going and going until the blood in my mouth isn't from my tongue anymore, but from my nose, my lip.

I think he's going to kill me. His eyes are wild, spit flies as he hits me.

Somehow, I get him off me, and he lands with a winded thud. I scuttle away from him, feeling bruising to my ribs. I cast around for something, anything, that might protect me from him, and I reach for a candelabra on Johnny's bedside table. Clutching it to my chest, I breathe, 'I will hit you if you come any closer.'

He's on his knees, breathing deeply, head bowed.

I stare at him, afraid to move, knowing that even if I tried, he would catch me. I'm too brittle, too broken. All I can think is that here is more evidence of what he is capable of, of what he's really like. If he's still here after Dwynwen has spoken to him, then she's given him another chance. But not now. Surely not when she sees what he has done to me?

A sob escapes Taylor, and my brow furrows. At first, I think he's playing with me, trying to make me think he needs help. But then he sits, and his face is alight with fresh tears, and he rubs at his face but the tears don't stop.

'I don't know what's wrong with me,' he says through wrenching sobs. 'I don't know why I'm like this. Why there's this ... this thing within me. This violence.'

He shakes his head, twisting the fabric of his T-shirt in his hands.

What am I supposed to say?

'The sick thing is,' he says to me, eyes trailing over my wounds. 'I enjoyed that. I enjoyed every bit of it.' He lets out a laugh, a horrible, wicked laugh. He crawls closer, and I lift the candelabra, finding courage in its weight. He doesn't flinch, though. Just looks at the stick and laughs again. 'There was a part of me that loved having you at my mercy. Loved that I was stronger than you could ever be. You tried to fight back and it didn't matter, because I was physically powerful.' His smile fades. 'Why do I enjoy that?'

I swallow. 'I don't know.'

He stares at me.

'You have made my years here hell.'

'I know.'

'And you've enjoyed it?'

'You're like a toy.' Taylor points at my lip. 'You've got blood dripping down your chin.'

I dab at my lip, wincing, before looking at my fingertips, stained red. 'I'm going to Dwynwen.'

Taylor nods.

'Why do you enjoy doing this?' I ask.

Fresh tears fall from his eyes. 'I don't know. It's like ... like I want to reassure myself that I can handle anything thrown my way. It's like...'

He tries to find the words, lifting a hand as if he might pluck them out of thin air. Eventually, he gives me a neutral nod, and a pitiful laugh. My nerves steady as I adjust my grip on the stick. 'You can't keep doing this to me, Taylor.'

Taylor wipes at his tears, composing himself with a shake of his shoulders. 'I know.'

'This is not how a man should act.'

'That's right.'

He gets to his feet, holding out a hand. 'I'm so stupid. So fucked.'

'Taylor—'

But he doesn't wait. He storms out of the room, leaving the door ajar. Somewhere in the distance the door of our common room closes.

When the pain subsides enough, I go to the nurse. I get signed off that I will be well, told to take it easy. I tell Dwynwen what happened. Everything feels like auto-pilot, and if it wasn't for the ache of pain, I'd feel numb. I sit in the shadow of the abandoned chapel on the school grounds until the sun sets. I return to my dorm room in laboured movements. When the boys return, I feign being asleep, thankful for the dark that covers my bruises.

Tomorrow is the next task.

Just get through it, Dylan.

CHAPTER 57

'Trick or treat, Mr Cecil.'

'But it's not Samhain.'

'Humour me.' Mother Mai extends both her arms, clutching two small leather boxes in her hands. I peer at one, then the other, trying to decide. 'Intuition, Mr Cecil.'

All well and good to tell me to use intuition when I can't fathom what is going on here, I think. How can she stand here and speak so proudly of keeping secrets? I want to question her, to find out exactly what it is she is hiding about Blake. What might she say?

For show, I close my eyes, put my hands behind my back, attempt to clear my mind even though it is fruitless, and I reach out with my left hand and touch the right box, because it feels like I've thought about the process somewhat.

When I open my eyes and look at Mother Mai, she is smiling. A good sign? She pockets the other box, and firmly grasps the one I have chosen. 'Your friend, Roman Edwards, is it?' I nod. 'He chose the other.'

'Oh?'

She holds out the box to me. When I go to take it from her, she pulls it back. 'Not yet, Mr Cecil. You see, today's task is about sacrifice. A perfect man must be willing to make sacrifices, and he must be selfless.' The late-morning sun makes her glow as we stand at the base of the stairs. She's wearing a black shawl, her wispy grey hair falling about her hunched shoulders. 'Your future partner requires you to look after her, no matter what the occasion. As a man, you are expected to care and nurture, and put your own needs behind you when faced with adversity.'

'I know, Mother Mai.'

'Do you, Mr Cecil?' she asks, equally coldly.

Paranoia makes me wonder if she knows something. I remember her collected tone as she spoke of Blake's death, and how easy it is for her to do what is right for the school. What sacrifices has she made? I wonder, as I look at the lines on her face; she's still beautiful, and graceful with age.

'But this is where the trick or the treat come into play,' Mother Mai says, her lips stretching into a beaming smile. 'Have you been to the nurse about those bruises?'

She points at my skin with a crooked finger.

'Yes, Mother Mai.'

She winces as she squints. 'Come. Let me take you to your task.' I follow her, slowing my steps. She's sprightly for her age, sure, but she walks glacially compared to everyone else here. It's almost painful, like frostbite on the edge of my nose. 'This task is unusual in the sense that you have influenced the outcome without even realising it. But you will still be questioned on your morals, and you will have to decide what is right. Not straightaway, I hasten to add. You are not expected to walk out of this task and choose, though if you wish to do so, we will not complain.' My brow furrows and she smiles at me. 'All will make sense once you get in the room.'

My stomach knots, and I try to keep my expression neutral, afraid that Mother Mai already knows too much and is waiting for me to slip up.

A doorway creaks and I turn, almost expecting to see the servants, but it is just another student, looking forlorn as he is guided away by Professor Tania. I hope the outcome of his test was good for him, and that I haven't just seen the face of a boy who has failed.

'Um, Mother Mai?' She nods, to show she is listening. We head towards a corridor I know well. A place that has names of dead alumni on a wooden plaque, my father's included. 'Did Roman Edwards get a trick or a treat?'

'I cannot say.'

Frustration ricochets through me. 'Okay, but *if* he got a trick...'

'Some boys will have to sacrifice things they never thought they would need to let go of,' Mother Mai says. 'Others will have to compromise.'

'Is there a difference?'

'Oh, yes. A sacrifice, in my experience, tends to be more painful than a compromise.'

She pushes open the door and we step into a dim, dead-end room. Mother Mai points to one of the doors opposite the names. Father's name is so easy to find, since I've been here so often, and I'm about to head into the room Mother Mai indicates when there is an anguished scream from the room next door.

'What the—?'

'Do not worry, Mr Cecil. Everything will be okay.'

She guides me into the room, stepping out after me. It's square in shape, barely wide enough for me to stretch out my arms. From where I can stand, both my fingertips brush either side of the wall, as if I might push them further away from me to create more space. As I turn around, she slams the door behind me, leaving me alone, lit only by a lantern on an old wooden table etched with the names of past students bored in classes. It's here that I take a seat, on a chair that feels dangerously unstable, despite the even floor. I lean against the table, realising two things: I can no longer hear the scream of my neighbour. I can see my father's name through the glass pane in the door.

I take small breaths, thinking the walls are coming closer and closer, and for one wild moment I think perhaps that is the task. Escape a room where the walls keep coming until they crush me into a pulp.

Father's name disappears as two figures approach the door. My breath hitches and I rise, instinctively, because the two figures that walk into the room are not servants. They're not men, either. They are women, one black, the other white, both wearing green form-fitting uniforms that glisten on the lapels with emeralds. They are makeup-free, their eyes neither warm nor cold, and they step either side of the room, only just, to let in another.

My legs wobble, the room lurches, but only for me. I swing back, landing with a thump on the delicate chair. Panic shoots through me because I know there is protocol, I know I'm supposed to do something other than look stricken.

The door closes behind the young girl who stands before me, and behind her, two other guards.

'This can't be real,' I stammer.

'Please rise for Princess Cerys Holly Celyn, of the Holly Court.'

CHAPTER 58

Shaking, I manage to stand, but my hands grip the edge of the table, fingertips sinking into etched names. I attempt a bow, but my body doesn't move, as if I'm afraid that taking my sight off her will lose her for good. Besides, I think I might faint if I make any sudden movements.

Princess Cerys steps closer, her hand touching the top of the chair before me. She also wears a form-fitting suit, which I think must be a one-piece. It shimmers like shales of a green mythical fish, and her soft white skin seems to brighten an otherwise dark space. Her lips are painted sage-green, and her eyes match them, I think. I notice as she takes her seat, telling me to do the same, that her clothing has green vines snaking across her stomach, her chest, down her arms. Like veins leading towards her heart, pumping her full of life.

She will wither and die in a room like this.

'I think you must be surprised.' Her tone is eloquent and tender, both commanding and safe. I wonder how many elocution classes she might have had to take to master it.

'Is this a trick or a treat?'

I instantly blush, thankful for the dim lighting. I sink into the shadows, cursing myself for such a boyish response to a princess sitting before me. She is the same age as me, I know that, yet she carries herself with a decorum that I've not seen before, not even in Dwynwen, or my mother. I suppose when you're brought up like she's been brought up, it is in your DNA.

Despite everything, Cerys smiles, as her guards stare above our heads at the wall behind me. 'I am a treat, Dylan.'

She knows my name, and she sings it like an old Welsh folksong.

'The rest of the boys must have picked tricks, then,' I say. 'Or are you here to visit every boy who picks a treat?'

Typical Ganymede's, to organise a royal visit for those who chose treat.

'I am only here to see you,' Cerys says. 'No matter how many times I visit Ganymede's, I'm always left with the same feeling. Revulsion.'

I blink, her words barely registering with me. There's a buzz in my ears as my heart rate increases, and the chair creaks beneath me as if unable to carry my fear.

'To see me?'

Cerys never once looks away from me, not even to inspect the room. 'Yes. Only you.'

'Revulsion?'

'I can speak with utmost confidence, yes?'

I laugh. 'You can speak however you want. You can do anything you like.'

One of the guards shifts, presumably at my tone, but Cerys doesn't flinch.

'I have only visited a handful of times, but each time feels worse,' Cerys says. 'Perhaps it's because I enter now as a young woman, instead of a young girl. The dynamic has shifted.'

'Yes. It must be like lathering yourself in the scent of a deer and walking through a lion's den.'

Cerys nods. 'Something like that.'

I don't say anything, and for the first time her calm demeanour shifts into something akin to uncertainty. Her eyes flicker to her sides, and I think for one moment she looks like she wants to ask her guards for guidance, but it's gone almost as fast as it appears. Thoughts running through her mind, no doubt, but brought back to something solid faster than I could possibly do it.

'You needn't be so quiet around me.'

'I'm not sure what to say to a princess.'

She smiles, though it looks sad. 'Not many people get this sort of interaction with a princess.'

'What interaction do they usually get?'

'Crowds, a few seconds, formal.' Cerys stretches her arms out, as if she's about to fly. 'But here I feel as though I can do whatever I please.' She smiles. 'That is what you said, isn't it?'

I shrug. 'You're the one with authority.'

'And you aren't?'

'I am just a boy.'

'Who is becoming a man,' Cerys says. 'And despite what society says about equality, be thankful you are one.'

Her words are laced with bitterness, and I lean forward, as if to see her better. To my surprise, she does the same, so that we are only a few feet apart.

'We have met before,' I say, because I'm not sure what I can say. Asking her what she means feels too polarising. I have to remember this is a task, and for whatever reason I've been given the biggest of all. 'Is the king here? The queen? Are they in the other rooms?'

Cerys lets out a warm laugh. 'No, Dylan, it is just myself.'

'Oh.'

'Back to your first statement, however. Yes, we have met before.'

'You remember it?'

'I do.'

'No, you don't.' I laugh. She seems surprised. 'Sorry, but you're being polite. You couldn't possibly remember me.'

'Why not?'

'Out of all those people you meet, and you remember me?'

'There are many reasons why I would remember you,' she says.

I lean back, crossing my arms. 'Go on, then. When did we meet?'

'You were outside on your family farm. You were doing something with potatoes. I don't pretend to know exactly what. It was a warm day, and you seemed to glisten in the sun. Your parents were there.' She softens here, and I realise it's because she knows what happened to them. 'They were kind. Your father spoke to my father. My world changed from that day. Yours stayed the same until a little while later, when it would fracture forever.'

'Stop it.'

How dare she? Is this what royalty has become? Entitlement to speak so openly about someone else's pain? How dare she tell me what I already know? How dare she reveal that she knows more about me than I know about her?

'I did not mean to offend,' Cerys says.

'You didn't offend,' I snap. 'I don't like that you are talking to me like ... like we're familiar.'

Cerys nods. 'I understand. I only do so because you have been familiar to me for a few years now. I appreciate that I have not been familiar to you.'

'Of course you have. We walk the halls funded by your family. You are familiar to me as the burning earth.'

Cerys's smile falls.

She rises, and I sit a little taller. Both of the guards shift, snapping their attention to her. She waves off one with her hand. 'I'm not leaving. Fetch me the book.'

The white guard ducks out, and Cerys doesn't stop looking at me. I want to shout at her to look away, to leave me alone, but I don't think that's proper. A few moments later, the guard returns, carrying a tome that I recognise.

'How did you get that?'

'I appreciate all of this must be rather overwhelming to you, Dylan, but I have to be honest, I thought you might be somewhat more curious about my presence,' Cerys says. 'Or do you see royalty every day?'

'Not like this.'

'No.' She resumes her seat, placing the book in front of her. 'And yet you are on a task that has given you a treat, but something tells me you rather think this might be a trick.'

I say nothing.

'Please, Dylan. Speak to me.'

I close my eyes. 'There is nothing to say. You are you and I am me.'

'Our social class does not separate us.'

'I think, on the contrary, it does.'

Cerys sighs. 'It would be easy for me to tell you straight why I am here, but if this is going to work, I want us to have all the information.' She holds out the book to me. Dwynwen's book. 'This is a Ganymede's treat. You decide if it is a treat for you.'

A treat, not a trick. My father's name, just visible over the shoulder of the guards outside. I'm doing all of this for him.

My hands reach out and touch the book, and up until that point I was hesitant. But here it is, right before me, with no professor to come and interrupt. No need to sneak within the office of Dwynwen's and hide under her table. All these restless nights wishing to know the truth, right here.

I look at Cerys.

'Please, be my guest.'

I flip through the pages, resisting the urge to see the names of the boys I know are Plutonians, and finally, there I am. My name is printed in ink at the top of the page, and there are three pages dedicated to me, with more pages left empty to fill in my future. A true record of my key moments that has brought me to this moment.

Scribbles from Dwynwen's hands, correlating to the text about my father that I took from her office. My birth date, with a note of my astrological signs. The first glimmers of talent that I was showing. The first record of working on the farm. Everything, every little detail, including...

A gasp escapes me and I move back from the book, dragging the chair with me, colliding with the wall. Cerys, for one brief moment, looks afraid, then she looks disappointed.

'This can't be right.'

'It's there plain as day,' Cerys says.

'But I don't understand.'

'Your parents made a deal.'

'You're wrong.'

Cerys moves the book closer to me, but I don't need to see it again. I don't need more confirmation of what I already saw. Because if I thought I was trapped before, I'm even more so now. The truth has come to light, and I must bathe in it.

My partner sits across from me, in all her regal attire.

CHAPTER 59

'Will you say something?'
I shake my head.
'Have I disappointed you?'
I meet her eyes, shaking my head.
'I know it's a lot to take in.'
'Why is this happening now?'
'You picked treat,' Cerys says, but then she leans forward. 'And because you have to stay focused, Dylan.' Her tone is imploring, low. Different to how she has been. The guards stare at the wall and give nothing away. 'They wouldn't allow this unless they thought they were losing you.'

My eyes rove over her beauty, and I think how any other guy would be on cloud nine to know they are partnered with Cerys. The ultimate, the royalty who help us all. Why me?

'Losing me?' My searching eyes implore her to go on, but she stares at me intensely, and frustration burns a hole through me.

'Your father, my father, they were friends,' Cerys says, when I have been silent for too long. 'They grew up together. Your father saw my father through Ganymede's, your grandparents were managers of the crown estate. Your father, my father, they trusted one another. They had a ... *special* ... relationship.'

My eyes widen. 'Wh-what are you saying?'

'I can only speculate. But I believe they had a unique affinity with one another. Inevitably, they had to go their separate ways, but my father always promised to look after yours. And I believe he did.'

It's laughable. If Carwyn had cared for my father, my father would still be here. She doesn't know what she's talking about. This is a trick, a test. And yet, even as she says it, it's like a cloud dispersing into vapour. Hazy, uncertain, but clearer than it once was.

'Can I go now?' I can't entertain this notion of her version of my father. I can't even begin to think that he was someone else. He always had a sadness to him, like a longing that wasn't satisfied. A deep thinker, forever lost in his own head. I now imagine him lost in rippling memories of a bond he never felt again.

'You can do whatever you want to do,' Cerys says.

I rise, then bow. She does the same. The guards don't look at me. The door opens from the outside and I leave them behind in the room where I thought I was going to suffer some twisted, cruel game – but really, they have broken me in a way I never thought possible. Somehow, I muster the strength to keep walking, not stopping to look at my father's name, because right now he feels like a betrayal to me.

What scares me most is feeling that I know everything, yet nothing at all. Like the article that said the king is always watching, I feel his eyes upon me now as I pass portraits of him and his family. They have all been watching me, and they are all-seeing, all-knowing, and nothing has been kept secret. Roman, the House of Pluto, listening to their words, taking their papers. Somewhere along the line I was not as careful as I first thought.

I'm not sure where to go, afraid that if I try and hide, someone will be waiting for me somewhere. So I keep walking, lost to the world, trying to put as much distance between me and that room and that book and the goddamn princess. I round the corner, heading to the main hall, when I collide with something solid. I stumble back, breath expelling from me in a gust, and I place my hands on my thighs as I right myself.

'I beg your pardon, Mr Cecil...' Professor Lawrence starts to say, before he pauses, takes stock of me. 'Mr Cecil, is everything all right?'

I want to tell him I'm fine. Want to put on a brave face and act like nothing has changed. But something snaps within me under his stare. He recoils, as if my tears have frightened him, and then he checks around him before he guides me to the door that leads down to his classroom. I find myself sat in his room, smaller than ever in the front row, and he comes from around his table, offering me a glass of water poured from a jug on his desk. He pours himself some wine, and I wish I could drink that instead. Father always swore by his wine.

And all the while, I know I can't trust this man.

'What's wrong? Are you worried about your task?'

'I've done my task,' I bite out, glaring at the water.

'Did it not go well?'

'I have no idea,' I say. 'How long have you known?'

'Sorry?'

'How long have you known who my partner is?'

Lawrence sits a little taller, but his fingers tighten their grip around the intricately designed goblet. He runs a finger over the ridges of flying eagles, before lifting it to his lips and taking a longer drink, eyes staring into the distance, at nothing in particular.

I could scream. I could let my anger fly out. I even consider striking him, because in that moment I know he's known everything about me and hasn't said a thing. But I'm a Saturn boy, and we pride ourselves on patience, on restraining ourselves, and I calmly swallow the bubbling anger and know that later I'll express it through the written word.

'I can't comment on any individual student's partners.'

'I just met her, Lawrence, drop the pretence.'

Lawrence sighs. 'Still. I cannot.'

'But you knew.'

'I don't know what—'

'Oh, please, Professor Lawrence, I'm not a child. Have some respect for me. Talk to me, man to man.'

Lawrence's eyes flash a dangerous warning and I roll my shoulders, roll my tongue over my teeth. He waits before speaking again, 'They let Princess Cerys meet you.'

'Yes.'

Lawrence's throat bobs, and he sips from his goblet again. 'And how are you feeling?'

'Oh, top-notch. One hundred per cent. I have made it in life and I am thrilled.'

Lawrence shakes his head.

'She showed me the book. Dwynwen's book. It said my parents made a deal.'

Lawrence stands, putting one hand behind his back, his other pressed to his chest, holding the goblet close to his heart. 'I see.'

'That's it?'

Lawrence peers at me, before walking towards the mural of the zodiacs, what was once my favourite feature of his room. 'Have you told anyone about this?'

'No. You were the first person I saw.'

'I see,' Lawrence says, strolling back to his desk.

'Stop saying, "I see".'

Lawrence tenses. 'And did you glean more information about her, your Princess Cerys?'

'She told me that the only reason Ganymede's brought her in, the only reason she showed me that book, is because the school thinks they're losing me. To keep me focused. What does that mean, Professor?'

'I cannot begin to speculate.'

I scream, and he recoils.

'Let it out, Mr Cecil.'

I think I might, but no more anger flares, only simmers. 'I'm fine.'

Lawrence sits at his desk, and for the first time he exhales, his hair rippling in the breeze of his fleeing breath. 'You must be ... surprised.'

'Surprised? I'm terrified. My partner has been chosen for me by interference. Not through technology.'

'You don't know that. She is your perfect pairing.'

I shake my head. 'That is not true in my case, and you know it.'

Lawrence holds up his hands. 'I'm telling you, I don't.'

'I don't believe you,' I say. 'Why else have I been looked after by you all these years? Why else am I looked after by Ganymede's?'

'We have a duty to our students...'

'Oh? Is that why boys have been disappearing?'

A wave of calm crashes upon the threshold of the room, before drowning us in its quiet. Neither one of us looks away. A thirty-something man, a seventeen-year-old boy, both abiding by the rules society has put upon us.

'I beg your pardon?' It escapes Lawrence in a whisper.

My hands shake, my voice waivers, as I say, 'I *know*, Professor Lawrence. Ganymede's has been removing boys they don't deem fit for graduation. I'm on to every single one of you.'

Lawrence leans forward, dragging his elbows across his desk. 'I don't know what you are implying, Mr Cecil, but you cannot throw such baseless accusations around.'

'Are they baseless, though, Professor?'

Lawrence looks away, reaches for his goblet, only this time his fingers knock the contents onto his desk. Red wine spreads, drips over the edge in rhythmic droplets, splashing like blood upon the stone floor, forever ingrained. He swears, half-rises as if to deal with the mess, but then falls back into his chair, staring at the offending spillage.

'I heard you,' I say, my voice low.

He pauses, but his eyes remain on the wine. 'Heard what, Mr Cecil?'

'Talking about Blake. He was murdered, wasn't he?'

He looks at me. 'Mr Cecil.'

'Lawrence.'

'This is not appropriate.'

'No, it isn't. And I know that, for whatever reason, my "partner" wasn't chosen for me in the natural way,' I say.

Lawrence shakes his head, barely, but I catch it.

'I've seen the evidence on that, at least. My parents struck a deal, didn't they? They agreed to sell me off to the monarchy?'

Lawrence sighs, but says nothing.

'You know my father loved the king. The king loved my father. They couldn't be together and for some reason he thought the king should look after me, too. That's why they were coming back for me.' My voice cracks, but I don't care. 'They were coming back because they regretted what they'd agreed to. And somehow, they died before they could get out of the deal. That's why Ganymede's has looked after me. That's why I'm still here. Ganymede's must uphold their bargain.'

I wait for him to speak, willing him to do so, to confirm everything that has dawned on me. 'Isn't it, Professor?'

I'm proud of myself for staying calm, proud of my measured approach, but my Saturn patience is being tested right now with the look on his face.

'Am I to be prince, Professor Lawrence?'

The tide of silence swells, resounding in a shattering crescendo as he says, 'Yes, Mr Cecil. You are.'

CHAPTER 60

A numbness follows me as I walk through the corridors like a ghost, unsure of what to do. I've said too much to Lawrence, revealed too much to him about what I know, and he has given me the biggest piece of information I could know.

The truth.

I am but a boy, a gay boy, destined to be the partner, husband, to Princess Cerys.

The father of her children. The prince that aids the line of succession.

A truly respected, powerful member of a generous and kind monarchy.

If I thought I didn't have choice to begin with, now I know that it is true.

Once Lawrence told me that I was to be prince, he poured me wine. Handed it to me. I smelt the sweet aroma, raised it to my lips. But at the last moment I didn't drink. I put it next to me, and I rose slowly, and I left Lawrence's room as calmly and diplomatically as possible. If it was a test in mindfulness, he would have passed me. The knowledge that my parents struck a deal with Ganymede's doesn't fill me with satisfaction as it might once have done. Instead, I wish to rid myself of it.

Climbing the stairs, exhausted, I'm about to open the door to my common room when a voice calls.

'Where have you been?'

Roman. The setting sunlight trickles through stained-glass windows, casting him in beautiful colours of red and green, amber and yellow, like autumn personified. He stands in vest and loose trousers, his feet in neat black loafers. His hands are in his pockets, his eyebrows raised, burnt orange with enviable genetics. He gasps when he sees the bruises from Taylor. 'Who did this to you?'

He hurries to me, hands outstretched. 'I'm fine.'

'Not fine. I'll get the bastard that did this.'

'Don't get involved.'

He lightly touches my face, tilting it this way and that to see the damage. 'Dylan...'

'You're okay.'

Roman pauses. 'Why wouldn't I be?'

I lean against the dormitory door. 'I didn't know if you chose a trick or a treat.'

'I was never in trouble,' Roman says.

'Was it a trick?'

'No.'

I collapse into him, sinking into his chest as he wraps his strong arms around me. Sobs escape me, muffled in the fabric of his vest. His arms tighten around me, and I let my hands explore him, running over his muscled back, hands linking together at the base of his spine.

'What's the matter?' he whispers to me.

'Did you meet your partner?'

Roman falls silent, but I know the answer by the way his hand runs over my shoulders, comforting me.

They're interfering in our tasks, I think. *They're on to us.*

'What did you think?' I choke out.

'She seems nice.'

I clutch my eyes tighter as the sharpness of his words hurts my bruised flesh. 'We're in trouble.'

'I know.' His hold on me tightens, secure.

'You liked her?'

'I don't feel anything for her, definitely not attraction,' Roman whispers, his lips brushing my ear, sending shivers down my spine. 'I can never feel that for anyone but you.'

I tilt my head to look at him, aware that my eyes are red and wet with tears, but he smiles at me, uses his right hand to wipe them away with delicate precision. Standing on my tiptoes, I tentatively rise to kiss him, and he exhales as he kisses me back. I never want to let him go, my fingers twisting his vest in my hands, relishing the warmth that radiates from him, that complements the rays of golden light that bathe us.

When our lips part, our foreheads rest together, our noses brushing, and our lips still inches apart, I whisper, 'My partner is Princess Cerys.'

'What?' Roman reels back, putting me at arm's length. A flash of fear in his eyes makes me wilt, and I think of pulling him to me again, a reassurance that he will always be there. 'What?'

'Yes,' I say. 'We are to be together. I am to be...' I choke, look away. 'I am to be prince.'

Roman breaks away, hands running over his shaved hair, before massaging his temples. 'I just kissed the prince.'

'You kissed *me*,' I say, stepping to him, gripping his shoulders. 'Me. Dylan. A boy not made for this world, not fit for society. You did not kiss a prince. You kissed a cursed man.'

I shake my head. 'She was waiting for me in the room opposite where my father's name is forever etched. It's like some sick, twisted game.'

'Dylan...'

'I know now why Ganymede's looked after me. Why I'm still here. I'm betrothed to the monarchy.'

Roman's head droops, and I crouch just a little, trying to get him to look at me again. But his eyes flicker, they close, and I can feel I'm losing him.

'Please, Roman,' I whisper. 'It doesn't change anything.'

'Doesn't it?' Roman asks. 'You aren't just being partnered with some regular girl from a hamlet. You're going to have a royal wedding. You're going to have a royal title. You're going to represent the crown, society. You're...'

'Fucked.'

Despite everything, Roman emits a delirious laugh, and I have to join in, because to not join in would be to succumb to the tears.

'You can't be ... we can't be doing this. We can't be kissing when you're ... when it's been decided...' he says.

'But *I* haven't decided,' I say, voice raised. 'I don't have a say in this matter. Why is that allowed? I'm supposed to carry on and accept graduation knowing what is planned for me? When all I want is to be with you? To kiss you? To hold your hand in public and walk through these halls with pride that I have the handsomest boy in the school on my arm?'

Roman shakes his head, biting his lip in an irresistible way.

'You say you can feel no attraction to anyone but me,' I say. 'But Roman, I can feel nothing but tortured love when I look at you. Every time I see you, you remind me of my truth. You bring me pain and longing and you make my heart race and my stomach flutter. You send jolts through my body when you meet my eye, and you keep me up at night when you're nowhere near me. You make me realise that there is no point to this life if I cannot share it with you. You are confirmation that I must fight for liberation. I must fight for you, and for people like us.'

Roman stares at me, the intensity of his gaze piercing me. There are tears in his eyes as he swallows something he wants to say but can't seem to find the words for. I fear rejection when he leans against the wall, sliding his hands into his pockets.

'I can't let you put yourself in danger.'

'I will do anything for you, Roman,' I say, joining him at the wall. Our shoulders brush, and just this touch alone is enough to make me close my eyes and feel the heat of the evening on my skin. 'Men have gone to war for love before. I will do it again.'

Roman shifts, so that he faces me. 'You can't go to war for me.'

'Would you fight for me?'

'Yes.' His quick response fills me with adoration.

'Then I will fight for you.'

Before he replies, the door to the dormitory opens, and I peer over my shoulder. Johnny blinks, seeing us together. 'Interrupting something?'

'Hmm, kind of, mate,' Roman says.

Johnny rubs the back of his neck. 'Sorry, man. It's just ... well, it's about Taylor.'

I grimace, his pain still on my skin. 'What about him?'

'He's gone. He never came back from his task.'

CHAPTER 61

We gather in our dorm rooms, Johnny leaning against his bed, Cameron sitting on the edge of his. Roman stands in the window archway, face turned to the landscape. I stare up at the ceiling, lying upon my mattress, lost in thought.

'I did this,' I say. 'I told Dwynwen about what he did to me.'

'I asked Professor Tania why Taylor had been disqualified,' Johnny says. 'She said he admitted beating Dylan up.'

Roman looks at me from the side. The weight of Johnny's words is clearer to the two of us than it is to the others.

'They put him through some low-stakes torture, from what I've gathered,' Johnny continues. 'It was enough to make him talk. He confessed to bullying you for three years, said that he beat you up in this very room. Then he said that he is afraid of who he is. That he thinks there is evil inside him.'

'Taylor told me he didn't know why he felt violent,' I say.

Cameron tuts. 'That's interesting.'

'Is it?' Roman asks.

Cameron makes a noise of affirmation, shifting on his bed.

'Taylor has always projected himself to be a boy of calm nature, so for him to admit that his education hasn't worked the way they thought it would ... well, that's a problem for them, isn't it?'

'He's not a perfect man,' I say. 'Not an ideal student. But more importantly, he's not fit for society.' I sit up and cross my legs underneath me. 'You said you saw him being escorted away?'

'That's right,' Johnny says. 'Professor Tania took him out of the room as I was leaving, and then I saw him handed over to two security lads.'

'What did they look like?'

'One was tall, the other a bit shorter,' Johnny says, brow furrowed. 'Probably in their twenties, and...'

'Ieuan and Gareth,' Roman says.

The sky is tinged blood-red. I imagine the trees breathing a sigh of relief that they no longer have to be at mercy of the heat for another night. They have no choice. They cannot escape the climate of the earth humanity has ruined. Just as the students at Ganymede's cannot escape the heat put on them to be perfect men.

'Do you think the other boys who have gone missing were taken away in the same way?'

'I don't know. Seems odd, though, doesn't it?' Cameron asks.

Johnny points to Taylor's part of the room. 'All Taylor's stuff is here. He wasn't even allowed to pack his bags.'

'I don't think he's coming back.' Roman eyes Taylor's bed.

We fall silent, possibilities coming to us and disappearing as quickly as they come.

'I don't like any of this,' Cameron finally says.

'None of us do.' Johnny sinks onto his bed, resting his elbows on his knees, and starts chewing on his thumbnail.

Roman goes to sit in the window seat, his back to the darkening sky. 'Maybe we should try and speak to the security guards. Ask them flat out where they took Taylor,' he says.

'Yeah, that's a great idea,' Johnny says, sarcastic. 'Oh, hey, guys, where are you taking all these students that are never seen again?'

Everything has changed. How foolish I was to think there was hope. That some boys in a school could do anything to make a change. I wish I'd never known about Princess Cerys. Wish that Ganymede's revelation to bring me back to their desired outcome for my life hadn't worked. Because yes, I was straying. Yes, I was ready to risk it all. Now I'm realising they will always have control over me.

Anything else is idealistic.

And as I look at Johnny and Cameron, I think my own realisation is reflected in their expressions.

'Fight or die,' Roman whispers to the room, but he looks pointedly at me.

CHAPTER 62

My sleep that night is broken by images of Taylor. Taylor coming back into the room. Taylor blending with the shadows at the end of my bed. Taylor gripping my collar and shaking me awake. At quarter to six in the morning, I bolt upright in bed, sweat gathered on my chest, surveying the still room. Taylor, of course, was nowhere to be seen, whereas only a second ago he had been right here, screaming for my help. Even when he's not here, he's disturbing me.

Giving up on sleep, I dress in joggers and vest, pack a tote bag with swimming shorts and a towel, and head outside. At the entrance to the school, the lake glistening in the already glorious brightness of the morning, is Roman. He sits on the top step, his hands in his lap, staring out at the landscape. The shade, where we both are, is enough to make me shiver, but Roman sits in it with a towel draped around his shoulders, and his feet bare.

'Roman.'

He startles, then rises, and stands before me, glistening with damp. His muscles rippling, and his shorts hugging his hips, creased. 'You gave me a fright.'

'Another swim?'

He kneels, picking up his own bag. I think he might leave me, and all I wish to do is hold him close, but instead he nods towards the water, and we walk in silence, the rustle of the dry grass against our skin. I keep my gaze fixed firmly upon the still lake, relishing the warmth as we emerge from the shadows into the morning sun.

At the banks of the water, Roman doesn't hesitate. His arms cut through the clear water, propelling him forward as his strong back breaks the surface of stillness. He takes a breath, legs kicking as he twists his body, floating atop the water like he is one with it. It laps at his skin with hunger, the same hunger that has my stomach churning and my heart pining. It drips over his chest, pooling at his sternum, disappearing with his waist.

'Don't just stand and stare,' he says to me, face glowing in the morning heat. 'Come in.'

I pull my vest off, feeling the warmth rush to my exposed body. My eyes flutter, so that all I see is shades of pink and orange and amber. I turn, drop my trousers, thinking I imagine the small gasp that comes from Roman. I take my shorts from my bag, slip into them, and when I turn back to the water, he's grinning at me. My feet break the surface, chilled, and my legs ache as I go deeper. My racing thoughts become louder as my nerves send signals for me to stop, to get back somewhere warm, but the numbness that pinches my skin is addictive. Waist in, an intake of breath, and finally I submerge, dipping my head under.

The racing thoughts quieten as I sink, and my body stops protesting and begins to relax. And then, as if the water cleans my body of the heavy toxins of thoughts, I float back to the surface. Roman greets me with bright eyes, a blushing face.

'That was beautiful. You're beautiful,' he says.

We swim away from the banks, heading to the middle of the lake, seeing a school of fish swim by underneath us. The heat prickles my skin, even though I am mostly chilled. I can feel my skin redden, but I don't mind. The UVs are not at their strongest yet.

'What are we going to do?'

I don't look at him, because I know what I'll see. Fear. And as I swim a little further into the lake, I think of what's going to happen when this place is no longer home for me.

'We don't have a choice, do we?'

'I know, but...' Roman, who urged me to make changes and fight for our right to belong, is pleading.

There's no current of water, but there's a current of us, and we are pulled together by something other. His hands graze my body and mine his, but we are aware we swim before a school full of our peers, of professors.

'It's a hard truth when you realise everything has been rigged against us,' I say. 'If we leave this all behind, then what's for us?'

'Somewhere we can live and be ourselves.'

I offer a sad smile. 'Where?'

'A hamlet will have us. My parents, they'll hide us. Hell, we could even hide in the open country and live under our tree.'

It's a touching, fond thought. Before Cerys, I would have believed in it.

'You want to live your life hidden away?'

'Or we'll find a home. Somewhere on the edge of society. We'll grow our own food and we'll work our own jobs and we'll get by.'

I reach for him, placing a hand underneath his chin. 'Boys

like us don't get to live in the same house. We don't get to work a job and be a partnership like everyone else.'

He leans into my hand as my thumb brushes against his lips. 'Then we change it. We rip society apart and we campaign and fight for our rights.'

'Just the two of us?' I say. 'Us against the world?'

'The Plutonians. Yesterday it seemed like you all kind of zoned out from it. I worry you're losing sight. You really are a worthy leader, Dylan.'

'But are we enough?' I say, though his words console me. 'If we fight, we become a public enemy.'

Roman pushes away from me, shaking his head. 'So, what? You wish to remain passive?'

'I hate the thought of being passive,' I tell him. 'But ... it feels impossible, fighting against the might of the system.'

It seems overnight we have both been sleeplessly thinking, but we have gone in opposite directions. Him naive, me realistic.

'We *can* be the change, though,' he says. 'All of us. Together. All it takes is enough voices to convince others. All it takes is the collective to overthrow the current power, and become the power. Not them.'

'But ... we are inexperienced, we're just boys.'

'We are inexperienced *men*, but we can fight,' Roman argues. 'Dylan. You can't lose sight of it. Remember our plan to get the truth out there. To get the truth to the Jolly Jester.'

I tread water carefully, looking at the hills that tower above us, keeping us in the valley, away from prying eyes. 'I want things to change. Of course I do. But my fate is sealed. It is predetermined.'

'No, it is not. I'm sorry, Dylan, but it's not,' he says.

There's silence, nothing but the sound of birds tweeting in the trees, or above us as they start their mornings. Shadows in the windows, movements as air is let into bedrooms, classrooms. Another day of perfection at the institute of sublimity.

'I think my father loved the king,' I say.

'Everyone loves the king.'

'Not the way my father did. I think the king loved my father.'

Roman's face twists into shock, then empathy as I tell him what Cerys said.

'They couldn't be together,' I finally say. 'For many reasons. I don't know why, but Father seemed to want me to be under the king's care. I think he regretted it the moment I set foot in Ganymede's.'

'That's awful.'

'I know.'

Roman swims closer to me, so that his skin brushes mine. His touch is the remedy to my pain, and I close my eyes, sinking into him as he submerges me.

'Does that not tell you what you should do?' he whispers. 'We can change it. We should change it.'

'Roman—'

'Dylan.' He cups my face, watching me. 'This world needs liberation.'

Tears fill the lake, salting my tongue, and Roman wipes his own tears before crying into my neck. Sunlight caresses our bodies, and when my hands run over his rust-coloured hair, and over his freckled chest, he kisses me, soft, gentle, but it says a thousand words, transcends languages. A foolish, reckless moment, for two foolish, reckless fools.

'Please don't throw your graduation away,' I say when we break apart. 'You're an asset to society. You have a solid future ahead of you. You can't throw it away.'

Roman's wounded expression is enough to set me on edge. 'What's happened to you?'

'What's happened to me?' I almost shout. 'I'm trapped. I've been given a death sentence, basically. Don't you see it? They got rid of Taylor because he beat me up. They're protecting me. He's a victim of whatever is going on because I've been deemed to be the perfect partner to the princess. That means you being with me is dangerous, Roman. If they've let you see your partner, they suspect. I'm going to get you expelled. I'd rather you go out in society and pretend to love a girl, but me? I have to pretend to love a princess, pretend to love my title, pretend to love the monarchy and the society that would see my kind eradicated for their uselessness. I don't even think they'd let me throw graduation away, even if I could. Even if I rebel. I'm done for. At least you can sneak away, Roman. At least you can put a mask on every day and deal with it in private. I may as well end it now.'

'Don't you dare say that. Ever.'

'Why prolong my suffocation when I could do it right now?'

Roman grips me, pulls me to him, and his hug is tight, full of fear and passion like he might lose me to the bottom of the lake. 'This won't happen to you. I won't let it. There's still time. There's still a chance.'

My hands caress his shoulders, as I say, 'I hope you're right.'

'It's not us that needs to change. It's them.'

I hold him a little tighter, to reassure him that I'm listening. But really, my touch is one of pity, for a boy who can't accept his fate.

CHAPTER 63

As the final task gets closer, my focus seems to wane. Every moment of my day is filled with seemingly hopeless thoughts of escaping this school and never coming back. I huddle in the library with Roman, both of us pretending to be absorbed in books. Our hands are linked underneath the table, our knees pressed together. We're lit only by the low lamplight, and as a torrent of summer rain pours down, our whispers drown beneath it.

'We would be selfish if we left this behind.'

Roman nods. 'I know. But wouldn't it be easier?'

'Privilege,' I mutter. 'To be able to leave others to deal with issues and say nothing, do nothing.'

Roman's hand tightens around mine. 'I know.'

'Why do humans have a tendency to ruin everything?' I say.

'I don't even think the brightest mind could answer that.'

Roman lifts his arm. I check the dim library, making sure it is deserted before I lean into him. Nestled into the crook of his neck, he flips through a copy of *Frankenstein*, not taking in the words.

'I've read it before,' he says to me, his voice low. 'Many times.'

'Oh, to have met Mary Shelley.'

'She'd sort this out.'

We hear voices somewhere near the entrance and break apart. He closes the book and looks at me. 'Come on. Let's find somewhere quiet so we can be together undisturbed.'

I smile, wishing there were somewhere truly private for us to be. The dark sky looms above us as we walk through the halls. Sweet, glorious rain pours, and wind rattles the windows. In the deserted hallway Roman briefly pulls me to him, as if to keep me warm. My laughter bounces around us, and he's grinning, even though there's nothing humorous about the situation we're in.

He sneaks us through an old servants' corridor, and we linger in the dark stairwell, holding hands.

'I think it's sad, when I think of my father.' I can barely make out his handsome features, but I know he's listening. 'What a sad life he must have had. I'm sure he loved my mother. That household was a house of love. I wonder if she ever really knew how much he loved the king.'

Roman hugs me, his scent familiar and safe. I nuzzle into his neck, my lips brushing it, before he brings my lips to his own. Pressed against the corridor wall, I get lost in his touch. He rubs my shoulder when the kissing stops, and we lean against one another like the pillar of the spiral staircase supports the rising steps. Even here we hear the dim sound of rain fall.

'You need to let me go,' I say, voice hollow.

'We should dance in the rain,' he says to me.

'Dance in the rain? Did you hear me?'

'We're young, we should be reckless, we should be foolish. Come and dance in the rain with me.'

'Roman...'

'Dylan. Please.'

I hold his gaze.

'Please, dance in the rain with me.'

And I do. We lollop over wet terrain as the rain washes over our bodies. I tilt my head to the downpour, as the heavenly droplets sink through the fabric of my clothes and chill me to the very core. Roman's laughter as he takes my hand and spins me around elicits giggles from deep inside, and I don't care for the cold that plagues me. I kick off my shoes, take off my socks and let my feet sink into the beautiful bounty of earth, and he does the same, and the grass tickles our ankles and we forget all of our harboured shame.

Sopping wet, droplets dripping from my hair, we chirrup with glee when thunder rumbles. I hold up my hands as a flash of lightning illuminates our cheerful expressions.

That's when I see them.

Unmistakably so.

Crossing the hallway of the bottom floor are some of the professors, grouped together, led by Dwynwen. Lawrence, Mother Mai, Dalia and Tania. They are staring straight ahead and haven't seen us; they're marching with what looks like determination. I tap Roman, turn him away from the swirling clouds and point to the windows, and he crouches, and pulls me closer to the wall. We conceal ourselves by sinking into the ivy that grows upon the school, and we follow them from the outside, peering through the window. Dwynwen slides open panelling that leads to a flight of stairs that descend underneath the school. As the professors go in one by one, I grip Roman's hand. We both recoil when Ieuan and Gareth appear at the door, look left, and then right, and then close the door behind them.

'What the hell are they doing?' I ask him, as a crash of thunder rattles my befuddled thoughts.

'I don't know, but let's find out.'

CHAPTER 64

Knowing that we have time, Roman joins me in my dormitory, Cameron and Johnny with us.

'Talk me through it again,' Johnny says.

'They disappeared underground and they were with security,' I say.

'I remember reading the history of this place.' Cameron stands looking out at the wet night, one hand behind his back, the other resting against the wall. 'The uses over the years. Ganymede's has been many things, but I remember reading about tunnels that connected the manor to the old church on the grounds.'

'You think there are tunnels underneath this place?'

'When the place is full of secret servants' corridors, I think anything is possible.'

'I'd love to get my hands on the blueprint,' Johnny says.

'Why?'

'So I can work out how I'd renovate the place.' He rolls his eyes good-naturedly. 'No. To get the lie of the land, obviously.'

'I say we go down there,' says Roman.

We all look at him like he's lost his mind. Maybe he's already catching a cold from the rain. We've lit the fire in our hearth, and both of us are wrapped in blankets, our discarded wet clothes piled in the corner. I try not to think of what he looks like underneath, stripped to his boxer shorts. But it's probably like the Greek god statues that line the halls.

'Good luck with that, mate.'

'Well, why not?' Roman challenges.

'You think the professors are going to be like, "Oh, hiya boys, yeah, come join us, why don't you?"' Johnny says. 'Nah. We'll probably never see the light of day again if we go down there.'

'You said Rory wasn't with them?' Cameron asks, looking at me over his shoulder.

'No. And if Rory knew about the tunnels, he would have told us, wouldn't he?' says Roman.

Roman's right. About everything. Seeing the professors sneak away like that has made me thirsty again for the truth. I might be Cerys's partner, but I still need to know the truth.

'So, let's find Rory,' I say. 'I know exactly where he'll be.'

Rory's office is on the second floor, small, and he squints at us when we knock his door. Behind him an old camp bed. It looks uncomfortable and I pity him. There's a scent of cigar smoke, the window opened a crack. He looks as though he has been caught red-handed doing something illicit.

'You're breaking curfew. You shouldn't be here.'

'We want to tell you what we just saw.'

Inside his cramped office, we hover at the door as he leans against the windowsill. He's dressed in a cream vest and shorts, hairs on his legs, his feet bare. I focus on his face. But that's hard to do, because for the first time I truly see Blake reflected back at me. To my horror, it's the same dejectedness like he's learnt something and everything has changed for him.

He listens to every word we say, and all the while I think of Blake, and when we're finished, he says, 'All this time they've been sneaking away and they haven't included me.'

'That's what you're pissed off about?' Johnny asks.

'Only because I thought they trusted me. Now I wonder if they've been keeping me at arm's length.'

'Be thankful for that,' Cameron replies. 'What do you think is going on?'

'I don't like that security has gone down there with them.'

'The same security who took Taylor,' I say.

'Yeah.' He looks out of the window, arms resting on the sill, and shakes his head. 'I wonder if Blake ever saw them going down there. I wonder if that's what he found out. Did any of them see you?'

Roman and I both shake our heads.

'Okay, good.' Rory sighs. 'All right. Clearly, we do need to go down there.'

Johnny groans as Roman says, 'Told you.'

'Listen, you didn't hear this from me.' Rory's voice drops to a whisper as he leans across the table. 'But the final task is an amalgamation of all that you have learnt. The chefs, the security, the professors, all will be leaving you for the day and the night. Myself included. They want to see how you go about your day, how you make your food, and they want to know you can be trusted to live independently.'

'Piss easy,' Johnny says.

'Maybe so. The point is, it gives you all a prime opportunity to get down there and see what is really going on.'

'Can you stay?'

Rory falls silent, looking to the graveyard. How horrible it must be, I think, to be in your office and be able to see where your brother lies dead.

'I'll do my best. Boys, tomorrow we find out the truth. About Blake, about this school, about every boy who hasn't graduated.'

'Tomorrow, Ganymede's falls,' Roman says.

CHAPTER 65

'Look around you and give yourselves a round of applause. It is almost time to graduate.'

Applause like thunder echoes around me, and I join in, though my stomach is churning. 'Why are we doing this to ourselves?' I mutter to Johnny.

'Smile and clap,' he replies through his teeth.

Johnny's so good at being chipper, I think. I could learn from him.

When the applause subsides, Dwynwen's joyful expression becomes serious. 'On this bright and early day, the summer solstice, no less, I want you all to reflect on what you have already learnt, and how you feel about that. This next task is to put into action everything you have known. This is true independence.'

I zone out as Dwynwen explains the task that I have already come to know, straight from Rory's mouth. He sits on the head table looking as relaxed as the other professors, staunchly looking anywhere but my corner of the Saturn table.

'We'll be wanting to ascertain that you can cook for

yourself, live by yourself, live with your fellow man, and yes, even fend for yourself should the moment arise.' At this, the breakfast hall breaks out into whispers, and Dwynwen quietens us by placing a finger to her lips. 'There is no need to worry. This task should be a breeze. Those who have made it this far are here for good reason.'

She smiles at the professors and they nod along.

'From ten a.m. today, you will be alone in Ganymede's for twenty-four hours. We will come back to collect you tomorrow, and should you successfully pass, you will graduate. Hopefully, we will return to a fully functioning school.' She laughs, though the smile doesn't quite reach her eyes, which swivel in my direction. 'Good luck.'

It's like she's saying it to me.

'I'm pretty domestic, I think,' Johnny says, loud enough for some of the other boys to hear. Lee and Jackson sit nearby, ignoring what's going on around them. Neither of them looked at Dwynwen during her talk. 'I can make a banging cuppa.'

Students are beginning to file out of the room now, and the professors are all standing, listening to Dwynwen, who has her back turned to the room.

'All right, boys?' Elis approaches. 'How we all feeling?'

I spot Roman coming over, accompanied by Ben. Despite it all, I smile, and when he sees me he gives me a wave.

'Anyone know how to cook?' Johnny asks our group. 'It was never my strong point.'

Cameron rolls his eyes. 'No, only you could manage to burn pasta, rice and apple crumble.'

'That apple crumble was still good, though.'

'Not something I'd want again in a hurry,' I say, as Roman sits next to me, his leg brushing mine. He drops his hand out of view of the others, giving me a pat on my knee. Biting my tongue, I look away from him, smiling.

At the top table, Headmistress Dwynwen moves to a door at the far end of the room. She opens it and the professors go in, single file. Dwynwen hovers at the door, looking over at us. Everything inside me wants to scream to look away, but I hold my nerve, and eventually she disappears from view, closing the door behind her.

It's like those remaining in the room have picked up on them leaving, because chatter breaks out louder. Some students look concerned, others look excited. With no professors watching us, we lean in closer.

'What are we going to do, then?' Elis asks.

'You've been briefed?' I ask.

'Roman told us,' Elis says. Owen, Stan, Ben and Kim have joined us now. Petro and Grady seem to have left.

'Good work,' I say to him. 'I've been thinking about what we should do, and I think it's the best thing for all of us.' All eyes are on me, so I plough on. 'Roman and I will meet with Rory, and we'll go through the door and see what is underneath this school. We'll come back and tell you what we find and we can go from there.'

'What, and the rest of us will just sit around and do nothing?' Elis asks.

'You have to focus on your graduation.'

'Fuck graduation,' Johnny mutters.

'Let's not argue about this...'

'You don't have to be the saviour,' Ben argues.

'I'm not trying to be the saviour.'

'But you're excluding us from helping.'

'He's not excluding you from anything,' Roman interjects. 'You lot wanted Dylan to lead you, and he's suggesting what we can do. He's thinking of you.'

Ben tuts, crossing his arms.

'I'm not putting you all at risk. Some of us have to get out of here with the knowledge of what is happening beneath us. If Roman and I get caught, Rory will be able to tell you what we found. You can continue while we...'

I don't voice the rest of it. There is no point dwelling.

'As much as I hate to admit it, you're probably right,' Elis says. 'The rest of us will see this task through to the finish line and when you come back, we'll decide what we should do next.'

'Do you have a plan beyond this?' Kim asks.

Roman shakes his head. 'Not really. We could get down there and find nothing at all.'

'I trust Dylan wholeheartedly. What better day to find out the truth when the professors are not watching us?' Elis says. '"Our doubts are traitors, and make us lose the good we oft might win, by fearing to attempt."'

Ben's jaw tenses, and without saying a word he stalks away.

'He'll come round,' Kim says. 'We might focus on this final task, but we'll be keeping an eye out for your safe return.'

I hope it isn't in vain.

CHAPTER 66

Roman's kiss is pure escapism. He holds me and I hold him, pressed against the walls of the disused shower room. Outside, we hear voices, but they fade, doors closing on their sound. We don't break apart. Our hands explore one another, from jaw to neck, to shoulder to chest. The lowest we go is our hips, and only when Roman pulls me closer to him.

He pulls me into a hug, and my hands rub his back and we sway in the middle of the shower block like we're doing a death dance. A melancholic melody plays in my memory, and maybe Roman prefers serenity, for he seems to move to his own notes.

We break apart, reluctantly, when the door to the bathroom opens.

'Thought we'd find you here.' Johnny and Cameron walk in, somewhat hesitantly.

'We were just...' Roman begins.

'You don't have to hide anything from us.'

'You make a banging couple.'

Roman's expression twists as he considers me, gauging my reaction. When I break out into relieved laughter, he grins and wraps his arm around me. Granted, it feels more like a brotherly hug in front of Johnny and Cameron, but it's a start. My friends, my Saturn boys, witnessing the whole thing with joyful smiles.

Perhaps this is our last day. If it is, I will remember Roman's lips on mine for eternity, when I am mere stardust and dispersed energy.

'Can I ask why you disturbed us?'

'We've seen Rory,' Johnny says. 'He's back.'

I don't stop to see what the others are going to do. I head out into the school, hearing the boys following me. 'Where did you see him?'

'He's in the library.'

I nod, hurrying towards the library. It's odd not to walk past any professors, instead seeing third-years lounging around looking slightly lost. Law and order is still in place, but I wonder what tonight might bring.

'Rory.'

'Boys, thank God.' He twists his hands together, standing at an empty library table. 'I found more newspapers today. The contrast is stark.'

'What did you find?'

'The official ones celebrated a fresh influx in newborns. Population rising, with unemployment levels at zero per cent. Then the Jolly Jester writes a whole article on how there are hamlets out there turning into ghost towns.'

'Still nothing on Blake?' I ask.

'Blake isn't on anyone's radar anymore.' Rory's lip quivers. 'And ... I can't get hold of our parents.'

He sits on the edge of the table, dropping his head. We head to him, and hesitantly I pat his shoulder. He's Blake's brother, I have to remind myself. He's not like the other professors.

'When did you last hear from them?'

'It's coming up to three weeks now. This is too long. I can feel it right here.' He touches his stomach, shaking his head.

'You're safe.'

'Fill me in on what's going on today,' he says after he composes himself.

'We are planning on going underground,' I say.

'Good.' Rory takes a breath. 'I'm coming, too.'

Half an hour later, Rory, Roman and I head to where we saw the professors disappear. My stomach leaps and my legs get heavy with every step, my body protesting at me to forget everything I've seen. Live a fake but safer life. But sometimes you have to go against the grain to make a change.

'If you want to go back, you can,' I tell Rory, and then turn to Roman. 'You, too.'

'You think I'm going to leave you?' Roman shakes his head. 'Honestly, Dylan, I thought you knew me better than that. I'm with you, every step of the way. Your battles are my fights.'

My hand twitches to reach out for him, but I don't quite trust Rory enough to do that. Instead, I take a breath, biting my lip.

'And it would be remiss of me not to come with you,' Rory says. 'I want answers, too, you know. But be prepared. If we go down here, everything could change. There is no going back now.'

Princess Cerys, a life of security, the most wealth I could ever have. I would never go without. Never be uncomfortable.

'It's a sacrifice I'm willing to make.'

CHAPTER 67

The scent of earth and incense smoke rises to greet us, and as we descend it only gets stronger. Rory closes the door behind us with a quiet precision, and for a moment we're plunged into darkness, until we get to the bottom of the stairs and find ourselves in a redbrick tunnel, lit by candlelight. Incense smoke wafts around us, and I stifle a cough, my eyes watering.

There's no sight of anything beyond. Just shrinking tunnel, flickering flames.

Roman moves closer to me, and I so desperately want to touch his hand, but I'm hyper-aware of Rory being with us.

'I'll lead the way,' Rory says. Despite his whisper, it still hisses around us like an unfurling, antagonised snake.

I notice how he's dressed in what he usually wears when teaching. An off-white Oxford shirt, black trousers and polished leather shoes. They click relentlessly over the surprisingly clean brick floor, and I wish he would walk more lightly, afraid he might give us away. But I don't see any entrances along this tunnel. No concealed doors. There seems to only be one way in and out of this place. If someone comes, we would have time to run.

Despite the flames, there's a chill, and the pungent earth smell is overwhelming in places. It's like inhaling dirt itself, seedlings burrowing within my lungs.

'What's that?' Roman whispers, coming to a stop.

What looks like a giant crow sits in the middle of the tunnel, guarding a flight of stairs. Rory presses his fingers to his lips and creeps closer. I hold my breath, staring at the bird, afraid of what might come.

'It's fake.' Rory shakes it, and pathetic feathers swan to the floor. 'It's like a papier mâché mask.'

I touch it, feeling the softness of real feathers, and the bumpy surface beneath. A part of it flakes off under Roman's touch, and he reels back, as if he's committed some huge sin.

'I guess we should go up there.'

Rory and Roman peer at the steps.

'Come on, then.'

We follow Rory, the steps going from narrow stone to fashioned wood, which creaks and groans underneath us. They begin to turn, and we emerge into a dusty room devoid of decoration. Small candles burn in a corner, shoved into an old brass candelabra. There's a small flight of wooden stairs leading to a pale blue door. Behind it, shadows move, light seeping through a gap at the bottom of the door.

'What the fuck?' Roman whispers.

'Any idea where we might be?' I ask Rory.

'Judging by the direction we've come,' he says, 'I think we've walked underneath the school and away from it.'

My head swims, and I have to fight to keep myself steady. Beyond, I'm sure I can hear voices, humming together. Roman is shaking his head, but we have to remain confident, we have to know what is really going on here.

'Are you sure you want to do this?' Rory asks us.

'Absolutely certain.' Roman sounds anything but.

Rory guides us up the stairs, and he places his hand carefully on the door handle. I give him an encouraging nod. Slowly, he opens the door.

At first, I think I'm dreaming. Amber light glows, purple, too. It seems to caress the stone walls like an elicit lover. There's music, which thrums against my eardrums and rumbles in my chest. It's played by human touch, the notes occasionally being missed, the rhythm off enough to make my hairs stand on end. The candlelight shines in all corners of the room, and the old church pews have been cast aside to make room for the function in the middle. Figures, standing in pairs, surround a golden altar, where a boy kneels, head bowed as if in prayer. They are all watching him.

The door we entered through slams shut and Roman swears.

Heads whip in our direction, but I can't make out features underneath, masked as they are in grotesque and twisted iconography. A crescent moon, weeping a single silver tear. A crudely shaped burning sun, eight spiked orange points coming away from lifeless eyes. A green leaf, a star, a single water drop. All of them have the same glossed-over eyes, and tight, pursed lips. Mirth escapes from underneath, so disjointed from their expressionless masks.

The figures are dressed in tight, form-fitting clothing, adorned in abundant leaves, which trail across the stone flagged floor, vines trailing around people's skin, as if they are growing on the human body. It's as if elaborate floral displays have come to life. The leaves whisper as the people come towards us.

'Stay behind me,' Rory instructs, eyes struck with fear.

'Ah, Rory, what a pleasure to see you.' The crying moon approaches, reaching with leaf-strewn hands to remove the mask. 'You have brought us new subjects?'

CHAPTER 68

Mother Mai stares back at us, the moon mask in her left hand. Her face is flushed, and she takes a few deep breaths, before she comes to us, reaching out to touch me. 'Mr Cecil. An interesting choice. And Mr Edwards. Care to explain?'

With horror, I look at Rory, wondering what he's going to say.

'What's going on over here, then?' The sun approaches us, a train of flowers trailing behind them. I know who this is before she even removes the mask. 'What are these two doing here?'

Headmistress Dwynwen looks at her mother, and back at Rory.

'Someone speak.'

'We've got new subjects,' Mother Mai says with a giggle.

The music is fading now. Whoever's playing clearly realises something new has come. Without its haunting tune, the room feels oddly still, the magic dying like a wisp of flame.

But all I care for is Rory's answer. His truth.

'Rory?' I whisper. *Do something*, I want to urge. But suddenly all of this feels foolish. We are unarmed, outnumbered, and we are nothing but fledgling men wishing to make their mark upon this earth. Judging by the boy knelt on the floor, unmoving, we've walked into something private between the professors, all of whom are now removing their masks, revealing their curious expressions. But none look fearful, none look ashamed. Omar smiles slightly, and Tania licks her lips.

'We've got to get out of here,' I say to Roman, reaching for him.

'Stop right there,' Mother Mai orders.

'Mother,' Dwynwen starts.

'Rory, please take our guests to the altar.'

Rory turns, grabs Roman and me by our wrists. We try to pull away, but I barely get him to budge. Roman manages to unsteady him, though, and breaks free, running further into the room.

'Roman!' My scream echoes around what I now realise is the disused church, stripped of its old Christian iconography, decorated with nods to nature, and the glyphs of the planets. Nature itself has broken through, with weeds growing through some of the stone laid to rest in the earth, and leaves dusted aside in each corner. It's like the Pluto crypt, I think, only this feels more alive, a reminder of what nature can and will reclaim if we let it.

'Calm down.' Professor Lawrence's voice comes from the other end of the church. He walks towards us flanked by Ieuan and Gareth, the two security members. 'There is no need for all this panic.'

'We've been betrayed,' I shout, as Rory drags me towards the altar. 'You are all betrayers.'

'We are nothing of the sort,' Omar argues.

'You forget who you are speaking to,' Headmistress Dwynwen snaps. 'Enough of this.'

'I don't recognise you. Any of you. This is not who we thought you were.'

Roman bangs on the door at the front of the church, trying with all his might to pull it open. 'Help. Someone help us.'

'Get him, right now,' Lawrence says.

The security guards run forward, flanking Roman. He tries to run, but Gareth trips him, and Roman splays across the floor, his breath heaving. Ieuan and Gareth lift him up and discard him at the base of the altar.

Rory squeezes me, shakes his head slightly and nods to the boy on the floor. Hesitant, I stand at the altar, seeing nothing inside the small bowl at the top. The boy doesn't move, but he's breathing. Rory stumbles away from me, and Tania drags him towards her.

'See? That's better,' Mother Mai says. 'What do we do with these two, then?'

The professors circle us now, Ieuan and Gareth blocking the only two exits out of here. I tap the boy, turning him to face me. I recoil in horror. Bruised, swollen-faced but unmistakable. 'Taylor.'

He doesn't react, eyes glazed. What have they done to him?

'Stay calm, Mr Cecil,' Dwynwen says.

'Calm? How can we stay calm?' I glare at Rory. 'How can you do this? How can you betray us like this?'

'You horrible, evil people,' Roman growls.

'You don't know that,' Dwynwen says, wounded. 'You have come here and I grant this must look sinister to you, but I can assure you it is not.'

'It is anything but,' Mother Mai says. 'This is sacred.'

'It's something,' I mutter.

'We praise our beautiful earth and you have come and ruined it,' Mother Mai says. 'You have interrupted a moment of summer solstice celebration.'

'Fuck your moment,' Roman shouts. 'This isn't beautiful.' He points at Taylor. 'This is perverse. What are you doing here with him? Where are the others?'

'Others, Mr Edwards?'

'The other students,' he says. 'Are they here, too? Buried beneath our feet?'

'How dare you,' Mother Mai reacts.

'It's about time you answered,' Roman continues. 'We're on to you. All of you. We know what you did to Blake.'

'What happened to Blake was an accident,' Lawrence insists.

'No, it wasn't, and you know it.' Rory's words make the professors still. Dwynwen and Lawrence exchange a look. Rory moves away from Tania, walks away from the circle, towards us. 'What's the matter?' He laughs. 'You really didn't think I'd want the truth about Blake?' He moves towards Dwynwen, but Mother Mai stands before her, mighty. Rory steps back, still laughing. It bounces around us and echoes in this horrible rotting church. 'Please. Tell me what you did to him.'

Rory moves towards us, as though he is our ally again.

'Stay away from us,' Roman tells him.

'I'm on your side. Trust me.' Rory clasps his hands together, as if begging. 'Please. You have to know that.'

'I don't know what to think anymore,' I say.

'No, I can imagine you don't,' Dwynwen says, breathless. 'They have seen enough.'

All but Dwynwen and Lawrence grin, reaching for their masks.

'What are you doing?' I move closer to Roman, standing in front of Taylor, protecting him.

The professors are closer now, closing any gaps, their leaf clothing forming like a big boundary line of growing nature. I can feel Roman trembling beside me, and I give him a reassuring nudge. It's not enough, but I want him to know I'm by his side, and I always will be.

'It's a shame this has to be done,' Dwynwen says. 'But threats must be eliminated.'

'What of Mr Cecil's partner?' Lawrence asks. 'The princess.'

'We will explain.'

'What are you saying?'

'They cannot leave here.'

Lawrence sighs. 'I'm sorry, boys,' he says, as though he is on our side.

'Tough luck,' Mother Mai says.

That's when a loud bang makes my head reel and Roman falls to the floor.

CHAPTER 69

They've shot Roman. That's all I can think in those split seconds of fear. My ears ring and my head aches.

I go to him, my hands roving over the parts of him I can reach. 'Are you hurt?'

He shakes his head. 'No. It wasn't me who was the target.'

I look around, brow furrowed. Rory, standing with a small gun in his hand, points at where Mother Mai had been standing moments before. She's on the floor now, hand to her chest, consoled by Omar and Tania.

'He tried to shoot me,' she states, pointing at Rory. There is no blood on her hands. No wound to be seen. 'Who employed this man?'

'Rory,' says Dwynwen, and he spins to point the gun at her. She raises her hands. 'You can't do this.'

'Tell me the truth, Dwynwen. Tell me what you did to my brother.'

Some of the professors gasp, whispers of 'brother' echoing around us. Dwynwen doesn't react, already knowing the truth.

Ieuan and Gareth leave their posts, coming towards us, but Lawrence shakes his head. 'Stay where you are,' he tells them.

Rory stands, pointing his gun now at Lawrence, now at Dwynwen. I stay next to Roman, finding his hand, taking it despite the situation we're in.

'Is that my gun?' Lawrence asks, his voice calm.

'I found it when I stole your newspapers.'

Lawrence's eyebrows raise. 'I noticed they'd been disappearing.'

'I will shoot every one of these professors until it's just you remaining, Dwynwen,' Rory says. 'I'm waiting for answers.'

'Can I check my mother is okay?' she says.

'No, you can't.'

'Please, lower the weapon.'

Rory swings his hands, shoots, and there's a yelp and a sickening wet sound. Mother Mai screams, and Omar swears, and Tania looks as though she wants to wrestle the gun from Rory's hand.

But it's Ieuan's scream that really hits me in the gut, and I know I shouldn't, but I look and see that blood splatters the wall where Gareth had been standing only moments before. His body lies lifeless, head mercifully turned away from us.

'Start speaking,' Rory orders.

'Okay, okay,' Dwynwen stresses. 'If I'm to tell you of Blake, I must tell you of everything.'

'No, Dwynwen,' Mother Mai says.

'Shut up,' Rory says.

'Do not tell my mother to shut up. If you want me to answer you, you show us some respect.'

Dwynwen and Rory glare at one another, and Rory gestures for her to continue. I want to tell him to stop, that he's being reckless. He's going to get us all killed.

'Mother, I will tell him. He deserves to die knowing the truth.'

My heart flips, and I get to my feet. 'No. You're not doing this.'

'Dylan, please. Let me explain.' She waits for us to fall silent, and when we do, she takes a moment to breathe, collecting her thoughts. It's a mindful technique I recognise from Lawrence. 'The collapse of society itself must never happen again. You see, in the past we had people who were weak. People who couldn't do the prime function they were here to do. And even now, we find ourselves suffering because of it.'

'Dwynwen, enough.'

'Mother, please.' Dwynwen sighs. 'Are you aware of the sickness?' She pauses like the flicker of a flame before ploughing on. 'Well, it's like a flu that sets your lungs on fire. People are choking on their coughs. Fevers are rising. It's taken many lives, many of our healthy people. When you're trying to rebuild a society, you don't need a sickness making it harder to do so.

'This sickness isn't a new thing, by the way. It has been around for many years, but it's only in the past few years that more and more people have not been recovering from it as it mutates. It frightened us, but more importantly, it has frightened the king. Ganymede's, and schools like ours around the UK, were instructed to ensure our students remained healthy by royal order. We were also given instructions to help society, more so than we already were.

'As you know, Ganymede's was set up to address the problem of men within society. Fertility rates have improved since we took over, and more and more healthy babies are being born, and healthy families are being raised. We have been mindful that we must not increase too fast, lest we end up in the same scenario we were in before, when society could not support so many people. So Ganymede's has always been a place for population control. What does it matter if here or there a few boys that would not amount to much are culled to keep the numbers down?'

My ears ring. It's like I've been plunged under water as ice runs through me and my hairs stand on end. Culled? Roman swears. Dwynwen closes her eyes, waiting for it all to subside.

'Now, let me explain. The king has a problem. We have a population that is still weak. We have an opportunity to eradicate that weakness. We carefully choose people for this task, and it is all under the instruction of the monarchy. When the time comes for your final education, you are not only being put through our technology to find you the perfect partner. We are checking that you are, indeed, perfect. That is to say that you don't get seriously ill. That you are healthy individuals. That you are emotionally well and calm and regulated. That you are capable of repopulation and loving your opposite sex. We know when students might not make it. We see it and we see if we can fix it. Conversion therapy, for example. Sometimes, we can't. We may discover that someone is already sick, they just don't know it yet. We may see a streak in someone's personality that the king does not want in society. We may determine that in a few years, you are to be diagnosed with something life-altering. Then there are those who might not be able to create life. Those who might refuse to procreate. There are those who aren't intelligent enough, or skilled enough. Those who are, in the eyes of the law, broken.'

My breath hitches and Roman shakes his head, swearing under his breath again. Heat prickles across my forehead.

'As you can imagine, there aren't many who are broken. Across all our schools, across our male and female students, only a small percentage are put to use elsewhere.' She says these last words like they're poison, and Lawrence clears his throat.

'It's a good thing,' Mother Mai chips in. 'Everyone has a purpose; everyone has a use.'

'What about Blake?' Rory questions.

'I'm getting there,' Dwynwen says, sounding defeated. 'Please, I know it is tough to hear, but the king wants perfection. What if we could create the perfect human, by identifying the traits we don't want, and fixing them? Eradicating them all together. Our king does not want to see us heading in the same direction as previous societies. There must be no perversions. He does not want so many people that the earth cannot support them. He does not want so many people that the earth gets destroyed to accommodate them. He wants emotionally mature children to emotionally mature parents. He wants skilled people, born to skilled parents. He wants a society of people who don't get ill, who can live and prosper until they die naturally. Don't you see? He does not care who you are or what you believe, as long as you are perfect and live how we naturally live. The monarch came to the decision that to have adequate societies, we would need to keep numbers at an acceptable level. We are pleased that the population is growing, but we have to level that out. We have to ensure that every time a child is born, they are born to be perfect. This is why our schools are here. You are here to be processed. You are here to be perfect. The king believes less is more.'

'But eugenics opens the doors to discrimination,' Roman says.

Dwynwen swallows, a quick shake of her head. 'Not quite, Mr Edwards, but thank you for your input.'

My stomach flips at the way she talks, like this is some class.

'The king believes that we can create the perfect human. Regardless of the perfect man, he believes that with the right studies, we can create the perfect society. He does not discriminate. His science does not discriminate. It is simple.

If you are perfect, welcome to society. If you are not, you should not be on this earth. It is kinder to society to let the riff-raff go.' Roman scoffs, and Mother Mai shouts. 'All races, nationalities, beliefs ... it does not matter, as long as you are perfect.'

'How?' It comes out as a croak, but Dwynwen hears me.

'You have seen Taylor.' Her words die, and we all stand for a moment looking at Taylor kneeling over. Gone is the confidence he once put out to the world. Dwynwen sighs. 'You brought to my attention his bullying behaviour, and after much conversation and thought, we knew he needed to be removed from society. So, we have brought him here, where he will be studied and put to use elsewhere. We must eradicate the violent man.'

Her words are so cold, I shiver.

'What of Blake?' Rory presses, impatient.

'Rory, I promise you, you will get answers,' Dwynwen snaps. She shakes her head. 'Sorry. Please. The king wants to know if there is a violent gene. If there is one, he wants to know how it can be removed. By manipulating our core essence, we can create the perfect society.'

'God save our king,' Mother Mai says, and some of the professors repeat the words, equally vigorously. Dwynwen and Lawrence do not.

'By studying Taylor, he can see what makes Taylor who he is. Taylor has already told us that he feels violent. That it consumes him and he doesn't know why.' Dwynwen observes him like he's a germ on a Petri dish. I pity him. 'He has agreed to collaborate and help us eradicate the violent gene once and for all.'

'This is barbaric,' Roman says.

'The bruises suggest he was coerced into collaboration,' I say.

'The bruises are my fault.' Ieuan steps forward. 'It's part of the studies. We wanted to see what neurological activity goes on when he is fighting. He was happy to fight.'

Taylor begins to shake, and I kneel down. He's crying. 'Shh,' I whisper to him. 'It's all right.'

'The king wants to know if we can *create* perfection, too,' Dwynwen says. 'We've been doing it through our education, through our pairings, but he wants to know if it is possible to create perfection from inception. The idea of perfection isn't new. The ancient Greeks had an ideal in mind when fashioning men out of marble. Da Vinci gave us the *Vitruvian Man*, and even then, he based it on other, similar, observations. Throughout the centuries, perfection has come in different guises.'

'In horrible guises, too,' Roman says. 'People have died because of it.'

'But the king is closer than anyone,' Mother Mai interrupts. 'It's about time.'

Tania nods.

'This is some sick cult.' Roman grimaces.

'This is *science*,' Mother Mai stresses. 'Pushing the boundaries of the realms of possibilities.'

'I don't follow how this sickness fits into what you're doing,' I say, voice shaking.

Dwynwen nods slowly. 'When we cull students – and it's not just the boys we cull, by the way; this happens across all our male and female schools around the UK. Small cohorts here and there, but the numbers add up. I like to think of it as trimming a manageable but overgrown garden.' She smiles at this, but only Ieuan returns it. 'When we cull our students, we use everything available to us. We might study their organs to see what didn't work, and see if we can find a way to make it work for someone else. We donate their healthy organs and we donate their blood and we sometimes extract their life force for further study. You see, these culled students help society in a different, less traditional way than those who graduate. They're just no longer around to see it.' She ignores Mother Mai's cold laugh. 'Because they are not perfect, we can determine why that is, and work on ensuring the next generation are. When you only have the perfect in society repopulating, eventually we only have perfect life force. But lately this sickness has been sweeping through the hamlets, and people we thought were healthy are finding themselves in trouble. So, we have been taking more boys, and injecting them with the virus, to study the effects and see if we can find a cure.'

I sway where I stand, head pounding.

'And do these boys consent?' I ask. 'Do they know this is what they are doing?'

Dwynwen pauses. 'Not exactly.'

'What about vaccines?'

'This virus is resistant,' Dwynwen says. 'The king is adamant that we can find a perfect cure to eradicate it completely.'

Rory raises the gun. 'This is disgusting.'

'Now, don't do anything rash,' Dwynwen says. 'They help us, and in turn you, in their own ways.'

'This is murder,' I say. 'It's dangerous territory. Ganymede's has blood on their hands.'

'Mr Cecil,' Dwynwen says. 'That is a narrow way of looking at this.'

'Narrow?' I say. 'This is not narrow. You are ... we are ... we are being farmed here. Every student that walks through this door is like cattle, and if they have TB, they're slaughtered. If they're fit and healthy, they go on to pastures new, used for something else further down the line. How can you let this happen, Headmistress? How can you oversee all of this?'

'It is not your headmistress's fault,' Lawrence says. 'We are at the behest of the monarchy.'

'Lawrence,' Mother Mai admonishes.

'The monarchy you are marrying me into,' I say. 'I can't love her, Headmistress. I can't love any woman.'

The weight of my words falls upon us all, and Roman gives me a proud smile. Lawrence scratches at his nose, and Dwynwen's features flicker from shock to nothing.

'Did I hear that right?' Mother Mai asks. 'Does that boy need conversion therapy?'

'Your parents—' Dwynwen begins, ignoring her mother.

'I don't care what my parents wanted or didn't want. They're dead, and they can't make these decisions for me anymore. In fact, it doesn't even seem we are allowed to make our own decisions. Maybe you should have set a decision task for us, Dwynwen. One last hope of us making one before we walk out wearing shackles. Are you telling us the king is that powerful? Are we really supposed to abide or die? Do I really not get a say in who I want to love or marry?'

Tears glisten in Dwynwen's blue eyes, rolling down her otherwise composed face. 'I'm afraid so, Mr Cecil,' she whispers.

'Enough,' Rory bellows. 'If you don't tell me what you did to my brother, Jupiter help me, I will shoot every last one of you.'

'That can get you arrested, young man,' Mother Mai says.

'I say we take him for studies,' Omar suggests. 'He's clearly motivated by violence.'

'Shut the fuck up.' Rory rounds on Omar, who stands his ground.

'Nobody is getting shot,' Dwynwen orders. 'Rory, please. Listen to me. What happened to Blake was a huge tragedy, I completely stand by that. What happened to him was not supposed to be his fate. He was the billionth boy, for king's sake. He was proof of success. Of perfection. He was ... he was perfect.'

She tilts her head, sniffing. 'What I told you, Dylan, wasn't the truth. Blake was always supposed to pass with flying colours. Blake threatened to go public with everything he'd discovered. That simply wasn't allowed.'

Rory screams at hearing this confirmation. He charges forward, straight at Dwynwen, who screams in fear. The gun is knocked from Rory's hands and clatters across the floor as professors move out of the way. Roman grabs my hand, pulls me away from Lawrence's approaching figure. My back turned, gunshots ring out, and someone shouts in fear.

'What have you done?'

CHAPTER 70

Rory bleeds at the altar, leaving streaks of red as he tumbles, kneeling, hunched over. Taylor, groaning, rolls over, but does not move.

'Rory.' A scream wrenches out of me and I run back into the church, gripping him, feeling his blood seep between my fingers and drench my palm. 'Stay with me, Rory. Stay with me. For Blake.'

'Blake.' Rory's eyes are wide with fear, and his right hand touches the wound in his chest. 'Go, Dylan. You have to run.'

Roman grabs me, pulls me away from Rory, and I try to fight, try to stay with him, with Taylor, but it's useless. Shouts assault me, but I don't try and make sense of them, too angry now at what has happened to a man who only wanted to discover the truth of his brother's death. Pulling me by the hand, Roman barrels towards the back of the church and barges through a door. The evening breeze sticks to the sweat on my skin, and for one moment I feel like this has all been some weird game. Roman yanks me away from the church, and we find ourselves running into the forest.

'Roman,' I gasp, breathless. 'Roman, stop.'

Somehow, I pull him behind a tree, the thick trunk shielding us. Roman leans against me, equally winded, and I hold on to him, keeping him close.

'There's no going back,' he says, breath brushing my face. 'We can never go back.'

'Roman. They killed Blake.'

'All of them did. I don't know.' Roman sinks to his knees. 'What do we do from here?'

It's a question that can't be answered. Surely we are dead men. Now that we know what Blake knew, our time is running out. Which leaves us with what option? Run into the open country and hope we can survive? Survive in a life of misery? Misery that will ruin what we are to each other?

There are footsteps coming, growing louder, and Roman grips me, pulls me to him so that I am pinned to his chest. I hold tight to him, wanting to run, and yet never wanting to lose sight of him.

'Dylan,' Dwynwen breathes, coming to us, Lawrence by her side. 'Mr Edwards. Are you both all right?'

'Don't come any closer,' I say.

'Dylan, please,' Lawrence says. 'What just happened...'

'Please, listen to me,' Dwynwen says. 'When morning comes, you will have a choice. Choose to graduate, and you will do so. Everything we have told you is true. You will be cared for and looked after. I will protect you, both of you, because you are bright boys that deserve a spot in society. It does not have to be a mark upon your record. Graduate, *please graduate*, and we can forget any of this ever happened.'

'And if we don't?'

Dwynwen sighs.

'I am not fit for society, and I am not fit to love the princess,'

I argue. 'There must be other suitors, other partners. I cannot go out there and pretend to be someone I am not.'

Dwynwen's lip wobbles, but she stands a little taller. 'And yet you must, for your partnership has already been decided.'

'But how can you let me go out there knowing ... knowing what I am?'

Dwynwen clears her throat. 'If you were partnered with any other female, Dylan, then perhaps this conversation would go differently. But you are a brave, strong, confident and sensitive boy who will be a gentle man that society craves. And you will be a man the monarchy needs.'

'But not the man I should be.'

'As I say, Dylan, I cannot and will not make this decision for you.' Dwynwen looks around the forest. 'If you graduate, nobody in that room will utter your truth. You will have a choice in the morning: whether you wish to graduate and greet society knowing what you know.'

'Which, by the way, nobody should know,' Lawrence says. 'If society were to know what these schools are doing at the request of the monarchy, there would be chaos. We cannot afford for this to get out there.'

'At all,' Dwynwen says.

Lawrence steps closer. 'In amongst all of this, one crucial thing is missing. Opposition.'

'The world needs opposition,' Dwynwen whispers, before looking over her shoulder. 'Now. We have to get back.'

Neither of them are themselves, I realise. Loss of composure, checking if they've been followed. They look afraid. Lawrence stares us down for a while longer before stepping away, as Dwynwen disappears towards the church.

'Sometimes life is meant to test ya,' Lawrence sings, 'that's why we thank the Jolly Jester.'

He's gone, long leaf coat swinging behind him. Roman gasps.

'What the fuck?'

Roman cups my face, looking at me, saying everything and nothing at the same time. My hands find his. I tilt my head to kiss his fingers, and he nods.

'You are still the prince,' he whispers to me.

'Roman.'

'No, listen to me. We don't have much time.' Roman hovers, as if debating if we should run. 'My feelings for you will burn as bright as the summer solstice sun. Our fates do not have to follow in the footsteps of Blake and Rory. Tonight, Dylan, we are more powerful than we have ever been. A daffodil always blooms.'

'But Roman, this isn't right. This isn't what I want.'

'No, and it's not what I want, either. It's not what anybody wants. This cannot go on.' Roman's hand trails behind my neck, his other hand tracing shapes over my heart. 'There's a reason the House of Pluto trusted you, Dylan, and we still do. You are the magician. The cards will always fall in your favour.'

'But I can't fight without my warrior.'

'Every man must lose to gain, and you are a battlefield I will emerge victor from,' he says. 'Dylan, some things are bigger than you and me.'

'Please.' Tears fall, salt upon my lips.

Roman's forehead rests against mine, his tears staining my shirt.

'Let's run. Let's hide. Together,' I plead.

'We will, but not the way you want to. We can't do that.'

'Yes, we can. We can evade all of this. They're letting us go.'

Roman shakes his head with sadness. 'They're doing anything but.'

'Roman.'

His lips find mine, questioning, slow, and when I kiss him back, he kisses harder. It's a kiss that is wet with tears, but neither of us mind. He spins me around so that he backs against the tree and I lean on him, squeezing his back, feeling his strength underneath me, a reminder of what he represents to every part of my being. His tongue brushes mine, and his hands rove through my thick hair, and a breeze shoots past, carrying the shards of my broken heart.

'This is the right choice, isn't it?' I whisper to him, when we've stood under the trees for what feels like hours.

'It's the only choice, and one we have full control over.'

CHAPTER 71

Boys stifle their yawns and rub at their eyes, but me? This tiredness is a normal feeling. Only now every movement aches, and every beat of my heart is like the prod of a fresh bruise. Dead on my feet, I stand shoulder to shoulder with Cameron and Johnny, wearing last night's clothes. Every student is here, some looking calmer than others. Roman stands at the furthest side from us, stonily looking anywhere but at us. I swallow down the rising fear that I'm going to lose him.

I trust that the House of Pluto group know what we discovered last night. Johnny, Cameron and I welcomed Elis into our dorm room, and he spent the night in Taylor's bed. I wanted Roman to be with us, but he said no, breaking me more than he could ever know.

Truly, I don't know what any of these boys plan to do. You can only ever trust someone so far. As the professors assemble on their seats on the stage in the assembly hall, I slip my hands in my pocket and stare at the grooves in the floor.

Dwynwen steps up to the stage, looking as calm and collected as ever.

'Good morning. Your final day of Ganymede's.' She looks well rested, much to my chagrin, and her hair is sleek upon her shoulders. She offers a warm, trustful smile to the students. 'Congratulations, firstly, to you all. You proved last night you are capable of looking after yourself, and living unsupervised.' Roman bows his head. How strange to think everyone else followed the task, oblivious to truth. 'You can choose to graduate and start the rest of your glorious lives, or you can choose to leave this school and forfeit everything on offer to you. It really is that simple. A choice. A yes or no. I think it is deserved, considering all you have been put through to ensure you are the true perfect men society needs.'

There are some murmurs of appreciation, and if I didn't know better, I'd like that Dwynwen recognises all the work we have done these past three years, and indeed, this past month. But it's hard to feel anything other than dread for what I'm about to do. In bed last night, somewhere between disjointed sleep and waking reality, I thought of everything Dwynwen and Lawrence had said. Their shedding of the truth, and how they could be so accepting of what was really going on. I'd replayed their words in my mind, and thought hard about what it is I should do when both options leave me doomed. Live a life of unhappiness, or allow them to take my life away from me?

'When I call your name, you will be asked if you wish to graduate. Say yes, and you may go and take a seat on the bus waiting outside, which will take you to your chosen hamlets, and your new lives. Say no, and you will be asked to stay in this hall, and will be given further instruction when the boys have left.'

Dwynwen begins calling names. A Mars boy says yes, a Mercury boy says nothing before finally saying yes, and then

Jackson takes the stage, mumbling yes. I don't know if he and Lee know the true fate of Taylor. All I know is that when Roman and I went back to the church before returning to Ganymede's, the place was deserted. No sign of Taylor, and no sign of Rory. Each boy that comes after, thinning the crowd, says yes. Faces I recognise, boys I've grown up with, each one saying yes with hearts full of trust and hope and longing. Even happiness.

'Cameron,' Dwynwen calls. I hold my breath, watching my friend, the smartest boy I know, take to the stage. 'Do you wish to graduate?' She shows no emotion.

'Yes, Headmistress.'

I exhale, and Johnny does, too.

Dwynwen nods, smiles, and Cameron walks out of the room, not looking at me or Johnny.

More boys are called, and then, 'Elis.'

Elis walks slowly to the stage, and it's almost as if I can hear the doomsday song that must be playing in his head. The same question is posed to him, and after a moment's hesitation, he says, 'Yes, Headmistress.'

He catches my eye as he leaves, offers me a small smile, and then he's gone. Roman looks at me, shakes his head, and I hold his gaze, trying to plead with him.

'Johnny.'

I turn to my friend, pat him on the back. 'Whatever you decide,' I whisper.

'I love you, man.'

He hugs me, much to my surprise, and then bounds onto the stage. Happy-go-lucky Johnny. I wonder if all this time, he's been switching it on, projecting a different image to the world.

'No need to ask me twice, Headmistress,' Johnny says. 'I am dying to meet my girl.'

His words punch me in the gut, and Dwynwen claps with the rest of us as he leaves the room.

'Roman.'

My stomach drops and I swivel, seeing Roman step out of formation. He doesn't look at me as he stands in front of Dwynwen, a curt expression on his face.

'Do you wish to graduate?'

This is it. He could say no. He could say no and run into the crowd and take us away from all of this. It's not too late, I think. He meets my eye, lip quivering, and I bite my tongue as tears well, shaking my head. Fight this, Roman. Stay strong.

'Yes, Headmistress.'

My head tilts back as applause rings out, celebrating the death of Roman and me. When I look back to the stage, he's gone, and my heart races.

Roman, come back.

But he's walking straight out of the hall, shoulders tense, not daring to look at me. I dab at my eyes, trying not to give myself away when the love I feel for that boy burns.

That's it, then. He's accepted his fate. Will I ever see him again? Will I ever feel happiness once more? Am I destined to be as empty and hollow as my father must have been when he lost the king?

'Dylan. Here, please.'

Dwynwen watches me, and while her face remains impassive, she must know how I feel. I clear my throat, trying to steady my emotions, when all I can think about is how the only person to ever make me happy has walked away from me, from us.

Numb, angry, afraid, I climb the steps to the stage. Dwynwen smiles at me, her hands clasped before her. 'Dylan. Do you wish to graduate?'

My legs threaten to buckle under the weight they can't hold much longer. Despite what we discussed last night, the reality is different. Roman has done nothing wrong, he's done what we agreed, but it is enough to destroy me. Lawrence gives a small nod. Mother Mai appraises me, and my other professors all look mildly bored. We are the only ones who share the common truth. The knowledge of Rory's death, no doubt brushed under the carpet like Blake's. I look back at the entrance of Ganymede's, from here the exit to a new life. My eyes widen, breath catching, as Roman watches me from the doorway. His fist to his chest, he lifts it to his lips and nods.

Everything within me tells me to do what I know I should do. What I know is right.

'Mr Cecil?' Dwynwen asks. 'Do you wish to graduate? It is your choice.'

I raise my head, meeting her eye, wondering if I imagine that flicker of pleading within. My mouth forms my answer. 'Yes, Headmistress.'

'Good work, Mr Cecil,' Dwynwen says, relief on her face.

She steps forwards and pulls me into a hug. An odd move, I think. But then her whispered words tickle my ear. 'Do not react. There isn't much time. Rory got away.' I go to move, but she holds me tight. 'Listen to me very carefully. I am the only one to know this to be true. Blake, he is alive. He is out there. Find him, Dylan. Make sure you find him.'

She lets me go as everything I've ever known shatters. I think of her confession, how she never actually confirmed that he had been murdered. I only thought she admitted it. How all this time the only person to ever actually see Blake dead was her.

Before I can say anything, before I can do anything about it, she says, 'Please, head to the coach. You will find there is a different one waiting for you for ... obvious reasons.'

What am I supposed to do?

I turn to the door, choking. Roman is gone.

My lip begins to shake and I know I need to get away from their eyes, because I'm going to lose all sense of control.

I'm at the door leading into the entrance hall now. Ever closer to leaving Ganymede's, and Roman, forever.

'Dylan.'

His voice is a swan song, his sun-dappled face a blooming rose.

His lip quivers, and his cheeks are flushed. My legs shake until he's upon me.

We hug, tight, swaying in the hallway of Ganymede's, under the watchful gaze of the statue, and surrounded by the art that has been such a comfort to me.

'I knew you would ruin me,' Roman whispers.

My tears fall and my grip tightens, because I know I'm letting him go. I know once we're out in the real world, he will forget about me.

'Roman, listen...' But he interrupts me as he plants a light kiss on my lips. I taste the salt of his tears. It's not enough, I need more, but then he's gone, wiping at his eyes, leaving me alone like I always knew he would.

With a heaved breath and a shattering heart, I step out into the warmth of the day, listening to the singsong call of the birds and the hum of bees. The boys on the bus look at me, Johnny nodding, but looking glum. I give them a wave, trying to see Roman, but he must be on the other side. I long to join them, to tell them the truth, but waiting for me is a golden chariot.

As I approach, the driver steps out, dressed in dark green. The insignia of the crown is upon his lapel. 'Ah, Prince Cecil. How wonderful to make your acquaintance.'

CHAPTER 72

What does it mean to be a man? Is it to stand on morals, and consider how the situation affects those around you, more than how it might affect you? Is it to be considerate of feelings other than your own? Is it to be the stability in someone else's life, offering them familiarity and comfort, a place to call home? Men come in different forms. Some are physically strong; others can help around the house. Others are good cooks, and some paint and write and provide art that makes others feel in ways they never thought they could feel before. Men should be compassionate and brave, resilient of mind, strong-willed and prepared for anything. But ultimately, a man should know when to make the ultimate sacrifice, and when to put someone else's feelings before his own.

As I stand at the altar days after my eighteenth birthday, dressed in a forest-green suit with a shirt patterned with blooming flowers, I withhold the beauty before me. She glows ethereally in the sunlight, dressed in a white dress that has real red roses sewn delicately within the fabric. Her skin is a flawless shade of white, and her lips are the sweetest shade of pink, and her eyes are a harmonious brown, almost honey-glazed. Her hair is long, curled, rolls over her shoulders and down her back, and a crown of holly seems to sprout from its roots as if she is life itself. Fitting, I guess, as she is offering me a new life.

She is perfect.

As I say my vows, she smiles wider, her eyes fluttering. This is the best day of her life, and everyone in this historic chapel is here for her, basking in the joyful rays she projects. To be a man is to look after your love, to provide, to care.

So it doesn't matter that I can't get Roman off my mind, and it doesn't matter that I wish I could be saying these words to him instead. I am to marry and tonight we are to start trying for our first child.

Everything I have learnt is for this moment. As the priest declares us husband and wife, as the audience cheer, as Cerys cries happy tears, all I do is smile and think about how I am making her day. How proud she is right now to be married to me. The whispering thought of how I am to disappoint her, to ruin her life, drowned out by the audience that now loves me and takes me as their own. A new prince. A prince who wants a boyfriend. A husband who wants a husband. A man who has had his hand forced in marriage.

But it doesn't matter what I want. A good man sacrifices his own desires, his own needs. Yes, he is looked after, but not as much as he looks after his wife. He lets her free, to be a beautiful butterfly in this world. He does not possess and he does not control. He encourages and cheers and delights, and he is the first to bathe in her joy and her successes. He does not disparage; he does not complain. Her success is his, and his is hers.

With a ring on my finger, under the gaze of the handsome king and the achingly beautiful queen, I am a man of honour, a man of power. Johnny smiles in one of the aisle seats. Cameron couldn't make it, but he sent me a letter. Elis, hair neatly cut and looking the most refined I've ever seen him, fixes a smile to his face. They know the true me, and yet they are men who keep their word. They look after their own and do not concern themselves with others.

When I saw them two nights ago, they told me that Ganymede's is set to welcome a fresh cohort of students in September. Now that I am royalty, I know that the monarchy is keen to see Ganymede's continue to provide what they need to provide to keep this society of ours functioning. I don't know every way of working for this monarchy, not yet, but I am to learn from the king himself. My wife, Princess Cerys, will be queen someday, and I king. She already knows her place. Me? An old farm boy with no parents and a lost love knows nothing.

I first felt dejected that Ganymede's continued, but I remember Dwynwen's words. That we are to all keep a secret. I have not told a soul what she told me before I left Gandymede's as a graduate.

But as I step out of the church and stand upon the steps, photographers snapping photographs of us together for the first time as a married couple, I remember why I did this. Yes, to be a good man. Yes, to put Cerys first. But also because as a man of power, I can make a change. Change is what I am going to do. Slowly, biding my time with the knowledge I have, but I will make it happen.

It was Dwynwen and Professor Lawrence who made me see the path ahead. My father and mother, too, even if their true decision is marred for me. My fate was sealed long before I knew the truth, but now that I have done what I needed to do, I can choose my own destiny. A leader of an oligarchy, or a liberator? Change starts from the top, but I don't plan to let it trickle down. I plan to let it flow to us all.

The king sidles up next to me to join the photos, his hand resting briefly on my shoulder before slipping down my back. 'You make an attractive groom.'

This is not the first time he has touched me. It isn't welcomed. 'Thank you.'

'Relish all of this,' he says to me. 'They love you.'

'They love Cerys.'

'They will love you, too.' He turns to me, beaming, but then it falters, just for a moment. 'You really do look like your father.'

I smile back at him, and his lips turn downwards. He shakes his head, just once, then fixes the smile on his face again. The cameras will not know how I truly feel for him, or what I wish to do.

Back at Ganymede's, I'd asked myself one thing: why did Dwynwen let me graduate even after I told her my truth? She risked me keeping her truth a secret, but mine? It could jeopardise everything. In that forest, she and Lawrence told me enough.

And Roman, so quick to dictate what path we should both choose. That conversation in the forest, which still haunts me. 'You must marry. You must let me go.'

That's when my decision was made.

Both Dwynwen and Roman let me go into society with a weapon, a strength. Not physical strength – training in archery and boxing – but strength of mind. Lawrence and Dwynwen encouraged us to sharpen our minds, and to become emotionally strong men.

They've let me rise into society because I have the truth. The truth that could make all these beaming people see this family that they so adored in a whole new way. Elis said I could be a figurehead, Roman said I am a leader. So, as I kiss Cerys for the cameras, trying to convince them more than I could ever convince myself that this was the right decision, I think about my next steps.

To be a man is to fight for the injustices in the world, and use your influence for the good of others, rather than for personal gain.

THANK YOU FOR READING
THE BOYFRIEND ACADEMY

IT WOULD MEAN SO MUCH IF YOU COULD LEAVE A REVIEW ON ALL YOUR PREFERRED PLATFORMS AND SOCIAL MEDIA TO HELP SPREAD THE WORD!

YOU CAN ALSO FOLLOW ME ON INSTAGRAM OR TIKTOK
@JACKSTRANGEAUTHOR
AND MY WEBSITE AT
WWW.JACKSTRANGEAUTHOR.COM
FOR ALL THE UPDATES ON MY LATEST WORKS.

Acknowledgements

The Boyfriend Academy would be nothing without the support of the full One More Chapter team. To Charlotte, Arsalan, and Jennie, thank you for trusting me with this story, believing in me, and guiding me when I inevitably went a little astray with all my ideas. I truly appreciate working with you to get this story as good as can be, and I hope I've done it justice and that you're happy with the final result. Thank you, Sofia and Kara, for your help in the final stages. Thank you also to Emily and Tony for your fantastic edits.

To Chloe, thank you always for making my dreams a reality. Thank you for your reassurances and your unwavering belief in me and my writing. This would be nothing if it wasn't for our little visit to my Hackney Airbnb outside a school that we both agreed would look good in a dark academia novel. Your excitement and enthusiasm always inspire me!

Similarly, to James, who is always there when I'm convinced that I can't do this, and who listened to every high and low emotion I went through when writing this. You always help me see sense and stay focussed.

To the cats who slept nearby as I wrote, and to the Strange fam: I know you're always the first ones to pre-order anything I write. Yes, that does include the cats.

To Dale at Clocktower Books and Tom at Gay-on-Wye. Your support for my last book was phenomenal, and I've loved every bit of interest you've shown in my up-coming works, including this one. Thank you!

To my writer friends, thank you for all of our conversations.

Finally, thank you, the reader. Whether you're new or you've come back to me after my debut, I'm so grateful to you and appreciate you. Thank you for reading this and for taking a chance on me.

The author and One More Chapter would like to thank everyone who contributed to the publication of this story...

Analytics
Imogen Wolstencroft

Audio
Fionnuala Barrett
Ciara Briggs

Design
Lucy Bennett
Fiona Greenway
Liane Payne
Dean Russell

Digital Sales
Laura Daley
Lydia Grainge
Hannah Lismore

eCommerce
Laura Carpenter
Madeline ODonovan
Charlotte Stevens
Christina Storey
Rachel Ward

Editorial
Janet Marie Adkins
Rosie Best
Kara Daniel
Charlotte Ledger
Jennie Rothwell
Tony Russell
Sofia Salazar Studer
Emily Thomas
Helen Williams

Harper360
Emily Gerbner
Ariana Juarez
Jean Marie Kelly
emma sullivan
Sophia Wilhelm

International Sales
Ruth Burrow
Bethan Moore
Colleen Simpson

Inventory
Sarah Callaghan
Kirsty Norman

Marketing & Publicity
Chloe Cummings
Grace Edwards
Katie Sadler

Operations
Melissa Okusanya

Production
Denis Manson
Simon Moore
Francesca Tuzzeo

Rights
Ashton Mucha
Alisah Saghir
Zoe Shine
Aisling Smyth

Trade Marketing
Ben Hurd
Eleanor Slater

The HarperCollins Contracts Team

The HarperCollins Distribution Team

The HarperCollins Finance & Royalties Team

The HarperCollins Legal Team

The HarperCollins Technology Team

UK Sales
Isabel Coburn
Jay Cochrane
Leah Woods

And every other essential link in the chain from delivery drivers to booksellers to librarians and beyond!

One More Chapter is an award-winning global division of HarperCollins.

Subscribe to our newsletter to get our latest eBook deals and stay up to date with all our new releases!

signup.harpercollins.co.uk/join/signup-omc

Meet the team at
www.onemorechapter.com

Follow us!

@onemorechapterhc

Do you write unputdownable fiction? We love to hear from new voices. Find out how to submit your novel at
www.onemorechapter.com/submissions